MORE PRAI[SE]

The Fifth Avenue Artists Society

"With *The Fifth Avenue Artists Society*, debut author Joy Callaway paints a marvelously detailed portrait of Gilded Age New York, and in Ginny Loftin, inspired in part by the author's own ancestor, she has created an affecting and appealing heroine. This is a delightful and memorable book."

—JENNIFER ROBSON, international bestselling author of *Moonlight Over Paris*

"With the warm glow and heavy drapery of Gilded Age salons as its inviting backdrop, Joy Callaway's engaging period novel explores the timeless struggles women face in the creative and working world, and the price some are willing to pay to protect all they hold dear."

—ERIKA ROBUCK, national bestselling author of *Hemingway's Girl*

"*The Fifth Avenue Artists Society* is an engrossing snapshot of 1890s New York City, where women were expected to cast aside their artistic aspirations in favor of marriage, motherhood, and social obligation. Filled with well-drawn characters and lush historical texture, this tale sweeps you into the midst of writers, artists, and musicians, some of whom wrestle darker muses than others. The era may be long gone, but the passions remain timeless."

—JILL MORROW, author of *Newport*

"[A] powerful debut. . . . Callaway paints an all-too-real portrait of the power of love to both create and destroy. . . . Readers will never see the twists around every corner. Beautifully written and solidly executed, Callaway's novel will captivate historical and romance fans alike."

—*Library Journal*

The Fifth Avenue Artists Society

The Fifth Avenue Artists Society

a novel

Joy Callaway

HARPER

NEW YORK · LONDON · TORONTO · SYDNEY

HARPER

P.S.™ is a trademark of HarperCollins Publishers.

THE FIFTH AVENUE ARTISTS SOCIETY. Copyright © 2016 by Joy Callaway. All rights reserved. Printed in the United States of America. No part of this book may be used or reproduced in any manner whatsoever without written permission except in the case of brief quotations embodied in critical articles and reviews. For information address HarperCollins Publishers, 195 Broadway, New York, NY 10007.

HarperCollins books may be purchased for educational, business, or sales promotional use. For information please e-mail the Special Markets Department at SPsales@harpercollins.com.

FIRST EDITION

Designed by Jamie Lynn Kerner

Library of Congress Cataloging-in-Publication Data

Names: Callaway, Joy, author.
Title: The Fifth Avenue Artists Society : a novel / Joy Callaway.
Description: First edition. | New York : Harper Paperbacks, 2016.
Identifiers: LCCN 2015042024| ISBN 978-0-06-239161-2 (paperback) | ISBN
    978-0-06-239163-6 (ebook)
Subjects: LCSH: Women authors—Fiction. | Sisters—Fiction. |
    Artists—Societies and clubs—Fiction. | New York (N.Y)—Fiction. |
    BISAC: FICTION / Historical. | GSAFD: Love stories. | Mystery fiction.
Classification: LCC PS3603.A4455 F54 2016 | DDC 813/.6—dc23
LC record available at http://lccn.loc.gov/2015042024

16 17 18 19 20   OV/RRD   10 9 8 7 6 5 4 3 2 1

To my daughter, Alevia

There are moments when a man's imagination,

so easily subdued to what it lives in, suddenly

rises above its daily level and surveys

the long windings of destiny.

—EDITH WHARTON,
The Age of Innocence

The Society attracted all sorts of artists to the grand drawing

room on Fifth Avenue. It wasn't the want for fame that

drew them there—though some certainly became

known—or even the anticipation of improvement.

Instead, it was the realization that for some, true art,

great art, is not won in solitude. It must first be lived.

—JAMES LAUGHLIN,
The Society

Prologue

omeone's coming." My best friend Charlie's lead-smudged fingers grabbed mine, stopping my pencil. A floorboard creaked beyond the door to his family's home library. I curled my shoulders, tucking my chin into the red soutache collar trimming of my cotton dress and folding my legs further into the cabinet. The paper in my lap crinkled and Charlie's hand clamped around my palm.

"Ginny, Charlie, I know you're in there. I've checked everywhere else." The brass doorknob began to jiggle.

"It's Frank," I hissed, as if Charlie didn't already know we'd appointed my twin brother the designated seeker. Charlie glared at me, willing my silence. He and I had always played hide-and-seek reluctantly—until we'd discovered the vacant cabinet below one of the walls of bookshelves in his library a month ago. Since then, we'd encouraged the game. We always emerged the victors—much to the chagrin of Charlie's younger brother, George, and my siblings—and it gave us time to work on our contribution to the Mott Haven Centennial Time Capsule without interruption. Just today, we'd played five games, buying us three hours to finish our illustrated story on Bronx history before the time capsule was interred at six.

"Come on," George's five-year-old voice whined. "The rules state that you have to hide where we can find you. A locked door doesn't count." Our brothers had joined together to find us. One of them swiveled the door handle again. Charlie shook his head.

"It's not locked," he whispered. "Sometimes the jamb sticks. And don't they know they're breaking the rules, too? There can't be more than one seeker." The smack of a bony hip pounded into the wood, followed by another. The hinge rattled, threatening to give way. Pressing my story to my chest, I flattened against the corner of the cabinet. I breathed through my mouth. Mrs. Aldridge just had the bookshelves French polished and the pungent scent of shellac stung my nostrils.

"I give up," George said. "I'm hungry and thirsty and my parents have already taken the sandwiches next door."

"I *will* get in," Frank growled, unfazed by George's surrender. His fist pounded into the door, followed by another series of bodily blows. We couldn't let Frank find us. Our hiding place would be lost forever.

"Come on, Frank." George tried to dissuade him once again. "Your mother probably has your lawn all set for the picnic and I'm sure your father and sisters are starved. It isn't polite to keep them waiting." Frank was silent. George exhaled and I could hear him withdraw into the foyer.

"Charlie," I whispered. Frank slammed himself into the door and it finally gave, sputtering open in a series of resigned groans. Charlie slowly lowered his drawing pad from his lap, setting his pencil across the finished depiction of George Washington's stay at the nearby Van Cortlandt Mansion. He pulled the cabinet doors shut, blotting out the summer sunlight and the back of Mr. Aldridge's leather sofa.

Frank's footsteps came closer. Neither of us moved. I barely breathed. Finally, I heard him stop and yawn.

"Honestly, if you're in here, wherever you are, I give up. Everybody's out on the lawn eating and George has likely already drunk all of Mother's lemonade like he did on Memorial Day." Charlie didn't budge, though my mother's lemonade was his favorite. We both knew Frank's cunning. My brother sighed, waited for a moment, and retreated from the room, his boots clopping toward the foyer. The minute the front door slapped into place, Charlie flung the cabinet open.

"Is your story finished?" he asked hurriedly. I nodded, glancing over my slanted cursive, hoping it was perfect. Charlie snatched the paper from my grasp, pressed it atop his drawing, and started to climb out of our hiding spot. "If my brother's consumed the last of the lemonade, I'll throttle him."

"Wait," I said, catching the tail of his suit. "You haven't read my story and we haven't signed our names to it." Charlie huffed and flattened the pages on a shelf below a row of *Encyclopaedia Britannica*s and my favorite book, Washington Irving's *A History of New York*.

"I'm sure it's magnificent," he said hurriedly. *By Charles and Virginia*, he scribbled at the conclusion of my story. Then, recalling he hadn't written our surnames, he leaned down and scrawled *Aldridge*. I waited for him to realize his mistake, to add my last name, but he didn't. Instead, he gathered our story in his hand and glanced at me. When our eyes met, his cheeks flushed, and I felt my own face burn. Had he meant to leave it off?

"Are you coming?" His gaze broke from mine and he walked toward the door, toward our families and Mother's lemonade.

I allowed myself to whisper it only once before I followed him.

Virginia Aldridge.

Chapter One

Staring at Alevia was pointless, but men always did. I snorted as this evening's gawker—a short fellow with a scraggly beard—gestured toward her so heartily he sloshed his punch down the corded silk collar of a golden-haired man in front of him. Forcing my eyes away from the shocked gentleman and the rest of the partygoers, I glanced at my younger sister's profile through the crack in the pocket door and prayed she hadn't heard me. The one time I'd mentioned a man noticing her, she'd blushed so severely I thought she'd literally burst into flames, and vowed never to play in public again. Thankfully, she was still playing her favorite piece, *Tristesse* by Chopin. Her deep brown eyes were closed to the music, a slight smile on her lips, oblivious to everything but the movement of her fingers on the piano keys. I looked out into the room and found the gawker still staring at Alevia, completely unaware that the gentleman he'd just doused had extracted his unbecoming silk flower from his buttonhole and was dabbing his collar with it.

Taking a step back from the door, I buried my face in the crook of my arm and laughed.

"What's so funny?"

I hadn't even heard the door to the library open, and didn't dare turn around lest I miss another effort by Alevia's admirer.

"One of your party guests has . . . noticed my sister." I could feel him behind me and leaned back against his chest, crushing his bow tie. I nodded toward the slight view, watching as the short man's attention snapped to his friend's glare and the wilted fabric in his hand.

"Oh," Charlie said, and laughed softly. "That's John Hopper—he's a writer, like you. Doesn't surprise me, he's painfully rakish when it comes to ladies. Perhaps I could use some of his nerve . . . Ginny, I have to ask you—"

"Why would you need it?" I cut him off, elbowing him in the ribs.

"In case I'm shamefully rejected by the object of my affection, of course." He pulled away from me and looked down, brows furrowing. I rolled my eyes and laughed at his dramatics. Charlie was charismatic and handsome. He could attract anyone he wanted. Even me.

"Your drawing is getting better," I noted, crossing the room. His sketchbook lay open on a table beneath the window, the only bit of wall unoccupied by ornate mahogany bookshelves. I looked down at the pencil sketch of my home, and then out the window to the real thing next door. "You got the color wash right this time, and the dimensions of the shed, though if the roof were drawn any steeper one could mistake it for Trinity Church."

I could see his reflection in the window. He was still looking down at his shoes, likely absorbed by some image in his head. I didn't bother to ask him what it was; a similar haze came over me when I wrote, so I ignored his silence and leaned down to grab my notebook and the old copy of Washington Irving's *A History of New York* from the arm of the leather sofa. Scanning the page I'd left off on, I shoved it back between the rows of other antique books lining the walls.

"Haven't you memorized that by now?" he asked. I stared at Charlie for a moment, past the sincerity of his smile to the green eyes holding a strange melancholy I couldn't place.

"Of course," I said, glancing away. "But there's something about seeing our families' names on the page." I didn't know how many times I'd read the book, though I knew it had to be over one hundred. Mother said I'd plucked it randomly from the shelves when we had first called on Charlie's family eighteen years ago, the day after our move into my father's childhood home. I'd been captivated by Irving's prose ever since—that, and his coincidental mention of both Charlie's and my family's ancestors, the Stuyvesants and Van Pelts, respectively, both old Dutch settlers who'd laid claim to the city long before the Vanderbilts or Astors built their palaces.

"Ginny, I tried to call on you earlier today, but you were still in the city. I need to speak with you." He pulled at one of his sideburns.

"I suppose I can listen. So long as I can blame the dullness of this story I'm writing for *The Review* on your interruption." A child's English primer read with more eloquence than the two paragraphs I'd penciled into the notebook I was holding. "Is everything all right?" His face paled, but he nodded. He was lying, clearly. "Tell me."

"Everything's fine, Virginia," he said. But Charlie's lips met my forehead and lingered there. Then his fingers clutched the back of my head, holding me as if it were the last time he'd ever see me up close. The only time I'd ever seen Charlie this troubled was at his younger brother's funeral fifteen years before.

"Mr. Aldridge?" I jerked from his grasp to find an older man I didn't know in the doorway. I felt Charlie step away from me. "Excuse me. It's only . . ." The man coughed, looking from Charlie to me and back again. "Your mother asked me to summon you. It's time." Charlie forced a smile and passed me without a glance.

"Yes," he said, stumbling over the word. "I-I suppose it is." What hadn't he told me? The last few days played out in my mind—our afternoon strolling on the High Bridge, my trek into the city this morning to purchase a notepad, seeing Mrs. Aldridge and Charlie deep in conversation on the front porch this afternoon. Mrs. Aldridge. She seemed in good health. Surely she hadn't taken ill. Not so soon after Mr. Aldridge's death. I followed after Charlie, despite my having planned to avoid the party tonight and enjoy the quiet company of the Aldridges' books.

Alevia was still playing. I could vaguely hear the slow notes of "Oh Promise Me," and the guests' laughter as I shoved past feathered hats and black-jacketed arms to follow Charlie. He stopped in the middle of the room, brought his fingers to his mouth, and whistled. I heard my sister's hands lift from the piano, leaving notes hanging unfinished on the air. Everyone turned to look at him. I took a deep breath, inhaled the sweet scent of someone's lavender cologne, and looked around for anyone I knew. Finding no one beyond Rachel Kent, one of Charlie's distant cousins, over his shoulder, her locks pinned under a purple cap adorned with a stuffed hummingbird, I fleetingly wondered if it was one of my sister Bessie's creations. Miss Kent nodded at me and I grinned back, relieved to find a familiar face besides Alevia's. The reception had been held in Miss Kent's honor, a reunion of sorts with her family acquaintances that she'd lost touch with since moving from the Bronx to White Plains years back. Mrs. Aldridge had begged Alevia to play for the party, and I'd come along hoping to write something profound. Ever since Charlie and I were young, the Aldridges' library had been one of our sanctuaries, the only place beyond our rooms where we could shut out the world and create.

"If I could have your attention," Charlie shouted, silencing the party's rumble. He glanced at me for a moment before he turned his gaze to the rest of the guests. "For quite some time I've wanted to share something with all of you and now, it turns out, is precisely the time to do it." Charlie cleared his throat and looked up, staring above the crowd to the windows in front of him. I followed his gaze, finding his mother looking the picture of health, grinning, hands clasped together in anticipation. I balked at my reflection in the glass and tucked a few unruly light brown strands back in their pins. "See, there's a particular woman I love and I cannot go on living without knowing she's mine," he said. "I've known her for as long as I can remember. As a young boy I admired her poise and beauty, and as a man, though I still love her for those things, I think I find the most joy in her passion—in her love of the arts that have been so important to both of our families. She is, quite simply, a reflection of what I've always dreamed." His words sounded in my ears, but I barely believed them. I'd longed for this moment for so many years. I glanced at the faces of the strangers around me, their smiles confirmation that they'd heard him, too, that this wasn't a delusion. He was finally going to ask me to marry him. My hands were sweating, balled in my skirt, and as his eyes scanned mine, I released the fabric abruptly, the striped gold and white satin falling back to the ground.

"Charlie," I whispered, but he turned and dropped to his knees.

"Miss Rachel Kent, will you be my wife?"

I took a step back, but stumbled, unable to move.

"Come with me." Alevia appeared from nowhere and pulled me through the crowd. Before I knew it, I was on the Aldridges' front porch, hearing the door click shut behind me. I couldn't register anything about the last minutes beyond Alevia's long fingers around my wrist and the faraway cheers of the guests.

Alevia turned right, toward our home. Her dress was a red blur, but I didn't follow. Nothing made sense. Surely I'd heard him wrong.

"I'm sorry," Alevia's voice came quietly behind me, bringing me back to reality. I could feel his breath on my face, his arm wrapped around my body. I believed that he loved me. Yet he hadn't chosen me.

"He came to me in the library. He . . . he asked to speak with me and then he held me and kissed my forehead as though he'd never see me again. I suppose now he won't. I've never heard him mention her name, let alone insinuate love for her. How dare he! Doesn't he know how I feel?" I was trembling, hands jammed into fists at my sides.

"Perhaps he doesn't. Know, I mean." Alevia's eyes were full of sorrow for me, and I stepped away from her, unwilling to see my pain reflected in her face. Less than an hour ago I'd leaned into his embrace as I had every time he'd ever reached for me. I'd never given him any reason to think me indifferent. If he didn't know I loved him, he was a fool. I suddenly yearned for Mae, my younger collected sister who always said the right thing, and cursed Hunter College for scheduling courses in the evening.

I kept walking in the wrong direction, past home after clapboard home, hearing the shuffle of Alevia's crimson brocade skirt behind me, but I didn't turn around. I couldn't go back home and face my family. The moon was round and bright red, appropriately hellish, and I shuddered as wind swept through the creaking trees.

"It's the money. You know her father inherited millions from his bachelor brother in Georgia and that the Aldridges are near penniless. Surely you recall Mrs. Aldridge asking Mother to loan her money last month." Alevia's voice was strange and I turned around to find her arms clasped tightly across her chest, anger apparently conquering her timidity. I'd forgotten the conversation. Alevia and I had been reading in the drawing room—only a room over—when she'd come to speak to Mother. Even though Mrs. Aldridge had spoken in a whisper, we'd heard. It had been such a shocking, desperate request, that Alevia and I had promised each other we'd never speak of it. After all, Mother hadn't had the money to give Mrs. Aldridge.

Alevia cleared her throat. "Family name only goes so far. You know that. We're all well respected, sure—The Intellectuals, as they call us—and history demands that the wealthy see us as important and invite us to some of their soirees, but that's not enough if your mother can't afford to outfit herself or entertain at her home." Her contempt was palpable.

"If that's the case, then he's spineless and I hope I never see him again," I whispered, stunned to realize that I meant it.

"Mrs. Aldridge looked as if she were about to be showered in gold coins." Alevia exhaled and tore her hat from her head, mashing the pluming black feather Bessie had spent weeks trying to find. "And he admires her passion. For what? Her paintings? Perhaps they've improved, but from what I remember they're poor at best." Her lips were pursed in a way that reminded me of myself as a little girl, furious I hadn't gotten my way, but unable to do anything about it. I laughed at the recollection, and Alevia's eyes widened in shock. "How can you possibly laugh when your heart is broken?" she asked softly. Kneeling in the dusty street, palm pressed to forehead, I could still feel Charlie's lips on my skin and finally started to cry. My sister's hand landed on my shoulder, her grip uncharacteristically strong.

"He . . . I should've known. I . . . I thought he was proposing to me," I said. "I was naïve." Standing up, I smoothed the lace overlay trimming the top of my skirt, and sniffed. "I had no reason to believe he loved me beyond what I felt. He never kissed me, never actually told me he was in love with me." I closed my eyes, but all I could see was his face. "It was my fault. My mistake," I whispered.

"No." Alevia's small voice cut through the night and her willowy frame pitched toward me. "No," she said again. "It wasn't. He needed you near him because you're his support, don't you see? It's not that he doesn't love you." She sighed. "He wanted to watch you as he made the biggest mistake of his life so that when he's miserable, when he wishes he were dead, he can recall your broken face and know that at one point, someone he loved also loved him."

Chapter Two

The Loftin House
BRONX, NEW YORK

It looks like everyone's asleep," Alevia whispered. I pushed the picket fence back in place behind me and sighed, hoping she was right. I didn't want to talk to anyone. The branches of the old chestnut tree screeched back and forth against the side of the white house, the deep red leaves of the Virginia creeper vine swinging freely from its tips. Alevia started up the porch and I followed, barely aware that I was moving. My eyes drifted toward the moon and then down to Charlie's library window next door.

"Oh, my good lord!" Alevia screamed. Pitching my skirt, I ran up the stairs, through the front door, and grit my jaw to avoid screaming myself. The shadow of some sort of winged creature seemed to float toward us from the drawing room. My heart jumped in my chest and I pushed Alevia forward.

"Go," I hissed, but she stood, frozen, as the shape loomed closer. "Alevia, *move*!" I shoved her, tripped over a bowed floorboard, and fell.

"That's not quite the reaction I was hoping for, but I suppose it'll do," Bessie said. I picked myself up and whirled around to find my older sister laughing, wearing a ridiculous hat adorned with white feathers and an enormous stuffed pelican.

"What in the world were you doing in the dark—" Alevia started.

"Are you serious, Bess?" I asked, unable to pry my eyes from the hat.

"Quite. It's Caroline Astor's. She wanted something dramatic for a celebration honoring some business accomplishment of Jack's. She's paying fifty dollars for it, so naturally I had to go all out." Bessie's knack for millinery—though she'd been making hats for our family for as long as I could recall—had been discovered by mistake. She'd gone to pick up Alevia's music for the Astors' New Year's tea, only to find Mrs. Astor panicked because her hat hadn't been delivered in time. An avid student of *Harper's Bazaar*, Bess created a new headpiece from Mrs. Astor's old ones. From that evening on, she'd been one of the most requested milliners in the city.

"It's certainly . . . striking. I only hope people don't run scream-ing when they see her in it," I said. Bessie rolled her eyes and care-fully removed the hat, letting her waves fall loose, framing her face. She ran her hands through the end of her hair, fingertips lingering on her collar lined with cut jet beads. Bess had spent thirty dollars on the "Princess Louise" dress last month—an extravagance that nearly caused our family a deficit—but the profligacy wasn't at all uncommon. She'd been infatuated with fine clothes since before she could talk—a consequence of our late socialite great-aunt, Rose VanPelt, treating her as the granddaughter she never had—but her obsession had deepened since she'd begun purchasing all of her supplies from O'Neill's millinery department, conveniently located on the same floor as ladies' clothing.

Alevia had mentioned her increased spending months back, when money had been so tight we'd survived on buttered bread for a week, but Bess had only reproached her, saying that she deserved to buy fine things because she was the oldest, had worked the longest, and brought in nearly as much money with her millinery as my twin brother, Franklin, did working as a salesman for J. L. Mott Iron Works—a profession he'd valiantly accepted though the demands of it had whittled his previous occupation—painting portraits—down to a hobby. Never mind that there were only six years difference between all five of us—Bess's twenty-six years to Alevia's twenty—and that Alevia's playing contributed a significant amount to our well-being, bringing in ten dollars for luncheons or teas and fifteen for balls, enough to buy our groceries for the month. The truth really was that Bess bought fine things because she believed she belonged among the wealthy, among Great-aunt Rose's people, among my mother's, instead of the working class we'd been born into. She was tired of struggling. We all were.

Alevia continued to stare at the pelican's beady eyes, button nose scrunched in disgust.

"Princess Victoria wore something very similar last month. They'll all adore it. Caroline has invited me to stay on for the party after the fitting. Everyone will be there—the Goelets, the Delafields, the Roosevelts—so of course I accepted. I guarantee that I'll have over fifty requests for hats exactly like it afterward. Just wait. Adelaide Frick was already asking about the other ladies' hats when I took her measurements this evening." Bess pursed her lips and smoothed the midnight blue silk evening dress hugging her figure. "Speaking of parties, Alevia, how was your playing tonight?"

"It was fine," she mumbled, looking down. Reminded of the image of Charlie down on one knee, my insides felt hollow, and I pinched my eyes together, praying when I opened them I would find the evening was just a nightmare.

"I understand it wasn't your ideal, Alevia," Bess said, drawing out her name. "It wasn't Carnegie Hall . . . but, as a consolation, I'm sure your performance caught the eye of at least one attractive artist." I could see the short man with the beard, feel Charlie's face against mine, and forced the thought from my mind. "Didn't it?" Bessie winked at me and nudged Alevia softly. She wasn't asking because she was interested. Bess had been jealous of Alevia ever since her playing had been noticed by New York's elite five years ago and had started landing her invitations to entertain at their parties at least three times each week. Bess was handsome, well respected, and sought after by the Astors and the Carnegies when it came to fashion, but it was Alevia, young, elegant, beautiful Alevia, who sat in their ballrooms, attracting the admiration of their men.

"Bess. Stop," I said. It had been a little over a year since Alevia had rejected her most recent prospect, banker Robert Winthrop's son, Frederic. Though she hadn't fancied him in the slightest, she didn't like to be reminded of his attention. The courtship had been a short one. He caught sight of her while she played for a small dinner party of Caroline Astor's last fall and had written to her on several occasions before asking her to accompany him to the premiere of Joseph Arthur's play *Blue Jeans*. The critics had lauded the play, and Alevia had been quite keen to see it, but Mr. Winthrop had talked through the entire performance, outlining his requirements for a wife. At the conclusion of his soliloquy he'd told Alevia that if she was fortunate enough to wed him, she'd have to relinquish her playing to focus on his social calendar. It wasn't the first time an interested society man had voiced this requirement. Rather than explain her passion for music and vie for his understanding, she returned home, swore she'd never marry, and never spoke to Mr. Winthrop again. I was glad she'd rejected him. I would have done the same given the ultimatum, but Bess had thought her an imbecile and told her so. Though Alevia had forgiven her, Bess's words had wounded their relationship.

"Tell me," Bess prodded with the tenacity of a novice dress-maker's needle. "I know there was at least one."

"Please. Not now, Bess," Alevia whispered. She tucked a strand back into her waved side locks that swept upward into a Newport knot. I knew Alevia was being considerate, so I braced myself and came out with it.

"Charlie asked Rachel Kent to marry him tonight." Bess's brows rose and she walked toward me, but I turned, starting down the dark hallway toward the light coming from the parlor. I could hear my mother laughing, followed by Mae's high-pitched voice, as I passed my late-father's portrait on the wall of the study. The warmth of the fire swirled around me and wood smoke filled my lungs. Mother and Mae were folded over a book in front of the hearth. "What're you still doing up?" I asked. Mother always re-tired by nine. It was well past eleven. She took one look at me, and stood from the longue.

"We were discussing Horace Mann's *On the Art of Teach-ing*. Mother was telling me old tales about her most challenging pupils—beyond us, of course—and warning me that my longing to become a mother might award me my most difficult trial as an educator as our children are often . . ." Mae stopped when she glanced up from the book.

"Ginny? What's wrong? What's happened?" Mother asked. Both of them stared at me, nearly identical blue eyes slanted in concern. I opened my mouth to reply, but found that I could nei-ther answer nor cry.

"Charlie . . . he asked Rachel Kent to marry him tonight," Alevia said quietly, materializing behind me. My mother's face paled for a moment, then turned an unearthly shade of red. Mae gathered me in a hug, and I wrapped my arms around her, suppressing the urge to run off to my room. Mae was my confidante, my best friend, but her sympathy made me feel pathetic, as though I'd been the only one to confuse Charlie's and my intimacy for love.

"I'll never speak to Ruth Aldridge again as long as I live," Mother said evenly. "She's put him up to this match. How dare she."

Bessie made a noise in the back of her throat and shook her head. I backed away from Mae to look at her. Bess skirted around Grandmother Loftin's Steinway grand piano to pluck a dead rose from a vase on the windowsill and twirl it between her fingers. The gold lining the green glass stone on her pinkie caught the moonlight. "Sorry," she said, and shrugged. "I'm sorry for Ginny, I am, but can you blame Mrs. Aldridge, Mother? She lost her little girl at birth, George as a child of five, and Mr. Aldridge just last year, leaving only Charlie and his dismal inheritance. You know as well as I do that she can't possibly survive on what little Charlie has left. It's only the two of them. We've barely been able to keep our bills paid since pneumonia took Father and there are six of us to help with work. In any case, it's not as if Ginny's writing would've saved them. She hardly makes enough to pay the monthly ice charge."

I froze, staring at my sister, who continued to twirl the dead rose between her fingers as dried petals fell to the floor. Bess and I had never been very close, but no one, not even she, had ever spoken of my dismal salary, or chastised me for my profession. I'd worked hard to earn a place at the *Review*, applying eight times before its publisher, Mr. Robert O'Neal, agreed to hire a woman. His selecting me had been mostly out of desperation—he'd run out of competent male applicants who would work for the minimal wage he offered—but I didn't care. I immediately resigned my post as a ticket secretary at the Mott Haven Canal. My father had been proud of me, of all of us, and had made it clear when he was still alive that our talents weren't to be cast aside.

We were all artists of some kind, save Mae and Mother, though their fervor for teaching was an inspired endeavor in its own right. The Loftins, my father's family, had all been creative. They'd never been famous or renowned, only common Irish folk who wrote and played and sang and painted to carry on the heritage of their small village, Ennistymon, and to provide tutors for the castle's children. Like their ancestors before them, my grandparents and my father had never focused on one particular form of art and had thus never relied on their talents for their livelihood. Father had always said he regretted it, but his job at J. L. Mott had afforded our family a decent living of $2,500 each year—a living that we had yet to meet since his death three years ago. So perhaps his path was as it should've been. Perhaps the pursuit of art could only result in poverty and grief.

"That's enough, Bess," Mother said. Her voice startled me. "Of course I blame Ruth. We've been friends and neighbors for eighteen years. We've shared everything—joys, disappointments, heartaches. We've watched all of you grow, and watched you and Charlie grow toward one another . . . I . . . I didn't think her capable of such selfishness." Burying her hands in her brown tweed skirt, Mother closed her eyes, no doubt trying to make sense of it all. In spite of my pain, I was thankful I wasn't alone in my confusion.

"Bess, why would you . . . how could you say that?" Alevia picked up where Mother left off. Her eyes were wide as she looked from my wrecked face to Bessie's empty stare. Alevia and I shared the same ardor for our art. She knew how hard I'd worked to obtain a position at the *Review,* and though it only awarded me a meager twenty-five dollars each month, it meant my writing had been given a chance.

"Because it's the truth," she said. "If he'd chosen Ginny he would've thrown away everything—his reputation, his lifestyle, his mother's well-being." My mind spun, unable to process her words. I'd never thought of writing as an obstruction to my happiness. I'd never considered anything beyond the fact that I loved Charlie, and I suddenly felt naïve, embarrassed that I'd ever thought it could be so simple. Mae squeezed my hand, then disappeared from my side, crossed the room, and snatched the stem from Bessie's fingers.

"You're a fool." Mae's words were pointed, but her voice was calm. "Is love worth nothing? Does it count for nothing? Charlie's just as shallow as you are."

"Girls!" Mother shouted, silencing Bessie's rebuttal.

"It's all right." I closed my eyes and forced composure. They were all looking at me. I could feel their stares. "Really it is," I said, wishing they would disappear. "It's not as if someone died."

"I'm glad to hear it," a deep voice muttered from the door behind me. "Now, let's have a glass of wine to celebrate the fact that I've finished traveling for a spell and don't have to work tomorrow." I turned to find Franklin, clutching a bottle of Madeira under his arm, Grandmother's emerald green wineglasses strewn between his fingers. His hair was disheveled, sticking up in the front where he always ran his fingers through it. I was surprised to see him and wondered how long he'd been home. Though it wasn't uncommon for him to travel week after week, he'd been in and out of the house for nearly a month this time, traveling through Connecticut from iron plant to iron plant selling parts for J. L. Mott, like my father before him.

Making his way through the room, his eyes met mine and he rolled them toward the ceiling, mouthing "sorry" over Alevia's head, apologizing for taking so long to save me. He knew well enough that even though my mother and sisters—save Bessie—meant well with their coddling, their sympathy would only make it worse.

Franklin set the bottle and glasses down on the marble tabletop between Mother's chaise and a small easy chair we'd inherited from my grandparents. An early sketch of Charlie's hung on the wall behind it, a pencil and watercolor interpretation of my ancestors' homeland in Ennistymon. He'd given it to Mae for her fifteenth birthday, after she'd told him how much she loved landscapes.

I watched as Franklin took the knife from the leather sheath at his side, plunged the tip into the cork, and pulled it out. He poured himself a tall glass and set the bottle back down on the table. Then he stepped over Mae and leaned languidly against the oak mantel, sipping and looking at us.

"Are you going to pour us a glass, Frank, or are we just going to stand here all evening mourning with Ginny and staring at each other?" Bessie asked, lips pursed at Franklin who shrugged, then grinned.

"Bessie, that's enough," Mother said evenly.

"For once I might agree with you, Bess. We should move on," my brother said, drumming his fingers along the mantel. I glared at him, but he winked. Sighing, he sat down beside Mother, long, lanky legs nearly reaching his chest. "I can't say that I'm sorry for Virginia, though. I like Charlie fine, hell, he's like a brother, but I have plenty of handsome friends who would love a chance with Ginny." The thought of another man struck me through. There could never be anyone else. How could there be? Charlie had held my heart for as long as I could remember. Bessie pursed her lips in disagreement and Franklin looked at her sharply, his eyes narrowing to slits. "Gin and I are only twenty-two. Aldridge losing his balls doesn't confine Gin to the nunnery, Bess, but your being a proper bitch might send *you* there." Frank and Bess had always been at odds. I looked away, biting the inside of my cheek to keep from laughing despite my heartache.

"You miserable—" Bessie started, but Mother cut her off.

"I'll not tolerate that language in my house, Frank. And Bess, I've already told you twice and I meant it. You'll never speak of your sister that way again. Do you understand?" Mother leaned forward and poured herself a substantial glass of wine. "Help yourselves," she said, looking around at us. "Last I checked, we don't have a maid and all of you have two hands." Something about the way she said it reminded me of my father, of the tone he used to knock us back into place when we acted pretentiously. I tried to remember the sound of his boots on the wood floor and the boom of his voice echoing through the house upon his return from work. I couldn't believe he'd been gone three years. The cool rim of a glass pressed into my hand and I took it from Mae. "Don't listen to Bessie," she whispered, straightening the collar of her white shirtwaist. "She's jealous of you, even now."

I forced myself to drink the wine, mostly to prove to my family that I was all right. I barely tasted it, swallowing the vinegary liquid down before it had a chance to sink into my taste buds.

"I'm so glad that you're home, Frank," Alevia said. She tilted her glass back, set it on the table, and licked her lips. Yawning, she turned, cracked her knuckles, and left for bed, followed shortly thereafter by Bessie, then Mae. Relieved that the room had been reduced to Mother, Franklin, and the popping fire, I sat down in the wingback chair across from them. The life I'd always envisioned had been reduced from structure and promise to ash.

My eyes drifted to the tabletop in front of me, to the photograph we'd taken this summer while picnicking on Randall's Island. It was a small photo, and of poor quality, but it had been free—an excuse for my aunt Cassie to try her new daylight Kodak.

Mother and Mae bookended the group, both perched like tiny chickadees on the craggy rocks next to Bess's hourglass figure outfitted in eyelet and lace, and Alevia hiding beneath the brim of her straw hat. Frank and I were in the middle. I was leaning into his arm trying my best to keep my lips together, my wide-set hazel eyes—identical to Frank's—squinted in laughter at something Aunt Cassie had just said, pert nose unbecomingly crinkled. In black and white, we all looked relatively related, the pigment evening out the discrepancy of our colorings, from Frank's and my light brown hair to Mother and Alevia's ebony, from Bess's olive skin to Mae's porcelain. My father was noticeably absent, his place behind Mother's right shoulder an appropriate blotch of bright sunlight.

"It's October third," Franklin said, interrupting my study of the photo. I smiled at his random revelation, not sure why it mattered. "Grandpa James's birthday," he reminded, then shrugged, eyes fixed to the flames.

"Someone has to tell the story," I said, remembering at last. I'd forgotten in the chaos of the evening. Growing up, Father always told the tale of his father, the fearless Civil War hero. Even though we were required to listen back then, I was captivated. I could still see my father's face, round brown eyes dancing as he sat in front of the fireplace talking about the fierce man who raised him. My sisters had never really cared about our history, but Franklin and I always had, begging our parents to tell us more.

"All right," Mother said, and grinned at me, likely relieved to find that I seemed livened by the distraction.

Rubbing her eyes, she straightened up against the longue, patted Franklin's leg, and reached for my hand. "It all began in

'49 . . . when your grandparents, who'd been living in a large brick home on five acres in the city, decided they wanted to sell it. At the time, the city had just started construction on a big park right in front of their home and they'd grown tired of the noise and commotion, so your grandfather sold the house and land for three thousand dollars and moved the family to the Bronx. Back then, this was country. You could hear wild geese calling and crickets in the summertime, and your grandfather knew that he'd build a home here . . . a country retreat, he called it." Franklin made a noise of amused disagreement. Today, the quiet call of geese overhead had been replaced by the whir of the trolley flying by every hour, the distant clanging from the iron factory, and the commotion of a thousand commuters hustling to the train station or to the ferry dock along the canal. "So, all was quiet and lovely, and everyone was happy . . . until Lincoln's call to arms." Franklin elbowed my mother and she smiled, nodding for him to continue. He crossed the room, plucked an armchair from the corner, and set it down in front of the blue and white Wedgwood tiles lining the hearth, in the exact spot where Father used to sit.

"He was a brave man. A man of another era," Franklin started, echoing Father's words. He paused for a moment and then proceeded. "He went to war honored to serve and came back from Gettysburg without a scratch . . . carrying that blasted creeper vine." Franklin gestured toward the front of the house. "Sometimes I wonder what possessed him . . . why he'd take the effort to dig up a vine from the battlefield and bring it all the way back home." I laughed, imagining the grandfather I'd never known digging while bullets flew around his head.

"Likely because it reminded him of himself—strong and nearly impossible to kill," I said, and Mother grinned.

"I imagine he wanted to remember what he'd seen sacrificed."

Franklin cleared his throat, and straightened in his seat. "Nevertheless, he came back, but just for a two-week furlough. And then he went off to Georgia, where he died valiantly during the battle of Peach Tree Creek. Captain Bundy's report said that he'd been shot nine times, three through the heart." Franklin brought his hand to his chest as he said it, palm resting on the corduroy vest. "He died in true Loftin family fashion . . . stubbornly. His strength was his heart, his determination. It took three bullets to kill him." Frank looked down at his hands, then up at me, eyes boring into mine. "We have to remember that we, too, are Loftins, and though our hearts may fracture, they will not falter. No one will stamp us out." Franklin leaned toward me, looping his arm around my shoulders. I lifted my hand to take his. Our parents told us he'd reached for me like this only moments after we were born and that my hand had lifted to rest on his. It made sense. Everything else disappeared when we embraced this way and all we saw were each other. Frank's forehead met mine. "No one," he whispered. "Do you understand me, Gin? We will always, *always* rise stronger."

Chapter Three

The Loftin House

BRONX, NEW YORK

*C*harlie came by my house the following day, and the day after that, and the day after that. Every day for two weeks and two days. He came at different times, but always looked the same—fingers tangled in his brown curls, eyes darting across the upstairs windows. I wanted so badly to go to him, to hear him say that he'd made a mistake and wanted me, but there was no guarantee of that dream and I wouldn't subject my shattered heart to a conversation to the contrary. Instead, I'd watch him come up the walk every day, flattening myself on the cushion of the window seat when he got close enough to see me. Alevia had fabricated an excuse the first time—that I was ill and resting. The rest of my family had thankfully followed suit.

I'd barely moved since waking the morning after the party. But it wasn't only sadness that paralyzed me; it was also inspiration. I wanted, needed, to write. From sunup to sundown, words poured from my mind. I wrote until my fingers could barely move from their clutch on the pencil and my brain began to confuse sentences. I wrote twelve columns for the *Bronx Review*, I wrote about my family, and when I couldn't put it off any longer, I began to write about Charlie. It started because I knew someday I'd forget what it felt like to be in love, to have him in my life—the comfort that came with his friendship. I could already feel his absence, and unable to bear it, I wrote down every daydream, all the things I'd always hoped for our future. By the time I was done, I'd written a book—about imagined adventures overseas, a pleasant domestic life surrounded by family and art, and finally, a parting at death that made me ache.

I stared at the words "The End" as if they were an inscription on a gravestone—an irreversible statement that at last forced me into the real world to face the truth of his betrayal. I ached for the words I'd written to come alive, to transform this bleak reality, but they never would. Charlie, my perfect match, had deserted me. Without him my dreams of love and marriage and children and art could never be. No one else had the same mix of passions and I wouldn't resign myself to someone lesser for the sake of companionship.

I set my notebook down and thumbed through the latest *Scribner's Magazine*. My fingers paused on a story from Octave Thanet—otherwise known as Alice French—titled *Stories of a Western Town*. She was criticized in some circles for hiding her identity, for choosing to remain a spinster, but she'd always been an inspiration to me, a woman who'd successfully broken through the iron gates of masculinity to grace the pages of the country's finest literary magazines. Charlie had known of my admiration, and after my fifth rejection from the *Bronx Review*—the day after the *Review* hired him for his drawings—he dragged me down to the library. Though I'd always been resilient, this time I'd thought to give up writing. It seemed impossible that someone could see past my gender. Charlie had made me sit at reception while he disappeared into the bowels of the library, returning with copies of Thanet's stories, *The Bishop's Vagabond, Knitters in the Sun,* and *We All.* He'd forced me to read them, sitting silently beside me until my defeat began to crumble.

I stood from the window seat and closed the magazine. There was no use in recalling our memories, the occasions I'd mistaken for love. My legs wobbled with disuse and I ran a hand through my greasy hair. I had no idea what day it was, only that today was ending. The sun was setting through the naked chestnut branches. I yawned, glanced down at the walk, and flung myself onto the floor. *Charlie.* He'd seen me this time, I was fairly sure of it, and I crawled to the foot of my bed knowing the only way I could avoid him was to hide. Mae had come up yesterday to say she was tired of covering for me. Franklin had said the same, practically begging. "Gin, he needs to talk to you. He looks awful," he'd said. At the time, my brain had been churning with words I needed to write, so I'd barely heard him. "Did he change his mind about Miss Kent?" I'd turned to look at my brother who'd stared back at me saying nothing, but whose eyes said no. "Then I don't care."

Charlie banged on the door below my window, shaking the walls. I could hear Mae's footsteps, quick and light, coming from the study on the opposite side of the house where she'd been writing her thesis and preparing lessons to teach the orphans at Saint Joseph's Asylum, as she did every Friday afternoon before attending her evening courses. I knew this week at the orphanage was especially important as Mae's benefactor and frequent volunteer, Mrs. Greenwood, would be in from her country home in Millerton. Mrs. Greenwood had noticed Mae's passion for teaching two years ago, and insisting that New York needed educators like Mae, had offered to pay for Mae to attend college.

I sniffed at my skin, revolted by the oniony musk radiating from it. I couldn't figure how I'd been sweating. We'd gone through the last of our coal and wood days ago. The house was frigid.

"Mae. Please. I know she's here. I saw her this time. Let me in." Charlie's voice was soft and desperate. I pressed my palms to my ears to drown him out. I could so easily give in to his distress.

"Charlie, you know we all love you, but I can't." I could hear Mae's high-pitched voice through my hands, and let them fall to my lap. "She . . . she doesn't want to see you." I knew it pained her, but relieved that she was going to turn him away after all, I took a deep breath. Avoiding him was torture, but I didn't want to face him—maybe ever. Mae yelled Charlie's name, and I heard something crash to the floor and shatter.

"Sorry! I'm sorry," he said. He must've pushed past her. I threw myself under the bed. His footsteps pounded up the stairs and I curled into a ball hoping he wouldn't look for me.

"No," Franklin said abruptly. His voice was close, probably coming from the landing, and I squeezed my eyes shut, thankful for my brother's presence. "You can't."

"Let me go, Frank," Charlie growled. I could hear them struggling against each other, the banister screeching as Charlie tried to shove past him.

"Leave . . . her . . . alone," Franklin breathed. "You've chosen." The commotion suddenly stopped and Charlie groaned.

"Ginny! You have to talk to me. Please," Charlie yelled. "You can't discard me so quickly." His footsteps retreated slowly down the steps and I crawled out from under the safety of the bed like a hunted deer emerging from the brush.

I stood before the mirror, staring at the startling vein-snaked eyes and pale skin that hadn't seen sun in weeks. Charlie and I argued constantly, but the last time we'd fought to the point of jeopardizing our friendship I'd been seven, standing in this exact spot. His younger brother, George, had just died and Charlie had been a wreck for weeks upon weeks, blaming himself for George's death because he'd been there to see it. I'd been there, too—walking home from sledding in Bathgate Woods Park with Charlie when George, who'd decided to sled down a small hill half a mile ahead of us, plunged into the street in front of a fast-moving sleigh. There was no way he could've saved him, but Charlie kept blaming himself until he was so gripped with grief that he couldn't move, just sitting in his room, barely blinking and staring at the empty bed next to his own. Each day, when his mother finally made him get up, he'd come over to sit on the edge of my bed and cry—until the night I told him that George had always been easily bored and unless Charlie stopped weeping, George would grow tired of watching over him and would move on to someone else. I'd meant to make Charlie laugh, mostly because I'd watched him weep for weeks and couldn't take his grief any longer. But the moment the words came from my mouth, I knew it had been the wrong thing to say. He'd yelled at me and threw my dressing chair across the room, shattering my window.

I couldn't help but smile thinking of that fight now, though it had been one of the darkest moments we'd ever shared. I stepped closer to the mirror, inspecting my face and soul for any trace of the little girl I'd once been. I could barely remember her, though if I concentrated I could feel the unbridled freedom of chasing Charlie and Franklin around the house while performing a play I'd penned about Buffalo Bill, or running into the Harlem River with my siblings, Charlie close on my heels. In those days, I didn't worry about my life, or what I'd make of myself. No, in those days my only thoughts were how long it would take for my body to warm to the cool water or if I was fast enough to catch the boys. I turned to the window, toward my notebook full of memories, determined to go back in time. My bones ached from sitting, but I sat down anyway and opened the cover.

The door flung open, smacking against the wall, and I turned to see Franklin glaring at me, lips pressed in irritation. I stared at him, blinking desperately in an attempt to clear the haze of the last few weeks. "You look terrible," he said. One of his hands snatched the pale pink sleeve at my wrist as the other yanked the leather-bound notebook from my fingers. I lunged for it and he pushed me away. "Honestly, Gin. I've never known you to wallow in misery, and I've had enough. So has Mae. If Mother hadn't been in the city for Alevia's audition for the last week, she would've dragged you out of your room days ago, so I'm going to do it for her."

My brows rose. "Is that so? I'm quite heavy." I was amazed at how strong my voice sounded after days of neglect. "I'm fine, Frank. Truly. I've just been writing. And well, I might add." I picked at my nails, noticing the dead circles of dry skin on my index finger. The blisters had popped up about the fourth day, but I'd simply gripped the pencil with my fingertips and continued.

"I don't care. I'll not have you wither away in seclusion like that Dickinson woman." I laughed and he looked at me sharply. "It's not funny, Gin. I've never in my life seen you so affected by anything. You're a strong person. Talk to him and move past this. For my sake if not for anyone else's. I'm tired of fending him off." Franklin sighed and lifted his hand to rub his eyes. His fingers from nails to knuckles were streaked with black and blue paint.

"Who've you been painting?" I asked, walking over to my armoire. Though Franklin couldn't afford to devote all of his time to painting, his portraits were incredible, somehow capturing not only a person's likeness, but the character as well. He stretched his hands out in front of him and grinned.

"Oh. Just Mae. She's the only one home save you. Bess has been in the city most days, measuring the society ladies for winter hats." He yawned. "It's been so tiresome watching Mae study all weekend. I don't think I'll ever understand why she's so enthusiastic about teaching."

"How can you not? It's the same as you with your painting, me with my writing, Alevia with her playing, Bess with her—"

"Yes, I see." Franklin cut me off, eyeing the robe draped over my arm. "Thank god you're taking a bath. You smell terrible." I rolled my eyes and started down the hallway.

"So do you," I called out. "Though in your case I don't think you can help—"

"Virginia." Charlie materialized from nowhere, grabbed my hand, yanked me into my mother's room, and shut the door. The last word of my retort to Franklin caught in the back of my throat, choking me. I swallowed it away.

"How'd you get in here?" I asked evenly. Wedged in the narrow doorway, I could feel the heat of his body inches from mine and smell his light piney sweat beneath his jacket.

"Funny, Gin," Franklin yelled, having no idea I'd been detained on my way to the bathroom. Charlie didn't respond and I pushed past him, lunging for the door, but he seized my shoulders and pulled me back into the room, hands digging into my skin. I hadn't looked at him yet, beyond a glance when he'd startled me, and didn't now as I shoved against his chest, trying to free myself.

"I waited until Mae went back to the study and Frank went into your room," he grunted, struggling against me.

"What do you want? Fra—" I started to scream for my brother, but Charlie's hand clamped across my mouth and forced my face to his. I closed my eyes.

"Ginny, please," he whispered. "Can't you just look at me?"

I swallowed hard, let the tension drop from my shoulders, and opened my eyes. His eyes were rimmed with black circles so dark they made the green seem luminous. The hair on his face was long, save a patch on the right side of his chin where he'd never been able to grow it. I must've winced, because he loosened his grip on my shoulders. He looked almost as awful as I knew I did. "That bad?" he said, and laughed under his breath. His fingers peeled back from my mouth, sliding slowly over my lips. I closed my eyes, letting my head drop onto his chest. His heart thumped wildly against my ear—a complete contrast to the hands slowly tangling in my hair and drifting up and down my back. I felt drowsy, as though I could fall asleep against him, but he shifted suddenly, smoothed my hair back, and kissed my forehead. As if his lips had broken some sort of spell, I jerked away from him. I couldn't believe I'd let him touch me, that I'd forgotten his abandonment so quickly. I crossed the room to the rippled glass window, past the photo of my father as a young man wearing my grandfather's Union army jacket on the dresser, knowing that if my father had been here he would've been furious with Charlie and demanded I stand my ground.

"Ginny, I'm sorry." I didn't turn around, but stared out at the night sky and then down to the darkened window of the Aldridges' library. I'd noticed that the library lamps hadn't been lit since the party, and hoped that his lack of work had something to do with missing me, that he couldn't create without confronting my memory. "You've been avoiding me. I've come to see you every day." I pinched my eyes shut and lifted a shoulder. "Why? Where . . . where have you been?" With you, I thought, remembering the lifetime I'd written in my notebook.

"I was writing," I said. "Why are you here?"

I turned to face him. He stared at his hands, opening and closing his grandfather's pocket watch at his hip, hair hanging in his eyes. I could see his profile in the mirror on top of Mother's armoire, his straight brows pinched, full bottom lip clutched in his teeth.

"I . . . umm," he mumbled, then looked up at me. Nerves curled in my stomach, forbidding the rest of my body to move. I stared at him—at the somber eyes and lips that had paused on an unspoken word. He held my gaze. "Ginny, I love you." His words shocked my heart and warmed me through. I'd wanted to hear him say it for so many years, sentiments I'd long felt but propriety forbid me to say. He wouldn't marry Miss Kent. He loved me. He'd come back to me. I reached down to take his hand. Clammy with sweat, his fingers were limp against mine.

"Charlie," I whispered. "I love you, too. I always have." He smiled thinly and looked down at our linked hands. "What is it?" He squeezed my hand so hard I flinched, and hugged me.

"I love you, Gin," he said into my hair, "but I . . . I have to marry her." I pushed him away and he stumbled back, catching himself against the wall.

"No, actually. You don't. You coward!" Heat burned my cheeks. He'd given me hope only to crush it once again. "Why would you bother coming here? Why would you tell me you love me if it doesn't matter?" I snapped, backing away from him. "To make yourself feel better?" My hands clenched at my side. His eyes were glassy, but I didn't care. I wanted to hurt him as much as he'd hurt me. He opened his mouth to speak, thought better of it, and stared down at his shoes. "You can explain yourself or you can get out," I said. Physically too weak to yell at him, anger still churned through me, stealing what little strength I had. Charlie straightened and started toward me. I put my hand out to stop him.

"Ginny, you know we don't have any money."

"We don't either," I said. My neck felt tight. "We barely have enough to spare for food by the time our bills are paid, but we're happy. How does that—"

"I . . . I haven't told you everything." He cleared his throat to compose himself. "Mother and Father . . . when they got married they didn't have the money to buy a house. My father's uncle, Harry, offered to buy it for them on the condition that they'd pay him back. It was working out fine, but now without Father, we can't afford it. The *Review* pays so minimally for my drawings that we're four payments behind. Harry's company folded a few months back. If we don't reimburse him in full by next month, he'll have to sell the house. Mother won't have anywhere to go. If I marry, we're saved. The initial three thousand from Rachel's father will pay Harry off and then when I inherit the estate and ten thousand from Rachel's family—"

"I don't want to hear her name," I said. He tried to take my outstretched hand but I snatched it away. "Don't touch me."

"I don't love her," he whispered. "My heart. You have it." He put his palm on the silk above my chest.

"Then marry me instead and risk ruin," I said. "We could find other jobs. Your mother could move in with us if she had to." I removed his hand from my chest, feeling the cold air rush over my skin with its absence. He didn't say anything, but closed his eyes and shook his head.

"You know she'd never agree to that," he said finally. "Our home is all she has left of my father, of George."

"Then you've made your choice."

"No. I can't. I don't want to lose you . . . please, Gin."

"What would you have me do? Wait for years until Rachel dies? Be your mistress?" He looked up from the floor and his body went rigid.

"I know that I can't will you to do anything," he said softly. "You'll do what you want. You always have." I laughed hollowly and caught a glimpse of my reflection as I turned away from him, stringy hair and ashen face harrowing in the dim evening light. I was a mess. Everything Miss Kent wasn't. I pivoted to face him. His shoulders were slumped, the dark rings around his eyes even more pronounced than before.

"I'll see you around the neighborhood, of course," I said as pleasantly as I could. Charlie had been as much a part of me as I was, but the man standing before me was foreign, a stranger to my soul. Charlie's brows furrowed and he crossed the room, gathering me awkwardly in his arms. I stood against him, puppet-like as he hugged me. "You need to go now." I untangled myself from his embrace. He backed away, staring at me as he went, and then finally turned. "Take care of yourself, Charlie," I whispered. As the door clicked shut, I stood in my mother's room alone, regretting my words and wishing that I could have been weak enough to keep him.

Chapter Four

I eyed the old wooden clock on my nightstand. Just past 5:20. Less than ten minutes until Franklin and Mae would appear in my doorway, tear the notebook from my fingers, and demand that I come with them, though I didn't want to go. Neither tolerated tardiness—or my need to be alone. Since Charlie's surprise visit a week ago, they'd barely left me to my own devices, appearing in my room to distract me every few minutes as if their presence could somehow cause me to forget. Instead, they were driving me mad.

I glanced down at the page and read the sentences for the tenth time. The first ran on and had to be fixed, but I couldn't figure out how. "*In all the time I'd known him, he'd never begged for anything, not because he was necessarily against it by principle, but because he'd always been perfectly intentioned in everything he did, and felt that if a person didn't react to his intentions in the affirmative, well then, they didn't, and life went on. So the fact that he was begging now startled me.*" I circled the sentences, slammed the notebook shut, and flung it across my bed. Perhaps my problem wasn't my ability to edit, but the fact that these particular sentences required me to recall the misery on Charlie's face. Even though I knew I'd done the right thing, Charlie had been my best friend for eighteen years. We'd grown accustomed to consoling each other. In spite of everything, it was strange that I couldn't be the one to cheer him, that he was the source of my own sorrow.

I glanced at the discarded notebook, not entirely sure why I was bothering to edit it in the first place. It wasn't as if anyone would ever read it. It was too personal, not to mention terribly written. I was a short story writer; I had no idea how to write a proper novel. I hadn't attempted a longer work in twelve years, since I was a child. My family and the Aldridges had gone to see P. T. Barnum's circus in Brooklyn, and the glitz and the wildness of it had left us all inspired. The next day, I was commissioned by Charlie and my siblings to write a book about the ringmaster. In my ten-year-old mind, I'd thought a story of a ringmaster who could speak to animals a genius idea. I'd written the fifty pages with great fervor, while Charlie sketched the scenes and Franklin painted dramatic depictions of the ringmaster. Even Mae, Alevia, and Bess had been convinced to participate. Alevia obligingly played *Gavotte Circus Renz* by Hermann Fliege over and over for inspiration, while Bess created replicas of the performer's costumes. When we'd finished the book, we were sure it would eclipse Stevenson's *Treasure Island* in popularity. Our hopes were only provoked by our parents. After Mae's dramatic reading, they'd deemed it brilliant. Father had bound the volume with two thin sheets of wood and Mother had covered it in a scrap of red silk. We'd given the finished copy to Charlie for his eleventh birthday.

I stood and crossed to my dresser, running my fingers along the chipping white paint on my windowsill as I went. Glancing in the mirror, I laughed wryly at the hints of black lead smudged across my cheeks and under my eyes as if I'd actually been writing rather than crossing out, erasing, and rewriting the same sentence over again. I thought of Charlie's library, of the one place I'd always retreated when I couldn't seem to find the right words. I knew that part of its magic had to do with Charlie's presence, his encouragements and suggestions, but within its walls, I'd always been able to sort my thoughts. He'd stolen my only hideaway from me.

I scrubbed the pencil marks away with the tip of my finger and smoothed the pink silk rose petals attached to the Brussels lace at my shoulder. It had taken Bess three nights to arrange all of them and affix them to the sleeve in the latest fall fashion. Bess refused to create anything short of perfection, even if the costume was being made for one of us.

Pulling my grandfather's worn copy of Irving's *The Sketch Book* from the drawer beneath my mirror, I flipped it open. How many times had I read it and found solace in its pages? Stopping on the title page, I stared at the colophon, "*published by George Putnam.*" Putnam and Irving had been fast friends, though Putnam had been Irving's junior by decades. Late in Irving's life, press after press had passed up the chance to publish an updated edition of Irving's work, but Putnam had decided to take it on, convinced that the words Irving had written were still relevant and needed. It was one of the most profitable decisions Putnam ever made, and the reason I'd been introduced to Irving's work as a child. My grandfather had started reading the new anthology and was so taken with it that he'd demanded his entire household read it. My father then passed it on to me.

I closed Irving and went to retrieve my discarded notebook. Perhaps it was a vain and foolish ambition, but the desire for someone to read and cherish my stories as I cherished Irving's swelled in my chest. I closed my eyes and ran my hand over the worn cover, imagining it as a threadbare hardback on the dresser of a girl I would never know. That possibility eclipsed the hole in my heart with a strange new sense of purpose, and I knew that the feeling alone was worth whatever would come next. I would make something of this manuscript—somehow. I would find a way to learn what it would take to transform my scattered words into something of worth.

"Well, what a welcome surprise." I jumped at the sound of Franklin's voice and whirled to face him. Propped against my doorframe in a black tailcoat, he grinned at me and flicked his gold pocket watch open. "Five-thirty precisely and you're actually ready."

"Good thing, too. At least for your sake," Mae said to me, materializing beside Franklin in the doorway. "I stalled as long as I could. I helped Mother with the laundry and even washed the dishes twice, but Frank said he'd be hauling you off with us at five-thirty whether you were ready or not."

"Oh really? And if I wasn't?" I laughed, narrowing my eyes at the two of them.

"I'd just sling you over my shoulder." Franklin shrugged and scratched at the corner of his mustache. He glanced down the length of my turquoise blue satin dress. "In any case, I have to admit that I'm relieved you're dressed. Mae and I were taking bets on whether or not we'd have to endure the Symphony next to the stench of that horrendous pink dressing gown." I grinned and snatched my small black purse from my bedside table.

"You would've survived," I said, shoving past them. "But I doubt I would've. I'm afraid the spectacle of a woman in her nightclothes wasn't the sort of entertainment Mr. Carnegie had in mind."

Chapter Five

Carnegie Hall

NEW YORK, NEW YORK

Franklin coughed, hand masking his face to keep from laughing out loud. I looked around wondering what in the world he thought was so funny, but saw nothing beyond Mae beside me fiddling with the ruched collar of her plain purple-velvet dress.

Franklin turned to face us, eyes glistening with hilarity. "Do you see Louise Carnegie over there?" he whispered, nodding toward the balcony across from us. All five stories of the new hall were packed tonight—the papers said that most of its two thousand eight hundred seats had been occupied for every performance since its opening in May—but I found Andrew Carnegie's sparse white hair and full beard as easily as a spotlight amid the darkness of his hall. I laughed under my breath at his wife next to him.

"You can't miss her. She's wearing one of Bessie's hats," Mae noted, no doubt thinking what we all did: that the joke was on Bess's customers. Mrs. Carnegie's head looked as if it'd been wrapped up like a Christmas package in red silk with a gargantuan gold bow attached to the side.

"The bow keeps hitting Adelaide Frick in the face." Franklin chuckled through the last word, pinching the bridge of his nose in an attempt to keep his composure. "I'm thankful Bess is busy sewing. We would've been subject to a monologue on her inspiration for that dreadful accessory." Unable to look away from the huge hat, I watched as Mrs. Carnegie turned toward her husband, sweeping one of the bow tails across Mrs. Frick's cheek. Glaring at the fabric hanging in her face, Mrs. Frick batted it and scooted away. I laughed out loud, and clapped my hand over my mouth, feeling the eyes of the patrons around me.

"It's a wonder she's not wearing that wretched stork hat she had Bessie make after Caroline Astor's party." Mae scrunched her nose, tucking a stray mahogany tendril behind her ear.

"I'm honestly shocked that anyone was inspired by the pelican hat enough to request anything remotely related," I said.

"I'm not. If one of them has it, the rest want it . . . well, not the same thing of course, something similar." Franklin rolled his eyes and fiddled with his new gold cuff links. "That's the only reason Bess has customers anyway. Hodgepodge a hat for Caroline Astor and they all come flocking."

"Frank, I don't want you to think I'm unappreciative. This is amazing," I said. Looking away from Franklin's expensive cuff links, I gestured to the Carnegie Hall stage right below me. "But you invited the whole family!" Franklin had been excited to invite Mother, though a headache kept her home. Her parents, Sarah and George VanPelt, had kept a reserved box at the Academy of Music since its opening in 1854. She often spoke of the performances she'd seen as a young woman—*The Barber of Seville, La Sonnambula, Don Pasquale*—though she rarely mentioned fond memories of her parents at all. Her mother, a hard-nosed woman, had passed on from some type of fever when Mother was sixteen, and her father succumbed to a ruptured aneurysm a few weeks before my parents' wedding—a match of which he adamantly disapproved.

"Frank," I said again, nudging his arm. "Surely we can't afford this. And those cuff links had to cost at least fifteen dollars." I didn't want to harass him about his spending, especially because his salary and Bess's financed the majority of our charges, but I knew that seats like this cost at least five dollars apiece and we'd only had twenty dollars to spare last month.

Franklin lit a cigar, puffing on the end. "We can't," he said out of the corner of his mouth. "I met a man on the train to Connecticut last month whose father—some entrepreneur sort—has reserved this box for the season. We got on quite well and we've kept in touch. They should be by to join us shortly." He took a drag and coughed. "And the cuff links only cost ten. They were discounted at Wanamaker's." He lifted his arm in front of his face. "Handsome aren't they? I've been saving a few quarters here and there and finally had enough to buy them."

I smiled, inhaling the charred smoke from Franklin's cigar. It reminded me of wandering past the Manor of Morrisania as a child before it was parceled off, of the old gardeners puffing away while they worked on the lawn.

Everyone suddenly stood around me and I joined them, pulling my skirt from the chair cushion as the players began to take the stage. Orderly and slow, black tuxedo after black tuxedo, they filed into their seats in front of the columns trimmed with gilded filigree, waiting for Walter Damrosch. I felt a bit guilty coming to see the Symphony. Franklin had hoped Alevia would attend, but none of us were surprised when she begged off to practice. She'd auditioned for the sixth time, and been denied, just a few weeks before, on the grounds that her playing wasn't satisfactory, though the truth was Damrosch didn't want to cause conflict between the male players by admitting a female. I'd grown tired of both the Philharmonic and the Symphony pretending that they were rejecting her based on the quality of her playing.

Walter Damrosch came on stage to a roar of applause, tipped his head, and forced his thin lips into a mediocre smile. His lack of enthusiasm annoyed me and I looked away, scanning the guests in orchestra seating. A woman in an elaborate red dress trimmed with rose chiffon and black velvet ribbon was doubled over laughing in the second row, her face nearly as crimson as the fabric. Righting, she drew her fingers to her mouth to whistle and I recognized her immediately as Anna Katharine Green, bestselling writer of detective fiction. She nudged a dark-haired man to her left and he turned to face her, the full beard, kind eyes, and wide smile unmistakably belonging to her publisher, George Haven Putnam, president of G. P. Putnam's Sons. I stared at them for what seemed like minutes, watching them laugh and clap like old friends, imagining Mr. Putnam's father and Washington Irving sharing the same camaraderie. My heart lifted in my chest. I wanted desperately to feel the excitement for my book alive in someone else, and knew, in that moment, that someone was George Putnam—a man whose literary ancestry ran parallel to the author I admired the most. Mr. Putnam leaned in and whispered something, pointing toward the velvet curtains drawn back from the stage. Anna's eyes followed. I wondered if they were talking about ideas for a new story.

"Excuse me. Sorry. I'm sorry we're late." A tall man with nearly black hair edged past Mae, disrupting my focus on George and Anna, and deposited himself in the empty seat beside me. He was followed by an older gentleman with round glasses and a long beard, and a younger man with golden hair and a straight, confident posture I recognized immediately to be the man I'd seen standing next to the author, John Hopper, at Charlie's party.

Frozen against the hard chair back, I leaned into the shadow of the box above us and shielded my face with my hand, wishing I could melt into the red velour upholstery. I couldn't let him see me. I figured there was a fifty-fifty chance he'd recognize me as the girl who'd stood heartbroken next to Charlie as he proposed to Rachel and I had no idea if he would have enough tact to avoid the topic. Franklin started to get up, but the Symphony launched into the opening notes of Berlioz's *Te Deum*, and he was forced to take his seat, thankfully leaving no time for introductions. Leaning over Mae and me, Franklin nodded at the row of men beside me and I turned the other way, staring at the velvet curtains hanging next to our box.

"What's wrong with you?" Mae whispered. "You're sitting as though that man next to you has some type of plague." Her eyes danced in amusement, and I looked down noticing I'd managed to fold myself onto about half of the seat, leaving at least six inches of space between myself and the gentleman beside me.

"Frank's friend, the one on the end," I whispered. "He was at Charlie's and I—"

"You're being foolish. I doubt anyone besides Alevia even suspected you were upset," she said. Pursing her lips, she sank back against the chair, fixed her eyes on the orchestra for a moment, and then turned back to me. "And even if he did notice, there's no way he would've known about you and Charlie. He doesn't even know you."

As the music continued, I grew bored. I'd heard *Te Deum* hundreds of times and the rhythmic piano chords that Alevia had played over and over in our home seemed to drone on and on. Though Mae's words had settled my worry for a moment, from time to time I would feel someone's attention crawling across my skin, and assumed it was the man I'd seen at Charlie's. The music reached a crescendo, every instrument in the hall moving to the jabs and swings of Damrosch's arms, and I felt a gaze again. Rolling my eyes, I turned sharply in his direction, but found the man next to me staring at Mae instead. Startled, he straightened hastily in his seat, and cleared his throat.

"Wasn't that remarkable?" he asked later, when the music finally stopped for intermission. He smiled in my direction, but his eyes drifted again beyond me to my sister, who had stood up to take a glass of sparkling white wine.

"The music was fine, but if it's her you're actually talking about, she is," I said bluntly, and he laughed.

"She looks familiar. I'm Henry Trent." As much as he was trying to look at me, he couldn't. His dark eyes kept darting from me to Mae and back again. "I'm . . . um. I'm a student at Columbia, studying English." Trying to pretend I didn't notice him glancing at her, I pinched myself to keep from either smiling like a buffoon or laughing. Mr. Trent blinked a few times as if he was trying to rid himself of whatever spell had overcome him.

"Lovely to meet you, Mr. Trent. That's probably how you know her . . . Miss Mae Loftin," I said, tipping my head toward my sister. I caught the eye of the man from the party who was conversing with her and Franklin and jerked back to Mr. Trent. My heart began to race. I didn't know what I'd say if he mentioned seeing me at Charlie's. Mr. Trent was staring at me, no doubt wondering why I was gaping dumbly over his shoulder. "You've probably seen her at a literary seminar," I said, forcing myself back to the conversation. "She goes to all of them at Columbia. I've been to a few with her if an author I like is speaking. We went to see Ambrose Bierce last month."

"I was there, too," he said, fidgeting with the corner of his gray tweed jacket. Finding his distraction suddenly more annoying than endearing, I stood up knowing I'd have to face Frank's friend at some point, and turned toward Mae.

Standing in the corner of the balcony, Mae shook her head at Franklin who was leaning a little too far over the edge, a second cigar balanced between his teeth. His friend stood beside him, cheeks eclipsing his marked cheekbones as he laughed at something Frank had just said.

"I'm just saying that I'd think twice about siring her child because there's half a chance it would turn out crazy," I heard the man say as I walked closer. I was thankful that I'd missed this gem of a conversation. The man chuckled under his breath and Franklin grit his teeth, nose scrunching in disgust. I wondered who they were talking about.

"I wouldn't touch her with a barge pole, though *you* didn't seem so averse last time." Franklin clapped him on the back, then noticed me standing there and straightened up. "Oh. Mr. John Hopper and Doctor Joseph Hopper, this is my sister, Miss Virginia Loftin." I blinked, confused, before I realized that Charlie had mistaken my inquiry of the short man for the one before me. I swallowed hard, determined to keep it together. I extended my hand to the older of the two and forced a smile.

"So you're an entrepreneur, Doctor Hopper?" I asked, automatically wishing I'd said something simple and polite instead of coming right out and asking about his profession. The older man smiled graciously, the same exact grin I'd just seen on his son beside him.

"Your brother is kind. I'm simply a doctor who prefers innovation to stagnancy." He removed his eyeglasses to clean them on the edge of his jacket and I looked around for Mae, finding her sitting behind me talking to Mr. Trent.

"I'm a writer," Mr. Hopper volunteered before I could ask, and I turned back to face him. Grinning goofily, he cleared his throat.

"Which means I bathe in money, employ many servants, and live in a tidy little mansion on Fifth Avenue." Mr. Hopper raised his eyebrows at me and Franklin choked on his cigar.

"Right. You know, I think we're neighbors," I said, straight-faced. Mr. Hopper started to say something, but Franklin stopped him.

"Ginny's a writer, too. She just finished her first novel," he said. I nodded, relieved that Mr. Hopper hadn't mentioned recognizing me—so far.

"You should join our little group then," Mr. Hopper said. His brown eyes were kind. "It's just a gathering of amateur artists, really. Well, artists, musicians, writers, and the like." He adjusted the sprig of Lilly of the Valley tucked into his buttonhole. "I was quite taken with the idea of creating a salon in New York after having the pleasure of speaking with Mathilde Bonaparte in Paris a few years ago. She hosted one of the most popular salons until her exile to Belgium." He laughed. "Not to say that mine is anywhere near as grand as hers was. In any case, it would be a pleasure to have you attend." I'd read something about Parisian salons recently, a brief citation in an article about Proust, mentioning that men and women were encouraged to mingle and collaborate. In a sense, in my own life, the fact that my brother and Charlie read my work was revolutionary and rare.

"Oh, you should." Franklin nodded at me. "Gin, it's wonderful. I've only been the one time, but I meant to tell you of it right after, to invite you with me the next time. I suppose I've been traveling so much that exhaustion has wiped my mind clean of functional thought. Forgive me." I smiled at Frank.

"I'll have to try it," I said, though in truth I thought it sounded like hell. Even though I'd dreamed of publication privately, the thought of sharing my writing—my deepest disappointments and joys—with strangers filled me with horror. My manuscript wasn't ready, and neither was I. In part because the last artists gathering I'd attempted in June—an all-male meeting of Charlie's early childhood friends from his old neighborhood in Brooklyn—had ended badly. Charlie had said that a female presence might not be the best idea, but I'd insisted on attending anyway. I'd been desperate for the camaraderie of other serious writers. When we arrived, the host, a pock-faced man named Wayland, had immediately asked me to leave, stating that a woman's attendance was improper. Charlie had defended me, prompting a heated exchange that ended abruptly when Charlie said that Wayland was too simpleminded to appreciate the complexity of my prose. Charlie had held my hand the whole train ride home. That was one of the occasions that made me realize I'd always loved Charlie, that he was my match.

The strings began to sing behind me, disturbing the memory. "Nice to meet you, Mr. Hopper."

"Likewise, Miss Loftin. I'll see you and Franklin next Friday," he said. "And if you don't show, I'll come fetch you. I know where you live." He winked at me and I stared at him, wondering how in the world he knew. He held my gaze, and I looked away, before realizing he was referring to our earlier exchange. I sat down and leaned over Mr. Trent and Doctor Hopper.

"As you should, judging by the number of times your carriage has visited my lawn. I've noticed several tire depressions in the grass. If you wouldn't mind telling your footman to keep to the drive, that'd be magnificent."

"Oh, the atrocity," he whispered. Dramatically placing a hand on his heart, he winked at me again and turned his attention to the players.

Chapter Six

NEW YORK, NEW YORK

You don't remember where it is?"

Franklin and I were walking down yet another unfamiliar cobblestone street in Manhattan. Passing mansion after mansion, the flicker of gas lamps flung shadows of elaborate gables and open-mouthed gargoyles onto the street. I knew we were somewhere near Fifth Avenue. Nowhere else—possibly in the world—was there such an abundance of wealth encapsulated in such a small area. Franklin's black evening jacket disappeared, then reappeared, in front of me as he stepped back into the light. He stopped for a moment, neck craning toward the door of a brick home that looked minuscule in comparison to the castle-like monstrosity beside it. Taking a few steps toward the door, he squinted at the number, shook his head, and kept walking.

"No. I do. It's just that I've always taken the New York and Harlem to Eighty-Sixth Street. I've never taken the elevated line in. We're farther south, so . . ." Franklin shrugged and stopped to wait for me to catch up. I walked faster. The black lace lining the white taffeta dress I'd borrowed from Bess was too long, catching on the edges of the cobblestones with each step. Bess didn't know I'd borrowed it. She'd been in the city all day, selecting materials at O'Neill's for a hat Alva Vanderbilt had asked her to redo for her fourteen-year-old daughter, Consuelo. She'd be livid when she realized I'd worn the dress, but Mother had insisted I look presentable, and I'd barely noticed which dress she was helping me into. Instead, I'd been lost in thought. I hadn't seen Charlie in two weeks—not even so much as a glimpse from my window—and though I knew my heart couldn't bear his presence, it ached in his absence. Every morning, I woke wondering if he'd come for me, if today was the day he'd come to tell me that he'd called off his engagement to marry me instead. But with each passing week my hope was fading. Even if he loved me, he didn't love me enough.

"I recognize that one," Frank said, gesturing toward an Italian Renaissance–style mansion with scrolled ornamentation edging the rectangular frame. I wondered how Doctor Hopper had the means to settle among the Fricks and Vanderbilts.

"I thought Hopper was a doctor," I said, breathlessly, finally catching Franklin.

"He is. This way." We turned down a narrow alley, past a wrought-iron fence protecting someone's garden. The light scent of English boxwoods drifted over the pungent wood smoke billowing from surrounding chimneys and I inhaled the November air, huddling into my grandmother's mink coat—a pelisse that Grandfather had given her on their wedding day.

"Not to discount physicians, but unless he's invented some new contraption, I don't understand how he lives here," I said as I tried to keep up. Franklin strained to see the numbers on another brick house.

"They're related to the Carnegies somehow," he said. Stunned at the comment, I watched as Franklin reached into his pocket, flipped his watch open, and glared at the time. "But I don't know the particulars." I thought of Mr. Hopper's comment at the Symphony, his joking—or so I'd believed—about living on Fifth Avenue, and smiled, finding my first impression, and the irony of the whole thing, hilarious.

"Frank, maybe we should knock and ask someone. Surely one of the housekeepers would know where they live." Franklin's nose wrinkled.

"It's nearly eight at night, Gin. I'm not going to go traipsing up to some stranger's door." He exhaled in frustration and the cloud of his breath drifted past me, disappearing into the night. I thought of Mother, who was likely already tucked in bed reading the new *Ladies' Home Journal,* and knew he was right. "Oh. There it is. Right there." Franklin tipped his head forward, toward a stream of light coming from a house at the end of the block. My fingers curled around the hard edges of the leather notebook in my pocket. I hadn't asked Franklin much about this gathering, mostly because I was afraid that if I heard the answer I wouldn't go. At once, the editorial rejections my writing had accumulated in the past crept to the forefront of my mind—*these characters are one-dimensional, the pace of this story is too tedious, the subject is dull.* I didn't want to stand in the middle of a circle reading a manuscript that I knew was far from perfect, reciting words that conjured Charlie. I also knew I wouldn't be able to hold my tongue if a man like Wayland questioned my being there or insulted my work, as most male artists were wont to do—a diplomatic way of reminding me that I should be at home needlepointing or cooking. Even so, I knew what I wanted and that was to shape this manuscript into something worth reading. To that end, I would need to embrace critique and seek opinions—honest ones.

Franklin was nearly to the door by the time I realized I was still in the road staring at the towering brick chimneys and limestone-edged turrets. He turned around when he didn't find me beside him and started back down the stairs.

"Come on, Gin," he said. His cheeks were pink and the front of his hair stood on end. I reached up and smoothed it back down in an attempt to forget the sudden flash of Mother's face in my mind, her smile when she'd seen me in Bess's dress. I'd been so occupied with wondering about Charlie's absence and how my writing would be received at the Society that I hadn't given her satisfaction much thought. But now, standing outside of the Hopper mansion, the realization dawned on me: Frank's friends, other men, wouldn't only be appraising my writing. They'd be considering my appearance, my wit, my suitability as well.

"I'm nervous," I said. He threw his arm across my shoulders.

"For god's sake, why?"

"I've had plenty of things published for the *Review*, but I've never read anything meaningful out loud . . . especially to strangers or to men . . . well, other than to you or Charlie," I lied. I'd never considered how other men perceived me, if they found me attractive or interesting. I'd never had to; Charlie's friendship, his love, had always convinced me that I was both of those things. But now, suddenly without him, I was unsure. I held on to the freezing metal railing and started up the scrolled concrete steps, hearing the muted sounds of laughter and voices behind the glass doors set in gilded wrought-iron frames.

"You'll never be forced to read anything aloud, though I've heard it can prove to be helpful," Franklin said, opening the door and pulling me inside before I could reply.

We started down a dark hallway and then turned into a drawing room. At first glance, it looked just like Charlie's friend Wayland's gathering—smoke so thick we could have been floating down a southern river with Mark Twain's Huck and Jim, everyone clutching a pencil or paintbrush—but the setting was different. The sweeping gold curtains, the fresco of flying cherubim along the ceiling, and the shiny Weber grand piano in the front corner of the room all pointed to the splendor reserved for the mansions industrialists built—a stark contrast to Wayland's plain home.

"Come on. Let's find Lydia," Franklin said beside me. Having no idea who he was talking about, I squinted into the smoke and dim, and his cold hand found mine. The room was packed. We passed by a few painters working on projects next to easels displaying finished pieces. I watched as groups of people shifted from one painting to the next, gesturing to their peers beside them, leaning into each work as if they were scrutinizing it. We skirted around the fireplace and nearly ran into an assembly of men and women laughing and talking in the middle of the room, as if this sort of intellectual mingling between sexes were common.

"That line about love was magnificent," I heard one of the women say to a bulky man sitting on a stool, "but the ending could've been written by a child." I waited for the man to respond with a retort about her juvenile scrawling, but only heard a deep chuckle. I dug my fingers into the swathe of black taffeta along my arm and pinched, stunned to find I wasn't dreaming. Somehow, it seemed John Hopper had located dozens of men who considered women's artistic endeavors profound. As if my thought conjured him, there he was, reclining in a corner a few feet from the fire in a yellow upholstered armchair, surrounded by a group of at least ten women. Mr. Hopper's notebook was open on his lap, and as he dipped his head to continue reading, a lady standing beside his chair casually brushed her hand across his shoulder. The gesture was innocent enough, but at once, I recalled Charlie's comment about Mr. Hopper's reputation. I recalled the ease of our conversation at the Symphony, the way his focus had given me the impression that he was fully interested in every word I said. Was that how he drew women in?

Frank's hand jerked me forward, away from Mr. Hopper and his admirers. I inhaled, choking on a particularly pungent cloud of burning tobacco. I heard the hollow wail of a cello beneath the noise and the higher trill of a violin suddenly stop mid-note.

"Frank! You're here." The smoke seemed to subside around us and I blinked to clear it from my eyes as a petite blonde shoved her violin into the cellists' occupied hands and lunged for my brother. Her arms circled his neck and he pulled her close, hands resting on the gray satin wrapping her tiny waist. The embrace was so intimate, so familiar. I stared at him, shocked that he'd clearly fallen in love without mentioning it—just like he'd failed to mention the Society. It was unlike him to withhold things from me.

"Miss Lydia Blaine, this is my dear sister, Miss Virginia Loftin," Frank said. I tipped my head to Miss Blaine who leaned in and hugged me.

"Oh, it's so wonderful to finally meet you," she said. "Franklin has been telling me all about your marvelous family and your incredible writing. Where are your other sisters this evening? I've been keen to meet the pianist." She smiled. Her blue eyes were kind and I forced a grin back despite my irritation at Frank, wondering how long they'd known each other.

"Well, actually, Virginia was the only one officially invited," Franklin said. Miss Blaine leaned over to pull him close. "We went to the Symphony with John last week and they got to talking, so he asked her to come."

"Frank tried to invite the others. We were hoping to convince Alevia, the pianist, to attend, but she's quite shy and doesn't like to waste her time socializing when she could be practicing," I said, rolling my eyes at the dedication I wished I had. "And Bessie wasn't home when we were getting ready to leave so we didn't ask her."

"Actually, I chose to leave her out," Franklin said bluntly. "I didn't want to coddle her all night. And Mae isn't artistic, though she was otherwise occupied in any case. She gives English lessons to the orphans at Saint Joseph's each Friday, and after she's finished tonight, she has plans to see *Mrs. Jarley's Wax Works* with Henry Trent."

"What?" The word came out of my mouth so quickly, Miss Blaine laughed. Mae hadn't told me anything. Franklin grinned, fingers drifting over Miss Blaine's hand, and I looked away, eyes locking on his face. "Why would she keep it from me?" Mae had always been private, but she usually confided in me. I held back my questions, though I kept my eyes fixed on Franklin's and then cast them toward Miss Blaine, hoping he'd catch my meaning. Why would *you* conceal so much from me? I thought. His lids widened, suggesting he understood and would tell me later, but then he shrugged.

"She didn't mention it to me either. I couldn't find her so I asked Mother if she knew where she was and she told me that Mae was at the orphanage, but had arranged to accompany Henry to the play afterward." Remembering how taken they'd been with each other at the Symphony, I hoped the affection would remain. Mae had always dreamed of a husband and children, and Mr. Trent shared her same passion for education. The thought struck me. Charlie and I had been well matched, too. Everyone thought so.

"I'm so glad you came," Miss Blaine said, interrupting. "In the three years we've been holding these meetings, I've met tons of people, of course—John tends to invite anyone with an affinity for art—but it's so rare and nice to meet a new friend." She reached to squeeze my hand. She was lovely and warm; I couldn't understand why Franklin hadn't spoken of her.

"I'm thrilled to be here," I said. "And so glad to have met you, too. Franklin has sung your praises." I shot a tight-lipped grin at Frank. He cleared his throat.

"Lydia is a remarkable violinist," Franklin said. On cue, she plucked the violin from the cellist, lifted the instrument to her chin, played an arpeggio, and curtsied.

"I can't give myself all of the credit. I'm mostly remarkable by force. My cousin is married to Walter Damrosch and my father has a great appreciation for the arts, so since I was a child, I've been encouraged to play and play well. I'm not sure why, considering all of this training will likely go by the wayside once I'm married. I don't really have much interest in it, anyway." Lydia's lips dropped into a scowl for a moment, then lifted back as she smiled.

"But what about all of the work you've put in? You must love it a little," I probed.

"I'd stop playing this instant if Frank asked me to, but you wouldn't, would you?" Inches from Franklin's face, he shook his head and lifted her hand to his lips. "Oh, I'm sure you'd like to say hello to John, wouldn't you?" Before I had a chance to reply that I didn't care, she had me by the wrist and was dragging me back through the smoky room, away from my brother who simply waved at me.

Insisting that I meet everyone, Miss Blaine had introduced me to at least fifty people by the time we made it all the way around the room. We listened to romantic poetry, paused to appreciate the matchless styles of several artists who'd drawn or painted everything from hay fields to street dwellers, and finally stopped in front of a cellist playing a piece that wailed with such heartache it brought tears to my eyes.

I blinked as the cellist lifted his bow from the strings. Lydia began clapping, and paced toward the stocky man whose head was still stooped over his instrument.

"Mr. Wrightington. That was divine." The man's eyes barely lifted. "The only bit of suggestion I have is that the eighteenth notes at the end could've been made a bit more legato." He finally raised his head and stared at Miss Blaine. His eyes narrowed. My fingers drew into my palm. Each time we'd stopped, Lydia had offered some type of comment to the artist, as had the other guests around us. Most of the time, she was complimentary, but a few times, she'd offered criticism. I'd expected at least one of the artists to lash out, but no one had. I'd mentioned this expectation after the second piece of analysis she'd offered, but she'd simply laughed and said that artists expected reactions at the Society, or at any salon for that matter. "No one forces you to put your art on display," she'd said, echoing Franklin's earlier words.

"You're right, Miss Blaine." The cellist's lips parted in a grin. "I thought the same directly after that measure." Miss Blaine beckoned me forward. I introduced myself, certain that I'd forget Mr. Wrightington's name the moment we departed his company. I'd met too many to remember all of them, though I desperately wanted to. Miss Blaine began to turn away and I followed, thinking that perhaps I was so eager to know them because they were such a contradiction to the flighty female artists I was accustomed to back in Mott Haven—the amiable sort that gathered in parlors giving lectures on novels and writing poems, affecting a love for literature until the topic turned to beaus and marriage. The neighborhood women meant well, but the artists here were serious about their art, and welcoming to boot. Each had put their paintings or notebooks aside to smile elatedly at my introduction.

"There's one more person I want you to meet and then I'll take you to John," Miss Blaine said, squinting through the smoke. I couldn't figure why she thought me so eager to get to Mr. Hopper, unless she assumed I'd been intoxicated by his mysterious charms like the rest.

"I'm in no hurry, I—" I thought to tell her that my heart had recently been broken and that I hadn't any interest in Mr. Hopper beyond a friendly acquaintance, but that would be entirely too forward.

We were standing in the middle of the room beneath a chandelier dripping with crystals, wedged between a cluster of writers sharing excerpts from their stories and an artist painting a plain-looking woman with an exceptional nose.

"Have you ever seen Franklin's portraits?" I asked her, watching the artist dunk his brush into the paint.

"Of course. They're incredible. He painted me at the last meeting. It's a shame he can't focus on his art full-time." She lifted her gloved hand, running her fingers over her blond hair done up in a fanciful fleur-de-lis coiffure. "My only complaint is that he was slightly too true to life. He even added the tiny scar above my lip—boating accident."

"Miss Blaine, how long have you and Franklin been, uh . . ." Unable to define what I didn't know, I shook my head. "I mean, how long have you known each other?"

"Lydia, please," she said, squeezing my hand. "And just a month or so." She pulled at the elaborate ivory silk gauze puff at her shoulder and then looked at me, blue eyes locked on mine. "We met at the last Society meeting and have rendezvoused a few times to visit the picture gallery at the Metropolitan Museum and to play a few games of whist with John, though Frank's traveling doesn't seem to allow him much time." She paused and leaned into me. No wonder Franklin had been so scarce at home. "Miss Loftin, it was one of those things . . . well, I don't quite know how to explain it, but the moment I met him I felt like I'd known him my whole life." I knew exactly what she meant, and my chest throbbed. "Oh, there he is." Lydia's words jolted me back. She took my wrist, cold fingers digging into my skin. "Tom always hides when he's writing." Wondering why this Tom fellow was so important, I looked over my shoulder toward the towering arched windows where I'd last seen Franklin and nearly stepped on a girl sewing some sort of shawl.

"Excuse me," I said, sidestepping her. I followed Lydia to an alcove adjacent to the drawing room. No larger than a closet, a circle of pink and white stained glass rained tinted starlight on a blond-headed man. His back was to us, pencil scratching furiously against the paper. Lydia cleared her throat. "Tom?" He didn't turn around but held up his hand instead. "I apologize. He's so rude," she whispered.

"It's fine," I said, understanding the annoyance that came with being forced to stop midsentence. Suddenly, Tom tossed his pencil down and slapped his hand on the desk, causing a tiny brown glass bottle emblazoned with a Celtic circle knot to tip over and roll into his lap. He snatched it, shoved it into his green windowpane plaid jacket, and spun around. Expecting to be greeted with irritation, I was stunned to find him beaming at me, perfect white teeth gleaming against the dim of the room.

"Hi. I'm Thomas Blaine . . . Tom," he said. He smoothed the front of his jacket. The sleeve of his right arm was rolled up to his elbow—likely to avoid smudge marks on his cuff—exposing an angry welt on his forearm.

"Nice to make your acquaintance, Mr. Blaine," I said. "I'm Virginia Loftin." He rubbed his thumb across the side of his forefinger and I noticed his fingers were rough across his knuckles—calluses from holding the pencil, just like I had.

"Tom's my brother," Lydia said. "And Tom, Miss Loftin is Franklin's sister. She's a writer, too."

"You can call me Virginia—or Ginny—please," I said. Lydia already felt like an old friend.

"Ah, yes. I think I remember Frank mentioning you," Mr. Blaine said. He dropped his hand to his side and seemed to stumble a bit, though he hadn't taken a step. I thought of the small glass bottle and wondered if he'd been drinking. It wasn't uncommon to have a drink or two in a social setting, but it was entirely unseemly to have too much. I'd only seen two people intoxicated in my life—my uncle Richard after my father's funeral and an old neighbor, Mr. Spivey, who'd consumed so much he'd fallen down his front steps. "I believe I met one of your sisters the other week. She was coming out of the Astors' place as I was going in." Mr. Blaine seemed to steady, his blue eyes, identical to Lydia's, met mine. His cheeks flushed. Apparently something besides simply meeting had occurred.

"Bess?" I asked, knowing without a doubt neither Alevia nor Mae had the capability or desire to discombobulate a man so severely. It wasn't that Mae and Alevia weren't as beautiful as Bess—on the contrary, I supposed we were all pretty in our own way. It was that Bess was the only one of us who'd mastered the skill of flirtation.

"Yes. I'm fairly certain that's her name." He sighed. "She's quite lovely." His face burned deeper against the natural pale of his skin and I coughed, feeling as though the walls of the small room were closing in around me. Mr. Blaine cleared his throat. "At any rate, have you had an opportunity to read your writing for the room?" I opened my mouth to reply that I hadn't, but he cut me off, continuing to speak. "It's quite an effective exercise. In fact, I read a bit of my new novel at the beginning of the night. Everyone seemed to find it smart and compelling. Several people begged me to share the next installment as soon as it was completed. I was re-lieved, though in truth I knew it would be well received. My stories often are and—"

"I'm so thrilled you've written another piece," Lydia thankfully interrupted Mr. Blaine's exasperating self-praise. "I should like to hear more about it, but we're on our way to say hello to John." My lips pressed into a smile.

"Wonderful to meet you, Mr. Blaine," I said. Lydia led us out of the alcove and into the drawing room.

"Isn't he amazing?" Lydia gushed. I nodded, knowing I didn't have the capacity to vocalize a lie at the moment. Though I thought him friendly and pleasant enough—and his passion admirable—I couldn't stand arrogance in men, especially in artists. "I told Franklin the minute he told me about you that I thought you and Tom would be a good match. You're both lovely and both writers. It's important to have similar interests in a marriage, don't you think?" Her words stunned me. The notion that I'd been paired with someone other than Charlie, even in conversation, filled me with grief. I glanced around the room, across the faces of countless men I'd passed by or met without thought, suitable men who were considered prospects. At once, I could feel sweat prickle my palms. I wasn't ready. "Virginia?" Lydia shook me and I turned to face her.

"I . . . I agree that he is a nice man," I stammered, "though it seems that he's quite taken with my sister Bess. Perhaps they'd be a better match." Lydia shrugged and exited the drawing room, leading me down a darkened hallway. I was relieved that she hadn't pressed the matter. Candlelight flickered against the walls and a cool draft floated over me. I shivered. The notion that I was about to entertain a conversation with another bachelor, and a womanizer at that, made my stomach tumble with nerves. I thought to turn around and find Franklin, but Lydia's hand found mine and led me further down the hall. Without bothering to knock, she opened the closed door. Caught immediately by a bear head on the alternate wall, I stared at its teeth bared in a snarl, barely aware that Lydia had left my side.

"Oh good. I won't have to come fetch you after all." Mr. Hopper's voice echoed across a room that was dark with mahogany walls, leather settees, and red and gold tapestries. His quip reminded me of something Franklin would say, and my unease settled.

"You know, I really didn't come here to humor you, Mr. Hopper," I said, avoiding his eyes by following Lydia's unnecessary path around the perimeter of the room.

"Oh?" He started to interrupt me, but I cut him off.

"I thought I'd asked you, quite nicely in fact, to keep your carriage off of my lawn. I simply came here to tell you that if I see one more divot, I'll have my gardener yank up all of your beautiful roses and plant them at my house," I said, raising my voice. I finally looked at him, finding his black leather boots propped lackadaisically on the bronze top of his gargantuan mahogany desk, his hands threaded behind his head. Mr. Hopper's lips turned up in a grin as he remembered our conversation at the Symphony.

"I'm um . . . I'm going to find Franklin," Lydia said abruptly. The thought that she was going to leave me unaccompanied made my chest tighten, but I took a breath. Mr. Hopper was a friend of my brother's, and a man who clearly had the means and charisma to draw the attention of any society woman or famed artist he wished. I was a modest writer from the Bronx with no fortune or acclaim. His interest would not extend beyond that of an acquaintance. I calmed at the thought. I smiled at Lydia and crossed toward Mr. Hopper, pausing in the middle of the room to watch as she made her way back around the perimeter and out of the door. The door shut behind me and Mr. Hopper laughed.

"I suppose you find it ironic that I do, in fact, live in a mansion on Fifth Avenue?" he said. I grinned, sinking into a leather chair across from him.

"I suppose you're right. What was wrong with her?" I asked, wondering why Lydia had taken such great pains to avoid crossing the room.

"What do you mean?" He swung his legs to the floor and set his pen on the desk. "Oh, you mean the way she walked around the room like that? She probably didn't want to walk on the rug. A very close friend of ours, Will Carter, was found dead in here a few months ago, laid out in the middle of the room. It was a terrible tragedy, and the loss was quite a blow to all of us." A cloud passed over his face, a pale that eclipsed his jovial countenance. "He was a talented man, a promising sculptor." Mr. Hopper met my eyes and the color slowly returned to his cheeks. "However, Will's greatest gift was his humor. He had the solitary ability to pull all of us out of the worst sorts of depressions. Father said it was heart failure that killed him. There was no sign of a struggle, but Lyd found him first." Somewhat relieved that he hadn't been murdered, a shiver crept up my spine all the same. I'd just walked across that rug. I swallowed hard, stifling the urge to look over my shoulder.

"I'm sorry for your loss," I said, though the sentiment was insufficient.

"It's all right. He'll always be with us, really." Mr. Hopper leaned back in his chair. My eyes drifted over his shoulder to a portrait of a gentleman in Union army garb. I laughed.

"What?" He leaned forward.

"No, I apologize. My amusement was misplaced. I was just looking at that portrait there. He's smiling." John looked over his shoulder. Though it wasn't uncommon to see a slight grin on the closed lips of a few portrait subjects, I had yet to see a portrayal quite like this one. His lips were parted, exposing a row of square teeth.

"Yes. You wouldn't be able to tell it without the beard, but that's my father. His mother asked him to sit for a nice, serious portrait. As you can see, it turned out quite well." He grinned at me, holding my gaze. "Are you enjoying yourself tonight, Miss Loftin?" He stood and rounded the desk. He was doing it again, the same thing he'd done at the Symphony. I couldn't tell if it was his tone, his proximity, or the use of my name, but in the course of a few moments, he'd made me feel at ease, as though he knew me and was genuinely interested in my response.

"Very much. Though I have to admit I'm overwhelmed, in a good way. My limited exposure to artist gatherings has consisted of ladies' groups, and——" Mr. Hopper coughed. "I don't mean to discount them," I said quickly. "It's only that they're not serious about writing. It's a pastime until they procure a proper husband, which isn't a dishonorable goal in the slightest, but . . ." I stopped. I didn't want to appear as though I thought myself superior, or come off as one of those women who looked upon marriage as declared warfare.

"You want something more," Mr. Hopper said, mouth quirking up. "You want to make more of your writing." I nodded, pressing my palms to the leather seat. "It's rare," he continued, leaning against his desk. "There aren't many women keen to make a career of their prose, even here." He gestured toward the drawing room. "I suppose most believe that men prefer the naïve over the ambitious and intelligent. It's unfortunate. Especially for a man who believes that the splendor of a woman's beauty is only magnified by a clever mind." He held my eyes, and I felt my cheeks redden, instantly hoping he'd mistake my color for the warmth in the room.

"It is," I said, composing myself. The thought that a woman would balk from her talents in order to please a man saddened me, though I knew it happened often. "I've only met one other female who aimed to make writing a career. She was an acquaintance of my sister Mae's, a student at Hunter College. We'd thought to begin meeting to share our writing, but she married and her husband had work in Milwaukee." I broke from his gaze. "I am so thankful for your invitation, Mr. Hopper. This, the Society, is incredible, the number of men and women sharing ideas, respecting each other's art. I was turned away from a men's writing group once, and when I walked into your drawing room, I was sure I was dreaming."

"Artistic interaction between the sexes is not at all uncommon in France. I'm convinced that it'll eventually become commonplace here, so long as people like us make a point to encourage it," he said, gesturing from him to me and back again. "I'm glad you're pleased. Have you met anyone of particular interest? I know Lydia mentioned wanting to introduce you to Tom." I kept silent and he smiled at me. "What is it?"

"It seems that he's already met my sister Bessie. Perhaps they'll be a match."

"You think he's that terrible?" Mr. Hopper grinned and held up his hand. "Forgive me. I don't know her. I've only heard the few stories Franklin has told me."

"She's undoubtedly more pleasant than Franklin has made her out to be. He loves her, but they've always been at odds. Frank can be so carefree, and Bess is always so calculated." Bess had been old enough to remember my parents' miniscule apartment in the city, the dirty, rodent-infested building we'd lived in before our move to Mott Haven. At times, she'd mention it, and I knew that those memories, coupled with Great-aunt Rose's influence, had impelled her to want more for her life, to desire the comfort afforded high society.

"So the sentiment that she's a fortune hunter is an incorrect one?" he asked, amber eyes dancing. He fit his hands in his pockets. "And what of your other sisters? What're they like? I feel now that Franklin might've stymied my understanding of your entire family."

I laughed.

"I doubt it. He's quite devoted to the rest of us. You met Mae; she's lovely, completely committed to education, and Alevia is beautiful and so talented on the piano. You've seen her before." The last sentence came out of my mouth before I could stop it.

"I have? She wasn't at the Symphony, was she?" His eyes squinted, as if the effort to try to remember was too much for them.

"Oh, right. Maybe you haven't," I said quickly, but he shook his head, thinking.

"I remember the name." He tapped his fingers on the table and then looked up suddenly. "Oh, Charlie Aldridge's party. You were there, too, weren't you?" His eyes flashed with emotion, then dulled, though the edges of his mouth twitched with an impending smile. "I thought you looked familiar at Carnegie Hall."

"Yes, I was at-at Charlie's," I stuttered, barely able to force his name from my lips, "but you and I didn't meet." I prayed that Mr. Hopper hadn't noticed my heartbreak that night. "I just heard your name."

"Did you now? Tell me. What did you hear?" Heat crept from my neck to my face. I knew how my words had come across. I cleared my throat.

"Nothing at all, really. It's just that . . . I was in the library during the party and at one point I looked out and noticed . . . well, noticed your friend with the beard staring at my sister, and asked Charlie who the man was. He mistook my inquiry. He thought I was asking after you." I got up from my chair. I'd embarrassed myself as well as Mr. Hopper and needed to go. I started to cross the room, but his hand caught my arm.

"Don't leave," he said. I turned, nearly colliding with his chest. He didn't back away or let go. Nerves tumbled in my stomach. I wouldn't allow him to assume that I could be another one of his conquests. "Please sit back down." He smiled and I broke from his stare to pace past him toward the chair I'd just abandoned. I needed to continue the conversation to reiterate that I hadn't been asking after him. "To be clear, that man is not my friend. Mr. Roger Williams is a first cousin of Miss Kent's . . . Rachel's. He's quite ir- ritating." The mention of her name was unwelcome. I stared into my lap, trying in vain to think of a topic that would steer my mind away from the worst night of my life. Mr. Hopper twirled his pencil between his fingertips and sighed, taking his seat behind his desk. "I asked who you were, too. I saw you standing beside Charlie and Rachel and didn't recognize you." He lifted his eyes and met my gaze. My mouth went dry. As much as I tried to ignore the image of Charlie down on one knee, I couldn't. Hurt echoed in my chest.

"Then I suppose we were both dishonest at the Symphony." My voice was strained.

"I wouldn't call it dishonest, just polite. We hadn't been properly introduced. I couldn't say, 'Well, hello, Miss Loftin. I asked about you at Aldridge's party the other week' without the connotation being misconstrued." He winked and I smiled gratefully.

"By some, perhaps, but not by me." I didn't feel the need to elaborate further. How could I explain that I'd never entertained the thought of a man's interest because I'd loved the same one, blindly, for so long? We sat in silence for a few moments and then he stood up and rounded the desk to face me.

"Would you tell me something, Miss Loftin? What do you write about? I'm just wondering. That's the purpose of all of this anyway, you know—to talk about it."

"Then why aren't you still out there?" I tipped my head toward the drawing room.

"After I hear reactions, I need to think," he said. "It's nice to read through a passage while listening to the music. But I can't concentrate enough to figure out how I'll change a piece until I'm alone—especially if I've received a bit of criticism as I did tonight. Some people could write through doomsday, but I need silence."

"Likewise." I sighed, fell back against the chair, and tilted my neck forward to look at him. "I write a monthly column for the *Bronx Review*, mostly about current events, though at times they ask me to write a women's opinion piece since I'm the only female columnist.

And I write down our family's stories for fun." I paused, considering whether or not I should mention the rejected article I'd submitted to *Scribner's* and *Atlantic Monthly,* and decided against it. "But the book I wrote is just a silly story about a man and woman who grow up together, find love in each other. It's my first attempt at a novel and I have to admit that I'm quite unsure that it's any good at all." I stopped, noticing John was looking up at the ceiling, studying the deep squares of crown molding, obviously bored. He didn't say anything but crossed to the opposite wall, opened a cabinet, and turned to me.

"What would you like to drink? Bourbon? Scotch? I don't have ice." I stared at his back, shocked at the forwardness of his question. Proper women never drank liquor and rarely alcohol, only imbibing a bit of wine behind the veil of their homes or a glass of sparkling wine at the theater. I started to get up. Why would he bother asking about my work? He clearly didn't care about my reputation or my writing.

"I've got to go find Franklin. It's getting late." It was. If Mother woke to find us absent at this hour, we'd be in quite a bit of trouble. Mr. Hopper turned mid-pour, sloshing scotch all over his black silk vest and down the side of the wall.

"Shit," he muttered under his breath. "I apologize for my language. Don't go. I want to talk about your book. I just thought it'd be nice to have a drink while we do," he said. I kept walking. "Please, Miss Loftin. I didn't mean to offend you by offering spirits. It's only that I've found having a small nip clears my head."

"Very well," I said, stepping gingerly across the expanse of the rug to Mr. Hopper's outstretched hand. I was desperate to talk about my writing with another author, with someone who had proficiently written a novel and could help me better my own. Feeling very defiant, I took a sip, inhaling the earthy smell of it, tasting the smooth hint of caramel on my tongue.

"Is it a true story?" His words took me by surprise and I choked on the scotch.

"What?"

"Your book. Is it based on real life?" I took another drink.

"No," I lied.

"That's a pity. I was hoping I'd get to learn more about you."

I fidgeted with the black lace that trimmed the end of my sleeve above my elbow.

"I'm afraid it's just a notion I had. Some romantic fantasy that will never see the literary shelves, but may entertain a housewife or two." Mr. Hopper's brows furrowed.

"Just because it's romantic doesn't mean it's not literature. The one novel I've had published had a bit of romance."

"But it was mostly based on some lofty theme, right? I mean, that's what all the greats do, write about something they notice in human nature." He leaned against the desk.

"You just got done saying that your story is about a lifelong relationship. If that's the case, then you're no different. You're writing about the test of loyalty—about how difficult it must be to stand by someone throughout an entire lifetime, yet how it's possible." I was impressed. He'd captured the purpose of my story without knowing anything about it.

"I suppose you're right."

"Isn't that what we're all asking ourselves? Who will stand by us? Who will love us?" He dipped his head for a moment, then lifted his eyes to the room and took a sip of scotch. "And yes. My novel is called *The Blood Runs from Antietam*. It's about war and what it is that makes men want to declare it."

"Let me hazard a guess. Blood, lust, and the want for power?" Mr. Hopper chuckled and shook his head. "What's the answer then?"

"You'll have to read it to find out," he said, winking at me again. Lifting his glass, he downed what remained. "I know you said you weren't ready to read your book to strangers, but since I'm at least a little more familiar, would you share it with me?"

I nodded, thankful that I'd taken the time to rewrite it without Charlie's name.

"I can't promise that it'll be good," I said.

"First drafts never are." Mr. Hopper set the glass down and held out his hand. I gave him the notebook, feeling as though I'd just severed a limb. "I'm eager to read it, Miss Loftin. Would you like me to tell you my thoughts or simply read it and keep my opinion to myself?"

"Of course I'd appreciate your thoughts," I said. "I'm well aware that publishable writing comes with the price of criticism." His eyebrow quirked up.

"You're serious indeed," he said, as though he questioned it even after I'd stated my intentions. "When I've finished revising my new story, I'd like you to tell me what you think of it. It's about a wealthy society man who flees his life to travel the world like a vagabond."

"Of course. But let me guess the theme. Something about the making of a man, whether or not he can escape the life he's been bred to live?" Mr. Hopper's eyes glinted.

"Something along those lines," he said, turning to put my book in the top drawer of his desk.

"I look forward to reading it." I started to stand. It was getting late. "It's been so lovely speaking with you, Mr. Hopper. I hope—"

"There's one more thing," he said, cutting me off. "Of course you don't have to take my advice, but you might want to speak further with Tom." He couldn't be serious. I wouldn't be pushed

into a courtship, especially with a man I found exasperating—
never mind the fact that he clearly fancied my sister. I felt my eyes
narrow and Mr. Hopper grinned. "No, not in that manner," he
said. "I'm not suggesting the two of you as a love match, but he *is*
a talented writer. You'll need more than one opinion if you plan to
make this a career, and it's helpful to know another writer striving toward publication . . . at least it helped me. You have no idea
how cathartic it can be to commiserate with someone else on the
prepublication seesaw of promise and rejection. The two of you
could share publishing ideas, read each other's writing." I cocked
an eyebrow at him.

"Do you?"

"What?"

"Share your writing with Mr. Blaine?" I asked. Mr. Hopper
shook his head.

"I used to. I don't anymore, but that wasn't my decision," he
said. "After I got published, he acted as though he didn't want
my help. It's just his pride. I know he hoped we'd be published
around the same time, but he's had a string of poor luck with editors and publishers alike." Mr. Hopper pressed his lips together and
shrugged. "I simply thought that knowing him—and his knowing
you—might be beneficial."

"Perhaps it would be," I said, "if he could stop praising his
work long enough to hear of mine." I clapped my hand over
my mouth. "Forgive me. I've spoken out of turn." Mr. Hopper
chuckled.

"It's been a pleasure speaking with you, Miss Loftin." He
swept my hand from my side and lifted it to his lips, the kiss he
placed upon it as light and quick as a butterfly landing on my
skin. "As to Tom," he said. "He's only trying to conceal his inse-
curity. Though if you do decide to make a habit of speaking with

him, it'd be wise to throw propriety out of the window and learn to interrupt him."

I found Mr. Blaine where Lydia and I had left him, hunched over the carved mahogany writing desk in the alcove. Lifting my hand to knock on the doorframe, I paused for a moment, arm suspended in midair, wondering if taking Mr. Hopper's advice would be a mistake. Then again, if this didn't go well, I didn't have to talk to either of them again.

Tapping my fist into the wood frame before I could second guess myself, I jumped as Mr. Blaine pushed back from the desk and slammed his hand on the top.

"What is it now, Lyd?" he said. "I told you I was in the middle of a scene the last time you—" Swiveling his neck around to look at me, he stopped midsentence and straightened in his chair. "Oh. Miss Loftin. I apologize."

"That's all right. I can come back later," I said, realizing as his blue eyes met mine that the nervousness I'd felt earlier had returned. My conversation with Mr. Hopper had settled me temporarily—or perhaps it was the scotch—but now, I felt nervous. I took one step backward and whirled toward the door, but Mr. Blaine started toward me before I could reach it.

"No. Stay, Miss Loftin. I-I wasn't really writing anyway," he said. His breath wavered across my face, rank with the stench of whisky.

"It looked like you were. Writing, I mean," I clarified, glancing down at the desk to avoid his eyes. I took a breath and forced calm. I'd only come to speak to Mr. Blaine as a fellow writer. There was no harm or expectation in that.

"Oh," he said abruptly as if he'd somehow forgotten how to speak. Running a hand through his cropped blond hair, he blinked and sat down in the desk chair. "I suppose I *was* writing, but not my novel, see. I just thought you were Lydia and wanted her to leave me alone. She always seems to break my concentration when I need it the most." He lifted a shoulder. "But your presence, Miss Loftin, is certainly welcome," he said. Leaning back in the chair, Tom grinned.

"I wanted to talk to you about publishing," I said.

"Publishing," he repeated. Biting his bottom lip, he leaned forward, shook his head as if to clear it, and glanced up at me. "What about it?" Mr. Blaine slumped down in the chair, posture completely different from a second before. Clearly he'd thought my presence driven by something else. Perhaps he'd assumed I'd come to request a private reading, lured back by the intrigue of his self-proclaimed brilliance.

"Well, I've been a writer my whole life—short stories mostly—but I just wrote a novel and haven't the slightest idea if it's good or not or how to go about getting a book published," I began.

"You're asking me about publishing a book." It was a statement, not a question. I nodded. "Why didn't you ask John?" The question came out airy and he plucked the pencil from his desk and twirled it between his fingers. I opened my mouth to answer, but didn't know what to say, if I should tell him that Mr. Hopper had suggested I seek him out. He glanced at me. "Oh. You already have." Mr. Blaine dropped the pencil onto the desk and stared up at the pink and white stained glass above him. "I don't know why you're here then. You've likely found all of the answers you need."

"Actually, I didn't ask him," I said honestly. "He's already been published and it's been quite some time since he's had to seek out a publisher." I was treading on thin ice. Surely Mr. Blaine didn't like to be reminded that Mr. Hopper had been published and he hadn't.

"That's true." Tom smiled at me and I felt the tension drop from my shoulders. "I suppose I'm a little sore over it taking me this long to find a publisher myself. Sorry for my tone." He paused. "Poker. You're familiar?"

"Vaguely. My uncles played in the war."

"Publishing is about as random as a poker hand—that is, if your material is good—the wild cards being who you know and what the publishers want—and their tastes are fickle."

"It seems that attempting acceptance in any of the literary—" I started to sympathize, to say that being well received by a literary magazine appeared to be as random, but Mr. Blaine cut me off.

"In my case, I know my writing is compelling, and I've got the first wild card in my back pocket. I have a rather known last name and am acquainted with plenty of publishers and editors, they just refuse to give my books a chance. As much as they say they want something different, they don't. For example, John's editor, Fred Harvey at Henry Holt. He read both of our books. He loved John's romanticized novel about war, but was disgusted with mine about the disparity between the classes."

"I doubt he was disgusted," I said. All of my rejections had been pointed, but polite.

"You don't believe me? I still have his letter. I'll bring it next time. He didn't like the way I made the upper class seem so unfeeling and, I quote, 'the lower class seem so disgustingly desolate.' He thought I was using class extremes instead of averages and was absolutely appalled by my love scene between a woman of the streets, if you will, and a man of means." Choosing to ignore the mention of a love scene, I was stunned by the brutal honesty of Mr. Blaine's rejection. I couldn't fathom that sort of dismissal—if I were ever brave enough to face publishers. "But, I've decided to go a different route." Mr. Blaine pushed a piece of paper off the top of a copy of

The Century magazine, and waved the volume in front of me. I'd already read this particular edition at least ten times over. "I've decided to read for a change." He paused to stare at the cover adorned with an illustration of a Greek goddess. "They say that Richard Gilder selects the best writers in the world for his magazine. I'm hoping their excellence will inspire."

"I often hope the same," I said. The magazine always included literary greats like Mark Twain and Henry James and the illustrator Monty Flagg, as well as articles and short stories from promising debut writers. Suddenly, an idea dawned on me and I plucked the magazine from Mr. Blaine's hand. He laughed as I flipped through.

"If you'd like me to procure a copy for you, I'm sure that John subscribes—"

"I've been rejected, too, Mr. Blaine. Never from this magazine, but from several others." I'd submitted the story of Grandfather James to *Scribner's* and *Atlantic Monthly* last March. The magazines had been running Civil War stories commemorating the twenty-fifth year of the Union's victory, and I'd thought my grandfather's story a heartening tale of American resilience. The editors felt differently, and I'd been so discouraged by their rejections that I hadn't tried other publications. "But I'm willing to give it another go and I think you should as well. We should write stories to submit to *The Century*. Nearly every name on these pages has made something of their writing."

"I think that that's a marvelous idea, Miss Loftin." Mr. Blaine pulled the magazine from my grasp and set it on the desk behind him. "And you're correct. It's commonly known that editors from all of the most prominent houses peruse it, even those with their own monthly publications—Charles Scribner's Sons, Henry Holt, G. P. Putnam's Sons, among others. G. P. Putnam's Sons are particularly interested in *The Century*'s writers, I've heard. It's as easy as one of them reading your story and loving your style."

"G. P. Putnam's Sons?" The name came out of my mouth before I could stop it, a girly squeak that caused Mr. Blaine to cock his head at me.

"Have your eye on that one, do you?" He laughed.

"Not really," I sputtered. "I mean, I suppose." I felt myself blushing and turned my head.

"It's nothing to be ashamed of. Everyone has their favorites," Mr. Blaine said, weaving his hands behind his head. "It's rumored that the Putnam brothers are especially loyal readers since their former magazine, *Putnam's Monthly Magazine of American Literature, Science, and Art,* was bought by *The Century.* If you're keen on catching their eye, submitting a story to Gilder would be a smart idea." He scribbled a few words on a loose sheet of paper. "Shall we agree to hold each other accountable for these stories? Perhaps read each other's work? I'd be happy to review yours if you'll take a look at mine." I barely heard him. I was sure I'd be rejected, but the possibility that my writing could be read by George Putnam made nerves fly madly around my stomach like a thousand fleeing bats.

"I'd love that," I said bleakly.

"Well, in that case, could you come over here for a moment? I've made a list of possible book ideas and suppose I could use one for my story. I'd like your opinion." I stepped forward to take a look. He shuffled the papers on the desk and flattened one on top. Barely able to see the letters against the dim of the room, I leaned closer to read the bullet-pointed list. *"Ben Franklin and his relation to the post; The French Huguenots and their exodus to the United States."* "I know that they're both superb ideas. Simply choose the one you find most appealing." I felt my eyes begin to roll, but stopped them before he could see me.

"I like both, but find the Franklin idea particularly interesting," I said, swallowing the compulsion to deem them both boring out of spite.

"Thank you, Miss Loftin," he said. "Do you know how I came upon it? I was up in Rye on holiday when I came across a marker of sorts near the road. It seemed to speak to me, to tell me that if I only regarded it long enough, it would give me an idea that would change the world. I know that—"

"I must go, Mr. Blaine," I interrupted, taking Mr. Hopper's advice. "I apologize for interrupting. I look forward to reading your story. Farewell for now," I said hurriedly. Opening the door, I stepped into the hallway before he could insist I stay to hear the last of his tale.

Walking quickly toward the trill of a flute over the lulling notes of the piano and someone shouting the name "Rebecca!" over and over, I eyed the large-faced grandfather clock with a carved shell motif, stunned that it was nearing two in the morning. I turned sharply into the drawing room, expecting a thinned crowd at best, even given the noise, but was shocked to find it just as crammed as before. Forcing my way through the throng, I looked for Franklin.

"Miss Loftin?" A short brunette girl wearing a gorgeous black gown with undulating bands of deep emerald velvet and gold braid materialized out of the dim. I nodded, wracking my brain for her name. Lydia had just introduced us. "What fortune that our paths crossed. I know you mentioned you'd just penned a novel. Would you mind listening to the opening paragraph of my story? I'm on my way to read it. I often write poetry and shorter works, but this is my first attempt at a novella and I'm afraid I haven't a clue what I'm doing. It'll only take a moment."

"I'd love to," I said and grinned at her, wishing she'd mentioned her name.

"Thank you," she said. "I would've read it earlier, but my husband, Teddy, summoned me back to my parents' home for a few hours to greet some friends going on to the country with us tomorrow. Never mind that I see them nearly every day back home in Newport." She paused. "He means well, but doesn't understand," she said, almost to herself. I followed her through the maze of people gathered around the fireplace and waited as she laughed with a lone harpist for a moment before leaning down and grabbing a disheveled stack of papers from a spot against the wall.

The woman sunk into a waiting armchair by the fire. I looked at the crowd gathered around me waiting to hear her words, and wondered why she'd felt the need to ask me to join them. She lifted her face to us and her eyes squinted, as though she was thinking. "I'll be reading a short passage, only the first paragraph of my novella, which is all I've got so far." She laughed, a high-pitched jingle that made me grin. "I haven't worked it all out in my head, but here's the premise: it's about a man whose career is falling apart, but who needs to be successful to marry his fiancée," she said, tapping her fingers on the mound of paper in her hand. The problem of money seemed to be a common theme, both in fiction and reality. I focused on her words. I wasn't going to let Charlie into my head. Not now. "Knowing there's no way to salvage his career, he searches his brain and remembers these letters he has from a famous, but deceased former lover, so he removes his name from the letters and sells them for a fortune. There will, of course, be complications with his plan, but that's as far as I've thought so far. Do you find it boring?" Hanging on her words, I found myself staring at her waiting for more, and shook my head, wishing I could've come up with a premise that seemed half as enticing.

"Absolutely not! It sounds incredible," someone said. Her thin lips drew up.

"I think you're all just kind." Sorting through the stack of papers, she yanked one out and set it on top of the others. "There's a chance that it'll be entirely awful. If it is, that's all right, but I want you to tell me. Be brutal."

"I promise," a thin man with a curling mustache proclaimed loudly. She smiled.

"I'll be counting on that, Mr. Daniels," she said.

"I've remained tonight for the sole purpose of hearing her prose. Her poetry speaks to me." A young woman who appeared to be no older than sixteen whispered in my ear, "It's incredible . . . what Mr. Hopper has created here." I turned my head in time to see her cheeks flush at his name. "Do you know that he was inspired by a Parisian salon? He spoke to me . . . privately . . . about how he came to form it." With her words, I felt foolish for thinking that Mr. Hopper was actually interested in my writing. His reputation was clearly valid: he was versed in making all women feel exceptional. "This society has inspired me to continue with ceramics, even though my parents don't approve."

"I'm glad to hear it, I—"

"Glennard dropped the *Spectator* and sat looking into the fire." The reading began. I was thankful for the interruption. "The club was filling up, but he still had to himself the small inner room, with its darkening outlook down the rain-streaked prospect of Fifth Avenue." She read with feeling. The scene reflected not only in her words but also in her face. "It was all dull and dismal enough, yet a moment earlier his boredom had been perversely tinged by a sense of resentment at the thought that, as things were going, he might in time have to surrender even the despised privilege of boring himself within those particular four walls." She looked across all of us, and then her lips turned up. "And that is all I have, I'm afraid." Everyone remained silent for a moment longer before the first bold soul offered an opinion. Soon the rest of her audience surged forward, and the sound of comments and praise were lost to the hum of the room. I remained standing where I was, reveling in the scene she'd created, wishing she'd written more. Her prose was so lovely and immersive, I'd felt as though I'd been in the room with Glennard.

After her audience had gone on to the next reading or painting, I made my way toward her. I tried to think of something critical to say, but was unable come up with anything. I wasn't going to be at all helpful in my critique. At first listen, it was perfect. I thought of my muddled manuscript in Mr. Hopper's drawer and cringed at the dissonance between the seamless brilliance of what she'd just read and my words.

"It's an exquisite start," I said loudly, my voice projecting over the small orchestra that had once again started playing. I felt like a fraud. What did I know of novel writing? I'd only just written one terrible draft myself. Bent over her friend Mr. Daniels's shoulder, squinting at his notepad, she jolted up, and plastered a hand to her heart.

"Good Lord, you startled me." She laughed and turned back to Mr. Daniels. "I like it. I really do," I heard her say to him, "but I can already tell where it's going. Sophie is going to choose Joseph over Harold, am I right?" He nodded and frowned at the page. "My advice? Even them out a little. Don't make Joseph such a catch and Harold such a dolt and it'll be wonderful," she continued. "Now if you'll excuse me." Turning, she grinned at me and nodded to a space near the doorway.

"Thank you for your sincerity, Mrs. Wharton," Mr. Daniels called out behind us and she nodded at him as we walked away. Edith, I remembered suddenly. That was her name.

"All right. Be honest," she said when we stopped. "I'm eager to hear the opinion of another female writer. The general consensus seemed to be that it was satisfactory, but I'm not so sure. Is it compelling enough?"

"I'm afraid I'm not going to be much help," I started. "I don't have much to say other than I wanted to read more. I was there. I was in that room with Glennard."

"Oh wonderful! That's exactly what I was after. Thank you." Mrs. Wharton clapped her hands. She bundled her stack of papers under her arm and began to walk toward the door, but I stopped her.

"Are you sure you don't live in town?" I asked stupidly. She cocked her head at me, no doubt wondering what I was after by asking. "It's just . . . I wish you did. I'd love to read more of your story and hear your thoughts on mine. There aren't many of us and it was so nice to run into you." I was babbling, but meant what I said. It had been evident by the crowd gathered around her and in the words of the young girl I'd stood beside that her poetry had already made its mark. I'd never been in the company of such a promising female writer, and found myself inspired. I knew the world would someday know her name. When it did, I wanted to be there alongside.

"Oh." She laughed under her breath. "Believe me, I wish I did, too. I lived here before I got married and used to treasure these meetings. Being around this many artists is good for the soul." Gripping my hand, she smiled and let go, walking into the foyer. "It was lovely to meet you. Thank you again, Miss Loftin."

I turned and shuffled back into the drawing room yawning. Squinting, I spotted Mr. Hopper leaning against one of the bookshelves, book between his fingers. He caught sight of me and beckoned me over.

"Do they ever get tired and go home?" I asked loudly, attempting to speak over the instrumentalists now playing what sounded like Bach.

"Eventually," Mr. Hopper said, grinning into the room.

"I just met the most talented writer, Mrs. Edith Wharton," I said. "Do you know her?"

"Perhaps," Mr. Hopper said, shrugging. "I don't recognize the name, but might know her face. Did you have an enjoyable talk with Tom?" I didn't say anything, so Mr. Hopper turned to look at me, grimacing at my pursed lips and tapered eyes. "Sorry." Chuckling under his breath, he shrugged.

"That's all right. I'm just being dramatic. It wasn't bad, really," I said, shaking my head. "We're going to exchange work and it was nice to talk about publication. I could do without the boasting, though."

"Perhaps you should work on your own bravado," Mr. Hopper nudged me. "It's quite irritating, I'll admit, though I'm glad talking with him was helpful. Come, let's find Frank. It's late and he's probably been looking for you." The thought of the hour made me fretful. Mother had always been clear that we weren't to ever be out past eleven, and that was only permitted if we were attending a performance. As glad as she'd been for me to attend the Society with Frank, I doubted she'd dismiss my absence in the wee hours of the morning if she woke to find our beds empty.

We walked past two people gathered under the chandelier. I looked over the shoulder of the taller man to find he'd almost completed a painting of the room. The heavy cloud of smoke had been left out of his depiction and the details of the room—the flames licking the etched fireplaces, the flying angels along the ceiling—were accurate and vivid behind the immaculately garbed crowd and the obvious focus on a lovely brunette woman tucked against the wall across from us. Mr. Hopper leaned into me as we walked past. "He might as well take advantage of the view while he can," he whispered, nodding toward the woman who was sitting alone, legs pressed against the wall as though she'd like to dissolve into it.

"Who is that?" I asked. She looked familiar, naturally flushed cheeks atop pouty lips. I looked away when she noticed me staring.

"Maude Adams. I'm shocked she's here."

"The actress?" I asked, recognizing her easily upon second glance. Her face was often plastered on the front page of the papers. She'd been on the stage since a child, most recently playing Dora Prescott in *Men and Women*.

"Yes. I haven't seen her off the stage in some time—I don't think anyone has." Mr. Hopper lifted his hand to wave at her, but she blushed and turned to face the wall.

"Really? Why?" The hum of the cello beneath the high staccato notes of the violin grew louder as we neared and Franklin materialized beside me.

"Where've you been? I've circled the room at least five times looking for you." Frank grinned at Mr. Hopper and I yawned.

"Talking to Mr. Hopper in the study and then Mr. Blaine and another author for a bit," I said, when my jaw finally settled back into place. Franklin's nose scrunched.

"I'd avoid going in there if I were you. Someone passed on in that room a few months back," he whispered to me, eyeing Mr. Hopper out of the corner of his eye.

"I'm well aware. It was a dear friend of Mr. Hopper's and Lydia's," I said.

Mr. Hopper crossed the room, toward Maude Adams, leaving Franklin and me to watch Lydia as she played. Her eyes were closed, brows lifting and dipping with the inflection of the notes, fingers flying along the fingerboard.

"Why didn't you tell me about her?" I kept my focus on Lydia, but felt Franklin's eyes on my face. I glanced at him, realizing he was actually looking over my head at Mr. Hopper as he attempted to talk to Miss Adams.

"It wasn't that I didn't want to," he said. "But she's . . . unlike any woman I've ever met. She is eccentric and fierce, unguarded. I didn't know quite what our relationship would become." He looked at me. "You are so devoted to me, to my happiness. I couldn't introduce the possibility without knowing for sure."

"Are you in love?"

"Yes," he said simply, and turned his eyes back to Lydia, smiling as he watched her play. "Like you are in love with—" He stopped midsentence and looked at me. "I didn't think, Gin. I'm sorry," he said quickly. I reached to squeeze his hand, realizing that this time my heart hadn't plunged to my stomach.

"It's all right," I said, but he shook his head, draped his arm across my shoulders and took my other hand. He clutched my fingers hard and stared at me.

"You'll not lose the next one," he said evenly. "I can't imagine if I lost . . . it's only been a short time."

"I'm all right, Frank," I protested, attempting to turn away, but his arm constricted around me.

"You're not, but you will be and you'll love again." He cleared his throat and his eyes narrowed, boring into mine. His jaw locked, lips pressed together in determination. "But I swear it, Gin, you'll not lose another on account of money. I will not let that happen."

Chapter Seven

DECEMBER 1891

Trellis Manor

RYE, NEW YORK

The sun shone on the coral wallpaper. I lifted my cup to my lips and swallowed, gritting my teeth at the bitter tea that had grown cold over the past hour. I was beginning to think coming to visit our former neighbor, Cherie Smith, had been a mistake. To start, it had taken several hours for all of us to get here—a lengthy carriage ride, passage on a ferry to Rye Beach, followed by another carriage ride—and we had yet to see anyone beyond the maid.

"I can't believe she dragged us up here. I'd like to see her, truly, but so far this is a waste of a day," Bessie whispered from across the room. She fiddled with the peacock feather on her hat, smoothing the golden strands along the edges. "I could've been working on my third attempt at Consuelo Vanderbilt's toque." Bessie's eyes rolled. "I certainly hope Alva's conjecture was right—that the other families will envy Consuelo's hat and will begin ordering pieces for their children, or all of this work is in vain." She withdrew four scarlet ibis feathers from her bag and began to slowly bend one into the form of a Christmas rose. I'd watched her attempt to create several unsuccessfully. Scarlet ibis spines were much too rigid to make the task an easy one. Mae snorted beside me.

"I was looking forward to seeing Cherie, too, but as I'm missing Mr. Trent's first grammar lecture at the orphanage—a lecture Mrs. Greenwood is also attending—to be here, I'd be much obliged if she'd grace us with her presence." I was happy for Mae. I recalled the way she and Mr. Trent had instantly been drawn to each other at the Symphony, and how seriously they both seemed to take their studies and students. I was glad she'd found such a perfect match, but the mention of her relationship stung. I'd glimpsed Charlie this morning, only for a moment as he'd walked out on his front stoop to retrieve the paper. He'd looked handsome in a gray tweed morning suit, pencil tucked behind his ear. He no longer consumed my every waking thought. I had the Society to thank for that. I'd never been so inspired, so determined to succeed. The influence of serious artists had the power to turn my soul to the page for weeks at a time. Even so, my feelings for Charlie were always present. I'd longed to run down the stairs and catch him, to ask him what he was working on, to follow him into the library and proclaim his illustrations genius, like he used to do for my pages. Instead, I remained where I was, blindly buttoning my dress, feeling my heart plummet into my stomach.

I yawned and resumed my slow inspection of the enormous room into which we had been ushered in an attempt to erase Charlie from my mind. At one point the decor had been quite lovely, but it was obvious that the doors hadn't been opened for months, maybe years. Dust dulled the gold-leaf crown molding along the ceiling and was stacked at least an inch thick around the frame holding a portrait of Cherie's mother and in the basin of an ornate pewter vase on the tea table beside me. The room would be a perfect metaphor for love lost—beauty built with painstaking care only to be abandoned. I had no idea why the maid had brought us in here instead of the drawing room, which I'd noticed was in much better condition.

Alevia rubbed her eyes, stood, and walked around Mae and me to the piano behind us. I heard the fall screech open, followed by what I assumed were the wildly out of tune opening measures of one of Mozart's concertos. It sounded horrendous, even to my relatively untrained ears, and Alevia stopped suddenly, likely unable to bear the grating disparity between the notes in her head and the awful noise coming from the piano.

"The notes are at least a half step sharp," Alevia whispered. "Grotrian-Steinweg is a fine make, however, and with a bit of tuning it would be lovely," she amended quickly, before any of us could deem her earlier comment snide.

"I certainly hope they don't entertain in here," Bess said, fiddling with the blue cut-glass stones circling her lace and ribbon–lined wrist. A tendril of auburn escaped the low braided coiffure at her nape and she hastily pinned it back.

"You'd assume, but then again, here we are," I said. "Perhaps the filthiness of the room is a new-fashioned manner of hospitality. It *does* bring out the gold and maroon in my new dress." I laughed, situating the mixed wool and silk skirt across my legs. In a rare gesture of selflessness, Bess had offered to lend me the money to order fabric for a new dress after noticing the threadbare sleeves on my other visiting costumes.

"I don't fully understand why in the world she'd ask Ginny to paint her," Bess said, propping both elbows on the table next to her. "I'm sure there are at least a few portrait artists around here, and she knows as well as we all do that Virginia's attempts end up looking like caricatures. Sorry." I shrugged.

"It's the truth, after all. I'm sure she only wanted company. We're her oldest friends." I inhaled the musty scent of moth-eaten upholstery, and sneezed. Mother had been adamant that we make the trip to see Cherie, though none of us had argued against it in the first place. She was good friends with Cherie's mother, Mrs. Norton, and thought the Nortons to be a fine family. Both Mother and Mrs. Norton had mentioned visiting Cherie with us before they realized that the annual Mott Haven Ladies' Christmas Tea had been planned for the same day.

"I can't imagine why she wouldn't ask Franklin to do the portrait," Mae said. "Maybe she was mistaken and wrote the wrong name in the letter." Cherie had lived across the street from us growing up, and though she was older than Franklin, they'd developed a friendly rivalry of sorts. They were both accomplished painters and had enjoyed jeering and bragging to each other about who they were painting. In actuality, it wasn't really a competition. Their styles were so different they couldn't be compared. Patrons hired Franklin for his honesty, his knack for capturing the very realistic feel of a person in dark and jewel-toned oil paints, while they sought Cherie for her optimistic tendency to portray not who the subject was at present, but who she thought they could be, using light pastels.

"That's what I thought at first," I said, sneezing again. "But in the letter she mentioned all of us by name, including Frank, and asked that I do it." I glanced down at the small trunk of paints I'd lugged from the Bronx and laughed, thinking of the lopsided mouth and uneven, melting eyes that usually characterized my attempts at painting people.

"I wonder if Cherie is accepting many commissions here," Alevia commented. "It seems such a shame that she had to move away from her friends and her patrons, her mother, all the people that love her . . . except for Mr. Smith, of course." Alevia had always been sentimental. If it was up to her, time would stop and our lives would remain as they were—save our artistic careers advancing. "It really is too bad that Frank is in New Jersey this week. Remember the contests they used to create? Both painting the same subject to see whose style the person preferred." She looked at us, then diverted her gaze back to the piano, staring at it as though she felt sorry for it.

"It's probably best Franklin didn't come," Bessie said. She swiped a finger across the table in front of her, leaving a clean line across the dusty wood. "You know there was always speculation that Cherie was sweet on him, and whether Frank knew it or not, I know Mr. Smith wasn't keen on the attention Cherie gave him during our last visit." Mae laughed beside me and shook her head. Cherie's husband, Mr. William Smith, a boring but wealthy financier, rarely attempted to disguise his feelings.

"I doubt that's it. He was probably just cross because Franklin swept him under the rug at cards," she said. I kept my mouth shut. Franklin had told me that Cherie had tried to kiss him the night before her wedding and that he'd refused. To Franklin, Cherie was like an older sister, and I knew he'd be relieved to hear that we'd gone to visit without him.

Cherie's letter had arrived last week, begging us to come see her as soon as possible. She mentioned that she was expecting a child and hadn't had friends from home visit since we'd been up to see her the last time—which had been nearly two years ago when we'd come up for a military ball. Although she was Bessie's age, she'd always gotten along with all of us. We'd been excited to visit again—that is, until now. Mae slumped down on the couch beside me, disturbing a bit of dust that settled on her white shirtwaist. She sneezed, too, tilted her head back, and shut her eyes. "I stayed up all night knitting a blanket for a little girl at the orphanage," she mumbled. "Wake me when she gets here." In a matter of seconds, Mae's body went slack. Three years ago, one of Mae's most promising students at the orphanage—the first she'd taught to read—had fallen ill and died of scarlet fever. Mae had thought of the girl as a daughter, a child she'd always longed for. Since then, every moment away from school had been occupied by the girls, as though if she visited and taught often enough she could spare the rest a similar fate.

Everyone fell silent. As I listened to the rhythmic ticking of an old grandfather clock behind me, my eyelids started to droop—until someone snored loudly and I shot up from my slouched position.

"Good lord, that's embarrassing," Bessie said. I glanced at Mae's open mouth. "It wasn't her." Bessie tipped her head at Alevia whose chin hung limply against her chest, one dark curl fluttering against her mouth as she breathed. "I wouldn't be caught dead sleeping." I lifted an eyebrow at Bessie.

"Really? Don't tell me you've forgotten about the opera last year." Bessie had fallen asleep in the middle of *Carmen* and woken at intermission with a drool stain on her chest. I laughed, remembering it.

"That was an accident," she said. She tried to glare at me, but couldn't keep it up and laughed under her breath instead. "Though I imagine I looked ridiculous regardless. I'd been up all night the night before working on Adelaide Frick's hat."

"A proper lady never allows the demands of the body to compromise her conduct." I quoted our great-aunt Rose, Bess's heroine—a woman who'd married rich and profited greatly, until both of her sons squandered her wealth after her husband's death—and smiled thinly, wagging a finger at Bess. "But truly,

Bess, perhaps you should allow yourself a break now and again." She looked up from the end of the feather that she'd begun to curl between her fingertips. "You've been working until nearly dawn every day for weeks on that toque, on the hat for Katherine Delafield, and on our dresses."

"I know." She stared down at the feather. "I know I need to, but I cannot. If I fail, if my income falters . . . I can't bear the thought of us wearing rags. We were bred for more, Virginia. Until art or marriage affords us luxury, I will not rest." Standing up, I walked over to her and clutched her shoulder.

"You have to stop worrying about the rest of us. We're all capable of making our own way." Bess nodded, but I knew she hadn't really heard me. I crossed to the window, unable to sit any longer without falling asleep. Cobwebs occupied the corners, stray strands fluttering in the frigid draft. The grass outside was winter brown and the bare trees rocked back and forth in the wind.

The door creaked open behind me, startling my view of the lawn, and I spun around in time to see Mr. Smith wheel Cherie into the room. Mae and Alevia's heads jerked up at once. Alevia yawned, quickly covering her mouth with her hand. Cherie was hugely pregnant. Her normally prominent cheekbones had been eclipsed by swelling, but she smiled at us and rolled her eyes at her husband. Apparently the wheelchair hadn't been her idea.

"I apologize. I've kept you all waiting so long. William refused to wake me from my nap even though I asked that he do so." Her lips pursed, brown eyes squinting in annoyance.

"You need all the rest you can get," he said softly. Mr. Smith smiled apologetically at us, but his blue eyes were cold. "Miss Virginia, do you have everything you need to paint my lovely wife?" I nodded, and Cherie ducked her head away from her husband to grin slyly at me. Perhaps she didn't want me to paint her after all.

"I'm honestly shocked that you didn't paint yourself, Cherie. You're so talented," I said, and she looked at me sharply. Mr. Smith laughed and shook his head.

"She did make quite an impression with that little hobby of hers once upon a time, didn't she?" Out of the corner of my eye I saw Alevia's mouth drop open and then close just as quickly. "I can't remember the last time she's had time to paint with the baby coming and all of the entertaining." He shrugged and Cherie's face paled as she turned her eyes away, refusing to look at us and our wide stares. The fact that such an amazing gift had been shut away stunned us all. He'd undoubtedly discouraged her work. She loved it too much to discard it voluntarily. No one said anything, so Mr. Smith clapped his hands together and started toward the door. "I'll let you get to it." He turned at the doorframe. "And Miss Virginia, please watch Cherie's proximity to the fumes. I'll not have our son exposed to toxins." I forced a smile and nodded. He shut the door and Cherie exhaled loudly as though her stays had just been loosened.

"I'm sorry," she said. She shut her eyes for a moment before bracing herself on the handles of the chair and standing up, hands clasped to her back for support.

"You haven't been painting at . . . at all?" Alevia glanced at the piano and then down at the wide panels of pearls and gold spangles along her skirt. I knew what she was thinking, that marriage was a sure way to lose the ability to do what you loved. Perhaps she was right. I'd never thought of the implications when I'd considered marrying Charlie. Primarily because I knew he'd never ask me to forfeit my writing, and secondarily because a profession wasn't an option for a marriage between two struggling artists, it was a necessity.

"You heard Mr. Smith. She's been busy, Alevia," Mae said softly, narrowing her eyes at our youngest sister, whose face flamed red at the insinuation that she'd spoken out of turn. Cherie walked past me and stopped at the window. I followed her, unsure if I should tell her where to sit or wait for instruction.

"No, I haven't. I either sit in the drawing room and read or take naps. I'd hardly consider that busy." Cherie's brown eyes were stony with anger and her lips pressed together. "He just doesn't want me to do it. It distracts—" She stopped midsentence, pinched her eyes together, and shook her head. "It distracts from the attention I give him and my need to tend to our social obligations and the house. Why the hell are we in here?" As if she hadn't realized where she was before, she swept her palm along the top of the piano, scattering dust on the floor. "If hosting in this filthy lounge is his attempt at encouraging you to leave quickly, I—"

"Cherie, I'm sure that's not the case," Mae said, interrupting. Bessie coughed and picked at the feather on her hat.

"I understand your frustration," Bess said carefully. "I love millinery and would be quite forlorn to give it up. But you have a lovely home and a husband with a respected last name—two blessings most of us aren't fortunate enough to have. He cares for you."

"No, he doesn't. He cares for the child." She pointed at her belly to enunciate her point. "He keeps referring to it as his son, as if he knows somehow." Cherie sank down onto the piano bench, head in her hands. "I'm half relieved Franklin didn't come. William knows his paintings. It'll be more believable this way," she whispered to herself. I crossed the room and knelt down in front of her, pulling her hands from her face.

"It's going to be okay, Cherie," I said. "Come and sit on the longue. I'll paint you." Cherie's eyes met mine and she laughed out loud.

"Ginny, you couldn't have thought I was serious. Don't you remember the one time you tried to paint me when we were children? My head was the shape of a potato and my eyes looked like they were running away from my face." She stood up, clutching the edge of the piano. "The truth is that I wanted to see you all, but I was absolutely going to die if I couldn't paint. Ever since that pretentious physician from the city found that William's closest friend died from heart strain after losing his wife and child, his smothering has been worse. I knew if you came, he'd leave me alone. Gin, how many canvases did you bring?"

"Three," I said, smiling.

"Good," she said, letting a giant breath escape her lungs. "He's hardly permitted me to pick up a brush since our wedding day, but over the past few weeks, my heart has been so heavy that I knew if I couldn't paint, my anxiety would just burst it." My insides felt hollow. I remembered the feeling of unbearable tension after Charlie left and couldn't imagine what would have become of me if someone had taken my notebook and pencil and forbidden me to write. Mae leaned down, opened the trunk, grabbed the edge of a miniature canvas, and shoved it into Cherie's hand.

"Sit down and paint," she ordered. Cherie ran her hand over the canvas and sat down on the gray longue next to the fireplace. I shivered, wishing someone had had the decency to light a fire, and dragged the A-frame easel next to her chair.

"Thank you," she whispered and grabbed my arm. "How've you been? Have you been writing?"

"She has," Mae said before I could answer. "A book." I grinned, wishing she hadn't spoken for me.

"A book? Ginny, you've outdone yourself." Cherie smiled as she smeared paint along the clean palette and dipped the corner of her brush into the green. "What's it about?"

"Relationships," I said vaguely. "Speaking of, Mae has a very promising new friendship." Pausing on the word, I glanced over at Mae's face, which flushed immediately at the mention of Mr. Trent. Cherie looked over at her and started to say something but I cut her off, sparing my sister the discomfort of detailing the yet undefined relationship. "And Alevia is going to audition for the Symphony again next month. A friend of Franklin's is a relation of Damrosch's and thinks she'll be able to convince him to take a woman." Cherie's eyes flickered at the insinuation of a female friend of Franklin's, but the diversion worked and she quickly launched into a conversation with Alevia about music, which led to Bessie piping in about the difficulty of procuring the scarlet ibis feathers for Consuelo's toque.

I was relieved that the conversation had turned from me and sat back against the couch. I hadn't thought about my book in two weeks—ever since Franklin and I had gone back to the Hoppers' for another Artists' Society gathering. Mr. Blaine hadn't been in attendance to go over our ideas for *The Century*, but Mr. Hopper spotted me as soon as we'd arrived and pulled me from Lydia's side to say that he'd read my book and had some thoughts. He'd said it with such a huge smile that I thought he'd loved it. Lydia had apparently thought the same because she'd piped in to gush about its genius, though she had yet to read a word. I found out later, when we'd met in the study at the end of the night, that Lydia and I were mistaken. Mr. Hopper started by saying that my writing was strong and that he thought the book had potential. I was dreaming of a vibrant career and publication, when he began doling out a series of blows that hit me one after the other until my stomach churned. He thought the characters were one-dimensional, that they had no aspirations beyond loving each other, and that their lack of motivation otherwise was unbelievable and boring. I'd nodded and thanked him, hoping he'd stop, but he'd kept on, mentioning that he'd actually hoped something bad would happen to them just to make it interesting. "Wasn't death at the end heartbreaking enough?" I'd asked, recalling my tears while I wrote it. Mr. Hopper laughed, shaking his head. "Death is a bit inevitable," he'd said, twirling his pencil between his fingers. "Plus, she's what, ninety when he dies? She'll be along shortly." His criticism in the moment made me want to pummel him. At the time I'd just finished reading his book, *The Blood Runs from Antietam*. True to life and war, the book was well written, but graphic and horrifying—following the lives of two generals on opposing sides during the Civil War. Every few pages it seemed that someone's head was getting blown off by a canon ball or prisoners of war were being hung then gutted for their crimes. I'd wanted to criticize his work as well, to ask him if anything beyond mutilation interested him, but had held my tongue, mostly because at the bottom of my heart I knew what he'd said about my book was the truth and that his comments would only work to improve my manuscript. I realized I'd never received a true critique. Charlie and my siblings had been as honest as they could in their feedback, but at the end of the day, they'd only been supportive. They were too loving to be anything else.

"Ginny." I jerked at the sound of my name and looked over at Cherie. Her cheeks were flushed with contentedness and she smiled. I nodded my head along with Alevia playing what I assumed was one of Bach's English Suites on the out-of-tune piano. I hadn't heard her play this particular song since we were children, when she first learned to play by ear on Grandmother's Steinway grand. I closed my eyes, realizing that I'd stopped hearing the sharp notes. "I think I'm nearly done with your portrait of me, do you want to see it?" Cherie asked.

"Of course," I said, glancing over to the windows where Mae and Bess were plopped on couches opposite each other reading selections from the adjacent bookshelf. Mae held *The Ancient Regime and the French Revolution* by de Tocqueville in one hand, brushing dust off the tea table beside her with the other. Bess flipped through an old *Harper's Bazaar*, paying no mind to Mae's compulsion to tidy. Something about the way Mae sat, eyes locked in a book made me think of Charlie. We'd been in his library at the beginning of the winter last year, watching the snow fall. I could still see the flakes piling up on the windowsill next to me. He'd been sketching an image of Benjamin Franklin for the *Bronx Review*'s Independence Day edition and I'd been writing a short biography on Founding Father John Jay. I'd felt Charlie's eyes on my face and had looked up in time to see him staring at me, pencil hovering in midair. "You know," he'd started, his voice almost a whisper. "It's been said that the sight of Franklin's wife, Deborah, stopped him in his tracks. He was walking down the street eating a piece of fresh-baked bread when he saw her. He never forgot it—the way she looked standing in the doorway of her father's house." Charlie had stood from the stool then and crossed the room. "This is one of those moments, Gin. The way you look right now with your hair half unbound," he'd pushed a lock back from my forehead, "the brown in your eyes surrendering to the green like it always does when you're writing, doing what you love. It's the most beautiful picture I could never begin to draw, but will always remember."

"Look." Cherie's voice jarred me back to the room. She turned the canvas around.

"Cherie . . . what?" is all I could make out. The painting was dark, swathed in black and dark green, completely unlike the optimistic portrayals she had been known for. She'd painted herself sitting in the middle of the room smiling, though her lips were tinged a disturbing gray. The skin under her eyes was so dark that her brown irises looked frightening. "Is that how you feel?" I asked, swallowing hard. She turned the painting back to face her and bit her lip, surveying it. Shrugging, she rose slowly from the lounge, plucked the easel from its place next to her and set it in front of me. "William will be back to get me soon," she said softly. "For what it's worth, tell Franklin that he wins, that his artistic vision was right all along. Somehow it makes me feel better to depict the truth rather than portray hope for a happiness that will probably never be." Cherie smiled at me and I grinned back despite the melancholy I felt at her circumstance, knowing that even if her life wasn't happy, in the past few hours she'd been free. "Do ask Franklin to call on me."

The door opened before I could respond to her request. Alevia's fingers fumbled on the keys as Mr. Smith appeared in the doorway. "Are you finished, darling?" he asked and Cherie nodded, hand resting protectively on her stomach. Mae flipped her book shut and walked around the edge of the couch, inhaling sharply when she saw the portrait. Mr. Smith didn't notice but took Cherie's hand, kissed it, and then righted, heading toward me. I inhaled the heavy scent of turpentine, heart pumping. I assumed he'd react one of two ways: he'd either curse me when he saw it or tear it up. He patted my shoulder, then glanced at the portrait. "That's lovely," he said, and I froze at his cold indifference.

Chapter Eight

JANUARY 1892
The Loftin House
BRONX, NEW YORK

I'd been staring out of my bedroom window at the chestnut tree for almost two hours and had only written four words. Mother and Mae were setting the table for lunch. I could hear the clatter of china and their laughter, and smell the pork fatback wafting from the reheated pot of brown beans. I pressed my pencil to the paper, as if the action would force the words, but nothing came. I was supposed to be writing a news piece for the *Review* about the upcoming Preakness Stakes at Morris Park Racecourse, but couldn't settle my mind. It was Charlie's wedding day. He'd be married in a matter of hours and the possibility that our friendship could be salvaged would be over. I'd made excuses to be home all week, thinking that at the last moment, he'd change his mind and come for me, but it was clear he was moving forward. Perhaps it was better this way. Our relationship had always been passionate, accented by arguments and apologies, but in the midst of heartbreak, I'd forgotten our fights, our immaturity.

I glanced at my dresser drawer containing my book, and then at the roaring fire next to it. The pages only reminded me of something that didn't exist. And, according to Mr. Hopper, it wasn't good anyway. I rolled my eyes at his chiding voice in my head telling me that that's not what he'd meant and reached into the drawer. I'd expected that it wouldn't be perfect, but he'd pointed out so many flaws in my writing I didn't know if I had the skill to fix them. Perhaps I was only fooling myself by thinking I could become a published novelist.

The notebook was worn and familiar in my hand as I flipped it open.

> *At a young age, you never have to try to be happy. You just are. That's how Carlisle and I were from the beginning— young and happy and carefree, unaffected by what we should do or who we should be.*

The base of my neck tensed. *"My heart. You have it."* As much as I wanted to ignore it, a naïve part of me believed Charlie. But he'd chosen. I caught my reflection in the mirror and swallowed hard as the image of Cherie's painting flew into my mind. That would never be me; I wouldn't allow it. Nothing, not the memory of what could've been or even Charlie himself could take my art from me. It was mine. I looked down at the page and closed the book, putting it back in the drawer. I couldn't burn it. I'd take Mr. Hopper's advice and make it better. I didn't care if publication was improbable. If it could make even one person remember who they were before adulthood set in with its social structure and rules, perhaps they'd be saved from the prison of Cherie's reality and Charlie's future.

"Mother!" Franklin's voice rang through the windows. He'd been scarce at home for a month—traveling up to Maine for work and then to a funeral in Stamford, Connecticut, of a friend I'd never heard of. At first I thought I was hearing things, before he yelled again. A strange chugging sound came from outside, like a metal ball being shaken in a tin can, and I ran to the window. I rubbed my eyes and looked again, but the automobile was still there, black paint gleaming in the afternoon light. Franklin lounged against the leather backrest, cigar clutched between his teeth, arm slung across the pink and white velvet ribbons along the standing collar of Lydia's long wool coat. Mr. Trent tilted his head toward Franklin, said something, and laughed, his breath vaporizing in the winter air. He straightened as Mother appeared below me, dropped the butter knife she was holding, and clasped her hands to her mouth. Not bothering to wait for her response, I flew down the stairs and out the front door.

"What . . . where did you get this?" Mother asked. Franklin swiveled a lever next to him to stop the motor.

"I just bought it from John Hopper. I worked out a deal before he went out of town for the weekend. It's yours. I had a little extra money and thought you shouldn't be walking to your errands anymore." I stared at it, unsure what to say or how he could've possibly afforded it. We'd been five dollars short on our bills last month. This kind of extravagance was reckless. We didn't even have anywhere to store it beyond Grandfather's old rickety garden shed out back. Franklin jumped down from his seat, helped Lydia out, and leaned to hug Mother who continued to gaze at it without blinking. I couldn't tell what she was thinking. She'd always been adamant that wealth didn't make a person happy, and had always encouraged us to be content with a simple life.

"We'll speak about this later, of course, but it's a lovely gift, dear." Mother smiled, giving none of her emotion away.

"Mr. Trent, did you know about this?" Mae asked, untying the white linen apron around her yellow velvet skirt. She shielded her eyes from the sun with one hand and wrapped her arm across her body to block the cold as she descended the remaining steps. Mr. Trent walked toward her, reaching to clutch her hands, and I thought of Charlie gripping my own but pushed the sensation away. It was time to move on.

"Not at all. I was just sitting in my room studying when I heard my name being shouted from the street. I looked out and it was ol' Frank yelling at me to come take a ride to the Bronx in his new Benz." Mr. Trent leaned down to kiss Mae's hand and my mother smiled at them for a moment before turning back to Franklin and the wagon.

"Do you like it, Gin? You haven't said a word." Franklin pulled Lydia behind him as he started up the walk.

"Ginny," Lydia said, breaking from Franklin to wrap her arm across my shoulders. "You know you've never seen anything more handsome in your life." She leaned in to my ear. "The Benz's nice, but I'm speaking of Franklin, you know. I've missed you since the last meeting. I hope we'll be sisters some day."

"I'd love that," I whispered back, squeezing her hand and trying to swallow the lump of irritation that had suddenly manifested in my throat. As warm and lovely as Lydia was, I wondered if some of Franklin's sudden tendency toward extravagance had something to do with impressing her. The neighbors across from us had taken notice of the automobile and were now congregating on their front porch staring at it as though a dragon had materialized in the street.

"So?" Franklin asked again, turning to look at me. "You like it, don't you?" I nodded, amused by the goofy grin on my brother's face.

"It's lovely, Frank," I said, leaning in to him, "but how could we afford it? We weren't even able to pay our debts last month. We haven't bought groceries or coal or . . ." I drifted off and stepped back to glance at the automobile once more. The silver spokes glittered in the afternoon sun. "Aren't automobiles nearly one thousand dollars?" Franklin cocked an eyebrow at me and shook his head.

"They certainly are. If not more than that." Bessie's voice came from the porch behind me. She was wearing a new dress made of blue and cream brocaded taffeta, complemented by long suede gloves with a mousquetaire wrist opening. Our accumulating debt hadn't affected her spending habits. "The Carnegies just bought a Million and Guiet Chariot D'Orsay the other week for well over two thousand, and it's not even motorized. At least that's what T—" She stopped abruptly and I turned to find her staring at Lydia. Bess's face paled, making her upswept auburn hair appear shockingly red against her skin.

"You're the woman I saw . . . who I saw . . ." Lydia stuttered, glancing over at my mother standing next to Mae and then back at Bessie. "That I saw talking to my brother the other evening." Bessie swallowed hard and nodded mechanically, causing the plume of turkey feathers jutting from the brim of her trilby hat to quiver. Alevia appeared in the doorframe behind her, grinning at Bessie's back. *Had Bess told Alevia about her and Mr. Blaine?* I wondered where Lydia had come across them and what exactly they'd been doing.

"You know Mr. Blaine, Bess?" I asked. Bessie's eyes met mine, wide and pleading.

"I do. We met at the Astors' one afternoon," she said softly. "He's very nice." Shooting me a thin smile, Bessie turned on her heel and walked into the house. Lydia grabbed my arm, and leaned into my ear.

"I caught them kissing in our laundry a few days ago. I had no idea she was your sister," she whispered, then shrugged. The thought that they'd been kissing shocked me. As far as I knew, he hadn't even attempted to properly court her. "I suppose I'd be more upset if I thought you were interested in Tom. You're not, are you?"

"No." I softened my tone. "He's kind and smart and we'll be good friends, but—" I started, but she smiled and shook her head, cutting me off.

"You don't need to explain," she said. "Sometimes it fits, sometimes it doesn't. I tried to make it work with my last beau for far too long. Only in the wake of his brother's death did it become evident that I hadn't been imagining his alternating tendency for seclusion and madness . . . and then I found your charming, compassionate brother." She patted my arm. "It's best to be true to yourself." She let me go and walked toward Mother, the hem of lace ribbons along her ivory dress fluttering from beneath her coat in the wind. Franklin started to follow her, but I caught his sleeve.

"Frank. How much was it and how could you possibly afford it?" I asked under my breath. He stared at me blankly and I tipped my head at the gleaming automobile.

"Oh." Franklin squinted toward the Benz. "Well, I got a raise at work—a large one—and thought that with the bonus I might get us something nice." I stared at him skeptically.

"Something nice is a new suit."

"I told you it's secondhand . . . if that helps you reconcile the extravagance," he said. "The paint is chipped off on the right side. John was trying to get rid of it and gave me a good deal—three-fifty—which is exactly ten dollars less than I had . . . after I paid the rest of our debt at the Building and Loan." I patted him on the back, hugely relieved.

"It's lovely."

"Don't be so disappointed in me, Gin. We won't be destitute because of it. I'll be making much more from now on anyway." His eyes broke from mine and he glanced toward Charlie's house, no doubt hoping they'd look out and notice that the Loftins weren't so poor after all, but the windows had been dark since yesterday. I'd watched them leave—the luggage, followed by Mrs. Aldridge. Charlie had come out of the house last. He'd turned around the side of the coach and looked up at my window. We'd stared at each other for a moment, neither of us bothering to smile. There was no reason to pretend. He'd lifted his hand to me before disappearing into the coach.

Something—perhaps the excitement of our new automobile— seemed to distract me from thinking of Charlie's wedding, and I'd retired to my room feeling as if I had enough strength to begin to revise my book. I went through the first half of it in a few hours—striking out sentences, tightening my prose—but when I reached the party scene, I stopped, unable to continue. I could still see Charlie's face, feel the heat of the bodies around me, smell the alcohol in the air. The tightness across my chest returned. I glanced down at the page for the fifth time and forced myself to read it.

And then he turned to me, got down on one knee, and asked if I'd be his wife.

From that sentence on, my book was a lie. In the haze of mourning, I'd created an alternate outcome that would seem beautiful to the reader, but it wasn't the truth. Mr. Hopper was right; it didn't seem real. That's what he had been getting at when he'd told me that he was bored with the characters' lives, that he found them flat and one-dimensional. His criticism still clenched my heart, but now I understood. If I was going to write a fictionalized account of our lives, it would have to be honest and I'd have to live the pain again—even if I chose to write us together in the end. Charlie would have to propose to someone else. I plucked my pencil from behind my ear and struck the sentence out. Flipping the page, I heard my doorknob twist, and looked up in time to see Bess walk into my room and close the door.

"Before you say anything, let me speak." She lifted her palm toward me as if I were about to launch into a lecture and sat down on the chair next to my dressing table. Her face was flushed. I opened my mouth, starting to say that she didn't need to explain her relationship with Mr. Blaine, but she made a frustrated sound in the back of her throat and waved her hand at me. "I don't know what nonsense Miss Blaine has told you . . . or perhaps it was Alevia, but I'd like the chance to set the account straight before you tell Mother." Bessie's eyes narrowed.

"When's the last time I tattled on you, Bess? Honestly."

"You jumped at the chance to do so outside, did you not?" She asked, voice rising in irritation.

"Calm down!" I hissed. "The last thing you want is Lydia hearing you."

"She's been gone for at least an hour. Frank took her home." Bessie drew a breath, pinched her full bottom lip and sighed, leaning against the chair back. "Mr. Blaine told me he met you and that the two of you were planning to exchange your work, so I figured it'd come out eventually, but I wasn't prepared. I didn't know that Miss Blaine was so familiar with Franklin." She picked at her fingernails and then looked at me. I pointedly glanced down at my notebook wishing she'd get on with it. "I was walking out of the Astors' one day after dropping off a hat and ran smack into Mr. Blaine coming through the door. It was like one of those things you read about. We stood staring at each other for what felt like minutes and then he reached for my hand and introduced himself. When my hand touched his, Gin . . . I don't know how to explain it. It felt like I'd lifted out of my body and taken to floating." Her fingers rose to her mouth, no doubt remembering his kisses a few days prior.

"I know how it feels," I said, remembering the light-headed feeling that always came when Charlie was close. The hair along my arms rose remembering the first time he'd held me. It had been at a ball celebrating Cherie's engagement about four years back. I'd been occupied most of the night by Cherie's much older, though handsome, cousin, Andrew Emerson, and had been quite taken with him—until Charlie, at the conclusion of our sixth dance, came behind me, wrapped his arms around my waist, and pulled me away. To this day, I'm unsure if Charlie was jealous of him or just tired of making small talk with well-meaning women, but I could still smell the wood smoke in his hair, the musky scent of exertion on his skin, and knew I hadn't taken a breath while we'd danced.

"Mr. Blaine must've asked Mrs. Astor where I lived, because I received a letter the following day asking if I'd meet him to walk along the High Bridge." Bessie smiled, ignoring me.

"And you went? You didn't tell any of us. You didn't even know him." My forehead scrunched, wondering how in the world she'd talked herself into meeting a stranger alone.

"He's a Blaine," she said. "I knew he'd do me no harm." I forced my lips into a grin to keep from groaning, knowing if William Hughes down the street had asked the same, she'd find it insulting.

"He's already done you harm," I said evenly. "You've compromised yourself and your reputation by . . . well . . . doing whatever you were doing when Lydia caught you." My face was hot and Bess laughed.

"That's ridiculous," she exclaimed. "We were only kissing." Bessie looked down and I knew then that she'd done much more than that. "Surely nothing you haven't already done with Charlie."

"He's never kissed me," I said softly. He'd never tried. Regardless of his supposed love for me, I'd been easy to resist. "And he's certainly never seen me undressed." I said it slyly to see if she'd take the bait and she did, hands bunching nervously in her blue skirt.

"He . . . he only lifted my skirt to my knees. I stopped him after that even though I wanted him to . . . I didn't want to stop him," Bessie stuttered. I gaped at her as she swallowed hard, composing herself. "To be honest, I would've married him then and there and still would. He's impossible to refuse. I'm not sure I'll be able to the next time." I didn't understand how she'd fallen prey to him. His egoism was hardly charming.

"If that's the case, then stop putting yourself in those kinds of positions," I said.

"I want him, Gin, and I'll have him. I'll marry him," she said fiercely, jolting forward in the chair as if someone had pushed her. "This is my chance, don't you see? My opportunity to be happy, to stop working so hard. Please don't take him from me." I looked at her as if she'd just sprouted antlers, wondering what in the world she was talking about.

"Why would I?" I grimaced and shook my head. "I don't find him the least bit appealing." Bessie's blue eyes widened at my words.

"Really? He mentioned that Lydia had introduced the two of you at one of Mr. Hopper's little get-togethers a few months back— something neither you nor Franklin had the decency to invite me to—because Lydia thought you'd be a good match for him."

I shrugged.

"That's Lydia's opinion." I couldn't imagine having to listen adoringly to Mr. Blaine's narcissistic stories for the rest of my life.

"Maybe you're telling the truth, but I think that Charlie's broken your heart so badly you'll try anything to get over him." I bristled. She knew nothing of how I felt. She hadn't bothered to ask. "I've got to get down to O'Neill's to pay for the order that Mrs. Goelet just canceled." Bessie stood up so quickly that the chair tipped backward, then dropped into place with a clatter. I knew she was hurt and didn't mean it, but her words stung. Her affection had been disregarded once before by George Vanderbilt, a man she had no business loving in the first place. Mistaking his kindness at parties for interest, she'd convinced herself that he loved her despite the disparity between our status and theirs—until it was announced that he'd proposed to Edith Dresser, a wealthy distant cousin of Charlie's. Bess was just afraid of being overlooked again.

I looked down at my scrawl in the notebook in front of me and thanked God for my passion for something other than the futile pursuit of men. I hadn't even chased after Charlie. Love was something I couldn't control, but I *could* control my words, and I planned to make something of them.

Hours later I was in the same place, reading over the same sentence, thinking about how I'd react if Charlie came back to me years later. I couldn't just throw this revision together hoping it would be better than the first. I needed to know it would be. I couldn't bear another brutal critique from Mr. Hopper.

"Ginny? Are you all right?" I turned toward the door to find Alevia looking at me, head tilted to the side at my unblinking stare out of the windows in front of me.

"Of course. I was just thinking," I said. Alevia leaned forward, craning her neck over my shoulder to glance at my notebook.

"Writer's block." She shook her head, fiddled with the single drop pearl on her necklace.

"Not quite. I'm trying to figure out where I want it to go next," I said.

"Oh, I see. The same thing happens to me when the music doesn't flow. I can't play." I smiled at her, doubting this happened very often, if at all. You could set about any piece in front of her and she'd play it flawlessly the first time. "Sometimes I play best when I'm in the warehouse at Estey. No one can hear me over the noise of the machines, so I just play through the wrong notes and bad tuning. That's where I figure it out. Maybe you need a change of scenery." I knew she was right. I'd confined my work to my bedroom for far too long. "It'll come to you." Alevia patted my back. For years she'd traveled down the block to the Estey Piano Factory once a week to test their pianos. I knew she'd started doing it as a favor for Mother and Father's friend John Simpson, who'd needed someone at the beginning of his and Jacob Estey's venture in the Bronx. After they were on their feet, Alevia had continued going for the money—or so I'd thought. I'd had no idea that she actually enjoyed it. "And if that doesn't work, try writing something else. Give yourself a break and then come back to it."

"Maybe I'll try," I said, and she smiled, brown eyes warming. "When's your next audition with the Symphony?"

"I'm not sure," she said softly. "Lydia said that she hasn't had an opportunity to speak with Damrosch about it yet. It'll be a wonderful opportunity whenever it happens."

"It's going to happen."

"I hope so, Gin. I really do."

After another hour of staring at the wall, I started down the stairs thinking I'd take Alevia's advice after all. I could hear her playing in the drawing room, the quick notes of Mozart's Piano Concerto No. 15 flying through the air.

I pulled my grandmother's old mink coat over my shoulders and walked two miles to the library in the blistering cold. I tipped my head at the librarian, Miss Gills, and made my way to the new Brittanica encyclopedias. If I couldn't think through my novel, I could at least attempt to find a topic for the story I'd submit to *The*

Century. The Century was known for its emphasis on history, especially little-known stories painting a romantic picture of American life. When dusk came, I left the library with a page of ideas from the historic importance of Anne Bradstreet's poetry to the story of Mary Musgrove. I had no idea which subject to choose, but at least I had a start.

I was exhausted when I reached home, but I made my way down the hall toward the parlor, thinking that I'd sit in Father's rickety old chair in hopes of conjuring his storytelling prowess. Passing the kitchen, I laughed at Mother covered in flour, mixing dough in a copper bowl. She glanced up, wiped the flour from her eyelashes, and pointed to a loaf pan in the open oak cupboard. The glass flour canister had tumbled over on the top shelf and white dust sprinkled down the ledges, pooling on the floor. I started to wipe the shelves, but Mother grunted and gestured to the loaf pan again.

"Have you lost your voice, or are you thinking of going into miming?"

She smiled and swabbed the flour from her face, taking the pan from my hand.

"Lord knows I can't stand to keep silent, but perhaps I should give it a try." She laughed. "It would make good sense for me to do something in the arts. My children are so very talented, but everyone knows your gifts come from your father, while your determination comes from me." She winked. From time to time she'd tell us of her childhood attempts at drawing and poetry and music. The stories were always amusing. Her parents had hired the best tutors, sure that their daughter had some sort of artistic talent that would woo a society man to her side, but Mother had always purposely failed, choosing instead to occupy her time teaching her dolls to read or write.

Mother spooned the sourdough batter into the pan and reached out to clutch my wrist. She glanced at the notebook in my hand and then looked up at me. "I know that your father understood your writing in a way I never will. Your soul is identical to his, just as Mae's is to mine, but I want you to know that I'm just as proud of you as he was, Virginia." Her eyes glistened and she released me.

"Thank you, Mother." I rested a hand on her back, on the worn checkered fabric, and headed for the parlor. Passing the dining room, I caught the small gold frame on the buffet as I went by. It held the only photo I'd ever seen of my parents together, standing side by side against the front door. They'd both always heralded their instantaneous love, saying that fate placed them beside each other on the ferry to Randall's Island that day. Father was going to meet his friends to fish and Mother was late for a family picnic. Neither of them made it to their obligations, choosing instead to ride back and forth from Manhattan to Randall's Island until the ferry stopped running. It had nearly killed my mother when he died. I wondered if love like that could occur even after two people broke each other's hearts. I wanted to think it couldn't, but I knew deep down that even though the tainted shadow of betrayal would never fully disappear, I would consider it if Charlie came back to me. The thought made me angry, more at myself than at him, but it was honest and I'd have to be honest if I was going to write about us.

I reached to push the door to the parlor open, but froze at the sound of Mr. Trent's voice. He finished his sentence and I heard my sister respond, her high pitch an indistinguishable blur to my ears.

"I know, my dear," he continued, "but I have to tell you so that you know, even if you insist the past doesn't matter." I could see them through the crack in the door. Mr. Trent's lanky frame was bent toward Mae across from him, dark heads nearly touching across the coffee table. I knew I should walk away but my feet refused to move. If he was about to tell her something awful, I'd need to know so that I could comfort her. Mae sighed and reached to hold his hand. I knew that she wasn't being dishonest; she really didn't care about his past. She'd always been that way, loving people for who they were at the moment. Mae whispered something to him. He lifted his hand to stroke her cheek and then bent forward to kiss her forehead. Leaning away from her, he kept hold of her hand and looked at her seriously.

"I've been married before." He said it so quickly that it took me a moment to process the sentence. His face was ashen and Mae withdrew her hand to stand up and cross to the window. She turned to face Mr. Trent when she reached the windowsill, the afternoon light catching her brown hair. Her forehead was creased in thought, but she smiled at him. He made a coughing noise as if he were choking.

"I was young." His voice was wracked with a tension that wavered with forced steadiness. "So was she. It was w-when Father and I were living in Vermont, when I was helping with his doctoring." He ran a hand through his hair, then dipped his head, holding his face in his hands. "Miss Loftin . . . Mae, I love you," he said abruptly and she nodded, still smiling, though I thought I saw tears in her eyes. "Her name was Emily. Father treated her mother for an infected wound and I helped. They . . . Father and her mother, I mean, thought we'd be a good match. I found her enjoyable and pretty, so I married her." Mae's face drained at the last bit and she began to fidget, lifting her wrist to stare at the brass button on the cuff of her hunter green sleeve.

"What happened?" Mae whispered, unable to look up from her hands.

"She's . . ." Mr. Trent cleared his throat loudly and coughed. "She's dead, Mae. So is our daughter. They died in childbirth." Mae looked at him, eyes wide in horror. I clapped my hand over my mouth. Mae moved from the window, crouched down next to him, and clutched both of his hands.

"I'm sorry. So, so sorry," she whispered. "Your poor wife and child." The hair along my arms stood on end. It wasn't that I hadn't heard of women dying in childbirth, it was fairly commonplace—but it had never happened to anyone close to me, and the thought of it swept over me like a frigid wind.

"Thank you," Mr. Trent said softly. "It was a few years ago." He was crying now and Mae lifted her hand to wipe his cheeks, letting the tears she'd been holding back escape her own lids. He sniffed and pulled her up from the floor, gathering her to him. "Mae, she's not my wife anymore," he said, smoothing a stray tendril back from her face. "And I loved her like a husband should, but I love you so differently, so completely." My heart warmed. Ashamed to be eavesdropping on a conversation so tender, I walked toward my father's study, thinking that if Mr. Trent didn't ask her to marry him right then, it wouldn't be long.

Whether it was Alevia's advice or Henry and Mae's exchange that spurred inspiration, I'd rewritten three chapters in an hour and a half. Heartache was easy to write. It was sadly familiar—the feeling of complete desperation, worthlessness, and the elusive hope that Charlie would come back. The fictional encounter of his return flowed out of my head and onto the paper as easily as the Harlem River into the East. But now I sat back, stuck again, having no idea what I'd write next, staring at the tiny deer head above the mantel across from me, wondering why someone hadn't taken it down after my grandfather's death. He'd apparently been very proud of killing it when they'd first taken up residence here, back when Morrisania consisted of a few brave houses surrounded by rolling hills. Now it didn't fit. Life would have been so different then—even in my parents' generation—so simple on the surface, yet tainted to the core by the dim complexities of war.

I remembered my parents talking about it from time to time, about the war and the battle that killed my grandfather at the age of forty-two. My father had never fully recovered from his grief. I glanced across the desk, eyeing a frame that held an old photograph of the Lincolns. Mother once told me that everyone had been so affected by the war and the valiance of the president during it, that when Lincoln's body rolled into town on its sixteen-hundred-mile funeral tour, she and her sisters had taken the train in from the country to see it, waiting five hours for a chance to pass his coffin. To this day, whenever the war or the president is brought up, she still comments on his face, saying that his wrinkles were deeper than any man's she'd ever seen and that it had almost made her happy that he'd passed on from his life of hardship.

That was it. An idea lodged in my brain and I pushed my notebook out of the way, snatching a clean sheet of paper from the top of my father's desk drawer. Remembering my parents' recollections had conjured the perfect topic for *The Century*, something I was sure Mr. Gilder would jump at the chance to publish—the controversial tale of Emilie Todd Helm. Emilie was Mary Lincoln's sister and the wife of an esteemed Confederate general. Straddling both sides of the war, she'd been portrayed as the strong, beautiful heroine of the Confederacy in some circles and the traitorous plague infecting the sensibilities of the White House in others. After the war, the controversy over her had faded, as controversies do, and her memory had mostly been ignored. But my grandfather, who'd met her once when she'd accompanied the Lincolns on a tour after her husband's death, had never forgotten "the young rebel woman with the kind face"—passing the remembrance along to my father who'd passed it to me.

The story spilled out of me and onto the page, and before I knew it, I was almost finished. I couldn't wait to read it at the next Society meeting and to show Mr. Blaine. The door creaked open, disturbing my focus on the last sentence, and I stopped to glance toward it, expecting it to be Mae and Mr. Trent sharing the news of their engagement, but it was Franklin. Lugging an easel and a blank canvas, Frank paused in the doorway, slung the canvas under his arm, and then carried both toward me. Amused, I grinned as he set it down on the oriental rug in front of the desk.

"What's that for?" I asked. Franklin straightened up and took a breath.

"Alevia told me you were having trouble with your book." He smoothed the edges of his starched cuffs with his fingers and looked at me. "Hopper told me that he sometimes paints whatever he's trying to get out. He says the words come easily after you have something visual, plus you've had all of the time painting to think it through." I looked at him doubtfully and Franklin rolled his eyes. "Try it."

"You've seen my paintings," I said.

"Your landscapes aren't bad, actually. In any case, I'm not suggesting you should be the next Thomas Eakins, but you could try to paint *something* to conjure the image in your head when you forget the words."

"It's worth a try." He smiled victoriously and I surveyed his suit. It looked different from the one he'd been wearing that morning. This one had light gray pinstripes. "Is that a new suit, Frank?" He looked down at his pants and pinched the fabric.

"No. Well, I mean, I suppose. I got it in Maine when I was on business there a few weeks back."

"Part of your bonus?" He glared at me, but nodded.

"I can't exactly go around looking like a ragamuffin. Especially when I'm working and trying to give off the impression that people should listen to me. Speaking of fashion, you should have a new dress made. We'll have more than enough and I'll give you the money when I get paid at the—"

"Are you sure all of this extravagance—the Benz, your new suits—isn't because you're trying to impress Lydia?" I interrupted. Franklin shook his head.

"She doesn't care about things like that." She didn't seem concerned with money, though I doubted that she was indifferent. She was society. That kind of influence didn't slip past without a little bit of it sticking to one's bones.

"On another note, where in the world are you going to park the Benz?" I asked. "It'll be ruined in Grandfather's old barn."

"I'll inquire after space in a carriage house," he said, exasperated. "In any case, I didn't come in here to be interrogated about my spending habits, Gin, I was just trying to help." He ran a hand across the top of the desk and then pointed to the drawer at my side. "I paint in this room sometimes. There are some oil paints in here if you decide you're going to give it a try."

"Thank you," I said. He started to walk away, but I stopped him. "I'm sorry for saying anything. It's just that it's quite difficult to stop distressing about money when we've lived so cautiously for years. I know you're only trying to provide for us with Father gone."

"Not just provide for us," he said bluntly. "I plan to make this family something again. A name people will have to respect, not just for our abilities, but for our innovation and our drive."

"What does it matter what people think? We're all happy," I said. "We don't have to live extravagantly just because you think that having things will remedy what happened to me and Charlie or keep them from happening to you and Lydia. If Charlie really loved me, he would've been with me regardless." Franklin's eyes dropped to the floor.

"Maybe," he said. "Oh, I almost forgot. John's out of town, but he gave me a note for you when I stopped by to pick up the Benz." Franklin reached into his pocket, drew out an envelope and tossed it to me. I pushed it to the side of the desk and Franklin stared at me. "Aren't you going to read it?" He looked at me as though all correspondence addressed to someone else should be shared, but as I didn't mind in this case, I ripped the flap open, unfolded the letter, and read it aloud.

> *Dearest Miss Loftin,*
> *I hope this letter finds you well. I wanted to send*
> *you a bit of encouragement as you revise your book. Your*
> *writing is truly remarkable and your sense of imagination*
> *is evident—not only in your novel, but also in your*
> *wit, an attribute that I've had the wonderful fortune of*
> *experiencing over the past several weeks. I hope you won't*
> *find this too forward of me, but I'd like to take you to the*
> *opera upon my return next week. They're performing the*
> *marvelous La bohème. If you agree, I'll come to retrieve*
> *you at half past five next Saturday evening.*
> *All of my regards,*
> *John Hopper*

His sentiments weighed on my heart. He was interested in me beyond friendship, beyond helping with my novel—at least that was what the letter implied, though I couldn't help questioning his words. I recalled the way he looked at me, the way he touched me. I could still feel the heat on my cheeks, attraction in the pit of my stomach. He was immensely talented, charming, easy to converse with, and undeniably handsome, but men of such character often were. And even if he hadn't made a habit of discombobulating women, I didn't know if I could bear the ambiguity that came with a courtship.

"So?" Franklin asked. Grinning, he smoothed the corners of his mustache. "Are you as fond of him as he is of you?"

"No," I said. The word came out much more quickly than I intended, and it was wrong. "I mean, I do enjoy his company, and he and I have a lot in common, but I'm not sure. People say that he . . ." I felt my face flush. His confidence was magnetic. Franklin laughed.

"How shall I put it . . . enjoys a variety of women?" He shook his head. "It's perfectly all right if you're not certain about him, but there's no validity to that rumor, Gin. John is friendly, likely the most social man I've ever met. He can hardly help acquiring such a reputation. I hope you'll give him a chance. For his sake as well as yours." I took his meaning and nodded, thankful that he hadn't uttered Charlie's name. Even so, the last time Charlie held me manifested in my mind, the way his fingers twitched with nerves as he'd brushed the hair from my forehead. I forced the memory away and thought of Mr. Hopper, the disparity between the two suddenly clear.

"I suppose I'd like to get to know him better," I said. Franklin smiled at me and tapped the doorframe.

"Perhaps he'll surprise you."

Chapter Nine

The Hopper House
NEW YORK, NEW YORK

As it turned out, Franklin was right. I was surprised by Mr. Hopper, but by his persistence more than anything else. The day after I received his letter, an enormous bouquet of white calla lilies landed on our front porch. I'd thought they were Mae's. Mae and Mr. Trent had gotten engaged—as I'd predicted—the day before. It had been a joyful day, but the moment I heard the news, Mr. Smith's cold eyes and counterfeit smile flashed in my memory. The only way I'd gotten over the possibility of my sister being regarded with such callousness was to realize that it wasn't an option. Mae wasn't an artist and she'd always wanted a family. There was nothing to stop her from giving herself wholeheartedly to the man that loved her save her teaching, and education was a perfectly suitable profession.

My mind was focused on Mr. Trent's ardent love for Mae, when Mae handed the calla lilies back to me. They were from Mr. Hopper. Then roses the next day. And they kept coming. He'd sent me a different bouquet of flowers every day with a letter begging my attendance at *La bohème*. Flattered as I was by the attention, as much as it suggested that Frank was right about his reputation—he couldn't possibly find the time to woo multiple women this way—I wasn't entirely convinced. Even though Franklin had done his best to assure me that overstated gestures were simply what Mr. Hopper did and that the flowers didn't necessarily mean anything, I still felt uneasy. What was I to him? Was I simply the most interesting prospect at the moment, or was he trying to court me? Neither possibility alleviated my confusion.

Yet somehow, despite my perplexed feelings, here I was, standing in the hazy drawing room after attending *La bohème*, watching Alevia—who Franklin had fooled into coming to the Society this time—walk toward the piano, arm crooked in Frank's. It had been a cruel trick. Alevia had thought she was going to have a quiet evening at the Blaines' talking music with Lydia while Franklin played cards with Mr. Blaine. The moment they arrived, Alevia found me in the foyer, pressing herself against me when we'd walked into the drawing room, hand clutching mine. It was something she always did in large crowds, an attempt to disappear, and the avant-garde mix of men and women was a scene that took getting used to.

Alevia sat down at the bench. Her shoulders relaxed as her hands found the keys. She looked like a painting, her silhouette poised in front of the long frosted windows displaying the starting flakes of a late-night snow. She was always comfortable behind the piano. A handsome man stepped from his easel displaying a photograph of the ocean and a craggy northern shore to stare at her, ignoring three women appraising his work. Lydia emerged from a group of string players and laid a hand on Alevia's shoulder. Alevia smiled up at her and Lydia lifted a hand to me.

As worry for my sister subsided, my head began to spin with thoughts I couldn't pin down. Mr. Hopper hadn't attempted to touch me beyond kissing my hand in greeting, or acted any differently than normal at the opera, but I'd felt his attention as alive as an electrical current. The knowledge of his attraction struck through me, and I looked around for him—for the eyes that had lighted when he saw me, for the wool tailcoat fitted to his broad shoulders. I found him walking under the chandelier, head bowed to a woman who looped her gloved hand through his arm. I felt nauseous. I should've known better than to believe Franklin's assurances about Mr. Hopper. He had baited me with his charm, he'd gotten me to concede my reservations, and in less than two hours, he'd transferred his infatuation with me to another. I felt idiotic and homesick for Charlie, for the ease of his friendship. For eighteen years, it had always been he and I, no one else. I'd never questioned our connection . . . until he blindsided me with his proposal to Miss Kent. I swore under my breath and pushed him out of my mind. I'd resolved not to think of him and I wouldn't.

I turned around, thinking I would assemble a few people to hear my story for *The Century*. As nervous as I was to read aloud, Mr. Hopper's critique had proven immensely helpful in improving my novel, and I was confident I'd glean something of worth from the comments I'd receive from a reading. I hadn't seen Mr. Blaine and wasn't going to miss the deadline for the next edition on account of his absence. Skirting around a crowd gathered to watch a play, I stared as the two characters dove at each other pretending to brawl. Someone pushed into me and I turned to find Mr. Blaine.

"Good evening, Miss Loftin," he said cheerily, and glanced over my head toward the gold curtains along the front windows. It was much more crowded than the past two Society meetings I'd attended, occupied mostly by musicians who'd come to practice for auditions the following week. I stared as a woman wearing striped trousers, the legs of them matching the style of her gigot sleeves, charged past me. It wasn't that trousers were entirely uncommon—women wore bloomers for riding wheels and actresses had begun to wear them on the stage—but I'd never seen them worn so confidently in a formal evening setting.

Ripping my eyes away from the woman, I found Franklin on the other side of the room, black suit blending into the corner. His head dipped as he alternated between glancing at the easel in front of him and his subjects—Lydia and Alevia next to the piano. I watched what I could see of his face in the dark—the gleam of his eyes and the grip of his teeth on his lip as he concentrated on the brushstrokes. Startled by the sensation of eyes burning my face, I realized I had completely forgotten about Mr. Blaine.

"I apologize," I said. "Where's Bess?" Mr. Blaine shrugged and his smile widened. He lifted a glass to his lips, taking a long drink of what looked to be scotch or bourbon.

"B-being stubborn," he stuttered. Blinking slowly as though he had suddenly lost his train of thought, he stumbled forward, nearly knocking into a girl in front of him. I grabbed his arm to steady him.

"Are you all right?"

He laughed.

"Yes. Of course," he said, taking another sip as I stared at him. I'd heard that drunkards were irresponsible, sloppy, and at times violent, nothing I wanted for a beau of Bess's. "I just meant that uh, that Franklin didn't want Bessie here—or so she thought—so she refused to come with me. It's all for the best though. I needed to get some . . . some writing in anyway and read your story, if you remembered to bring it." He shivered, rubbing his arms. "I'm freezing." I wondered how he could possibly be cold; in close proximity to two roaring fireplaces and over one hundred bodies pumping heat into the room, I was sweating myself.

"I remembered," I said, choosing to ignore his strange revelation. "In fact, I was on my way to read a bit of it when I ran into you." I turned to the cluster of players tuning at the front of the room. Though I knew I needed to read my work to perfect it, nerves still twisted in my gut at the thought. "Perhaps you wouldn't mind taking a look before I read it?" I ran my fingers over my waist, decorated in gold Indian embroidery adorned with beetle wing cases—a gift from Franklin—and scanned the guests in front of me. Most were well into their work by now, noses in notebooks or sketch pads.

"Of course," Mr. Blaine said. I caught something moving out of the corner of my eye and glanced toward it. It was just a man sitting by the fireplace writing, but his hand shook wildly, pencil moving so quickly I had no idea how in the world his brain could keep up.

"Do you know him?"

Mr. Blaine was still shivering.

"Are you sure you're all right?" My worry for Bess's future had transformed to concern for Mr. Blaine. He seemed terribly ill.

"Yes, quite," he said. "Who?" He asked, referring to my earlier question. I tipped my head toward the man who stopped writing momentarily to dig in his jacket pocket, withdrawing a new pencil and a small brown bottle emblazoned with a Celtic circle knot that he shoved back into his jacket as quickly. Mr. Blaine's eyes narrowed. "Oh. Yes. That's Marcus Carter. We grew up together. His brother Will's the one who passed away in the study. He and Lydia used to be engaged until . . . until they weren't anymore." Mr. Blaine's words were beginning to slur together. I recalled Uncle Richard's impromptu eulogy following Father's funeral and recognized the similar smearing of consonants. Mr. Blaine was clearly intoxicated, but I ignored my worry for Bess at the moment, stunned by what he'd said. I stared at the man crouched over his notebook, arm flying again, wondering whether Franklin knew and why Lydia hadn't married him. I recalled her speaking of a former beau the day Frank bought the Benz. Was this the same man? I would have to ask her about him later.

"What happened?" I asked, but the musicians started to play and my question was lost. The tune was hauntingly beautiful and I watched Alevia's eyes close, fingers resting on one chord after another. Suddenly, the bass and cello struck two sullen notes and her eyes opened at once, hands sprinting the keys to the tune of a powerful war march. I glanced in the direction of the man who had noticed Alevia earlier to find him intermittently conversing with an older gentleman in front of him and gazing at her.

"Tchaikovsky's *1812*," Mr. Blaine said. He tipped his glass to his mouth and swallowed what remained. I thought to ask him how many drinks he'd had, to remind him that gentlemen were never to imbibe more than two in public, but decided against it. He'd been groomed in manners. He knew the rules. "That'll be the first Philharmonic performance next season." As the music began to crescendo, the bows moved violently with the demand of the eighteenth notes. Lydia was at the back of the string group, a half beat behind, completely out of sync with the others, though her eyes were trained on her music as though nothing was amiss. I looked over at Franklin, thinking that he would notice, but found him glaring down at his canvas.

"Is Lydia all right?" I whispered to Mr. Blaine.

"Yes. She finds that run challenging. It's a gift, you know, to master a craft so easily that you don't often have to rehearse it." He cleared his throat. "I attempt to steer away from conversation about my writing with Lydia. My first drafts are typically quite close to perfect, and she has to work so hard at her music. I feel bad for her." I grimaced at his pompousness, and looked around for Mr. Hopper, but he was nowhere to be found. Perhaps he'd decided to entertain that woman elsewhere. "I have told her often that my secret is to outline first, to know where your mind should be so that—"

"Let's exchange stories now," I said, before he could enlighten me further. "Do you want to or not?" I asked. His face paled and he rocked into me.

"I'm sorry," he said. "I don't feel well." He swallowed and straightened his posture, the color returning to his cheeks.

"Perhaps you should consult with Doctor Hopper," I snapped. His affliction was clearly self-imposed.

"No need. I was just a bit dizzy." He grinned. "I have been quite busy with a new novel idea and haven't written my story yet, but I would be happy to read yours. I decided on the Ben Franklin piece, in case you were interested. I'll bring it next time." Slightly irritated that he hadn't upheld his end of the bargain, I reached into my pocket and withdrew my story anyway. I knew it was good; I felt pride whenever I thought of it and couldn't wait to see Mr. Blaine's reaction.

He sunk onto a tufted ottoman and began to read. I forced my eyes to the front of the room instead of trying to decipher his facial expressions, knowing that if he so much as furrowed his eyebrows I would worry.

Alevia was still playing, though the other musicians seemed to have taken a break. A cluster of men and women were gathered around the piano watching her, until she transitioned into the flowing introduction to Charles Everest's "Beautiful Moon." Alevia wasn't overly fond of contemporary pieces, generally preferring the classical greats, but I knew that she enjoyed this song. A powerful alto voice suddenly soared from the crowd around Alevia, "Beauti-

ful moon, thou queen of night, beaming with thy placid light." My
sister grinned as a short, plump woman stepped out of the group
to stand beside her, her voice so hypnotizing that the room seemed
to silence.

"Miss Loftin." Mr. Blaine pulled on the sleeve of my dress. I ignored him, mesmerized by the woman and Alevia. "Miss Loftin,"
he said again, this time yanking my chiffon sleeve so hard I fell
onto the ottoman and half on his lap. Scooting away, I pulled my
eyes from the piano.

"What is it?" I asked, wishing he'd waited for the song to end.

"I've finished reading." He shrugged and tossed a bit of hair
out of his face.

"Oh. Good," I said, wondering if I would gain any insight at
all from a man who'd consumed much more alcohol than he could
handle. "Go on."

"You write spectacularly," he started. "Your words are vivid;
your sentences are beautiful." He paused and pressed his lips together, drawing them into his mouth and then out again. "However, I'm concerned about the subject matter. Honestly, I find it
a bit shallow." He laughed under his breath. I felt my forehead
scrunch, but forced my expression blank. I'd asked for his opinion.
I couldn't show him that he'd already offended me. Great writing
required honest criticism and I needed to embrace it. My acceptance of Mr. Hopper's comments had already made my manuscript
stronger. "Emilie Todd Helm, Miss Loftin? She's barely a blip in
history. It's not as if she fought in the war herself, so her story really
had no impact on the American public, beyond making our kind
angry. I'd advise against your reading this story here. It's—"

"Our kind? What does that mean?" The questions came out
too quickly, too defensively, and Mr. Blaine's eyes narrowed.

"Yes, our kind. The Yankees. The victors." Alevia's hands

lifted from the keys and Mr. Blaine's last word rang over the quiet that had befallen the room. "Listen, Miss Loftin, I'm not telling you that your writing is bad. It's truly lovely and you can submit what you want." He sighed and shook his head. "All I'm saying is that I don't think a story about an unimportant traitor will be seen in a very sympathetic light by a New York that still very much remembers the war. Hell, *The Century*'s editor, Richard Gilder, fought the blasted Confederates." I took a deep breath and let the tension drop from my shoulders. He wasn't being unnecessarily brutal or trying to offend me by disliking my idea. I'd overlooked the editorial prejudices of the magazine. That was my fault.

"I suppose you have a point," I muttered. "Thank you."

"I'm sorry to disappoint you," he said softly, patting my hand. "But I didn't want you to get turned down on account of the subject matter. It's already difficult for women to break through, and you're much too talented. Do you have any other ideas?"

"Too many. I had a page of them, and then I thought of the story on Emilie. Most of the other topics were also historic women—Anne Bradstreet, Mary Musgrove, Sacagawea, Alexandrine Tinné, Isabella Bird. I suppose I could write about famous women explorers and their lack of recognition in history. Ouch!" Someone slammed into my leg as they shoved through the hordes of people gathered around us. I looked up in time to see the glint of narrowed green eyes beneath cropped curls. *Charlie?* I blinked a few times, certain I was seeing things. Craning my neck over a group of violinists behind me, I could barely see the man anymore, but watched the motion of his shoulders, familiar and broad, as he pushed through the crowd. "Mr. Blaine, excuse me. I'll be back." On my feet in an instant, I went after him. I knew that I shouldn't. I'd never pursued him before, purposefully leaving our fate in his hands, but he was here.

"Charlie!" He was only a few feet in front of me. Lunging toward him, I snatched his wrist, half praying I had it wrong, half praying it was him. "Charlie!" He stopped under the arched doorway leading into the drawing room. Fingers drawn into fists, he didn't try to sling my hand away, but paused for a moment, then turned to face me.

"There you are, Gin." His voice was low and breathy. He looked almost as miserable as when we'd stood in Mother's room—eyes watery with emotion and fatigue, bags hanging loose and dark at the base of them. I wouldn't feel sorry for him.

"What are you doing here?" I swallowed hard, feeling the weight of his hands on my back as he'd held me, hearing the desperation in his voice when he'd told me he loved me. He gently pulled his wrist from my grip and stared over my head at the chandelier.

"I'm . . . I'm having trouble. *The Times* wants my drawings and Valentine and Sons has asked me to try my hand at etching for their penny cards—"

"What could possibly be the trouble with that? Charlie, that's wonderful!" Illustrating the news and creating card company prints wasn't the same as collaborating with a writer as he'd always dreamed, but it was a step toward it.

"I can't. I can't concentrate . . ." he stuttered. His jaw clenched and he took a ragged breath. "I went by your house. Your mother said I would find you here." After everything, I was surprised Mother had told him where I was. No one save Franklin had mentioned Charlie or Mrs. Aldridge since his engagement unless I'd brought one of them up. It was as if the moment he'd broken my heart, the Aldridges ceased to exist to my family. "I must go. I'll miss my train." He'd been on his way out—in a hurry—when I'd caught up to him. He'd come looking for me, but changed his mind.

Charlie stared down at me. His mouth opened as if he was about to say something else, but didn't. Instead he twisted the wedding band on his left hand and closed his eyes, likely trying to contain emotion he didn't want to show. Before I could stop myself, my hand lifted to his cheek, palm flat against the spiky stubble. Instantly angry with myself, I pulled my hand away, forcing my arms to my sides.

"Charlie, I'm—"

"I-I can't," he whispered to himself. Charlie's eyes flashed with something I couldn't place and he stepped away from me. Turning to walk into the elaborate foyer adorned with a cornice of spiral rose vines and a twin chandelier dripping with crystals, he strode toward the door without a glance back.

"Wait!" I ran onto the porch, following him, but he was already halfway down the block. Pitching my satin skirt to my ankles, I flew into the darkness of the vacant street, hearing the heavy glass door click into the gilded iron frame behind me. "Charlie!" He kept walking without looking back, a figure vanishing then reappearing in the flickering glow of the Fifth Avenue streetlamps. "Charlie, stop!" My voice echoed against the brick and limestone. Finally stopping, he turned around, but didn't look at me, staring down at the toe of his Balmoral boots instead. I wasn't naïve enough to think he'd come back to me— I'd learned that lesson last time—but I deserved to know why he'd sought me out, why he'd come all the way in from the country to find me.

"Where are you going?" I said when I reached him. I forced a smile to break the tension, but he didn't return it.

"I can't . . . shouldn't be here, Gin."

"What do you mean?" I asked. "Surely you haven't been exiled from Manhattan." I laughed.

"Nothing. Nothing makes sense anymore," he said softly, ignoring my teasing. Charlie shoved his hands in his pockets, scuffing his boots along the road. I sobered.

"Look at me." He complied, eyes still watery with whatever had driven him to find me in the first place. "Has something happened?"

"No!" he barked. I flinched at his tone, and stepped away from him, but he grabbed my hand.

"If nothing's happened, then why were you looking for me? Why did you come here?" I yanked my hand from his grasp and his eyes tapered.

"I don't know!" he yelled. Charlie drew a deep breath. "I won't argue with you, Gin. Not tonight." He stared up at the cloud-streaked moon and then back down at me. The streetlamps' flame cast shadows on his face. "Nothing at all has happened, but I just thought if I could see you, Ginny, if I could talk to you, I could find clarity, everything would be all right." He leaned into me, eyes holding mine as if he were about to tell me he couldn't live another day without me, but I knew better. I'd been here before. I didn't owe him anything, and yet, it was as if I had no other option. His thumb drifted across the back of my hand and my fury crumbled.

"I'm here." My free hand found his jacket and his palm closed over it. Shutting his eyes, he wrapped his arms around me. I could feel his breath against my ear, and let my head drop to his chest. He sighed and pulled away from me, but just barely.

"I know I'm not making any sense, but nothing about my life makes sense anymore. I can't draw. She consumes me. She's stolen every thought, every moment." My fingers went slack in his clutch, the elation of seeing him quickly deadening. His grip tightened around my hand. "Ginny, I'm worthless . . . so worthless. I . . . I miss you."

"You're wrong," I said. He had just told me that he loved someone else. He couldn't possibly miss me. "You're worth at least three thousand." Charlie's eyes widened and he dropped my hand. "Surely you're happy. Surely the money made up for your loving me." He grit his teeth and shoved his hands into the pockets of his black wool overcoat.

"It's getting late. I need to go. My wife will be worried." His voice was emotionless and dry and he started to walk away. "I never should have come. This was a mistake." I opened my mouth to say something sharp, but nothing came, so I stood in the shadow of a turret, watching him go until he finally disappeared into the night.

*B*ack inside, I began to wander aimlessly through the room, past clusters of guests laughing and appraising art, while the writers next to them kept their heads down scribbling and solitary artists mixed paints or brushed careful strokes on their canvases.

"Miss Loftin. You'll do." Recognizing the thin man with the curling mustache as Mrs. Wharton's friend Mr. Daniels, he motioned for me to follow him toward a group of people clearly in the middle of a heated discussion. "Oscar is trying his hand at writing a play and there's some conflict about the main character. His reading spurred quite a disagreement. We need one more person's opinion to break the tie on the matter," he explained as we neared. Having no idea who Oscar was, but figuring I'd met him at some point in Lydia's series of hurried introductions the first time, I nodded.

"All right. Should I know anything about the play before—"

"Thank you for so kindly settling this dispute. I'm Oscar Wilde, and you are?" A man with a long face tipped his head at me and I stared, stunned that I was standing before the famed Oscar

Wilde. His lips turned up and he straightened under a peculiar red velvet cape tied around his neck with a silk ivory bow.

"Mr. Wilde," I said when I found my voice, "I've just read *The Picture of Dorian Gray* and—"

"Ask her," Mr. Daniels said, nudging Mr. Wilde and interrupting me. I hadn't even introduced myself. The two women beside him, clearly sisters judging by their identical swarms of black hair and cat-like eyes, looked angry—arms crossed, mouths pressed into twin scowls. Mr. Wilde cleared his throat and pushed a lock of wavy shoulder-length hair behind his ear.

"My main character conceals an indiscretion from his wife, a business dealing made when he was young. It happened many years prior to their marriage and he is ashamed of it, but his fortune was made as a result," he said, his Irish lilt rising and falling with the words. He flipped his wrist. "As with most dishonorable transactions, it surfaces years later and he's forced to tell his wife. She's angry. Should she forgive him?" His eyebrows rose with his question and the women stared at me, waiting for my reaction. Stunned that Oscar Wilde was asking my opinion, still reeling from seeing Charlie, I shook my head.

"I don't know. You're correct that he's at fault," I said. The women started to nod, thinking they'd won, but I wasn't finished. "But I think it would depend on her love for him and if her love could triumph her anger."

"Hear, hear!" Mr. Daniels shouted.

"Thank you for convincing me that I'm not crazy after all," Mr. Wilde said. He took my hand, turned it over, pushed Mother's gold linked bracelet to the top of my wrist, and kissed my palm. It was a strange gesture, but he was famously unconventional. "That is exactly what she does eventually. She forgives him."

"I'm glad for it," I said, avoiding the glare of the others. "It was lovely to meet you. If you'll excuse me." I circled toward the windows, toward Franklin and the musicians who'd begun to play again, this time Vivaldi's *Winter*. I looked back once, astonished that I'd just met Oscar Wilde. Thinking on his question made me wonder about Rachel, how she would react if she knew of Charlie's motivation for marrying her. I forced the thought from my mind, craning my neck over the crowd in the hopes of spotting Alevia and Franklin.

A glass pressed to the back of my hand. I inhaled the exotic scent of cloves and gardenia in Mr. Hopper's cologne and surveyed the amber contents in the crystal tumbler.

"I couldn't. Not in front of all of these people," I said, gesturing around me. "But thank you. They've put on quite a performance tonight." I wanted to ask where he'd been and if he'd had an enjoyable time entertaining that woman, but I nodded toward the musicians instead.

"Please come with me right now." I stared at Mr. Hopper, half-expecting him to burst into laughter, but he didn't. His face was stony, square jaw tipped away from me as though he couldn't bear to look into my face.

"Why?" I whispered, but he'd already started to walk away. I trailed him from the drawing room down the hallway, mousseline de soie along the hem of my new dress shuffling along the wood floor. The burning sconces along the wall cast flickering light across his back. In the hours since the opera, something had come undone. His black jacket was rumpled, hugging tensed muscles, and his hair stuck out in the back as though he'd been pulling on it. I followed him into the study.

"What's wrong?" I asked. Mr. Hopper's lips dropped into a scowl. He leaned across his desk and grabbed my notebook, raising it in front of me. I wasn't near finished, but had given him a few chapters to see what he thought.

"This. This is what's wrong," he said, slamming the notebook on the table. I rolled my eyes, unsure what I could've written that would've upset him so much.

"Why? What's the trouble?" I sat down in the leather chair, thinking through the early chapters. There was nothing of offense. Unwilling to look at him, I glanced over his head at the absurd portrait of his father. Mr. Hopper didn't answer, so I sighed, and met his narrowed eyes.

"He will not get away with this." He started toward me, thought better of it, and crushed his fist to the desktop. He'd lost his mind. I started to stand.

"If my characters have upset you, then by all means, don't read the book," I said, anger drumming in my chest. He wasn't making any sense. "It's a novel, Mr. Hopper. Please don't allow a fictional character to get you so out of sorts." He barked out a laugh.

"Surely you don't take me for that much of a fool." Mr. Hopper's brown eyes, usually so alight with gold, were nearly black. His lips pressed together, gaze steady on mine. "You told me it wasn't based on your life, but your character, Carlisle, is Charlie Aldridge." He didn't stutter or mince words as Charlie had an hour earlier. Mr. Hopper wasn't asking. He was telling. My breath caught.

"N-no," I stammered. "That's ridiculous. He's a family friend of course, but—"

"If you regard me with any sort of care at all, Miss Loftin, don't lie to me." I rose from my chair, and he turned away without apology and crossed the room. I didn't understand his anger. Even if he knew the truth, why would it affect him? Mr. Hopper opened the doors of the bar and braced himself against the frame. The careless way he'd accused me echoed in my mind. Perhaps he was accustomed to having the last word, but he wouldn't have it this time.

"I don't owe you any sort of reassurance, but I will not allow you to call me a liar, Mr. Hopper. It's fiction," I said bluntly and he whirled on me.

"Maybe a part of it, but it's him. I saw you together tonight. Anyone would've been able to deduce you were lovers." I shook my head, blood rising in my cheeks. Charlie was a married man, a man who'd never even kissed me. I opened my mouth to argue, but Mr. Hopper continued. "And the party in the book? I was there. I was at his party, remember?" Even across the room I could see that his knuckles had gone white around the rim of his green crystal lowball glass. "When I picked you up tonight and realized you lived next door to him, I should've known." Was he jealous? Surely not. I'd seen him in the company of another beautiful woman only hours before.

"That's absurd," I said, finally composing myself enough to speak without my voice shaking. "I told you. He's a family friend. The party in the book isn't remotely similar." I hoped he could be convinced. I'd changed the location of the party to a random industrialist's ballroom, afraid that readers would connect the dots. Apparently one had regardless. I cursed under my breath for running after Charlie like a lovesick fool and mentioning that I'd seen Mr. Hopper at Charlie's party in the first place.

"I don't believe you," he said evenly. Turning to the bar, he rummaged through the drawers. I walked across the rug, hearing the clatter of bottles behind me followed by the slap of his palm on the wood when he couldn't find what he was looking for. I looked back once, in time to see him tip a glass of scotch to his mouth. I was nearly to the door when something shattered behind me and a thud punctuated the aftermath. I whirled around, finding Mr. Hopper's broad frame crumpled against the cabinet, shattered crystal clutched in his hand.

I ran toward him and lifted his head from his chest. His eyes rolled back in his head, full lips quivering. Fleetingly, I wondered if he was dying and began to shake him.

"Mr. Hopper?" He blinked, and I jerked away from him, startled by the white occupying the expanse of his eye sockets. I rose, stumbling toward the door to fetch Doctor Hopper. I turned back to find him rubbing his eyes—his irises swung back into place. He groaned, a guttural sound that echoed through the room, and then his eyes met mine.

"What happened?" Mr. Hopper's voice was a hoarse whisper. He didn't bother to get up, likely because he couldn't. "I was so angry at him, so angry for you, and then I . . ." He trailed off, and cast his gaze to his lap. He still wasn't making sense. I knelt down in front of him.

"It seems you fainted," I said, though I had never seen anyone look as he had. He shook his head as though the prospect was an impossibility. "We should summon your father."

"There's no need. I feel fine now." He ran a hand across his face and straightened against the cabinet, but didn't attempt to rise. "I'm terribly sorry for my behavior, Miss Loftin." I tipped my head at him and started to stand, but his fingers swept across my arm, stopping me. "My words were misplaced. I didn't intend them; anger overtook me. I'll understand if my behavior has tainted your perception of the man I am. But before you go, I'd like to explain." Mr. Hopper's right hand curled into a fist and he dug it into the oriental rug. Whatever the reason for his rage, it hadn't cooled. "That night at Aldridge's party I lost Miss Kent, the only woman I've ever loved." I blinked at Mr. Hopper, shocked. His jaw clenched. Mr. Hopper had loved Miss Kent the way I'd loved Charlie. "And then I saw him tonight, stalking around the room like he was looking for someone. Eventually, he found me and asked where you were.

I'd been reading your book right before. I remembered the proposal, and it struck me that there were similarities . . ."

He looked at me, and something in his gaze quickened my heart, pumping fury through my veins. Is that why he'd decided to pursue me? Because Miss Kent had broken his heart and he needed a replacement? Her face flashed in my mind—her doll-like eyes and rosebud lips gilding what I recalled as an ordinary personality. I turned away from Mr. Hopper, disgusted. And then I remembered the way I'd felt watching Charlie propose—rejected, small, pathetic. Mr. Hopper had likely experienced the same debilitating heartbreak. I couldn't blame him for wanting to move on, to forget her. Hadn't I accepted his invitation to the opera because I wanted the same?

"You were there when Charlie asked Miss Kent to marry him, as Eleanor was present for Carlisle's proposal. You lived next door to Charlie as Eleanor lives next door to Carlisle," Mr. Hopper continued. He reached for my hand and I let him take it. "And in your novel, Eleanor trusted that he loved her. She trusted Carlisle her whole life and he broke her heart. The thought that Charlie hurt you, a woman so worthy of admiration and love . . . it made me hate him more than I already did." I diverted my eyes, blinking back tears. Charlie's rejection, the disregard he'd shown me tonight, had freshly seared my heart. "So I lied to him, Miss Loftin. I told him that I hadn't seen you. I couldn't stand to look at him for a moment longer, so I asked him to leave. It took all of my strength to keep my hands from him, to let him leave unscathed. If I'm right, if he broke your heart—"

"Why? Why didn't you say anything before?"

Not that I'd confessed either, I thought, but he'd barely reacted when we'd talked about seeing each other at the party. Then again, neither of us had mentioned the proposal and because of that, I'd been able to keep my composure, too.

"I suppose I don't prefer to suffer pity. I didn't want you to feel sorry for me," he said. "I was ignorant to think I could lure Miss Kent with my money." Mr. Hopper waved a hand at the mahogany walls and the tapestries. "We met at a talk I gave at Columbia right after *The Blood Runs from Antietam* was published. I saw her in the audience and, as cliché as it sounds, I loved her immediately. She was sitting next to her father sewing a handkerchief. It was clear that she'd only attended to humor him." Mr. Hopper's lips quirked up just slightly and he ran a hand across a poppy woven into the rug. "After the talk, her father came over to speak with me. He'd loved the book, and so out of curiosity, I asked Miss Kent if she'd read it." He laughed under his breath. I fiddled with the lace cuffs around my wrist in an attempt to distract the jealousy I felt at the repeated mention of her name. "She said she pitied me, that anyone with the capacity to write about that level of brutality must be in need of kindness." Mr. Hopper's eyes creased. "Miss Kent was always honest. She never loved me, Miss Loftin. At first I thought she was put off by my despicable reputation." He paused, doubtless trying to decipher whether I knew of it, too. When I didn't ask, his lips pinched. "It is like a cancer, and entirely untrue, a blemish on my character won by being friendly, I suppose. I've no idea of the origin or reason behind the rumor. In any case, she knew I wasn't the philanderer others assumed, but she still didn't love me. I knew that and yet I kept making excuses to see her, to hold on. It was pathetic and desperate, embarrassing even. She's always loved Charlie. She talked about him often, reminding me of her talented illustrator cousin in case any writers I knew ever needed an artist. He never seemed to give her the time of day though until—"

"Until he needed her money," I interrupted, and Mr. Hopper gawked at me.

"What?" His forehead crinkled.

"Of course you were right. The story—it's about us, about Charlie and me. I loved him, but tonight—" I stopped midsentence, unable to talk about the disgust on his face when I'd mentioned his love for me. "But that night at his party," I started again, "he chose Miss Kent and her money over me because he thought he needed it." Mr. Hopper shook his head and his thumb drifted over the back of mine. Despite my heartbreak, my stomach fluttered at his touch. He wasn't the man I'd thought him to be. His interest was genuine and he cared for me enough to feel protective.

"It's a beautiful story, Miss Loftin," he said softly, "beyond the fact that the truth of it has destroyed both of us." His sleeve brushed against my arm as he moved closer to me.

"Thank you," I whispered. I closed my eyes and saw Charlie's face in the dim of Mother's room. I heard his voice as clearly as if he were standing in front of me, *"Ginny, I love you"* and then felt his mouth on mine. His lips were soft, but his stubble was rough against my skin. He tasted like vanilla and oak as his tongue tangled with mine. I pulled away, opened my eyes, and gasped.

"I have already lost her to him. I will not lose you," Mr. Hopper whispered against my mouth and I felt the color drain from my face.

Chapter Ten

Though Mr. Hopper had returned to normal rather quickly, his fainting still unnerved me. I hadn't expected to think about it after the meeting, but I had. I couldn't stop wondering about the contradiction between the man who'd looked as though he was at the precipice of death and minutes later kissed me so tenderly I could still feel it on my mouth. In my mind it was still Charlie, but the astonishment that it had actually been Mr. Hopper was starting to wear off. I'd always thought that Charlie would be the man to kiss me first. We'd be in his library and he'd find an excuse to walk over to my writing perch on the settee. He'd sit close, his hand drifting to my knee as he pretended to read. And then he'd look at me and tell me he loved me, that he always had, and he'd ask to kiss me—a short, sweet kiss with the promise of more.

I lifted my hand to my lips. My first kiss had been nothing like I'd envisioned. My breath caught remembering the surprise of it. Mr. Hopper had been sure and deliberate, his lips slowly moving on mine, taking the time to draw me in. I pulled my hand from my mouth and cleared the memory from my mind, wariness overtaking my attraction. Mr. Hopper was handsome, chivalrous, and intelligent, a man willing to fight for me. The combination was a dangerous temptation, one that would be difficult to resist, but the more I thought of the implications of a courtship, the more I knew I might have to—for my heart, for my writing.

"*I told him I was too occupied with my music.*" Alevia's words echoed in my mind. The man I'd noticed watching her at the Society had approached when she'd finished playing and asked her to accompany him to hear the London Philharmonic Choir. "*He had the audacity to tell me that he admired ambition in women.*" She'd rolled her eyes. "*Of course he would say that now, before he's had the opportunity to understand the time my music requires, but he'd eventually change his mind. He's a Roosevelt. A man of society can't, in good faith, accept a striving wife. The social requirements are too great. My time to rehearse would be eaten up planning teas, soirees, and dinners.*" At the time, she hadn't any idea of Mr. Hopper's advances and was likely speaking from her experience with Mr. Winthrop, but her words had resonated with me. Perhaps I was naïve, but I wanted to think Alevia was wrong to discard the idea of marriage so quickly. My thoughts flit to Mr. Hopper, to the image of him crumpled against the open cabinet.

I'd meant to ask Franklin about Mr. Hopper's health, but the days following the Society had been busy for him. So busy, in fact, that it had been two weeks since I'd caught a glimpse of my brother—he left for work before I woke and didn't get home until I'd gone to sleep. But, as absent as Frank had been, his newfound wealth had certainly been at hand.

We'd each ordered two new dresses and winter coats at his insistence, feasted on roast turkey and mince pie, and followed dinner with chilled champagne. Mother had seemed more contented than I'd seen her since Father's passing—baking for friends, taking us for drives in the Benz. She'd even been forgiving when she'd woken at eleven-thirty the night of the Society to find three of her children still out. It was peculiar, the luxury of having more money than we needed, though at times I still worried. It could be taken as quickly as it had come. Mae and Mother were nervous about it, too. Both of them had been grateful for new costumes, but had asked Frank not to buy them anything else for the rest of the month.

I tapped my pencil on the empty pad in front of me, hearing Mae practicing her lecture in the study and watching Bessie bite her lip as she pinned the final scarlet macaw feather on a day cap for Ava Astor. Mrs. Astor had demanded that Bessie make her something that would stand out. This bright red hat pluming with over fifty feathers certainly would.

"Does it look dramatic enough?" Bess asked. "It must, you know. I've become known for sensational pieces over the last year. It's the reason business has been so steady." She shielded her eyes from the sun pouring into the parlor windows, the glint of it landing on the silver and turquoise cuff around her wrist. I nodded, inhaling the savory scent of mutton roasting in the kitchen. Mother and Mae had spent hours dressing it with the perfect blend of spices this morning before they'd gone down to the stationer's to order Mae's wedding invitations. "I wish I had Great-aunt Rose's old *Harper's Bazaar*s. I can almost remember a hairstyle in the June 1872 issue. It was elaborate and serpentine and would make a striking design for the gold threading along the band of this hat, but I can't recall the details."

"Well, it's already strange enough that I wouldn't wear it," I said, answering her question. Bessie laughed.

"It's perfect, then." Ever since she and Mr. Blaine had become somewhat steady a month ago, Bess hadn't been nearly as harsh as I was used to, and I wondered if we'd be friends in our old age after all.

"Let's see what you've got," she said, stepping toward me. Her brows lifted when she noticed my notepad was empty. "You haven't written one idea in three *hours*?" I grimaced, resenting the fact that she was pointing out the obvious. As hard as I tried, as deeply as I concentrated, I couldn't come up with new ideas. It had begun to bother me that I wasn't writing. Before I'd been content to write as-needed for the *Review* or whenever I was inspired. Now, if I wasn't working on something, I felt as though I was squandering my progress. My compulsion had been worse since the last Society meeting. Though I'd been horrified in the moment, the way Mr. Hopper had so easily seen my real life in my work meant that my words had been so vivid he'd figured they could be true—a sure sign my writing was improving.

I thought of the books and magazines stacked in my room. Even reading hadn't inspired a premise. I'd read the monthly editions of *Scribner's, Atlantic Monthly,* and *The Century* from cover to cover, along with every new book I could acquire from the library—Arthur Conan Doyle's *The White Company*, W. B. Yeats's new volume of poetry, Mark Twain's *The American Claimant*—only to find myself intimidated by the genius of the prose in front of me.

I'd sent my story about noteworthy female explorers, "The Invisible Pioneers," to *The Century* a week ago, after Mr. Blaine, who'd stopped by to pick up Bess for a show, read it and deemed it perfect. I hadn't written since—other than to work on my fast-concluding revision—and knew I'd have to come up with another novel idea in case an editor or publisher wondered what I planned to work on next.

"Perhaps it'd be best for you to stick to short stories and columns for the *Review*. It takes a different skill set to write novels, you know—at least that's what I've heard—and you're already so good at the shorter pieces." Bessie's lips pursed as she surveyed the hat.

I rolled my eyes, refusing to let her words diminish my resolve, taking back my earlier thought of eventual friendship. We would always be sisters, but beyond moments of understanding, we would never be friends. Everything from our aspirations to our personalities was different.

I plucked Mother's discarded copy of the *New York Times* from the table next to me. Bess was right, novel writing was an entirely different skill altogether, but I would learn it just as well. I skimmed the headlines. *A Woman's Ambition: Starting as a Typewriter, She Became a Successful Lawyer.* It struck me as an interesting tale—a woman of a humble profession rising in education and intelligence to the rank of lawyer when there were but a handful of female attorneys in the country. I wrote the subject in my notebook and turned back to read the article. It started out well, touting the intelligence of the attorney, and I'd begun to admire the *Times* for printing such a piece, when I got to the last paragraph—an entire section focused on the valiancy of her railroad tycoon husband for sending her to school. *"Her every desire and ambition were gratified by her husband, and when she expressed a desire to study law, he sent her to take the course at Ann Arbor."* I set the paper down.

"I'm going to find Franklin," I said abruptly, unable to read further. I needed to talk to him, needed to ask about Mr. Hopper so I could stop wondering.

"He's at work," Bessie mumbled, holding a pin between her lips.

"I know, but he's at the office this week and it's only a few blocks away."

"More like half a mile," Bess called as I walked out of the door.

Bessie was right. On warm days, the walk downtown felt like a block at most, but today the blistering wind chapped my face. Finally reaching the two-story limestone building, I flung the door open, and stopped for a moment to hang my grandmother's mink coat on the rack. This little block of offices and the plant on the bank of the Harlem was all that remained of J. L. Mott's former headquarters in Mott Haven. They'd moved the warehouse and the main office to Manhattan a few years back, but Franklin had fought to share my father's old office in this building with three other traveling salesmen. I walked through the lobby, by the old leather couches cracked and dusty with disuse and past a sketch of the twenty-five-foot cast-iron fountain Mr. Mott had debuted at the Centennial Exposition in '76 on my way to Frank's office.

"Hello, Mr. Brooks," I said, finding one of Franklin's counterparts lounging back in the desk chair, clearly not working. Spinning around, he straightened quickly, and smoothed his jacket over his sizable belly.

"Miss Loftin," he sputtered, as though his boss had just caught him sleeping on the job.

"Have you seen Frank? I need to talk to him." Mr. Brooks's brows furrowed and he twirled a pen between his fingers.

"No . . . he's not here." He tilted his head at me. "Haven't seen him in months, actually."

"I know. He's been traveling a lot," I said, "but he's home this week, working from here."

"No, he's not. Actually he's not working this week at all." My heart began to race. "Surely you know that he asked to be taken down to part-time. It's a damn nuisance to Rich and me, having to pick up the slack and all."

"I didn't," I said. "Why . . . why would he do that?" All of the extravagances—the Benz, the fancy new suits—jumped into my head at once. How could he possibly afford all of it on part-time wages? The sudden thought of my mother panhandling for coins, all of us thrown from the comfort of our home, made my stomach turn.

"Surely you know the answer to that," Mr. Brooks said, exasperated. "To help your mother around the house of course, since none of you women seem to be up for the task." I stared at him as though he'd sprouted two heads, wondering what in the world he was talking about. "I don't mean to be insensitive, but it's about time she abandon her paralyzing grief. Your father passed three years ago."

"Just a moment. You're saying Frank's been part-time for three years?" I expected my voice to shake, but it didn't. Franklin had been lying to me, to all of us, and we'd suffered the consequences. I recalled December last year, a month we'd made so little money that we'd had to forgo coal and firewood to afford food. My hands were clenched at my sides and I gripped them tighter. Mr. Brooks laughed.

"No, Miss Loftin. Just the past four months or so. You know, about the time your mother fell down the steps and decided she would rather go be with your father than get better?" His lips turned up in a sneer, no doubt thinking I'd lost my mind.

"Oh . . . uhh . . . that's right," I said, clearing my throat. My mother of course hadn't fallen down any stairs. "Well then, good day to you."

I stumbled home unable to grasp what I'd heard. What was he doing? Where was he going when he said he was going to work? Where was the money coming from? Whatever it was, I would find out. My brother was a liar, but I wouldn't let him ruin us.

I avoided my family the rest of the evening with the excuse

that I was writing. Instead I paced back and forth across my room waiting for Franklin to come home, wondering what I would say to him, imagining his protests and my demands. I eyed the small wooden clock at my bedside. It was nearly eleven in the evening. Where was he?

I plucked Mr. Hopper's new manuscript from the top of my dressing table. I'd returned from Frank's office to find a package from Mr. Hopper with the mail. He hadn't written a lengthy letter, just a short note to say that he'd only had time to revise a bit of it, would appreciate my thoughts, and was looking forward to seeing me upon his return from visiting a cousin in Philadelphia. I couldn't help but think of the society women he was sure to meet while he was away, torturing myself with visions of his tall frame bent over a beautiful face, his mouth against her ear. Though I wanted to believe that his reputation had only been won by innocent sociability, I wasn't entirely convinced.

I sat down on my bed, huddled close to the oil lamp, and tried to force my mind blank. Mr. Hopper thought me talented enough that he wanted my opinion. I couldn't bog my mind down in jealousy or worry over Frank. Whenever Charlie used to ask me about a piece, I would wait until my mind was completely clear to appraise it. The thought made me realize how little my opinion should've mattered. I'd always been honest, but what had I known of sketching? Charlie had needed to consult with other illustrators, just as I'd needed the thoughts of other writers.

I closed my eyes, ran my hand over the paper, turned my gaze to Mr. Hopper's words, and began to read.

"*Middle of a scene, well into the last third of the novel.*" He'd scrawled at the top. "*Mr. Michael Wells finds himself in Newport, penniless. He's been gone from his wealthy family for five years and has been making his way round the world, as I mentioned to you earlier.*"

Mr. Hopper wrote out of order. I'd heard of other writers drafting this way, but hadn't ever done it myself.

> *It was summer again. June, to be exact. It was raining, but the salt-air breeze still wavered over Mr. Wells. A horn sounded from the sea, signaling to the ferry docks in front of him. Newport in the summer. It was familiar, a thousand memories. He walked closer and sat on a boulder along the carriage drive. Drivers scurried from their coaches holding umbrellas, some two to a hand. The ladies mustn't ruin their fine clothes. Mr. Wells looked down at his saturated trousers and dirt-stained shirt. The brim of his tattered felt derby barely provided relief from the driving downpour. The passengers were disembarking now. He would know most of them.*

The front door creaked open, startling my reading. Rushing down the stairs, I caught Frank just as he was closing the door, his gray bowler hat under his arm, fingers clutching his black brief-case. He turned toward me and jumped.

"Ginny," he breathed. "You about made my heart stop." Franklin set his briefcase down. Relief flooded through me, but I ignored the urge to convince myself that Mr. Brooks must have been mistaken. "What're you doing up this late?"

"Where have you been, Frank?" He stared at me as though I should know the answer and started to tell me so, when I cut him off. "I went by your office today and you weren't there. Mr. Brooks said that you'd decided to go to part-time on account of some fabrication about Mother's grief and her falling down the stairs? Why would you do that? What's going on?" I hissed. I wanted to yell, but didn't want to wake the others. Franklin sighed.

"That was just a tale Mr. Mott came up with so Bob wouldn't know I was getting promoted and he wasn't, to explain why I wasn't around," he whispered. Mr. J. L. Mott was the big boss, the owner, and Franklin's boss. The other rank-and-file workers similar to him were under various department heads or executives, but because Father had grown up across the street from Mr. Mott's father, Jordan—the founder of J. L. Iron Works—Franklin was advised by Mr. Mott only, which had turned out to be a blessing and a curse.

"Oh," I said, feeling foolish. "I'm sorry." Franklin edged out of his camel hair blazer.

"Poor Bob. If you want to come find me again, Gin, you'll need to go on into Manhattan. I'm at the warehouse now . . . whenever I'm home, that is." He grunted as he lifted his black briefcase from the ground, random bits of iron clinking around as he did. Relieved, I began to follow him up the stairs. Without the anger that had been keeping me wide awake, I was exhausted. He stopped in front of me and turned around.

"I forgot to ask why you'd come to see me in the first place," Frank whispered. He set his hat on top of his briefcase on the steps and sat down next to it, waiting. I ran a hand along the long braid down my back, unsure if I should even bother explaining.

"I had a question about Mr. Hopper," I started. Franklin nodded for me to go on. "We went to the opera and everything was fine, but then at his house something happened. He was terribly angry at Charlie for . . . for everything, wracked with fury, actually, and he'd had a bit of alcohol. He fainted, Frank, right in front of me, but it was different somehow. He was trembling and his eyes were rolled back." Hearing the words come out of my mouth made me realize how frightened I'd been. Franklin was looking down at his hands, brows furrowed, twisting Grandfather's gold wedding band on his pinkie. "I want to know if he's ill . . . if you've ever seen him that way."

"No," Franklin said softly. "No, I haven't."

"After he woke up, he begged me to forgive him. I think he startled himself as much as me." Franklin nodded, keeping his focus on Grandfather's ring.

"I have no doubt. He cares for you." I nodded, glad for the reassurance that he did. "Without question," he reiterated. Something in his words made me think of him and Lydia and of her former fiancé. Was Frank sure of Lydia's feelings?

"Do you know that Lydia was once engaged?" I blurted the words, suddenly feeling a need to tell him, to protect his heart. Frank's focus jerked up from Grandfather's ring, a grin on his lips.

"Of course," he said. "Marcus Carter. The man's a lunatic. Wasn't always, according to Lydia and John, but after his brother passed on, something changed. Apparently he became reclusive, keeping to his room for weeks at a time, only emerging when he'd had too much liquor and was in the mood for violence. During one of these outings he found his way to the Blaines' in the early morning, kicked the servant's door in, and pulled Lydia out of bed demanding they marry that moment. His intrusion woke the servants who got to her room in time to dismantle the gun he'd placed to his head after she told him she was calling the engagement off." Frank paused. It was then that I realized I was holding his hand, stunned at the horror of what Lydia had had to encounter. "Evidently, Marcus has recovered now. He's tried to reconcile with Lydia, but she swears she can't bear to look at him and that her heart is mine." Worry coursed through me.

"Please be sure, Frank. The thought that she could break your heart—"

"My affection isn't misplaced. I promise," Franklin said, patting my leg. He started to stand. "But if John collapses again . . . in fact, if anyone is ever hurt at the Society . . . you should summon Doctor Hopper."

"I was on my way to do just that when he woke up," I said.

"You never fail to know what to do." Franklin leaned down from the stair above me and wrapped his arm across my shoulders. I took his hand. "I'm glad that you asked after John. I hope it means your heart is beginning to heal." Franklin let me go and started to stand. "There aren't many men worthy of you, Gin. I'm certain of that. But John might be one of the few."

Chapter Eleven

I looked down at John's hand clutching mine and wondered what I was doing. I questioned our involvement from time to time even though we'd been getting together for months now—attending operas, concerts, and plays with Franklin and Lydia, and meeting in his study to discuss progress on our novels each week.

It wasn't that I thought us unsuitable. We were practically the same person in terms of our passions, our motivations identical. But still I wondered if our connection was best for me. It wasn't that I questioned his reputation anymore—he'd proven it incorrect in his singular pursuit of me—but I'd known Charlie for eighteen years and thought I'd been certain of his feelings, of his intentions. I'd been wrong. How was I to trust John? It made me feel uneasy, as though I were walking a tightrope that could at any moment snap.

At first I'd tried my best to lock my heart away, to keep myself from feeling for him, but despite my intentions, the iron was eroding. My affection for John was growing and it terrified me.

It was unfamiliar and new, completely unlike the passion I'd felt for Charlie. I couldn't define it. Though our bond seemed much deeper than attraction, I couldn't be certain, and from time to time when I recalled that both John and I had loved others so deeply before, I worried that we were only using each other to heal. Even so, I couldn't deny the way John made my heart quicken, the way we understood each other.

John turned to look at me, eyes black in the dimness of the hall and smiled, squeezing my hand as though he somehow knew what I was thinking. Perhaps that was the point. Perhaps whatever Charlie and I had shared was merely a consequence of familiarity and immaturity. My relationship with John was built on a foundation much steadier than the seesaw of emotions that had kept my heart tethered to Charlie. We respected each other. Ever since the incident in the study, John had been a perfect gentleman, and I'd been happy in his company. He still apologized for his anger that night at least once a week—even though I knew it had been on account of his care for me—and assured me that he'd never before collapsed. I knew he'd spoken to his father about the episode and Doctor Hopper had found nothing amiss. I was relieved and reassured—it wouldn't happen again.

The hall was empty save a few people scattered here or there waiting for their loved ones to come onstage to audition. I held my breath as the back of Damrosch's head tilted to the music stand in front of him to read another name.

"James Browning," Damrosch's throaty German accent echoed through the auditorium and I leaned back against my seat, wondering if he would ever get to Alevia. John's coach had dropped us off nearly two hours ago.

"Darling, I've been meaning to tell you something, and I apologize in advance if it upsets you," John whispered. He avoided my eyes and smoothed the front of his gray sack coat. "I waited to tell you in here so that you wouldn't be able to kill me without a witness." He chuckled and I wondered what he'd done.

"It's dark enough. I think I'd be able to pull it off." I tried to lift my fingers from his, but he tightened his grip.

"I gave your book, *The Web*, I gave it to Frederick Harvey." At once, I wanted to both kiss and throttle him, but did neither, gaping at him instead. I'd just finished the latest revision last week—my fifth—prompted by my reading at the Society in March. Several people had commented that Eleanor's character could be deepened and I agreed. "Are you pleased?" he asked. I didn't know. On the one hand, it meant that John truly thought my book—we'd begun to call it *The Web* after the fact that life was never a straight line, but rather a web of interconnected circumstances—was truly ready to be considered for publication. But, on the other hand, he'd taken the liberty of giving it to his editor without thinking to consult me first. In a way, it felt like cheating. The only reason Mr. Harvey had agreed to take a look was because of John.

"You know, it's just that—" I started.

"I know. I should've asked you, but Harvey and I went to lunch to talk through my gentleman-turned-vagabond story and I shared your brilliant comments. He inquired about you, *The Web* came up, and he asked to see it. I thought you'd want me to give it to him right then instead of risking that he'd forget about it, but perhaps I'm wrong."

"Alevia Loftin." Hearing Damrosch's voice state her name interrupted any thought of my book and I sat forward in my chair. Alevia walked slowly across the stage in her handsome new silk performing jacket with ruched organza sleeves, tipped her demure black hat to Damrosch, and slid onto the bench. I closed my eyes and prayed that she would play perfectly. Admittance to the Symphony would make her whole. She desired nothing more, save the love of her family. Though she'd always been perfectly clear about her hopes and desires to all of us, John and Franklin had attempted to introduce her to several of their friends recently, thinking that despite her protests she must be forlorn to be the only one of us without a beau. Mother had tried in vain to encourage a romantic interest, but Alevia had dismissed every prospect.

"Johannes Brahms, second concerto, second movement," she stated. Her voice shook, but only slightly. Lydia had spoken quite earnestly with her cousin-in-law a week prior about her possible admittance to the Symphony as well as Alevia's—if their skill sets were equal or above their male counterparts—and he'd agreed to take them, as well as the backlash for their participation, if he did so.

"It's all right," I whispered and saw Damrosch's head tip toward her, inviting her to play. It wasn't the first time she'd auditioned for him, but it was the first time she had an actual chance. Brahms's second concerto wasn't a safe choice for an audition, in fact it was notorious for its difficulty, but I knew that if she could manage it, he would be impressed. She'd played it flawlessly at home this morning; she could do it again. Alevia's hands hovered over the keys, eyes fixed on the music.

"Come on," John said under his breath. She was stalling. Damrosch cleared his throat and Alevia's hands finally lowered to the keys, flying over the keyboard as they introduced the stormy theme. I held my breath as each note fell into place, and relaxed as Alevia closed her eyes, sinking into the music. I watched the back of Damrosch's head tip and turn with the notes, showing an interest he hadn't demonstrated in her previous auditions. As impressed as he was with her, I knew his open reception was mostly due to Lydia's influence.

"She's wonderful," John whispered, leaning into my ear. "And you, my darling, are going to be just as marvelous. Harvey is going to love you." His thumb drifted across my knuckles. I squeezed his hand. Though Mr. Harvey wasn't George Putnam, he was highly respected and well known just the same, and the thought that my book was in front of an editor of his caliber thrilled me.

"Thank you for all that you've done," I said, truly meaning it. As Alevia's fingers lifted from the keys, Damrosch stood from his chair and clapped. Goose bumps prickled across my skin as my sister smiled. He hadn't so much as moved at the end of anyone else's set. I looked over at John who was beaming at the stage and realized, quite suddenly, that even if the realization of our dreams were helped along by our friends, it didn't matter. The important thing was that they happened. John glanced at me.

"Never thank me again, Virginia," he said sternly, though his lips were turned up in a grin. I stared at him for a moment before remembering my last words. "An editor would have been impressed without me." He lifted the back of my hand to his mouth and kissed it. "If anyone should be doing any thanking it should be me. You forga—"

"I know I did," I said, interrupting him. "And it's forgotten. I'm going to say the same. Never thank me again."

"Thank you." He winked and stood to greet Alevia.

Chapter Twelve

A breeze from the open windows stirred the edges of the white damask tablecloth beside me. The sweet scent of gardenias wafted through my nostrils from the enormous bouquet between the windows, a gift to Mae and Henry from Mr. Blaine.

"Do you suppose they've all gone?" I asked, watching our last guest, ninety-year-old Mrs. Murphy toddle down the sidewalk. The parlor was silent for the first time since ten this morning when it seemed that every woman Mae had ever laid eyes on had embarked on our house for tea and to appraise the array of wedding gifts arranged on tables around the room. The grandfather clock in the drawing room chimed three. Her reception was a bit earlier than was customary—a week before the wedding rather than a few days—but as she and Henry had chosen to marry at his parents' country church in Rye, a tea closer to the ceremony was impossible.

"It's hard to tell, really," Lydia said. "At some of the receptions I've attended in the city, women breeze in and out until well into the evening." She was perched on the edge of the couch next to me, fanning herself and pinching layers of floral-printed silk from her legs. Her face was flushed and sweat beaded on her chest.

I watched the postman making his way down the street and shut my eyes. With all of the day's festivities, I'd hardly thought of the scathing rejection I'd received from *The Century* only yesterday. Mr. Gilder had found my writing disjointed and my illustration of the women unfeeling. Stupidly, I'd opened the letter at dinner, expecting elation. I'd barely heard my family's sympathies. Instead, I'd retreated to my room to tear the letter up and to question my pursuit of writing altogether. I thought my craft had greatly improved in the almost year since I'd begun attending the Society, as did John and Mr. Blaine. But perhaps they hadn't been entirely honest with me; perhaps they'd sugarcoated the truth in an effort to salvage our friendship.

"I'm grateful for everything, really I am," Mae said, interrupting my thoughts. She swept her hand at the tabletops brimming with Belleek fine china, silver teapots, gilded vases, a gold-plated toothpick holder, hand-painted candy dishes, and embroidered linen napkins from the girls at the orphanage. Few of the gifts were functional. Most were an extravagance, but that was the way of our time—at least that's what Mother always said. Weddings were cause for celebration, for lavishness. Even so, a year ago we would've never dreamed of such opulence, though I suppose Mae would've been showered with fine things regardless of our situation.

"But I don't believe I'll be able to smile again for some time. My cheeks are sore." Mae remained slumped against the blue tufted settee Franklin had dragged in from the sitting room. Even in her exhaustion, Mae looked beautiful. Her pale pink and white dress drew up in layers at the front, sweeping into a high French bustle at the back. Bessie had embroidered pink English rose vines on the hem of each tier, a wedding gift that had taken nearly two months.

"I'd smile for weeks if it would award me silver this fine." Bess leaned across Mae to pluck an oyster fork from the display of Tiffany silverware spread atop the Louis Vuitton trunk John had gifted her. "It's even inscribed with your new initials."

"Do you suppose she's in love with my brother or only interested in the finery?" Lydia whispered beside me.

"Both." I grinned.

"Don't get too attached, Bess. I'm returning that fork to whence it came." Mae yawned and retrieved the silver from Bess's hand.

"Why ever would you do such a thing?" Mother asked, coming in from the kitchen. She set a plate of leftover blueberry scones on an empty bit of tabletop beside Alevia, and brushed a few crumbs from her navy-and-white-striped bodice. Mae's eyes met mine.

"The set is from Mrs. Greenwood, as you know, but that fork is from Mrs. Aldridge," she said slowly, as though the reminder of Charlie still had the power to maim me. I'd grown quite used to his absence, though I couldn't pretend that his memory had fully escaped me today. I'd always thought I'd be the first to marry, only because I thought Charlie and me such a sure match. "She left the gift on the doorstep yesterday. As she wasn't invited to the tea, I don't feel I should accept it."

Mother pursed her lips and ran her hand over the top of Bessie's brimless straw hat ornamented with orange silk flowers. Mother hadn't spoken to Mrs. Aldridge since Charlie's proposal—just as she'd sworn that night—and as far as I knew, Mrs. Aldridge hadn't attempted to mend things either. The loss of an intimate friend didn't seem to bother Mother. She'd simply poured the extra time into us and into other women at church and in the neighborhood. Even so, I'd often thought to tell Mother to forfeit her anger toward

Mrs. Aldridge, because despite breaking my heart, Charlie hadn't ruined my life. But I knew it wouldn't matter. Once Mother set her mind to something, nothing could undo it.

"She wouldn't have given it to you if she didn't want you to have it," I said. "Regardless of our current relationship, you were a part of her family for years."

"Things change so swiftly." Alevia's voice came in a whisper. She swept her mother of pearl and feather fan in front of her face, but not before I noticed that her eyes were shining. Surely she wasn't upset about the Aldridges. "At one moment, a family is intact, and the next, a person is stolen away. It will never be the same." She hastily left the room, her yellow silk train overlaid with tulle and lace shuffling behind her. Mother turned to follow, but I heard the drawing room door click shut.

"I don't suppose that was about the loss of your neighbor's friendship?" Lydia's eyebrows rose. The melancholy notes of "The Last Rose of Summer" drifted in from the hallway. The song had originated as a poem by the Irishman Thomas Moore. It was a favorite of Father's. He'd always sung it while Alevia played. I could hear his voice now if I concentrated, his rough baritone floating through the house.

"No," Mae and I said in tandem. "Alevia's trying her best to conceal it for my sake, but she's upset about my moving away, even though I am only going to the city," Mae said. Mae and Henry planned to take up residence in the Trents' guest cottage in Manhattan until they found teaching posts.

"We've always had each other to lean on," I said. "She worries that our relationship with Mae will fade when she's gone and that we'll never see her." Bessie snorted.

"You say it as though we stay up every night gossiping and braiding each other's hair." She laughed. "Miss Blaine, we rarely see one another as it is, save at mealtimes when Mother insists that we're all present. Our interests consume the majority of our time. Mae, you would be an utter dolt to refuse Henry to retain our company. He is a man of worth and you love each other. Your life will be grand."

Lydia nudged me, doubtless questioning Bess's intentions yet again. Alevia had stopped playing, and I could hear Mother trying to console her. Bessie was right to a degree—some days we were so busy that we barely spoke to each other—but I knew it was the thought that Mae would no longer be available on any night that she needed her was what bothered Alevia most. The thought of Mae's absence made me dreadfully sad as well.

"Even so, I shall hate to leave this house," Mae said. She looked down at her hands. "I love you all so very much. But, I love Henry, too."

"Dear, don't worry so," Lydia said. "Life changes, most certainly, but you'll never lose the love of your family." Lydia clutched my hand and squeezed. "And as you said, you'll only be in Manhattan."

Lydia and I had discussed a similar subject at a production of *Maid Marian* the week before. She'd asked if I thought Franklin would ever propose and if I would be terribly upset at her for taking him away if he did. I'd told her that of course I wouldn't. A part of me was lying. I'd miss him supremely, and though I was fond of Lydia, I worried that she'd eventually grow weary of being a salesman's wife. Frank was faring well, but his income would never afford Fifth Avenue.

A chugging noise cut through the momentary silence. I glanced out the window to find John and Mr. Blaine frowning down at the gilded dash of John's Peugeot buggy, while Franklin reclined in the back, an amused look on his face. Mr. Blaine and Franklin had gone out sailing during our tea, and the exposure to sun and salt air was apparent. Frank's face was golden-brown beneath his straw boater, while Mr. Blaine's cheeks were burned deep red, his hair lightened blond white. John's forehead creased under his white felt hat as he tried to shut the automobile off. I hadn't expected to see him. He'd been so busy as of late. Today alone he'd had a reception for designer Gaston Worth, in from Paris, followed by a luncheon with a physician friend of his father's. I thought he'd likely stay at home and write after the luncheon—something he hadn't done for weeks—instead of making the trek to Mott Haven.

Lydia and Bess lifted from their seats in tandem and went to greet the men. I began to rise as well, but Mae caught my arm. She waited until they'd left the room then pulled me down to her, her blue eyes dancing.

"I've been wanting to ask you for weeks, but haven't had a chance to speak to you alone," she whispered. "I want all of you— Bess, you, and Alevia—beside me at the ceremony, but I'd like you to be next to me, my maid of honor . . . if you'll agree."

"It would be my honor," I said. As if there was any question of my consent. A loud crash startled me, and I turned to the windows in time to see John smack the dash. I laughed watching him regard it for a moment longer before shrugging and stepping down from the driver's seat.

"Goodness! Has someone been hit in the street?" Mother careened in from the hallway, a hand on her heart.

"No. It is only John's buggy," I said. Alevia smiled behind her, apparently revived from her melancholy.

"Oh, how delightful that he's come," Mother said. She squinted out of the window. "And Franklin and Mr. Blaine have returned as well." She clapped her hands together. "If only Henry were here." Mother gripped Mae's shoulder. Henry had already departed for the country to fish and sail with his older brother, Andrew, before the wedding. "What a lovely group," Mother said, watching the five of them making their way toward the house.

It was fortunate that Mother approved of all of our beaus. At first I'd wondered how she'd react to all of us courting members of the same elite group she'd chosen to abandon by marrying my father. It wasn't that she'd ever discouraged our interaction with the upper class—on the contrary, she'd only been complimentary of the families she'd grown up with—but she hadn't been close with anyone from that circle since her marriage. If she felt trepidation about being thrust back into her old world, she hadn't shown it. In fact, she seemed thrilled at the prospect of all of our matches.

"Have the last of the hens departed?" Franklin's voice bellowed through the house. He removed his hat, exposing tousled locks. Lydia swept a hand across the side of his head, a gesture that didn't do anything to tame his windblown hair.

"I certainly hope so." Alevia sighed.

"I doubt it. I've heard guests are in and out all day at these sorts of things," John said, echoing Lydia's earlier words. He stepped around Franklin and Lydia, lips lifting when his eyes found mine. He looked handsome in a beige-and-brown-checked jacket.

"In our case, I'm glad to say that all of our guests have taken their leave," Mother said. "Unless I was incorrect in my counting." John leaned down to glance at Mae's silverware, though he kept his hands behind his back, concealing something.

"Looks as though it's all there," he said. "Forks, spoons, knives. They look sturdy enough, silver." He righted. "Are those the types of comments you receive?"

"Of course not. It's a *Tiffany* set, John." Franklin laughed.

"They usually don't comment at all," Mae said. "The response has mostly been in squeals and claps."

"You'd think no one had ever seen china before," Bess said. "Mrs. Bouchard and her daughter lingered so long in front of the Belleek display that the rest of the guests decided to join in. They spent at least an hour appraising the design." It *was* an impressive set—all white with a raised floral pattern along the edges. Though Mrs. Trent hadn't been able to attend, she'd had fifteen place settings delivered. The rest of the items—the platters, the gravy boat, the dessert trays—had been given by Henry's grandmother.

"I suppose some china deserves the appraisal," Mr. Blaine said in an attempt to dismantle Bess's foray into negativity. "Certainly the level of detail can be quite artistic." Mr. Blaine patted Bessie's hand looped through his arm. I wondered if he'd received word from *The Century*.

"I have something for you, Miss Mae," John said abruptly. Mae sat up from her chair back.

"But you've already given me the lovely trunk, Mr. Hopper."

"Please call me John, all of you," he said. "And, I know." John flipped his hand at the trunk. "The trunk is a practical gift, but I wanted to give you something of meaning. You are so very dear to my Ginny." *My Ginny.* The sentiment struck my heart.

John pulled a briefcase from behind his back. It was old, but very fine, made of alligator skin with a curved walrus tusk handle. He knelt down in front of her, setting the bag on her lap. "It was my grandmother's," he said. "She was a teacher up until the end of the war. I thought you should have it. Perhaps you could make use of it." Mae ran her hands over the briefcase, unhinging the bronze clasp at the top. "My mother kept it in her room, to remind her of my grandmother, but since Mother's death, it hasn't been appreciated. I hope you like it." I knew how much it meant for John to part with something of his mother's. He'd told me not long ago that she'd died of consumption when he was ten, despite the desperate efforts of his father.

"It's lovely," Mae whispered. "I'll cherish it." She clutched the bag to her chest.

"I'm glad to hear it." John laid a hand on top of Mae's, then crossed to me and sat down. I reached for him and his fingers laced through mine. He knew how much Mae meant to me. All of the lovely sentiments in the world could not equal the depth of feeling for me that his gift had shown. As touched as I was, my stomach tumbled with nerves. We'd only been courting for five months. Surely he hadn't thought of marriage. But the possibility wasn't entirely unlikely. It wasn't uncommon for couples to become engaged quickly.

"That was kind of you," I said softly, forcing the thought of our future from my mind. I was likely overthinking things. John squeezed my hand.

"It was nothing," he whispered. "Nothing at all. The friendship your family has given me, the lo—"

"We've run out of ice, and I know the weather's blistering, but would anyone care for tea? The kettle's still warm," Mother interrupted.

"I'd love a cup," Frank said. He'd folded himself on the Donegal Irish rug beside Lydia. Mother started to turn in to the hall, but I stopped her.

"I'll fetch it," I said. She'd been catering to our guests all day.

"Miss Virginia, would you mind waiting a moment? I'd like to share some good fortune with the room," Mr. Blaine said. I stopped in my tracks. Surely Bessie hadn't become engaged without mentioning it. She would've been too excited to keep it secret. Mr. Blaine cleared his throat. "My story has been selected for *The Century*." My heart sank to my stomach. I knew the feeling was unfair, but I couldn't help it in the wake of my rejection. Lydia clapped excitedly, while Alevia began a string of congratulations. Mr. Blaine reached into his pocket, withdrawing a letter and a small brown bottle. Surely he hadn't been drinking in the middle of the day. He shoved the bottle back into his linen jacket and extracted the letter from the envelope. "Mr. Gilder says here that the prose is smart and that the story is an important tale of Americana . . . of course I already knew those things, but it was nice to hear them anyway." I felt my face pale and immediately forced a smile in hopes that my family and John wouldn't notice. Mr. Blaine turned to me. As jovial as his expression was, his eyes seemed weary.

"I'm thrilled for you, Mr. Blaine," I said. "Absolutely delighted." In truth, I was. He wasn't my rival or my competitor. It was only disappointment that clouded my elation.

"Tom, please," he said. "And it's all because of you, Miss Virginia. Had you not challenged me to submit a story, this opportunity wouldn't have come."

"I'm so glad for it." I started to retreat into the hallway.

"You'll surely receive word of your own acceptance in a day or two," he called after me. "The post is faster in the city." I nodded and turned into the kitchen. I braced myself on the cool cast-iron rim of the stove and breathed, forcing myself calm. Had Mr. Gilder rejected my work because I was a woman? Many women had been turned away on account of their gender, but I'd thought a publication such as *The Century* was progressive enough to appraise my work honestly. I shook my head. That wasn't the reason. Mr. Gilder published female writers. Just this month, stories by Virginia Frazer Boyle, Sophie Bledsoe Herrick, Dorothy Prescott, and Amelia Gere Mason had been included. I had to remember that this story wasn't my only chance. There would be other opportunities. I thought of the possible novel premises listed in my notebook. None of them inspired me yet, but at some point something would. I was sure of it. Not to mention that Mr. Harvey was going to read *The Web*. I wouldn't let the sting of failure stifle my voice. I was stronger than that. Perhaps Tom's work had simply been better than mine. I reached up to open the wooden cabinets, withdrawing Mother's Foley tea service.

"You mustn't worry about it." Alevia's voice startled me and I nearly dropped the creamer. "I know how it feels—to hear someone's good news before you've received anything positive at all. It's difficult." I didn't want to acknowledge my dejected, pointless feelings. "Your work is superb. Art is so subjective."

"She's right, you know." John appeared behind Alevia. "Your writing is eloquent, honest, unique." He stepped around my sister, his gaze steady on mine. "Your words are a pleasure to read. I'm certain Mr. Gilder—and Mr. Harvey—will feel the same."

"Thank you, John, but I'm afraid I've already been denied by *The Century*." John's eyebrows creased.

"Gilder's judgment is clearly flawed. I'll have a word with him the next time our paths cross." John's lips pinched. "Perhaps this is a sign, Ginny, that you are to be a novelist, not a story writer." His face was resolute. "I know that Mr. Harvey will love your book. Trust me, your time is coming." John's words, his irritation at my rejection, reminded me of Charlie. The first time I'd been turned away from the *Review*, Charlie had been over for lunch. We'd had rabbit stew. I still couldn't stand the taste of it. Mother had brought the letters in and I'd read my dismissal at the table in front of everyone—a mistake I couldn't believe I'd repeated. My eyes had immediately blurred with tears and Charlie had punched the table so hard he'd nearly overturned it.

John reached out to take my hand. I clutched his, suddenly wishing he could kiss me. His touch might soothe the sting of rejection. Instead, I let him go and turned back to the tea.

"I appreciate it. Both of you. But don't worry about me. My moment will come. Today Tom's news is cause for celebration."

"I suppose you're right," Alevia said.

"Your writing will be celebrated soon enough." John reached above me and extracted the teapot from the cabinet. He lifted the kettle from the stove, removed the pot's lid decorated with pale blue and white lilies of the valley, and poured the boiling water in. Then he arranged the sugar and creamer in front of the teapot on Mother's silver tray. I watched him work, amused. When he'd finished setting the cups on the saucers, he turned to me, a grin touching his lips.

"What is it?"

"How'd you learn to do that?" I asked. Arranging a tea service was a basic task, but even the simplest of chores was a baffling one for a man who'd employed servants his whole life.

"Learn to do what?" His forehead creased. "Pour water into a pot? Surely you don't think me that daft." Alevia laughed.

"Not quite. Though I did wonder how you'd learned to arrange the service." He shook his head.

"Some secrets I must never divulge." He chuckled and lifted the tray too hastily, clanging the cups. "Come along now, before I break the set."

Chapter Thirteen

"She's making a fool of herself," I whispered to John who didn't bother to look, but held me tighter instead. Lydia stumbled over the silver-beaded hem of her ciel blue silk gown. She leaned against Franklin as they danced, as though she'd lost all strength in her backbone.

"I assume you're referring to Lydia." John's hand drifted a little too low, settling on the ruched yellow silk at the small of my back as we swayed to Alevia's solo introduction to Johann Strauss's "The Blue Danube" at the other end of the ballroom. I inched away. "Have you seen Tom? He's not much better. I suppose they've both got low tolerances for sparkling wine." I spun around him in time to see Bessie crane her neck away from Tom's attempt at a kiss. His eyes narrowed at Bessie's rejection and guests began to stare. Luckily, she whispered something to him that seemed to calm him for the moment and interest slowly started to drift away from them and back toward Mae and Henry dancing in their wedding finery in the middle of the ballroom.

Bess and Alevia had insisted that Mae abandon her typically plain fashion for the wedding and she'd agreed, selecting an ornate silk dress with scalloped satin stripes and a bodice embroidered with pearls, pastes, and gathered silk lisse. It had been a lovely wedding. They had been married at Rye Presbyterian, the church Henry's family attended during the summer while they were living in the country. An old Gothic building with soaring ceilings held up by Corinthian pillars, the lancet windows were Tiffany's stained glass etched with fleur-de-lis designs trimmed in blues and reds. The sanctuary had been filled with hundreds of white hydrangeas and the sound of the Society's best musicians playing Handel's *Water Music*. The same musicians—all recruited by Alevia in the course of several meetings—were playing now after a filling supper of stewed oysters, galantines, and glasses of wine. Besides Lydia and Tom, however, the rest of us were able to remain upright.

John's hand squeezed mine. I could feel his eyes on my face, but ignored him, fixing my attention toward Mae and Henry instead. John had been by my side all night, stroking my hands and holding me to him. As much as I adored him, I needed a bit of space, just for a moment. When I'd pulled away to greet our family and friends at dinner, he'd followed, hand pressed to my back. In truth, there was nothing wrong with the way he was conducting himself. He'd been gentlemanly and considerate all evening. My irritation wasn't his fault. It was mine. From the moment we'd entered Westchester County, I'd thought of Charlie and hadn't stopped. I knew it was just because we were less than ten miles from his home with Rachel. Charlie didn't deserve my attention, still, it seemed odd that he wasn't here, celebrating with friends that had once been as intimate as family. Breaking from my view of Mae and Henry, I met John's eyes and smiled, trying to stay present.

"Hello there." Mother danced up to us, arm in arm with Franklin who winked and twirled her. I wondered where he'd deposited Lydia. "Isn't it a marvelous evening?"

"Just lovely," John said.

"The seating at dinner was unfortunate. I hope the two of you weren't bored," Mother said. I snorted.

"On the contrary. George Hoffmann talked the entire time about his new chicken coop, mainly about the eggs. He might as well have hatched them himself." Franklin laughed.

"Well, the benefit of having your own wedding is that you can choose where you sit," she said, winking at John. Franklin grinned at the prospect of my marriage to his best friend and I suddenly felt as though the walls were closing in around me. I forced a smile at my mother and brother.

"Excuse me. I'm going to get some fresh air," I said. Leaving John on the dance floor, I walked quickly toward the terrace, toward the rows of orderly English boxwoods standing sentry at the base of each pillar along the colonnade. I pushed past clusters of talking couples—men dressed in black tuxedos and white bow ties, women adorned with flint diamonds, lace, and ribbons atop an array of bright summer hues. I flung the French door open and it closed mercifully behind me, silencing the orchestra and the deafening sound of guests. I reveled in the warm summer air, glad to be alone.

On one hand, it had been one of the best nights of my life. My loved ones were all in one place, I was overjoyed that my sister had married her match, and I was in the company of a man that I was beginning to care deeply for. On the other hand, it had been awful. John's affection had encouraged nearly all of my friends and family members, including Cherie and Mother, to hint at an impending marriage. My insides numbed with each mention, but John had only encouraged their hopes, leaning over to kiss my cheek or hand each time. It wasn't that I didn't want him. I did. It was the thought of marriage that frightened me. It would change things, certainly, but there was no way to predict how. We were perfect as we were. Our writing wove us together, our passion for our art driving our passion for each other. Social obligations could consume us as a married couple—eating away at our writing as they already ate away at John's. And when we lost the time to sit and think, to create, we would blame each other. We could grow to resent each other. Even so, I couldn't blame John for thinking of marriage. That was the point of courtships, after all, but I realized at Mae's wedding that I had ignored the thought of that end, hoping instead that we could go on as we were in perpetuity. I felt hollow and scared thinking of what was to come. With Charlie, I'd had eighteen years to think about what he meant to me, to know that I loved him, to imagine what marriage would be like. I wouldn't have that luxury with John. Sooner rather than later I would have to come to terms with my feelings for him, to define the strength of my attraction, the magnetism that drew me to him, and the strange recoiling at the hint of marriage. In spite of it all, one thing was certain: I didn't want to lose him. I needed him, but I also needed to be honest with myself.

I descended the stairs and walked along a dirt path following a serpentine stone wall that separated the Trents' formal garden and the lily pads floating along the bank of the acre-wide pond. The crickets' droning chirp rose in crescendo and the light musk of antique roses wafted over me with the summer wind, tousling my fleur-de-lis coiffure and unsettling my skirt.

"Virginia!" Someone barked my name behind me and I whirled around. I blinked, wondering if I'd gone mad. *Charlie.* He ran down the terrace steps and through the garden to where I stood. He always appeared when I least expected him. He looked disturbed. His hair had grown much too long and he'd gathered the strands behind his ears. Feet from me, he tugged at the bottom of his untucked white shirt. His eyes didn't break from mine, and I saw that they were swollen, lids swathed in gray.

"Charlie," I started to ask what he was doing here, but he snatched my elbows and started shaking me.

"John Hopper?" He snarled into my face. "You can't possibly be with him. You . . . you can't." I could feel the heat of Charlie's glare on my face. That heat quickly turned to anger as I recalled the last time we'd stood this close.

"I'll do what I want," I said quietly, meeting his eyes. He'd lost any say in my life when he'd chosen someone else. He nodded once, as if to say that he already knew.

"Do you love him?"

I stared back, unwilling to answer.

"Ginny, answer me," he said softly, though his voice sliced through the peaceful summer air like a blade to my wrist. He straightened to face me. I knew I should walk away. I didn't owe him the satisfaction of an answer. Instead, I nodded once.

"You do?" Eyes going wide, he clutched the stiff fabric across his chest.

"Why do you care?" I'd meant the question to come out softly, but I spat it, and Charlie paused, fingers hovering in front of him.

"What do you mean by that?" he barked. He stepped toward me until I could feel him against my chest. I closed my eyes, trying to ignore what he was doing to me—a tingling warmth blooming—and prayed he wouldn't touch me.

"I meant what I said," I whispered. "Why would you care? You don't love me anymore; you have no claim to me. Why are you here? Where's your wife?"

I felt him step away from me and opened my eyes. As wrong as it was, as much as I knew he wasn't mine, I wanted him to want me, to love me instead of her.

"Not here. What do you mean I don't love you? You . . . you don't even know what it's like to see me in love with someone else." He stumbled over the last word and I blinked at him. I'd been standing right in front of him when he'd spoken of his love for Rachel the last time and beside him when he'd proposed to her.

"You said that she consumed you, that she was your every thought."

His brows furrowed. "No. No, Gin. That's not what I meant. She wants me around her all the time. I can't escape her love. It's like a cage around my heart," he said. "But you . . . I've been forced to watch you with him. I heard the wedding was today and thought to stay away as I wasn't invited, but changed my mind. I just got here. I've been sitting in the damn corner watching John touch you and you letting him. I couldn't . . . I can't stand it, Gin."

"I had to watch you and her," I said.

"That was different. I've never loved her." Charlie swallowed hard. "I wish I did. She's kind, a good wife. She deserves better, she deserves my heart, and I've tried, but the last time I saw you, I knew it was a worthless endeavor. I wanted to tell you that I loved you so badly. I was a coward. Ginny, you can't imagine the torture of pretending to love someone while the woman you love is still out there, reminding you of what you could have had." I opened my mouth to say that he'd chosen, but he clapped his hand over my lips. "And before you open your mouth to tell me it's my fault, I know. I know I've gotten myself into this hell."

He removed his hand and stepped forward, pushing against me. I stumbled into the wall, feeling the edges of the granite boulders dig into my back. Charlie's hands circled around my hips.

He'd never been so forward. I knew I should push him away, but couldn't move. He reached for my hand, his fingers trembling around mine, and slowly placed my palm where our bodies separated on his chest.

"My heart has always been yours," he said. "And you're mine. You have no idea the number of times I've woken with your memory on my mind." I couldn't breathe and didn't try, but ran my fingers up his back to the nape of his neck. He made a strangled noise in the back of his throat, leaned down, and kissed me, vanilla wedding cake on his tongue. My eyes closed and I could feel my mouth open as his teeth bit down on my earlobe. One of his hands drifted up to my bodice, fingertips parting the thin organza. He reached under my shift, stroking my breasts and then I felt the warmth of his mouth replace his fingers. Desire pooled in my stomach and I pulled his shirt up, running my hands along his chest. His eyes closed and his head tilted back for a moment as I touched him and then he lifted my skirt from the ground, fingertips grazing my stockings. The summer air hit my legs as he paused at my thigh and leaned in to kiss me again.

"Charlie," I said, barely conscious of anything beyond his hands on my body. I wanted him badly, but he wasn't mine. "Charlie, stop," I said, against every bodily instinct. It wasn't right. His lips lifted from my skin and he dropped my skirt.

"I'm sorry," he said softly, still pressed against me. "I didn't mean . . . I couldn't help it. Please. I love you, Ginny." His eyes were warm and pleading, fingers gripped to my arm plastered against the stone.

"I know. But you promised you would love Rachel whether you do or not. She loves you. And this is wrong." He turned his eyes to the ground.

"I'd rather be dead," he said quietly.

"Ginny, Charlie." Franklin appeared from nowhere. His face was pale as the clouds against the night sky, eyes wild. "Have you seen Lydia?" His voice trembled and he glanced over my shoulder.

"No. What's happened?" I asked, smoothing my skirt. Frank stared at me for a moment, then shook his head as if to clear it.

"Marcus Carter, Lydia's ex-fiancé. He's dead. We just received a telegram with the news and she ran off." I remembered noticing Mr. Carter at the Society, his hand flying over the pages, and the story Frank told me about the way Mr. Carter and Lydia ended. I wondered how he'd died.

"Will's brother, Marcus?" Charlie asked and Franklin bobbed his head at him, barely allowing the kindness of a glance his way. "Damn. Mr. and Mrs. Carter have lost both of their sons."

"What happened?" I asked. Franklin was pacing back and forth, looking over the wall at the garden and then at the pond.

"I don't know. The butler found him at four this morning on his bedroom floor next to the fire. They don't know the particulars yet." Franklin hiked the leg of his tuxedo up and started to climb over the fence to the bank of the pond. "I've got to find her. John's looking through the woods around the front lawn." The mention of John struck me through. I'd betrayed him. Frank paused halfway up the wall to glance at Charlie standing next to me. "I've told you once, but I'll tell you again and I mean it. Stay the hell away from my sister. She's been getting on quite well without you." I felt Charlie's eyes, but didn't look, watching Franklin disappear over the fence instead. Franklin was right. I'd been happy without Charlie. But *he* showed up tonight. *He* kissed me. It'd be easy to let the memory of this night confuse everything I'd grown to love without him, but I wouldn't let it. Charlie had chosen his future and it wasn't with me. It could never be with me. As much as I despised Rachel for coming between us, she was his wife and she loved him. She couldn't ever find out that he loved me. I wouldn't be able to live with myself knowing I'd healed my heartache by causing hers. I lifted my hand to my lips to remember the feel of him one last time. Then, I turned to face him. Charlie looked worse than he had before, tall frame slumped in defeat.

"I know he can't help but hate me. I know what I've done to you and I'm sorry . . . so sorry," he said, his voice breaking. I knew he meant it. I knew him as well as I knew myself. "I chose wrongly and I'm paying for it. I'm tortured every second that I don't have you, Ginny. I don't know how I'll go on without you, but I suppose I'll have to."

"You'll be fine," I said, reaching for his hand. I felt sorry for him. He was trapped, and as much as his rejection had killed me in the past, I was free to move on. "Try to forget me. It's easier that way." Charlie shook his head.

"I'm afraid that's impossible," he whispered.

*I*t was close to midnight and no one had even caught so much as a glimpse of Lydia. Though initially I figured she'd only gone somewhere to cry and would turn up, I was beginning to worry. When Franklin and John had returned to the ballroom after an hour of searching with no luck, the entire party, including the newlyweds, had pitched in to try to find her. I could see Mae now, white dress a light splotch against the darkness as she combed the edge of woods on the other side of the pond. Nearly one hundred guests were spread out everywhere searching. The elderly were the only ones who had avoided involvement entirely and most of them had stayed behind to enjoy what remained of the reception, though they'd been escorted to their coaches hours ago.

Turning away from the view of the looming French-style cha-
teau, I started south again, deeper into the thick hardwood forest,
following a crude path that Henry had mentioned forked at some
point, leading to thirty-five undeveloped acres of wilderness on one
side and the Long Island Sound on the other. It probably wasn't
wise to go alone—I couldn't see but a foot in front of me at most
and had no idea if the path had split yet—but I wasn't afraid of the
dark. I only hoped that when I finally turned around I'd be able to
find my way back.

The woods were silent except for the random calls of hunting
owls and the scuffle of dried leaves as they snatched their prey. I
took a deep breath, inhaling the tinge of sulfur and salt coming
from the Sound in an attempt to calm my alarm at Lydia's absence,
but it didn't work. A faraway shout came from behind me and I
whirled around, squinting through the shadowy trees.

"Nevermind!" In the night silence, I could hear Charlie's retraction clearly even though I was at least a mile away by now.
I couldn't believe I'd let him kiss me. I'd thought my heart had
finally numbed toward him, but in the moment, the deep, old feelings I'd buried had welled up. To anyone else, his gestures would
seem appalling. I knew that and blamed him for it, but I also
knew what he was struggling against, what he was still trying to
come to terms with: the fight of heart versus responsibility. And
even though he loved me, Charlie would choose responsibility in
the end. Divorce wasn't something he was willing to consider and
I couldn't say, in the same situation, that I would either.

Staring at the moon, I wondered where Lydia was, then
stopped dead, catching myself on the trunk of scrawny tree. I stood
there looking out at the sporadic flashes of lantern light on the fish-
ing boats—and then, I heard it.

The sobbing came from below me, to my right. I caught the

gleam of Lydia's blond hair in the moonlight and gasped. She was waist deep in the water a short distance away. She stretched her hands out in front of her and then submerged them. I didn't know what she was planning; all I knew was that if I yelled her name she'd startle.

I had to reach her. I ran through the woods along the edge of the bank. The skirt of my bridesmaid's dress caught on briars and twigs and I hiked it to my shins. Lydia had taken a few more steps now, her blue dress floating around her. I stopped above her, unsure how I could get down to the water without falling. Eyeing a channel of dirt next to me, snaking between the rocks, I veered toward it. I made my way down the bank slowly, gripping the stones, making sure my silk satin shoes didn't get caught between them. Lydia had stopped sobbing, but she was still crying. I could hear the deep hiccups of her breath as I got closer. Two more steps down and I'd be on the bank. Without warning, Lydia pushed forward, the water rising to her chest.

"Lydia!" I screamed. I didn't know if she could swim, but I'd never learned. I couldn't do anything to help her if she lost her balance in the waves.

"What're you doing? We've all been so worried," I yelled. The wind was picking up, bringing the tide in. She turned to face me. My breath caught. I'd never seen her this way. Lydia looked like a patient who'd somehow broken out of the asylum. She was holding her arms out, trying to balance, though she stumbled back and forth in the water, her long hair torn mostly out of her updo, tangling in the wind. She blinked at me, blue eyes bloodshot and serious, though her lips were turned up in a garish smile.

"Marcus is dead," she called flatly, though the grin remained. "I'm going to find him."

"What about Tom?" I shouted. "What about your parents? Come out of the water. I'll walk you back." I glanced around me, frantically looking for something I could extend to her if she couldn't make it out alone, but found nothing.

"I loved him." Tears poured down her face, but she didn't bother to wipe them away. "But after Will passed . . . Marcus changed. He wouldn't talk to anyone, not me or anyone, and I was angry. I left him."

"It's not your fault, Lydia." I started to remind her of his madness, but stifled my words, unsure if the memory would make her feel worse. "He and Will are together in some place much better," I said, attempting to reassure her, wishing someone, anyone, were here with me.

"You didn't know them," she said. "I want to go there, too." Her eyes dried and the eerie smile returned.

"What about Franklin?" I asked, fierce defense for my brother suddenly overtaking my pity for her. "I thought you loved him. He loves you. We all love you. We're going to be sisters, remember?" Her eyes narrowed.

"You don't understand and he doesn't care," she shouted. I didn't think she'd blinked the entire time we'd been speaking, but she did now—so slowly I thought she was closing her eyes. "He barely touches me," she said more softly, though her expression remained the same.

"Of course he does," I said. "He thinks you're the most beautiful woman he's ever seen and practically lights up when you're around. How could he help it? I do, too." My mind was spinning. "I'm sure you're the love of his life and—"

"Lyd, you're going to let us get you back to the Trents' safely." John's voice came from behind me, strong and matter-of-fact. In the hysteria of the moment, I'd almost forgotten he existed. Lydia started crying again when she saw him over my shoulder. He worked his way down the hill and shot me a quick glance, brows furrowed in worry. I nodded, at once feeling like I'd been reduced to the size of an ant. Even as Lydia's fate hung in the balance, I remembered my lips on Charlie's and hated what I'd done. John loved me and I'd betrayed him with a man who'd stolen his only other love. "I've lost them, too, you know," he shouted, eyes fixed on Lydia. He started to edge out of his jacket. "They were like brothers to me. Marc wouldn't want this for you, Lyd, you know that." Lydia began blubbering, and nodded.

"Thank god," I whispered. John walked past me to the water's edge, squeezing my hand as he passed. His starched white tuxedo shirt hugged his tense shoulders.

"Will you come back, please? I can't lose you, too. Frank can't lose you either. He's been worried sick." John began to push his shoes off. He stared at Lydia, waiting.

"Very well," she said. She looked at the water around her and then back at John and me on the bank.

"Just focus on me and start walking," John said. Lydia collected the length of her floating skirt in her fist, bit her lip, and started forward. I exhaled, relieved. "I hate to tell you, but you missed the cake," John said, no doubt in an attempt to keep up conversation. "It was marvelous. The most decadent butter cream I have ever tasted." Lydia smiled. The wind picked up, tossing the water around her.

"I suppose I—" She suddenly lost her footing, disappearing into the waves. Her head bobbed up. "John!" she called, before she went under again. John dove into the water, his arms propelling along the surface to where we'd last seen her. I stepped forward, my body racing with the urge to do something, but I was helpless. John disappeared below the surface, only to reemerge again moments later.

"Has she come up?" he bellowed. I started to reply, but he dove under again, not waiting for my response. I was shaking. I felt desperate, helpless. I closed my eyes and prayed for God to spare her, to keep John from harm. Just then John emerged from the water, his arm gripped around Lydia's chest. She was coughing, her hair hanging in tendrils across her face.

"Thank goodness," I whispered. My teeth chattered, the alarm of her near peril still coursing through me. As John swam closer, I could see Lydia's fingers gripped around his arm, though her head had begun to bob with each forward stroke.

"Gin, I think she's fainted," John panted. He stood, lifting her body to his chest as he shuffled out of the water. "Do you have any salts?" I stared at him for a moment before realizing I did.

"Yes," I said, reaching into the small pocket at my side to extract the bottle of Bull's Head smelling salts I'd carried to the church in case any of the guests had need of them. John set Lydia down, propping her up against a rock. She was snoring now, a high-pitched whistling noise. I couldn't help but smile. She was safe. I knelt down and began to open the cap, but John's fingers caught mine. He lowered to the gritty bank beside me and lifted his hand to my face.

"Thank you," he whispered. "If you hadn't found her—"

"John," I started. I had to tell him about Charlie. As angry as I knew he'd be, I couldn't hide it from him. "I have to tell you someth—"

"Whatever it is, I don't care," he said. "I just need you now." Pulling my face to his, he kissed me. His mouth moved slowly on mine. I could feel the softness of his lips, taste the sweet cigar smoke on his tongue, and something in my heart responded. A part of me belonged to him. He pulled away and I lifted the salts to Lydia's nostrils. Her eyes fluttered open.

"Ginny."

"You scared me," I whispered, wrapping my arms around her. She clutched me to her, her saturated dress soaking through mine.

"Never again, Lydia," John said over my shoulder. "Promise me." Lydia blinked hazily and then nodded.

"I'm so, so sorry," she muttered, stifling a sob. "I promise." I released her and stood.

"I know you are," he said. "Now let's find a way to get you up this bank." John squinted up at the rocks and I looked over at Lydia realizing she'd fallen fast asleep.

Chapter Fourteen

AUGUST 1892

The Hopper House

NEW YORK, NEW YORK

I couldn't understand why they'd decided to go ahead with the Society meeting other than the fact that they thought Mr. Carter would want it that way. I was only here myself because Lydia had begged me to attend. John wasn't even in town, but had graciously allowed Tom to open the house for a meeting anyway. John had taken a train to Georgia with his father late last week saying something about needing to help him with his research, though I doubted John, who had no interest in medicine, could be of any assistance in whatever experiment Doctor Hopper was doing. Frank casually mentioned John had really gone away to distance himself from the tragedy, to take time to mourn his once friend in his own way. I couldn't blame him, but I missed him terribly. I didn't want to be here either.

I was sitting in the corner where we'd spotted Maude Adams on the first night, still trying to think up an idea for a new novel. I glanced at the first idea I'd written down. *The immigration of my grandparents.* Their story was a heroic, heartbreaking tale, and though their lives had greatly improved a few years after their arrival in the city, I didn't know if I had the strength to live the calamity of their passage and early years as Americans. They'd fled to escape the Irish famine, leaving their parents and siblings behind. Losing two sons to disease on the ship over, they hadn't been able to find work when they got here, forcing my father, his three siblings, and my grandparents to live with three other families in an apartment in the slums until Grandfather found a post with D.F. Tiemann Color Works, a position that eventually made them quite comfortable.

I closed my eyes in an attempt to recall anything striking I'd read as of late in the newspaper or magazines, trying to mute the roaring white noise of hundreds talking and laughing at once, and the eerie undercurrent of suspicion. Familiar faces I'd never met but had seen here often kept walking past me, circulating around to each artist's display, their eyes bright with a strange optimism I didn't understand given the melancholy of the day.

Marcus's funeral had been that morning at Trinity Church. I hadn't attended, but Franklin had said it was horrible. Mrs. Carter had apparently turned around after she was through receiving everyone, climbed up on the casket, reached in, and pulled Mr. Carter's corpse from the pillow, hugging and shaking him while crying hysterically as though she could wake him up. Lydia had vomited and passed out next to Franklin and he'd had to carry her out of the church. Her behavior was concerning and foreign, entirely unlike the bubbly, poised woman I thought I knew.

I glanced over at Lydia now, stunned at the difference in her demeanor. John and I had promised we'd keep quiet about her episode in the sound—we'd told everyone save Franklin that she'd lost her diamond bracelet in the waves and that she and John had

gone to retrieve it—but for someone so affected by Mr. Carter's
death a week ago, her loud laughter hours after she'd fainted at his
funeral didn't make sense. Then again, nothing about grief ever
did. Lydia tipped her head back, dangling her hair in Franklin's
face as she laughed with a girl in front of her. Turning abruptly, she
took Franklin's face in her hands and leaned in to kiss him. Franklin shook his head, scowling at her brazen behavior. He'd been in a
sour mood ever since John had left for Georgia without him. He'd
asked to go along, needing to get away from our grief-stricken
peers as much as John did, but Doctor Hopper had requested the
trip remain father and son. I watched, waiting for Lydia to react
to Frank's dismissal, but she only grinned and scanned the crowd.
She paused on me and began to walk over. I closed my notebook
and waited, hoping she'd confide in me. I understood pain, the way
sorrow rose and fell in waves. The only way I'd gotten through the
loss of my father was to talk about him. So far, she had yet to utter
a word about Mr. Carter to Frank or me, but I prayed she would.
Perhaps speaking of him would alleviate the misplaced guilt she
felt in his death. Something had to settle her mind. She couldn't
continue on this way.

Lydia exhaled and sat down on the damask ottoman beside
me. Her lips were still turned up, but her eyes narrowed at Frank
across the room. I could only see the top of his head—a crowd had
gathered in front of us to hear a poem accompanied by a flutist.

"What do you suppose is wrong with him?" she asked without
looking my way. I didn't want to point out that her behavior was
a bit forward for a public gathering, so I shrugged. "I love him. I
do, but I can't figure it out. Half of the time he acts as though he's
repulsed by me, not even letting me kiss him—"

"He's not repulsed by you in the slightest." I laughed and
reached out to clutch her hand. "You're beautiful, and he loves

you, you know that. But you're in public." Lydia's head whipped toward me.

"No, we're not," she said. Her shaking hands fingered an enormous ruby necklace hanging from her neck. "We're among friends," she stuttered. I looked into her eyes, finding them blood-shot and glassy. Was she intoxicated? I recalled the way she'd been at Mae's wedding. She'd had too much wine then, too. "And it's not like anyone knows what's g-going on anyway." She dropped the necklace and swept her hand across the display in front of us. The poem had concluded and most of the group had moved on to other presentations, but the few still gathered were an interesting sight. Some weren't talking, staring blankly at the people around them, while others chattered and laughed with each other, unaware of anything amiss. The cellist who usually played with Lydia was sitting by herself in the corner opposite us, bow driving angrily across the strings.

"Are you all right? I can tell that you've had—" I started to tell her that imbibing too much liquor would do nothing to bring Mr. Carter back, but Lydia cut me off.

"Your brother and John are optimists. They've tried to cheer me, to cheer everyone, but right now, it's impossible. My sorrow is too great." The last word was forced from her mouth. She was right. Neither of them could stand watching people wither in grief without trying to cast light on whatever it was. That's why John had left this time, I thought. He was too close, he couldn't do it. But Frank could.

"Lydia . . ." My heart broke for her. Even though her grief for a man that wasn't Frank made me defensive, I could feel her anguish. She'd left things undone with Mr. Carter, a man she'd clearly loved. I started to say that he'd known how much she cared for him, but I had no idea of the reality of their past beyond one story. "Frank's only trying to liven you because he cares for you so deeply," I said, choosing words I absolutely knew to be true. I glanced in the direction of my brother. He hadn't mentioned the toll Lydia's grief had taken on their relationship, but I knew it had to be weighing on him. "We all care for you." I drew my arm around her shoulders.

"I know." Turning toward me, the corners of her mouth twitched. I wondered what had suddenly convinced her. "He gave me this earlier and said h-he did." She plucked the necklace from her chest.

"How? Where did he get that?" Disbelief floated over me. The ruby was at least five carats surrounded by tiny diamonds. Lydia lifted a shoulder. I reached for my notebook and pencil, flipping the blank pages to busy my hands. What was he doing? If he had to buy her jewelry to prove his love, he couldn't afford her. I doubted he had enough money, even given his promotion, to afford our expenses, our dresses, his suits, the Benz, and Lydia's necklace.

Suddenly, Lydia flung bolt upright. Her face drained as she stared up at the cherub mural and her lips grayed. I grabbed her shoulders and shook her, but she just made a low gurgling noise in her throat. My heart pounded. She needed a doctor, but Doctor Hopper wasn't here.

"Lydia." I dug my nails into her shoulders, but her head bobbed limply with each movement. She laughed and I jumped and let go. She rocked forward once with the absence of my hands and then jolted as though she'd woken from a dream where she'd been falling.

"H-he's here," she whispered.

"Who's here?" I asked. My voice shook, wishing I could somehow get Frank's attention or Tom's, though I hadn't seen him all night.

"Marcus." Barely able to get his name out, her teeth began chattering and she rubbed her arms, staring blankly into the room.

"No, Lydia. He's gone. In heaven, remember?" I tried to speak as calmly as possible despite the alarm roaring through me.

"I know that, but I feel him," she spat, glaring at me. The base of my tailbone started to tingle and I straightened in my chair. As ridiculous as it was, I couldn't help glancing about, hoping I wouldn't see a ghost. "I killed him. Will killed him. He died of a broken heart." A sob caught in her throat and I clutched her wrist.

"Listen to me," I barked over the sorrowful wail of the cello and the clashing far-off notes of someone much less skilled than Alevia playing the piano. "He and Will both died of a heart ailment, not a broken heart." That had been Doctor Hopper's findings anyway, though the idea that both men had succumbed to the exact same condition was a bit peculiar. I'd voiced my doubt to Bess and Alevia while Franklin and Lydia were attending the funeral, but neither thought it odd in the slightest. Bess had shrugged, saying that Doctor Hopper was one of the most renowned physicians in Manhattan and that we should trust his expertise, while Alevia paled and ignored the conversation altogether, turning to Grandmother's piano and playing "Abide with Me." Mother had come in to sing along with Alevia's playing, afterward giving me a hug and telling me that tragedies like this were simply difficult to understand. But, sitting here, listening to fragments of whispers around me, I knew I wasn't the only one to question Mr. Carter's fate. The most common story seemed to be that he'd died of an alcohol overdose, but that Doctor Hopper had been convinced to mask it in order to avoid a social scandal.

"You don't know anything," Lydia said. "He's *here*!" She screeched the last word, stumbled on the long train of her black mourning dress, caught herself on the wall, and ran from me.

Looking over her shoulder, her face was gripped with worry as if Mr. Carter was chasing her. I stood to go after her. I had no idea how to calm her, but I had to try. Out of nowhere, Franklin materialized in front of her, grabbing her in a hug. "I'm sorry," Franklin mouthed to me over her shoulder. I watched Lydia's head drop to Frank's chest, and let out the breath I'd been holding. Grief and guilt had the ability to consume, to sink a person so far into the depths of melancholy that for a while, they could hardly function. I hated that Lydia had to endure such pain and hoped she could overcome it.

I forced my attention to my notebook and tried in vain to ignore everything else. I flipped the first page, finding two ideas scrawled on the second. Both came from some form of real life: a fabricated story about the Society and an undefined idea about what it was that made people go along with class expectations. The latter made me think of Charlie. I could still hear the desperation in his voice, feel his hands on my body, but the memory of it, of him, no longer made me miserable. I knew he loved me, and a part of me would always love him, but fate had drawn us separate paths. Without thinking, I lifted my eyes to the room to look for John before I remembered that he was absent. Though I was surrounded by people, it felt lonely without him.

"Hello, Virginia." Someone tapped me on the shoulder and I turned to find Edith. She smiled, though her eyes held the same sadness as everyone else's.

"Edith! I'm so happy to see you." I closed my notebook.

"I'm surprised you recalled my name. It's been nearly a year since I last visited," she said, running her gloved hands over the black lace overlay along her skirt.

"One doesn't easily forget writing as profound as yours . . . or the discovery that there's another woman out there chasing the same dream." I glanced down at my peach dress as I extended my hand to her, suddenly embarrassed that I'd worn something so cheery. "I'm sorry about Mr. Carter," I said. Her eyes were lined with bags. She shook her head.

"It's quite a tragedy, though I can't pretend that we were ever very close. I came in for the funeral at the request of my family. Marcus and I traveled in the same circle, of course, but I suppose most of my melancholy comes from thinking of his poor parents. I can't imagine the heartache of losing both sons, especially to the same condition." She pursed her lips, making her already youthful face appear even more childlike. "I know that I shouldn't utter it, but I wonder about the rumors. Ever since William's death, Marcus drank excessively. I can't imagine Doctor Hopper agreeing to report dishonest findings, but it *is* a stroke of luck that Marcus didn't pass on from drunkenness months ago." Edith shook her head. "In any case, I didn't come over to depress you with talk of death. How's your writing coming along?" Her face brightened at the subject.

"Is it strange if I say that I'm unsure?" She shook her head.

"Of course not; I'm not sure either. I thought that I'd struck gold with the novella I asked you to read, but I got stuck, so I put it away . . . much to Teddy's elation, who has made it clear that he's enjoying a respite from my lamenting over characters' fates and complaining about my lack of time to write. There is never enough with all of the social obligations." She pursed her lips. Perhaps I wasn't insane to think my work threatened by the potential commitments of the upper class. Clearly John wasn't the only one with this problem. "I'm working on a home decorating guidebook right now, another hobby of mine." Her eyes swept the tufted couch, damask ottoman, and gilded settee situated around us. "There is so much wasted space in this room," she muttered, and then sighed.

"If I keep on collecting hobbies, I fear that I'll never accomplish anything. Do convince me to pursue something, Virginia, to choose one course and focus." I laughed, but she reached out to grab my hand, her eyes serious.

"Surely you know my opinion. I haven't read about Glennard in nearly a year and still think of that passage wondering what became of him," I said. "Please continue his story."

"Perhaps I shall," she said, raising her chin. "And what are you working on? Surely something." I told her about my rejected story, my struggle to begin a new novel, and about John giving *The Web* to Frederick Harvey. I'd barely spoken of it in case doing so would somehow doom it to failure. I hadn't heard anything from him yet and it had been months. "Oh! This is wonderful news!" Edith pressed a hand to her heart. "I'm only jealous that Mr. Harvey is monopolizing it while I so desperately wish to read it."

"I wish I could share it with you," I replied. "I've made a few copies, though I'm afraid I didn't bring them with me tonight. Are you sure that you can't convince your husband to return to the city?"

"Perhaps someday. Teddy is so very fond of Newport. However, I'm planning to return early next year for an extended holiday while Teddy goes on a hunt. Perhaps we could plan to exchange our work then?"

"That's a marvelous idea." A year seemed like forever. "It will give me ample time to write something new." Edith bounced up and down on the toes of her embroidered silk heels.

"I'm so very excited. I'm isolated in Newport and—"

"Darling, are you ready?" A man with slicked hair and a straight mustache appeared at Edith's arm. She startled.

"Of course not. I'd live the whole of my life at this Fifth Avenue artists society if I could. But, if you're asking if I'll go home with you, I suppose I'll agree." Edith extended her hand to him without a glance his way, and leaned in to kiss my cheek. "Until next year, my dear."

"It was lovely to see you again," I said. She tipped her head at me and turned, arm in arm with her husband as they wove around a swarm of guests in the middle of the room acting out a play. I turned my attention back to my notebook determined to choose an idea and begin plotting the story, emboldened by the thought that I'd found a female writing companion.

"It's all so sad, isn't it?" Alevia whispered. She appeared from nowhere and I stared at her as she turned from me to survey the room. I was surprised to see her. I had no idea she was coming tonight. Ever since we lost Father, Alevia had been traumatized by the thought of death and tended to avoid the reality of it at all cost. Her fingers curled around her black horsehair mourning bracelet.

"When did you get here?" I asked. Alevia sat down on the same ottoman Lydia had occupied earlier.

"Perhaps thirty minutes ago. Mae sent me down with the Trents' coach to retrieve you and Frank whenever you were ready to go. I only had to play for a few hours at the Vanderbilts'. I didn't realize it was just a dinner. I went over to Mae and Henry's after and then here." Mae and Henry's residence—the Trents' guest home along the East River—was quaint and warm. I loved visiting them and was glad we were staying with them tonight rather than traveling all the way home.

"How are the Vanderbilts?" I asked. Alevia grimaced as some- one began to play the piano, tripping over the notes so that making out the tune was impossible. A man with a loud bass voice started to introduce a story behind us.

"They were kind, as always," she said, turning back to me. She laughed softly, tucking a stray black strand behind her ear. "Mrs. Vanderbilt kept going on about a tea luncheon she wanted to throw for a cousin and Mr. Vanderbilt's conversation with Mr. Astor, whatever it was, was putting him to sleep. I tried not to notice because it would make me laugh, but Mr. Astor's eyes kept shutting."

I caught Tom emerging from the alcove room across to where Alevia and I were sitting. Alevia must have noticed, too, because she smiled.

"He seems all right, thank goodness," Alevia whispered, as though he could hear us a room away. "Bessie asked me to send her a telegram if we didn't see him tonight. I suppose he's been grieving and she was worried that with the funeral today he'd be inconsolable." Bessie had remained at the Trents' House in Greenwich following the wedding. She'd been inundated with business as New Yorkers gradually left the city for the summer and thought it would be better to fit and craft the forty or so hats in the country.

"I'm sure she's told you about Tom saying he wanted to marry her at the wedding?" I asked.

"Yes. She's very excited. I told her I was going to attend James Helfenstein's organ recital at Grace Church last Sunday and she asked me to go down to Great-aunt Rose's grave at the VanPelt cemetery in Richmond Town afterward to tell her. I felt a little peculiar going without Bess, but I know that Aunt Rose would be proud. I'm thrilled for them, for her." She sighed, looking around at the painters and writers and musicians scattered around the room. "I know it's practically blasphemy to say this, but do you ever think that perhaps you don't want to?" Alevia's eyes were cast down at her lap. "Get married, I mean." I knew it took great courage to admit she felt that way. I'd only dared say it a handful of times myself, though I thought it often.

"After Charlie, all the time. And then when we saw Cherie, I thought that if I had a husband that forbade me to write, I'd die. Now—"

"Why do things have to change?" Alevia blurted, cutting off my confession that I was altogether confused by the prospect of being faced with a proposal. I tried my best to avoid the topic; it was the only way I enjoyed my growing feelings for John—whatever they were. Alevia looked at her hands, at the fingers that had worked tirelessly to make her one of the best pianists I'd ever heard. "I know I've asked the same question before, and I know it's silly, but I miss Mae. And I think that if I had to move away, I'd miss you and Mother and Bessie . . . and the freedom of spending as much time as I wanted with my music."

"I miss her, too." Mae had always been my voice of reason when things were overwhelming. Over the past week, I'd headed down the hall to her room twice before realizing she wasn't there.

"Mae has always wanted a family to care for. And she and Henry are both passionate about teaching. Most men still believe that music is a profession that should exclude women. And even if I found one that didn't abide such nonsense, what if I was a better performer than he? What if I was more successful? I'm afraid that sort of reality would mutilate the pride of a man. My dreams could sour a marriage, and I wouldn't forfeit my aspirations to save it." Alevia took a deep breath. "I suppose I've just been thinking a lot about the Carters and the thought that any day I could drop dead. The thought makes me want to sit down at the piano and never get up."

"You wouldn't want to spend your final day eating cucumber sandwiches and bragging about your husband?" I laughed, but Cherie's dark and harrowing portrait leapt to mind, a vision of life with the wrong person. I knew there were happy marriages—Mae and Henry's were one of them—but there was a certain type of apprehension that came with marriage when you were a woman and an artist.

"Virginia." Lost in thought, I looked up to find Tom.

"Hello, Tom," Alevia said, turning her eyes only briefly from the string quartet tuning next to the piano. Tom grinned at her and then looked back at me. He seemed all right, but I knew he had to be suffering. "I'm glad to see you're holding up. I'm so sorry about Mr. Carter." I placed a sympathetic hand on his shoulder.

"If you must know, I'm fine. Happy even," he whispered. "Not that I'd tell anyone else because I'd probably go to hell for saying it, but I hated the man. He hurt my sister." I still didn't know all of the particulars of that relationship and wanted to know for Franklin's sake, for Lydia's.

"Tom, I've been wondering. Whatever happened with—"

"Can you come with me for a moment? I want to show you something."

"I would be happy to later. Alevia and I are about to listen to the quartet." I gestured toward Alevia whose brows furrowed as the cellist turned away from the piano, letting the fallboard strike the key bed.

"Actually, it's quite all right if you need to go," she said. I was surprised at her boldness. She rarely allowed her family to leave her side unless she was playing. "I think I'll speak with that cellist about the care of an instrument as fine as a Weber." She crossed the room, the ends of the purple ribbon affixed to her black skirt fluttering as she went.

"Good," Tom said. He walked toward the alcove and I followed, glancing around for Franklin and Lydia. I supposed Frank had taken her someplace to calm down.

A swarm of embellished silk caught my eye, a grouping of ladies gathered around a very handsome dark-haired man who seemed to be enjoying the attention. He was reclining against the fireplace palming one of the carved lions along the legs, smiling as the women laughed at something he was reading.

"Hamilton Revelle." Tom tipped his head in the direction of my gaze. "Aspiring actor, skillful philanderer." He coughed. "Ladies always circle around him like ravenous sharks."

"It seems to me that he wouldn't mind being devoured."

"That's true." Tom chuckled, though his merriment seemed strained, almost nervous. "In fact his reputation has been confirmed many times, unlike John's—" He stopped midsentence, cheeks reddening, likely unsure if I'd heard the rumors.

"I've heard. And no, I don't believe it. I know he's a gentleman." Tom tipped his head and opened the door to the alcove. He collapsed onto the chair, eyes gleaming in the pink and white moonlight raining in from the stained glass.

"What is it, Tom? The suspense is killing me," I said.

"Well," he started, sinking back in the chair, "the time has finally come."

"You're writing to ask Bess to marry you, aren't you?" After all of the chatter I'd had to endure from Bess, I was elated he was going to ask.

"Of course not," he breathed, nose scrunching as though it were the most asinine question he'd ever heard.

"What do you mean by that?" I snapped. Regardless of our strained relationship, she was my sister. "I asked you a question." I stepped toward him. "What did you mean by that?" Inches from his face, my hand started to rise at my side, ready to slap him.

"That I'm going to wait until she gets back from the country to ask her?" His eyes went wide and he shrugged as if I'd gone mad.

"Oh." I backed away.

"I do love her," he continued, "in case you're wondering, and it won't be long. Heaven knows we won't be able to endure a lengthy engagement either without . . ." Tom bit his lip and looked down. I studied my hands, disgusted by the thought of Tom running his fingers over Bessie's body. He coughed. "In any case. My news is of a more professional nature." He turned to the desk, rifled through some papers and withdrew a magazine. He held it out to me—the new edition of *The Century* magazine. I stared at the drawing of a colonial streetscape of New York on the front, steeling myself to see his name printed on the page instead of my own. "I just received it in the post today. I thought you should be the first to see it." I forced a smile at him.

"Thank you for showing me. I'm so very thrilled for you." I flipped through the magazine, scanning the pages for his name.

"It's on page 158." He edged to the front of his seat. I found the page and read the title: *The Traitor in All of Us*. There was a small illustration next to it, a woman in a hoop skirt glancing over her shoulder. The drawing was a peculiar accompaniment for the topic he'd chosen. I lifted my eyes from the magazine. Tom's forehead was creased, lips pale. He was nervous for me to read his work, though I couldn't figure why. Mr. Gilder had already sung his praises.

"Did they give you a chance to review the illustrations? It seems strange that they would complement a story about Ben Franklin's wartime spying with a woman dressed in the clothing of my grandmother's time."

"Oh, no," Tom said. "I didn't write that story. I mean, I started to, but Ben Franklin's contribution to the post seemed a little dry." Leaning back in the desk chair, he looked away from me, tapping his fingers on the knobby arm. "Come to think of it, I came up with the idea after one of our conversations. The story is about unity, really, about the humanity of both the Yankees and the Confederates. I used Lincoln and his Confederate relatives to illustrate the point." I gaped at him, feeling as though the wind had been knocked from my lungs. My eyes fell to the page.

Mrs. Emilie Todd Helm was an enemy of our nation. Her soul was for the Southland, stamped with the stars and bars of the Confederacy, and her heart was no different, belonging to a man who died with the blood of Union soldiers on his hands. She was a proud Rebel, unwilling to compromise her loyalty, unwilling to surrender, but in her hour of greatest grief it was President Lincoln's White House, the home of her sister, Mary Todd Lincoln, that offered her sanctuary.

The words were mine. Blood rushed to my head, dizzying my senses. I reached a hand out to steady myself on the wall as the realization dawned on me: Tom hadn't returned my story after he encouraged me to abandon it.

"This is my writing. You stole my work." My voice was full of rage.

"No, I didn't. I came up with this idea quite on my own." Ignoring my anger, he swiveled away from me and plucked his pencil from the desktop, twirling it between his fingertips. "Stole your idea," he scoffed. Before I knew it, I'd launched myself across the room. I snatched his jaw, fingers pinching so hard into his shallow skin I could feel bone.

"Liar," I snarled. "It is my writing. Every word. You stole it because you knew it was better than yours." He shook his head to disagree, but didn't try to break free from my grasp. "You'll answer for this. You'll admit it to me and you'll confess to Mr. Gilder." He still didn't say anything. I tightened my grip on his face.

"I'll admit that it's similar to yours," he said finally through pinched lips. "But our ideas are different." I couldn't draw a full breath and felt light-headed, my vision fuzzy. Suddenly, his hand clasped the nape of my neck and pulled my face to his. "I find your anger . . . amusing," he whispered. "Accuse me of anything you wish, Virginia. Tell everyone. It won't matter, you know. No one will believe you." His breath, rank with liquor, hovered in my nostrils. I jerked away from him. He was right. I'd shared the story with him before anyone else. There was no reason for anyone to believe me. No one else had ever read it. "You're a woman . . . with no husband and no name. Why would I plagiarize *your* work?"

"You may have made it into *The Century*, but you'll never really amount to anything," I said. "Charlatans never do." Whirling on my heels, I threw the door open, making a beeline for Alevia who'd returned to the damask ottoman.

"Tell Franklin, wherever he is, that I've gone to Mae's. I'll see you there." My breath was still coming and going in short spurts and Alevia's eyes went wide. I had to get out of there. I had to come up with a plan. Tom wouldn't get away with passing my work off as his own.

"What happened?" she asked. "I'll come with you."

"Tom has . . . he's stolen my story. The article in *The Century* is mine," I sputtered. As angry as I was, I couldn't bear to rehash it, not now. I just needed to leave. "And I plan to make him answer for it."

Chapter Fifteen

The Loftin House

BRONX, NEW YORK

As furious as I'd been at Tom for stealing my idea, I hadn't mentioned it to anyone other than Alevia until my copy of the magazine arrived the following day—primarily because I wanted to believe that I'd been wrong. The idea that Tom, a man who supposedly loved my sister, would do such a thing was despicable—a desperate attempt to gain acclaim because he couldn't come up with anything good on his own. But as much as I'd hoped to be mistaken, I'd read the magazine again, and the words were mine. I'd wanted to speak to Frank about it, hoping that he could reason with Tom, but Frank had been called out of the city for work. Instead, I'd gone to Mother and Alevia. Both agreed that the story was my work, both had been appalled, but neither had been able to come up with a way to trap Tom in his lie. I hadn't intended to tell Bess right away—at least not until I'd worked out a plan myself—but Alevia had been so outraged upon reading the story that she'd immediately marched up the stairs and told Bess she would have to part ways with Tom. In a matter of moments, Bess was shouting at Alevia saying that the writing wasn't mine, that I was lying because I was jealous. The words stung, though I'd expected them, and when Bess came to tell me that she would believe Tom over me, I wasn't surprised.

My anger was consuming. I was furious that I couldn't do anything to remedy his plagiarism. Even Mae, who'd responded to my hysterical letter with a visit, hadn't been able to think of anything smart. Tom had stolen my only copy.

Mother had been the one to finally drag me from my overriding need for vengeance. She'd said that Tom's dishonesty may have worked once, but it wouldn't always. Eventually, even the most carefully crafted deceptions were exposed by the light of truth.

So instead of moping about my misfortune, I'd taken matters into my own hands and sent a copy of *The Web* directly to George Putnam with an accompanying letter detailing my admiration of him, his father, and Irving. Feeling quite brave, I also sent the story to another publisher, Arthur Scribner, as well. I knew it was a bold gesture and that women writers weren't often considered by publishing houses unless they had a connection, but I didn't care. I thought it wouldn't hurt to be assertive since my book was already in the hands of one of the country's top editors.

I wiped my forehead. It was one of those rare sweltering days in the city. Even at ten in the morning, sweat prickled my upper lip and I could feel the dampness under my arms as my hand drifted across the notepad. Bess and Mother were arguing downstairs about Bess's refusing to apologize to me—white noise on top of Alevia playing Chopin's Piano Concerto No. 2. A draft filtered in from the open window in front of me and I held the page down to read.

"To begin with, the Society was an anomaly, something I never could have imagined—artists being social." I shook my head, scratching the sentence out. My brain wasn't working today other than to obsess about whether George Putnam had received my package yet

or if Frederick Harvey was ever going to get back to me about my book. I couldn't seem to move past the world I'd built in *The Web* to start building another. I'd tried everything, even painting the Hoppers' ballroom as Franklin had suggested. It hadn't worked. The only inspiration it had given me was the urge to finish writing and get out of the room and away from the fumes as soon as possible. Even though my windows were open, the piney turpentine radiating from the paints stung my nostrils and left me dizzy.

"He might be lying." I turned to find Bess in my doorway. She looked uncharacteristically plain in a white shirtwaist and pink skirt, though her hat was quite elaborate—made of gray felt, pluming feathers, and two layers of tightly curled white-and-pink-striped ribbon lining the wide brim. I was thankful she'd at least had the decency to admit the possibility of what the rest of us knew.

"I know how difficult it must be to realize," I started gently. "I know that you love him and want to think he's a noble man, but—" Bess pressed her lips together and shook her head, cutting me off. Her eyes dipped and she scuffed her leather boot along the floor. When she finally looked up, her lids were pooling with tears and the tip of her nose was tinged pink.

"Even if he's a fraud, even if he's done something terrible to you, I can't . . . I can't let him slip through my fingers." She sniffed and straightened. My eyes narrowed at her.

"A man like that won't make you happy," I said. "Surely you don't want to risk the chance that he'll continue to do things like this."

"Perhaps you're stronger than I am. I love him, and he's my way out of this life, just as John is yours." I bit back the retort on my tongue. I had never shared her desires—the glitz, the exorbitant wealth—and certainly didn't view my relationship with John as a way to escape. I wasn't even sure I'd marry him if he asked, despite the fact that by societal standards, he was the most advantageous match I could ever hope for. "Our family is doing well now, but I'm still working so very hard. We'll never be the Vanderbilts. I'm tired. Aren't you? Don't you want the leisure you're due?" She stared at me, waiting for a response I didn't give. I didn't want to argue with her. The only opulence I dreamed about was the acknowledgment that my writing was worth publishing. "And I don't believe that he's made a habit of lying—if he has at all. He's been discouraged with his writing. Perhaps this story has given him the acclaim he needs to finally break through."

"Of course it has!" I rose to my feet, cheeks flaming. "And what of my struggle? Of my need for recognition? Are you suggesting I stand by and let Tom bask in the praise of *my* writing?" Bess's teeth clenched, the traces of her earlier softness now vanished.

"I'm suggesting that you leave him alone . . . for my happiness." She whirled on her heel and slammed my door behind her.

I stared out the window, past the fluttering linen curtains to the white clapboard homes across the street. I couldn't do anything about Bessie or Tom. Thinking of them was a waste of time.

I heard a hawk caw once and then again, watched finches fluttering to and fro between the oak trees that had graced this land long before Mott Haven existed. I inhaled the humidity and the sweet honeysuckle growing on our fence. Something moved to my left and I glanced down at the Aldridges' walk, finding Mrs. Aldridge standing on the edge of her porch, fingering the last yellow blooms of her Lady Banks rose. Even though I blamed her for Charlie and my unhappiness, I pitied her. I could tell she was lonely.

I closed my eyes, remembering last summer. Mrs. Aldridge held a picnic on the lawn for Charlie's birthday with Mother's lemonade and chicken salad sandwiches and petit fours. All of the neighbors had come and the lawn was packed with blankets. Laughter filled the August air late into the evening. I could still see Mrs. Aldridge's face in my mind as it was then, her wide dimpled smile exactly like Charlie's as he hugged her after they'd lost a game of charades to Franklin and Mother. Charlie had come over to me right after, smashing into me as he flopped down on my blanket, nearly toppling the torch behind me.

"If I'd had you on my team, Ginny, my dear," he'd said, eyes inches from mine, "I know we would've beaten your blasted brother." I'd desperately wanted to kiss him then. I could still feel it in my stomach. The memory of his lips on mine just weeks ago forced its way into my thoughts. I opened my eyes to stop the sensation and thought of John, of the way he'd reached for me after saving Lydia. I could still feel his arms around my body, the intensity of his slow kiss. I'd wanted him to keep kissing me. It hadn't only been my body calling for him in that moment, something in my heart had responded, too. The hawk cawed again, from some tree branch nearby, remained, even though everything around it had changed. The thought comforted me. I realized that like the hawk, I could learn to live, to love, in the presence of Charlie's memory, as he remained a part of me.

"Ginny! Stop daydreaming and come down!" I jolted at the sound of Frank's voice and looked down in time to see him run up the walk, hat falling back on his head. Lydia laughed behind him and straightened it. I hadn't planned on Frank arriving back home until the end of the week. I set my pencil down, nerves tumbling in my stomach. I couldn't avoid thinking of what Tom had done. I'd have to tell them, both of them. It wouldn't be welcome news, especially for Lydia—if she believed me.

"Yes, do!" Lydia echoed Franklin. I was relieved to see her in a merry mood. "We have some wonderful news to share." She winked and pulled at her black ribbon–trimmed collar as she ran behind Franklin, no doubt roasting in the heat. Thinking Frank had finally proposed, I catapulted off my window seat, smoothed my cotton shirtwaist, and barreled down the steps with Bess on my heels.

"If my younger brother gets engaged before Tom finally finds the courage to propose, I'll scream," Bessie whispered.

"Thank you for the warning. I'll be sure to cover my ears," I said. Franklin and Lydia stood in the corner of the drawing room grinning, as if they were about to burst at the seams with their secret.

"Well, what is it?" Bessie asked, as Mother appeared behind us.

"What's all the commotion about?" Mother's eyes were wide, doubtless thinking there had been another row about Tom, before she realized that Franklin and Lydia were smiling.

"Where's Alevia?" Frank asked.

"We can't say a thing until she's here," Lydia said. They looked at each other and started laughing while the rest of us stared.

"'Levia!" Bessie yelled and rolled her eyes as though she was irritated with the delay. I heard Alevia's footsteps start down the hallway and then she appeared in the doorway, wiping at a pencil smudge across her cheek.

"Here I am." She seemed annoyed, before realizing Frank and Lydia were standing awkwardly in the corner of the room smiling at us. "Oh."

"Now that you're all here," Lydia said. She held her hand out to Franklin who dug in his pinstriped vest. He pulled a letter out and handed it to her.

"It's for you, Alevia," Frank said. Alevia's forehead scrunched. She stepped forward, taking the letter from Lydia's hand. I watched her face pale as she read the return address.

"I'm not sure that I want to open this here," she said softly. I looked over her shoulder. It was from Walter Damrosch. Alevia started to walk away, to retreat to the sanctuary of her room.

"I think you might," Lydia said reassuringly, catching her arm.

Alevia didn't seem to register what was happening. It wasn't another rejection.

"Open it," I urged. Alevia tore the envelope slowly, running her finger along the edge. None of us spoke or moved as she withdrew the letter. Her eyes scanned the page, face still so pale I hovered behind her in case she fainted. Lydia squealed and clapped at my sister who continued to stare at the letter as though she were having trouble reading it.

"Did you make it in?" Mother's eyes glittered. Alevia blinked, turned to us, and nodded.

"I . . . I think so," she said. Unable to help myself, I threw my arms around her, clutching the indigo-and-gold-striped fabric across her back.

"He was absolutely enthralled with your playing," Lydia exclaimed, when we finally broke apart. "We had a family dinner right after the auditions and he couldn't stop talking about the Brahms concerto." I knew the wait had been as agonizing for Alevia as it had been for me. For the first couple of months she would run to the mailbox every day, but the last few without a reply had seemed hopeless, even though she understood that that's how it went between Symphony seasons: she wouldn't find out until she was needed.

"I can't thank you enough," Alevia said softly, beaming at Lydia. "I wouldn't have had a chance without you."

"Of course you would've. He admitted that he should've accepted you long ago. Following the Brahms piece he said that he would gladly undergo any complaints from the men because none of them could hold a candle to your playing."

"What about you?" Alevia asked. "Did you make it in?"

"Afraid not," Lydia said, shrugging. "Honestly, I don't really care."

"Frank, do we have any champagne?" Mother asked, teary-eyed. "This is cause for celebration. We have a world-class concert pianist in our midst." I squeezed Alevia's hand. I'd have to wait until later to speak with Franklin and Lydia about Tom. I couldn't spoil the joy of Alevia's news with the unpleasantness of my own.

"We do," Frank said. "But I have one more letter." He reached into his vest, pulled out an envelope, and shoved it into my hand. "Here. It's from John. He had it delivered to my office inside a letter to me. He wanted me to tell you two things before you opened it: first, that he knew it, and second, that he really wants you to think on it." I ran my thumb across the rough paper, feeling a small tear on the corner as I began to rip the seal. I wished they'd stop staring at me and start talking amongst themselves. The silent anticipation was making me nervous.

> *Dearest Virginia,*
> *I can't wait to be home and see your face. I suppose right now you're thinking that I shouldn't have got Franklin involved just to tell you that. You'd be right if that were the case, but it isn't. You're all I've thought of while I've been away, so I couldn't help but say it first. There's something I've got to ask you, and I will, though first, something more important. I received a telegram from Fred Harvey last week asking for your address. It seems that he's read* The Web *and is keen to make you an offer of publication.*

I read the sentence again and started sobbing.

"What is it?" Mother asked, but I couldn't speak. Someone liked my book enough to publish it. I ran my fingers over the sentence, barely able to read through the moisture pooling in my eyes.

Tom's efforts hadn't ruined my chances. Alevia started toward me, but I stopped her, needing to read the rest before I shared the news.

> *I expect he'll be in touch in the next few days if he hasn't already, but I wanted to tell you first if I could, because you have no idea the joy I felt when he told me. It was better than when it happened to me, my darling. In that moment I realized something I think I've known since I saw you that night at the opera—that I love you and I can't live without you. You're in my mind all of the time and this time away from you has been a terrible torture. To touch you and kiss your lips again . . .*

My face burned beneath the tears.

> *I wanted to wait until I got back to do this properly, but I can't. Every moment that this is left unsaid makes my heart ache. I'm writing you now in part because I know you'll need time to think this through. I want to marry you. I want you to be my wife. You make me the happiest man in the world and I love you entirely.*

I'd stopped breathing. My heart began to soar, but my mind weighed it down. I couldn't tell him the same, that I loved him entirely. I didn't know. Though my feelings were deepening, my heart wasn't sure. Charlie's face flashed in my mind as though my soul thought to ask—what of him? And yet, despite his absence, despite the fact that I couldn't choose him, considering John's proposal felt like I was betraying him.

Alevia's hand found my elbow, and at once I recalled her words at the last Society meeting, *"What if I was a better performer than* he? What if I was more successful? I'm afraid that that sort of reality would mutilate the pride of a man. My dreams could sour a marriage, and I wouldn't forfeit my aspirations to save it." I wouldn't either. Cherie's agony flashed in my mind, the way Edith spoke about her marriage as though it was a hindrance to her writing. John's question and my indecision had tainted the news of my publication. Franklin was staring at me; I could feel his eyes on my face and knew then that he knew, that he wanted me to marry John. I needed to be alone. I forced myself to read the rest of the letter.

> I'll be back in two weeks and will ask you properly then. Please consider it, Virginia. We're kindred spirits you and I.
>
> > All my love,
> > John.

I folded the paper slowly, wishing he would have waited. Everyone was looking at me. I couldn't stand their hopeful stares. I didn't want to talk to anyone. I looked at Franklin. His eyebrows were lifted in question, a wide, goofy grin plastered on his face, no doubt expecting me to rejoice at the news of my publication and the prospect of a husband. Instead, I forced my eyes to the floor so I wouldn't meet anyone's gaze, and started to walk wordlessly out of the room. I passed Bessie and Alevia without issue, but Mother caught me by the wrist.

"What does it say?" she whispered, and I gently pulled my arm from her grip.

"My book will be published," I said matter-of-factly, "and John wants to marry me." I turned from her and walked into the quiet sanctuary of the hallway, relieved to be alone.

Chapter Sixteen

No, that's not what I meant. It's rare, but not unheard of." Frederick Harvey's wire-framed glasses, the same kind my father had worn, had fallen to the tip of his nose. He stared at me over the top of them, thick gray mustache shifting up and down as he chewed. "You *are* on the young side, but I'm smart enough to know that by your age most people have figured out what it is they want to do with their lives," he continued. Shrugging at my silence, Harvey cut another sliver off of his Chicken a La Keene—a Delmonico's specialty. My mouth was dry but I forced a bleak smile. It was good that he assumed I had my life together. In reality, outside of writing, I was a disaster.

"I didn't mean to offend you. If I did, I apologize," he said. I forced myself back to the conversation, realizing I'd been staring over his shoulder at a stone pillar behind him. He'd just finished telling me that he only had two other authors my age—John and a girl who'd claimed to be a relative of Henry Wadsworth Longfellow, but who later admitted she wasn't. In response, I asked if he'd been reluctant to take me on because of it, if he was worried that I wouldn't produce to the quality of his older clients.

"You didn't offend me at all," I said politely. I caught a glimpse of my dress in the mirror beside me, lifting a hand to the gold beading at my bodice. Bess had talked me into ordering the costume for the fall season, saying that the mulberry satin cowl neck drew the eye to my face.

I cut a bite of English muffin topped with Lobster Newburg, inhaling the buttery steam as I lifted it to my mouth. "I suppose I only wanted you to know that I'm serious about my career, Mr. Harvey, and I promise that if you take a chance on me, I'll be your hardest-working author." He laughed, belly jiggling under the blue pinstriped suit hugging his stomach.

"That was never a concern. I knew that before I met you," he mumbled between bites. "Your reputation precedes you." I was slightly annoyed that he already knew so much about me from John. I wanted the opportunity to prove my character on my own. Then again, I also knew that John's reference and the influence of him and his artists' society were the exact reasons I was sitting across from one of the most well-respected editors in the world in the finest restaurant in Manhattan.

"Is that a good thing?" I grinned, and Harvey nodded.

"Quite. Everything, in fact, that Mr. Hopper has said about you has been glowing and I have to say, upon meeting you, that I agree with him." He lifted his napkin from his lap to dab at his mouth.

"Thank you. I'm fond of him as well." Harvey's eyes lifted at that and he smiled at me. I wondered how many people John had told about his proposing. Probably as many as he'd come across since he decided to do it, I thought, knowing he couldn't contain himself when he was excited. It was one of the things I loved about him, but in this case, I wished he would've kept his proposal to himself. Harvey cleared his throat.

"Well, before we get into personal matters, I suppose I should tell you the specifics of the deal I'm offering. As I said, I want your book and because I do, I'm willing to give you eight hundred dollars for the rights to publish it. If it's a hit and sales go over eight hundred, we'll be talking royalties. You'd get ten cents for each copy sold." I coughed, nearly choking on a bite of English muffin. Eight hundred dollars was more than I earned in a year writing for the *Review*. Harvey grabbed my water glass and thrust it toward me. I swallowed a few sips, and set it down. My eyes were still watering from my coughing fit and I wiped tears.

"Are you all right?" he asked.

"Yes . . . well, I suppose I will be once I recover from shock."

"There is one condition though, and I hope you'll agree to it." Harvey shifted in his chair and I braced myself, trying not to breathe so that the tickling sensation shooting down my throat wouldn't make me cough again. "You're going to have to revise it. She can't accept Carlisle so soon after he proposes to Sarah, the other girl. It makes her seem weak and she's not. They can be friends their whole lives, but she cannot concede to him so quickly after he broke her heart. It's not natural and it won't make her likable to the reader." I blinked at him, feeling the euphoria of his offer disappear. I didn't know if I could change that plot point. Theoretically, I knew that I could, but I wasn't sure if I could bear it. The last draft had been poured straight from my heart.

"Would it seem weak if she took him back much later in life? If she put him off for years and then finally in her older age accepted him? It doesn't seem right that he'd have to live in misery if he's proven that he loves her." A knotty sensation had developed in my throat and I tried to swallow it away. I stared over his shoulder beyond the ornate fringed curtains out the window, to the procession of top hats and deep jewel-toned satin dresses promenading along South William Street. Harvey grunted, eyes squinting in consideration, and then he looked at me through his glasses.

"I suppose that would be all right. Just give it a go and I'll let you know my thoughts after I see the revision." The tension in my neck gave, and I relaxed against the back of the wooden chair.

"All right," I said. The thought that I was agreeing to publication with Henry Holt instead of G. P. Putnam's Sons, my dream, flitted across my mind, but I forced it away. The notion that I would decline a chance at publication with a reputable publisher in hopes that George Putnam—a man I only *thought* would be perfect for my career, but had never met—would offer me a deal was ludicrous.

"So, you're happy with my proposal?" he asked. I held out my hand in answer and he shook it.

"I'm so glad," he said, exhaling loudly as though there was a chance I'd say no. Even if he told me to destroy my manuscript and start over, I would have accepted knowing I'd eventually find a way to see through my personal reservations to his suggestions. He lifted his hand to the waiter and said something about champagne, but I barely heard him. I'd just accepted an offer from a publisher who loved my book, a publisher who was going to pay me eight hundred dollars to publish it.

When we'd first been seated, Harvey had told me that *The Web* stuck with him because of its true-to-life honesty and its vivid characters. For that reason, he thought people would go mad for it—for that and the romantic tension that I suppose would come through even more now that Eleanor, my main character, wouldn't accept Carlisle as early on as I'd written it, or at all. Like all successful businessmen confident in their decisions, he said that he knew everyone would be dying to get their hands on it and that he had no doubt it would grace the coffee tables of all of the fine homes in America from the White House to the mansions along Fifth Avenue. That vision had been in my wildest dreams, but now I could hear the society women I knew whispering about it at the dinner table and my peers back in Mott Haven wondering who the characters really were.

"Miss Loftin?" Harvey was staring at me as though I'd lost my mind. I had, but he should be used to erratic behavior. He brought dreams to life, after all.

"I'm sorry. What did you say? I'm so excited I'm afraid I drifted off."

"Ah, the sign of a true artist." He grinned. "I was just asking you if you'd heard from Mr. Hopper since he's been away? If he's written you?" Harvey leaned back against his chair, fiddling with the napkin in his lap. My excitement disappeared, replaced by annoyance. The question was inappropriate. I was his business client and didn't owe him a conversation about my personal life. John may as well have been here with me throughout the whole meal. I twisted my hands in my lap, cotton napkin threading through my fingers. I didn't know what to say. I couldn't tell him that I had because then he would ask me what it said and I certainly wasn't prepared to talk to him about the proposal—especially since my answer was still so unclear.

"I'm afraid I haven't." My voice sounded far away, and meek.

"Oh. Well, good." I was taken aback by his response, thinking he'd been hinting at John's proposal. "I didn't want him to ruin the surprise. I know how taken he is with you so I was afraid he'd tell you I was interested before I had a chance to do so myself. I've told him before that being able to write an acceptance letter to an author whose work I love is truly my greatest joy, so I'm glad he decided to humor me in that regard."

"I was astonished, honestly," I said, neither conceding to his assumptions nor giving John away. The waiter returned with two flutes of champagne. Mr. Harvey held his up in invitation and I did the same.

"To the start of a profitable friendship," he said. Our glasses clinked, a bright bell-like tone amid the hum of voices and the clatter of pots and pans in the kitchen far away. I took a sip, feeling the bubbles slide down my throat.

"One more thing." Harvey held up his hand and downed the rest of the champagne in a gulp. "You and Mr. Hopper. I know you're . . . involved." My cheeks began to burn and he noticed, waving his hand at me. "No need to be embarrassed. I'm simply asking if you would be able to separate the personal from professional if . . . if something were to happen, either to further your relationship or end it." I nodded, though he had just articulated part of my reluctance in accepting John.

"Of course." I forced the words from my mouth, truly not sure. Even if John had the capability to put rejection behind him if I turned him down, I didn't know if I could. The prospect of facing him, knowing I'd hurt him, would mutilate me. But I hadn't made a decision yet, and even if I said yes, I didn't know if we'd continue to be a perfect team professionally. The countless possibilities of how marriage could change our dynamic whirled in my head. I wanted to believe that he would encourage me and I him for the rest of our lives, but it wasn't so simple.

"I'm sorry that I had to bring it up, Miss Loftin. I know it isn't pleasant to speak of such things, especially endings, but I'm glad for your honest response. I encourage my authors to work together, to read each other's work, and as you've already developed a working relationship with Mr. Hopper, one that I think has profited you both quite well, I would hate to see it go by the wayside."

"I agree," I said mechanically. My heart once again felt as though it had been torn nearly in two, seeming only to be held together by a tiny shred of hope that I'd get hold of myself and choose the path society and my family would have me choose: John.

I'd headed for the station, toward the train that would carry me across the Harlem River home, but turned back at the corner and instead started to Mae's. I walked thirty-three blocks barely aware of how long I'd been walking or of anything going on around me. As monumental as the day had been, my mind always tended to focus on the unsettled, and so I'd said goodbye to Frederick Harvey with my conflicting emotions toward marrying John still at the forefront of my thoughts. I hadn't seen Mae in nearly two weeks—she and Mr. Trent had begged off our weekly Sunday dinner to attend a birthday celebration at the orphanage—and needed to talk to her. I craved her level head and her clarity.

The streets were crowded today. Scruffy panhandlers gathered in clusters against the buildings, pleas rising as the next group of immaculately dressed businessmen in fitted suits hustled past. I wove through the masses, muttering a continuous strain of "excuse me." It was a beautiful day, the leftover summer humidity broken in steady intervals by the relief of an early fall breeze. Even so, I was sweating badly. Trails of moisture ran from my hairline down my neck and I wiped them away with the back of my hand, lifting my hat from my head. Crossing the street without looking, I followed the path of a bright purple umbrella—the only color I'd seen in blocks—heard a horse whinny, and jumped out of the way as a carriage thundered past. I coughed, noticing everyone around me was doing the same, most burying their nose in the crook of their arm as they walked to ignore the city's stench. I hurried toward the riverfront.

Two streets over, the walks were unoccupied and clear. I glanced at the East River and then back at the last of the purple clematis blooms creeping across the Trents' white picket fence on the corner ahead. I snaked through the grass between their enormous brick home and a limestone monstrosity next door. Mae and Henry's windows were open, sunshine baking the little white guesthouse. I knocked. Mae huffed followed by a cheery, "Coming!" She flung the door open, and laughed.

"Thank god. I thought you were Lucille. She seems to pop by every few hours and stays until the next meal. She has a cook. I don't know why she insists on taking every meal with us." Lucille was Henry's mother, an ex-socialite busybody who'd rather talk to a brick wall than keep silent. Mae couldn't wait to move away from her.

"She likes you," I said, grinning.

"I'm glad. Truly I am, but I wish she'd find someone else to visit." I followed Mae into the house, past the study to the tiny dining room in the back. Her third-grade teaching books were stacked on one end of the table and two were open.

"Sorry to call so suddenly. I didn't tell you I was coming because I'd planned to have lunch with Mr. Harvey and go back home, but . . ." Mae whirled on me, her plain gray skirt wrapping around the legs of a dining chair.

"You had lunch with Frederick Harvey? What did he say? Is there any way he can help you with Tom or Mr. Gilder? You didn't write to tell me!" Mae's lips pursed and I knew then that I'd left her out—accidentally, of course, but I had. It was easy to remember to tell the others, but Mae wasn't home, and at times I simply forgot to write. "And if I ever hear that you've been in Manhattan and didn't stop by I swear I'll beat you senseless." She glared at me and sat down at the table.

"No. He can't," I said, answering her last question. "Mr. Harvey deals in books, not magazines, and the story in *The Century* wouldn't matter to his business with me anyway. I'm afraid nothing can be done about Tom, as much as it horrifies me that he'll get away with passing my work off as his own." I was still furious at Tom, but the news of my deal with Henry Holt dulled it a bit. I looked up to find Mae still glaring at me. I hadn't explained why I hadn't told her of my news. "The meeting was a bit last minute," I said, sitting across from her. "Mr. Harvey only sent a letter a few days ago and I figured you and Henry would be at school or at the orphanage."

"If you thought that then why did you come calling?" Mae's cheeks flushed and her eyes were hard. She was clearly upset about something else.

"Because I needed you. I took a chance." The words came out in a whisper, all of the emotions of the past hour flooding back in the seconds it took to utter them, and Mae's face softened.

"Did Mr. Harvey . . . did he reject it?"

"No. He asked that I revise it, but he loved it. He's giving me eight hundred up front and ten cents per copy if sales go over that amount." Mae gasped.

"Eight *hundred*? That's more than Henry and I will make in a year at our jobs." I squinted at her, unsure if I'd heard right.

"Jobs?"

"Oh. We found out several days ago that we'll both be employed by Grammar School Eighty-Five, in the twenty-third ward, starting in August. Miss Culpepper at the orphanage gave us a very complimentary reference, as did Mrs. Greenwood and—" Mae's jaw set and her face flushed again, no doubt realizing she'd kept something from me as well. "I'm sorry. I suppose we both forget to write sometimes." She looked down and I knew I'd been right. Mae wasn't acting like herself.

"Are you all right?" I leaned across the table to grab her hand and she nodded, before shaking her head. Tears blurred her eyes and she blinked them away.

"No. I'm not," she sniffed. "I can't stand it here, but Henry insists that we stay. I prayed we would find jobs in the country because I knew if we found positions here, we would have to stay in this blasted shed, living behind his parents." The last words came out in a hiss and she wiped her eyes. I'd had no idea that she'd been so unhappy.

"Have you told him?"

"Of course," she said, "but he thinks it's best for us to stay. I know it's because of her . . . his . . . his wife that he's scared to move away." Mae closed her eyes and took a deep breath. "You know that she died in the country. I think our wedding was the first time he'd been out there since."

"And he's scared you'll die, too?" Mae's shoulders lifted in a lackluster shrug.

"Either that or it would remind him of her, I suppose." Anger on my sister's behalf ran through me like a flame and I stood from my chair, hands clenched at my sides.

"If that's the case, he's being ridiculous. She's dead," I said, fully aware of how insensitive I sounded. The knowledge that Mae had to sacrifice even an ounce of her happiness for the sake of Henry's filled me with rage. I'd thought their relationship near perfect, but clearly didn't know the full picture. "I heard him that day, the day that he told you. He said he hadn't loved her the way he loves you. Was he lying?" I half-hoped Henry was home to hear me shouting.

"It's okay, Gin. Sit down. No, he wasn't lying," she said, a slight smile drifting across her lips at my fury. "He loves me. Only me. I'm the only one he ever has and I know that. It's just that he feels guilty, I think, that he didn't love her the same way and she died." I felt the anger drain. Mae sighed. "I think he thinks that if we stay right here where we met, if we never change, I'll be with him always. Instead of being excited about our life together, he's petrified that I'll get pregnant while I'm praying that I will." I didn't know what to say, so I stayed quiet. "I'm fine living in the city. Actually, I never really cared to go anywhere else. But I can't stay here, living behind his parents." I knew she was telling the truth. Mae had never wanted to travel. Adventure had really only appealed to Franklin and me, but as I sat listening to her new worries, I realized that this life was much different from her life in Mott Haven. She'd gained Henry, but she'd forfeited the everyday company of our family, and the excitement to start her own was lost in Henry's fear. The realization struck me. Every marriage required surrendering something. The only way a union would be a truly happy one was if love for your spouse eclipsed all other devotions.

"You came to talk to me about something and I've burdened you with my problems." Mae closed the books on the table and looked at me. "Enough about me. Tell me about you."

"It's nothing," I said, unable to have an unbiased conversation about my possible marriage when she clearly had worries of her own. "I only missed you and wanted to say hello."

"I don't believe you." Mae tapped her fingers on the table, puffing air into one cheek and then the other as she thought. "Let's see, you went to see Mr. Harvey who knows . . . have you given John an answer?" She held my gaze. I knew she could see my answer without my saying it, but I shook my head anyway.

"No. That's why I needed to talk to you. I can't stop worrying and thinking about it. I don't know what to do."

"Yes you do," she said. I withered with the implication of her words. At times, the answer was so clear that I knew I could either accept or reject him right then—and that was the problem. It was never the same answer from day to day or even hour to hour. I knew that would be Mae's point, that my reply should be immediate and constant if it was right, but even though I knew it had been that way for her and Henry, I wasn't sure it always had to be.

"How would I know, Mae? I'm so confused that at times I feel like my brain is about to explode with the strain of trying to make sense of what I want. I care for him, deeply. At times I think that it's love, but I don't know for certain. It was so different with Charlie, so gradual and so clear. John and I . . . it's happened so quickly. He's my friend. He encourages me. We make sense." I knew my words were jumbled, but the thought of telling John no, of breaking his heart distressed me to no end. "How could I refuse him?"

"You can't take him if your answer isn't wholeheartedly yes. It's not fair," she said softly, but bluntly, and my heart dropped.

"It is sometimes," I protested. "I told you before that—"

"You don't love him. Not enough or you wouldn't question it. And I know you, Gin. You're so worried that marriage will prevent you from doing something extraordinary with your life that you won't allow yourself to go through with it. The only man you would've taken a gamble on was Charlie, because when you love someone like that, you know you'll be happy even if none of your plans work out." Mae sighed and squeezed my hand. "But if you marry John and something happens . . . if your next book doesn't sell or you find yourself too busy with family life to write as much as you want, you'll resent him because a love as deep and powerful as the love you had for Charlie won't be there to remind you why you married John in the first place."

Mae didn't fully understand. My indecision wasn't only about my muddled feelings. She was right: I'd loved Charlie, a part of me always would, but I hadn't questioned marriage to Charlie because I knew my writing would always be a necessity, a living that couldn't be sacrificed. If I married John, I would want for nothing. I'd write for self-fulfillment alone, a luxury that could be buried under other commitments when life became too busy. Even though I knew John would loathe the loss of his art as much as I would, I couldn't risk a life of regret and bitterness.

"I don't know if I'll be able to tell him no. He'll hate me." Something in the back of my mind kept urging me to marry John, to make him happy and to save both of us the heartache. "Why did he have to ask me? Why couldn't we just go on like we were? We were happy." I slapped my hand on the knotted oak table.

"You can tell him the truth. He might be hurt, but he won't hate you," Mae said, ignoring my emotional second statement. My mind flitted to my brother, and I took a sharp breath.

"But what about Franklin? What will I tell him?" My brother had been adamant about the fact that John and I were perfect for each other and that I was brainless and naïve if I thought otherwise.

"What do you mean?" Mae's eyebrows scrunched. "I know John is his best friend, but he can't expect his sister to marry someone just because he wants her to."

"After the proposal, I couldn't even look at anyone. I was so flustered that I went up to my room to think and Franklin followed me. I could tell he was disappointed that I wasn't excited. He knows my concerns about marriage well enough." Mae rolled her eyes.

"I don't know why he's trying to push you into this," she snapped. "You won't marry John. Do you understand me? You won't. Every time you mention it, I think of Cherie's portrait. She talked herself into marriage. You won't do the same. Henry and I have our problems, Ginny, everyone does, but I never questioned marrying him. That's the difference." Mae stood from the table, pushed the chair in with a screech, and disappeared into the kitchen. She wouldn't allow me to marry John and a strange mix of comfort and unease drifted over me at that thought.

Chapter Seventeen

Fifth Avenue
NEW YORK, NEW YORK

It was only early September, but the leaves were beginning to change. In the late-afternoon light you could see tinges of red and orange around the green veins. I tried to focus on the colors as I walked along Fifth Avenue instead of dwelling on what I was about to do. I tipped my head at a young girl pushing a pram and tilted my head back up toward the branches. John was home. Franklin had mentioned that he'd returned yesterday, just in time for tonight's Society meeting, and I knew right then that I'd have to go see him. It was either face him now or avoid him until he tracked me down. The latter wasn't fair, but I couldn't wait to talk to him at the Society meeting either. I hadn't told anyone I was going to see him. Franklin would've tried to reason with me, Bess would've laughed at my stupidity, and Mother and Alevia would've wanted to talk about it to death.

I spotted the brick turrets on the next corner and my heart began to race. One of the Hoppers' Irish maids was hunched over sweeping the front stairs and each swish of her broom seemed to leave me more light-headed.

"Can I help you, miss?" The maid spun around at the sound of my feet on the walk and I swallowed hard.

"Yes. I'm here to call on Mr. John Hopper," I said.

"Oh, well, come in. I'll go fetch him. What's your name?" She eyed my burgundy morning dress, doubtless wondering why I hadn't changed, and I pinched the wool at my side in reflex.

"Miss Virginia Loftin. We're very well acquainted, in fact . . ." I started to say nearly engaged, but stopped myself, stunned by that instinct. "So there's no need to make a formal introduction of my being here. Do you know where he is?"

"I suppose he's in the study, though I really do think I should—"

"Thank you," I said, opening the door and throwing myself inside before she had a chance to insist on making my presence known first. I paused at the entrance to the vacant drawing room. My eyes drifted from the cherub mural to the chandelier, down to the Weber piano, and across to one of the twin etched mahogany fireplaces. This room, the relationships I'd formed at the Society, had changed my life over the past year. The thought that I'd never see this room again was heartbreaking. If I changed my mind and accepted him, I could keep the Society. I could live in this house that had become such a part of me with a man I loved. The notion passed through my mind as quickly as a lightning bolt, warming me through, but shocking me at the same time. I'd never allowed myself to truly visualize what life with John would be like without trepidation eclipsing all else.

"Are you all right, Miss Loftin?" A familiar, crackly voice sounded behind me and a wrinkled hand touched my arm.

"Doctor Hopper. Yes, I'm fine." I smiled, though my palm pressed instantly to my chest as though it would slow my startled heart. "I was just . . . trying to figure how all of those people fit in there each month," I said stupidly. The room was huge.

"It's quite a large room," he said, lips curling up. The hallway was so dim that I could mainly see the gleam of his glasses.

"Yes, I know. But so many people come and—"

"Are you looking for John?" Doctor Hopper interrupted me and I saw his grin grow wider at the mention of his son.

"I am. I understand he's in his study?" Hopper nodded.

"Has been for hours. Writing, I think. He'll be thrilled to see you. You're all he's talked about from the time we left until the time we got back."

"I'll go find him then," I whispered. By the time I got to the study door, I was shaking with nerves. My hand hovered over the doorknob and I nearly turned around and went home, but steeled myself and opened it. John's eyes met mine. He was sitting at his desk, feet propped lazily on top of it, and he slowly lowered them and stood. I didn't look away, but held his gaze as I walked toward him. Neither of us said anything, but his lips transformed into a hesitant smile as he reached for me. He pulled me close and I let him, wrapping my arms around him in turn, reveling in the comforting weight of his body pressed to mine, knowing I'd never feel it again.

He took my face in his hands and kissed me, tasting like his scotch, vanilla and caramel. I wanted him more than I ever had before. I could feel it swimming in my stomach and couldn't tell if it was simply my knowledge that I would leave him or that in the course of a few minutes I'd changed my mind. His teeth bit down on my bottom lip. He was being tender, but I could feel his desire, ferocious and wanting, in the grip of his hands in my hair. He started walking forward, lips and arms still locked on mine, and I stumbled backward, tripping and falling onto the edge of the leather couch. Undaunted, he kept kissing me, burying his face in my neck and lowering his lips to my shoulders. I arched up as his fingers found the ivory silk bow and pushed the fabric down. John's hands held my waist as his mouth dropped down my chest. I closed my eyes, fingers gripped hard to the back of his head as his lips trailed from my breasts to my stomach. I reached under his jacket to lift his linen shirt, and he looked down at me, eyes full of longing, and leaned down to kiss me. Skin to skin, I could feel the warmth of his body, and thought that maybe I'd been wrong to question my feelings for him. Though it felt different from how it had with Charlie, it felt consuming and true, like love all the same. John's mouth broke from mine and he lifted his neck to look at me, smoothing the hair from my face.

"I love you," he whispered. "And I want you so badly, but I can't. Not here, not now." He kissed my collarbone and pulled the burgundy wool back over my chest. My heart felt as though it had stopped beating, afraid of what he would say next. John smiled, lifted off of me, and knelt down beside the couch. Finding my hand, he clutched my fingers in his, and I sat up. "Ginny, you know I love you and you know I want you to be my wife. We're the same, you and I. We'll push each other; we'll fight for each other's dreams. Please . . ." He stopped midsentence. I could feel his nerves, the wild vibration of his heart, and felt my own pick up. "Will you . . . will you marry me?" The tears I'd been holding back suddenly began to fall.

"I love you, but I can't." The last bit, the words I'd rehearsed, sounded foreign and wrong preceded by sentiments I hadn't planned. He jolted away from me, eyes wide. He turned toward the wall, his head bowed. I began to sob, but didn't retract my words. There were other things to consider besides the answer my heart wanted. I'd made up my mind.

"You love me, and you'd have me right there on that couch, but you won't marry me?" John spun toward me, jaw gripped in hurt. I didn't know what to say; I didn't have an answer. I covered my eyes, trying to hide from his face. "Answer me . . . please," he said softly. I heard his footsteps, slow and steady, start toward me. "Ginny, I know I'm not him. I'm not so naïve to think that you love me like Charlie." I cried harder. John's words slayed me. I couldn't stand that he thought my answer was based on the notion that I didn't love him as much as I loved—or had loved—Charlie.

I dropped my hands from my face and glanced at him standing above me, looking miserable. "John, you have to know it's not that." My voice was a series of screeches and whispers. "I'm only—" I started to explain myself, to tell him my fears, but he cut me off.

"It is. If you loved me like that you wouldn't hesitate." John sat down in an oversized chair next to the couch. "I suppose I should tell you that I went to see Rachel last night." He stared down at his hands. I felt a jolt of jealousy at this declaration, making me wonder if I was torturing myself by saying no. He didn't elaborate, so I cleared my throat and asked.

"Why?"

John shrugged. "I don't know, really. Only that you're all I've thought of for months and I suppose I needed to know if she'd lost her effect on me. It wouldn't be fair to offer myself to you if she hadn't." I watched his lips move as he spoke, lips that had, just minutes ago, been on my mouth, my skin. "Not that it matters now, but I felt nothing when I saw her. Charlie wasn't home so I saw her alone in their drawing room, but when she walked in all I wanted to do was turn around and come home to you." He dropped down in front of me. His hand grasped mine, fingers wrapping hard around my palm. "Ginny, if you can't be with me, tell me why. That way, I'll at least be able to confront the heartache instead of wondering."

"I'm afraid," I said, reaching to wipe a lingering tear from his cheek. "John . . . I'm so sorry." He raised himself up and hugged me. I clung to him, letting my tears soak into his tweed jacket as he held me.

"It's all right," he whispered. I sniffed and stopped crying. He pulled away and sat down beside me.

"I'm worried that marriage will change me . . . that it would change us. We're so good together just as we are." He grinned at me, the first time since I'd walked through the door, leaned in, and kissed my cheek. "What if our shared life consumes us to the point that we become too busy to write? What if one of us is more successful? We could end up resenting each other, John. We could lose everything we love—our writing, each other."

"I promise we wouldn't change. Even if the whole world tempted us to forget why we married in the first place, I wouldn't let it happen. I promise you, Ginny. I wouldn't let us end up miserable. We have everything." I looked away from him. The answer wasn't clear. My mind held true to my response, but my heart begged me to change my mind. I could be making a horrible, horrible mistake. He took me in his arms again and I pressed my head against his chest as his fingers wove through the upswept hair at my nape.

"If your life doesn't work out as you planned it . . . professionally, I mean," I whispered, remembering Mae's words. "If you never publish another book and you're left with just me, would you be happy?"

"Yes," he said immediately and goose bumps rose along my arms. "But my dreams are important to me, as are yours. I think we can make them happen together. I wouldn't have asked you to spend your life with me if I thought it would stop you from doing what you love the most." His lips met the top of my head and lingered there. "I want to marry you because I love you and I want to be with you always, not because I want to control you or have you spend your life organizing luncheons."

I laughed a little at the thought. "Thank goodness," I said. "John, I do love you." Something in my soul lightened with the reiteration of those words, and the strain in my chest burst at last. Perhaps I'd questioned my feelings for so long that reason had eclipsed my true affection. I tilted my head to meet his eyes.

"I know you do." He leaned down and kissed me. I closed my eyes. I could feel the melancholy in the stilted movement of his lips, in the way he pressed down on my mouth. He pulled away from me, but I reached up, holding his head against mine.

"I mean it. I love you. So I'm not saying no," I said against his lips. "But could you give me a little more time to think about how it would all work?" John smiled and pecked my mouth.

"Of course," he said. "But, god, Virginia, how you break my heart."

$\mathcal{H}$is words kept ringing through my head as I lay wide awake staring at the ceiling hours later. We'd talked about other things after—about my deal with Frederick Harvey, about what we'd been doing since we'd seen each other last, and of Tom's plagiarism. A copy of *The Century* had been among a pile of mail on John's desk, and he'd read the story immediately. He recognized my writing from the first line, his face burning with rage. John vowed to expel Tom from the Society and to speak with Mr. Gilder at an International Copyright League luncheon the following day.

Even though the conversation had shifted away from his proposal, I couldn't forget what he'd said to me or how the threat of his heartache had affected me. I shifted against my pillow and buried my face, hoping to force sleep. It was nearing early morning. The Society meeting would be almost wrapped up and everyone, possibly John included, would be retiring. The thought of him made my chest clench and I flipped back over on my back to stare out the window at the moon. As much as I'd thought myself confused for so long, I'd realized, wrapped in his arms, that it was a lot simpler than I'd made it to be. I'd been so worried about misreading my heart and about the implications of my career if I married John, that I'd been blinded. I'd only needed to feel his presence and to speak to him, to hear his adamant vow that my art would never be forfeited. I'd been right to hope for both all along; perhaps with John it was possible to marry and sustain my writing. Something in his words or his touch had allowed clarity. He'd been right about us. We had everything in common; furthermore, we were equals. We would only sharpen each other. More than anything, I wished I would have accepted him right then, instead of postponing. But I'd wanted to collect my thoughts first, to make sure my decision wasn't based solely on the flood of emotions I'd felt in his presence.

No one knew we'd talked, though I wondered if John had talked to Frank about it tonight. I'd arrived home in the early evening, in time to have Bessie plop an understated hat on my head, decorated only by a tiny praying mantis on the brim, and ask me what I thought. She hadn't actually cared. What she'd really been after was my attention to tell me that she knew Tom was going to propose before a showing of the play *The Masked Ball* tomorrow evening. I knew she was waiting for a reaction, for my disapproval, but I gave none. As much as I wanted to tell her that John believed me about Tom, that he was planning to dismiss him from the Society and speak to Mr. Gilder, I held my tongue. None of it would matter. Bess would accept Tom regardless. I hoped she'd be happy.

I tucked the thin cotton sheet under my chin and felt blindly across my nightstand for *The Century*. I hadn't read it. I couldn't bear to when it had first arrived, but now as I sat wide awake in bed with the knowledge of my deal and John's promise to remedy Tom's wrong, I flipped it open.

I leaned into the moonlight, landing on a story about Andrew Jackson's resolution following the Battle of New Orleans. I scanned it, rather bored by its dry tone. The next page displayed the article's companion illustration—a gold pen and ink sketch of a two-sided coin. I recognized it immediately as Charlie's work. Jackson's face was contoured perfectly on one side, the detail on his uniform vivid and precise. I smiled, running my hand over Charlie's scrawled signature before closing the magazine. His work had finally been noticed by an editor. My happiness for him surprised me, making me realize that as much as he'd hurt me in the past, I had been able to move on with time and John's love. I wished him the best. I hoped he was finally happy, as I hoped to shortly be.

I sunk back against the pillows and my mind wandered back to John. I'd missed Alevia and Franklin's departure for the Hoppers' as I'd planned, but wished, after the house was emptied and I found myself alone with Mother and my thoughts, that I could've talked to Frank for a moment, if only to tell him to remind John to wait for me.

Instead of the chaos of the Society meeting, I'd enjoyed a delicious dinner of chicken potpie in front of a roaring fire with Mother. She'd asked me once about John and when I told her that I hadn't decided, she let the subject drop. I'd appreciated the gesture. I could tell from her eyes that she'd wanted to ask more— she missed Mae's unguarded confidences—but held back. Instead, we'd laughed and talked for hours about Franklin and Lydia and Bessie and Tom, wondering what Bessie would do if it was Franklin who proposed instead.

Yawning, I closed my eyes again as I recalled Mother's laughter, realizing something I hadn't thought of before—she was alone.

I wondered how many times she'd sat by the fire by herself after Father's death. It had to be lonely when all of us were out. I couldn't help thinking of the contrast between how her life must be now and how happy it had been with Father. I could still picture them together if I concentrated, his large calloused hand engulfing her small one as they stayed up talking late at night, and thought, quite suddenly, that that's all John was after: a hand to hold in the small hours, someone to laugh with at the end of a long day. I wanted to be that person.

Chapter Eighteen

The Loftin House

BRONX, NEW YORK

Someone screamed, a bloodcurdling yell that blasted straight through my bones. I jerked upright in bed wondering if I'd dreamed the scream, but I heard it again followed by the sound of a man sobbing. I hurled out of bed, crossed to my armoire, threw on the first dress I found, and ran down the stairs.

"What in the world is going on?" I heard Mother say as I sprinted down the hallway. The wood was cool under my feet and I could smell traces of wood smoke from our fire last night. I waited for a reply to Mother's question but didn't hear one, only hiccups coming from the front parlor. Tom's bow tie hung unbound at his neck, face red with hysteria as he looked down at Bess crouched on the floor in front of him. Neither could speak, that much I knew. Bessie's face was buried in her tiered lace nightgown, arms across her knees, shoulders shaking wildly. I was surprised that she was home in the first place. I thought she would've been off to a fitting in the city by now. I could feel Mother's concerned eyes on my face, but couldn't look at her. Suddenly, Tom lifted his hands to his mouth and began to sob again. Unease churned through me. Mother crouched next to Bessie and rocked her shoulders gently.

"What? What do you want?" she said, half-sobbing and then folded herself back into a ball on the floor.

"Tom," I said, forcing my voice to work. "What's happened?" He took a heaving breath, wiped a hand across his nose and mouth, and looked at me. His eyes bore into mine, heavy with such a deep sadness and anger that it made the hair along my arms bristle.

"My . . . my . . ." He started sobbing again, unable to get the words out. I reached down, snatched Bessie's forearm, and yanked her up to face me.

"Tell me what's happened . . . now," I said. She stared at me blankly. Her face had drained with whatever news Tom had shared. "Bessie," I said. "Now."

"It's . . . it's Lydia," she whimpered. "She's . . . dead." My stomach flipped at once and I gagged. Mother began crying softly.

"What happened?"

I felt strangely displaced from my body as if I were still dreaming. I pinched my eyes shut until they blurred and then opened them, finding I was still clutching Bessie's arm, still hearing Tom groan with agony behind her. And then, I thought of my brother. "Tom . . . Bessie, where is he?" My voice rose hysterically and I walked toward the door. I had to find him. Wherever he was, he'd be inconsolable.

"Damn your brother, John, and his devil doctor father!" Tom yelled, stopping me midstep. Mother grabbed my arm as I gripped the doorknob, but I barely noticed. I slung her off, pulled the blue velvet yoke of my dress around my neck, pushed my feet into my boots, and slammed the front door as Tom's fist hit the window.

The glass shattered, tinkling over the sill and the sidewalk, but I didn't turn back. Lydia was dead and my brother and John were in trouble. The tone of Tom's voice followed me as I ran down the street toward the train station and the canal. The trolley screeched passed me, and I skirted a pile of fresh manure, thankful that the street was mostly vacant. If John and Franklin had somehow been involved in Lydia's death, they'd be riddled with grief and guilt. The thought swept through me. What if John had dismissed Tom from the Society and there'd been a brawl? What if Lydia had been caught in the middle? Surely they wouldn't have allowed any harm to come to her. They both loved her.

The station was empty, the roman numerals on the clock pressed into the crumbling redbrick reading six-twenty. The next train wouldn't be here for another thirty-eight minutes. A whistle cut through the crisp early-morning air, followed by another. Shooting over the railroad tracks, I sprinted toward the canal right beyond it, and down the splintered wooden dock. Passing by shrimp boats and industry tugs, I crossed the gangplank to the ferry just as the side-wheel paddles began to chop the water.

"Your fare, miss?" I stared blankly at the brass New York Ferry Company buttons lining the old man's uniform. I hadn't thought to bring money. I hadn't thought of anything beyond getting to the Hoppers' as quickly as I could.

"I—"

"You'll pay me on your trip back," he said hastily, withdrawing a dollar from his pocket and jamming it into the other as the ferry pushed away from the shore.

I stood at the railing of the steamer watching Manhattan grow closer. My fingers tapped anxiously on the railing. I couldn't accept the possibility that they were accountable. I absolutely could not, yet the thought kept pushing into my mind. Maybe Tom's words meant nothing. Even so, I couldn't shake a haunted feeling. They'd all been together at the Society. What had happened? I closed my eyes, trying to force my thoughts to silence, but Lydia's wide Cheshire grin popped into my head, blue eyes dancing with merriment. One of my friends, a woman who could've been my sister, was dead . . . *dead*. A whimper came from my lips as reality sunk in, and suddenly, another series of images jumped into my head, startling me so intensely that my eyes flew open. I had no idea what had killed her, but the answer buzzed in the back of my mind as if I just needed to find the words. I felt her fingers trembling against my skin, words jumbled as they came from her mouth. I saw her playing next to Alevia, arm limp and lifeless against the bow, face deep in concentration as though she hadn't any idea. *Alevia*, I thought. Where was my sister?

"Are you all right?" My eyes snapped to the left, toward a black man with a long beard like Doctor Hopper's. I tried to form words, but couldn't. I lifted my hand to my mouth, realizing just hours before I'd been kissing John, considering marrying him, and now here I stood wondering if he'd even be alive when I got to his house. I didn't know how I'd go on if he was dead. The man beside me was still staring. I could feel his eyes go from my unbound hair to my dress to my boots.

"Yes. I'm fine," I said quickly, unable to stand his gaze. I glanced down at my dress, realizing a swathe of brown paint was smeared down the side—a consequence of attempting to conjure words by painting. The steamer stopped at the dock and I fled from the railing, shoving past musky-smelling fishermen and pretzel, hot tamale, and candy peddlers readying for a day of selling their wares. I scanned the passengers lined up for the Bronx, but all I saw were strangers staring me up and down, wondering why I was running off the ship in such a state of undress. I bolted down the street, rounding left at Park Avenue.

I looked up and down the avenue for them, but found only a few foreign faces as I went. It was early, not even seven in the morning, and the street was mostly deserted, save a few random coaches idling under the banners of laundry strung from apartment windows overhead.

The stench of sewage and rotting garbage stung my nostrils. I breathed through my mouth and kept my eyes fixed to the brownstone on the corner of the next block, ignoring the cold filth squishing under my boots. I couldn't believe I'd been born into an apartment similar to these. Someone called out at me, his Italian accent echoing between the buildings as I sprinted right on 106th and then barreled down the clean cobblestones on Fifth.

Squinting out at the park, I slowed to a walk. A footman yawned on the stoop of the red brick and limestone Vanderbilt mansion, stretching in the early-morning sun. I took a deep breath, trying to free the strain of a cramp in my side, and was relieved to smell only the sweet fragrance of freshly cut grass. One more block and I would be there.

I stopped dead at the gate. The front door stood wide open. My body felt stiff and I made my way up the steps. Everything was eerily quiet. Even the maids, who should've been cooking breakfast by now, were absent. I reached the porch, walked slowly through the front door, and a sob convulsed in the back of my throat. The ornate Italian table in the entry was toppled over and a few chairs in the parlor lay scattered on their sides. It looked like they'd been robbed, and they may have been, though I knew that wasn't the case. Everyone had fled. Had all of the Society witnessed Lydia's death? I swallowed hard, forcing myself to walk past the destruction and down the hall to the drawing room. Surely my brother and John were here. They had to be.

I tripped over the leg of a stained-glass lamp in the hallway that lay shattered on the floor, catching myself on the wall. I tiptoed around the glass, but the edge of a shard pierced the sole of my boot. John was gone. I could feel his absence acutely. I closed my eyes for a moment, praying I'd find Franklin in the drawing room. Instead, I looked through the door, and screamed.

"John? John!" I screamed his name. My voice echoed through the house, hysterical and breathless. My lungs convulsed. Lydia's body lay in the middle of the floor under the chandelier. Her face was turned toward me, tongue curled in the back of her open mouth, eyes wide open. Her legs were bent, bare toes scrunched against the floor as if she'd been trying to hold on. As much as I tried to look away, I couldn't. My head began to spin, static taking over my vision, and I stepped back, forcing myself away from the sight. I couldn't faint. Not here, not now. Forcing saliva down my throat, I screamed again. "Franklin! Where are you?" My stomach lurched to my throat and I vomited. I fell to my knees on the sharp glass and shoved myself against the wall, hugging my knees. In a matter of hours, everything I had known, my entire happiness, had disappeared. I tilted my head back to look down the hallway toward John's study. If he was in there, he hadn't answered, and if I found him dead . . .

I stood, clutching the top of a table still standing in the hallway. Closing my eyes, I tried to force the memory of Lydia's face alive and laughing, but couldn't. All I could remember was the stiff look of death. At once, a chill drifted up my spine and I ran from the house. I heard people's horrified comments as I ran past, but I kept running, smelling the stench of the vomit in my hair. Where had they gone? They couldn't have left long ago. Tom had likely come to find Bess as soon as he realized Lydia was dead, but why? If one of my siblings had died, I wouldn't have left their body lying in the middle of a drawing room just to find John. And suddenly, the answer was clear. He hadn't come to tell Bessie. He'd come to find Frank.

I pounded on Mae's door, first with my fists, then smacking hard with the palm of my hand. "Mae!" I yelled. I half-nodded at the neighbor's gardener who'd stopped watering the plants to stare at me. The door finally opened and Henry stood in the foyer, grin lifting half of his mouth as he stared at me. Obviously, he hadn't heard.

"Ginny, are you—"

"Where's Mae?" I pushed past him.

"She's upstairs. We were just about to depart for a lecture on Johann Herbart. What is it, Ginny? What's wrong?" I didn't bother to turn around or answer him, but sprinted up the stairs. I yelled for Mae. She was talking to someone. I could hear her high-pitched voice coming from the ladies lounge next to her bedroom. I yelled again and her voice stopped when she heard her name.

Mae materialized in the hallway, took one look at me, and her eyes went wide. I began to cry as much with relief at the sight of my sister as with fear and sadness, and she ran toward me, flinging her arms around me, despite my filth. I squeezed her, comforted by the familiar lavender scent in her hair, the tight grasp of her arms, and then I saw Alevia. She craned her neck out of the lounge smiling, but her lips dropped immediately when she saw my face. I sobbed, disentangling myself from Mae to hug her.

"Thank god," I whispered. I should've known she would come here. Alevia pulled away, eyebrows scrunched at me.

"What is it, Ginny?" Her eyes bore into mine. "You've been sick and you look frightful." Even though she'd been at the Society last night, she'd apparently left before anything happened. I could feel Mae behind me and turned to face them both.

"Have you . . . have you seen Franklin or John?" Mae shook her head, but Alevia shrugged.

"I did last night. They were taking Lydia to the study to try and calm her down when I left. Franklin seemed like he was embarrassed. She was pitching a fit and crying hysterically over Mr. Carter." Alevia looked down at her blue wool bolero jacket and shook her head. "I felt sorry for both Frank and John. John had already dealt with enough last night. No one seemed to notice, but he and Tom had quite a heated exchange at the beginning of the evening and Tom stormed out." I swallowed hard, strangely relieved that her death hadn't been a casualty of a brawl between Tom and John over Tom's plagiarism, over my honor. Then again, why would it? They were both gentlemen, and even when I'd seen John angry—livid at Charlie for hurting me—he'd never resorted to violence.

I took a breath.

"Lydia is dead." My sisters stared at me as though they hadn't heard me. Then slowly, Alevia brought her hand to her mouth and sunk to the floor. Mae pressed her hand to the burnt orange satin at her chest, trying not to cry, though her bottom lip trembled.

"How?" Mae whispered. Henry appeared in the doorway behind her, white-faced.

"I don't know," I said. "I woke up to Bess screaming this morning. Tom came by and told her, although I think he was looking for Franklin."

"Oh, poor Franklin. He'll be shattered when he finds out," Alevia sniffed.

"I think he knows." My voice shook as I said it and everyone's eyes snapped to my face. "When I left . . . when I ran out of the house to try to find him and John, Tom's words were, 'Damn your brother, John, and his devil doctor father.' I can just feel it, he was there, he knows." Henry turned and punched the doorframe.

"Then where is he?" Mae asked calmly, though I could tell that it took considerable effort for her to maintain her composure.

"I don't know." I looked down, fiddling with my collar, seriously questioning whether or not I'd gone insane. I thought about turning and going back to the Hoppers', thinking I'd surely been mistaken. Lydia wouldn't be dead. John would be sitting in his study writing and I'd walk in and tell him that I would marry him after all. "They're gone," I said, as reality set in once again.

"What do you mean 'they're gone'? Who's gone?" Henry's voice was strong, but it broke on the last word, and I remembered how close he was to John.

"I'm . . . I'm hoping Frank's gone home, but I know for sure that John and Doctor Hopper have vanished. I'm not sure where. I went straight to the Hoppers' after I got off the steamer and the front door was wide open. The tables and chairs were overturned. And Lydia. She's in the drawing room." I cleared my throat. "They left her there. She . . ." I started to explain the way I'd found her, but stopped myself, unable to vocalize what I'd seen. Alevia was staring at me, waiting for me to continue, but I shook my head. I ran a hand through my hair, and pressed my temple hoping the pressure would get rid of the aching beginning to pound at the sides of my head.

"That's ridiculous. They must've been robbed or attacked." Henry paced to the other side of the room. "I'm sure Lydia's death was shocking, but why would they run? It doesn't make sense."

"I suppose if they had something to do with it," Mae said. She glanced at me apologetically for the statement.

"I don't know how they would have. They couldn't possibly," I said. I prayed that the uneasy feeling in my gut was wrong, that they hadn't fled after all. I thought of the gentle way Frank loved Lydia, the way John had saved her after Mae's wedding. Even if she'd died in their presence, her death had to have been nothing more than a horrible accident—something to mourn, but nothing to run from. I was amazed that I could think at all, let alone discuss this situation. "The way she died . . . the way I saw her body. She wasn't murdered. At least I don't think so." Alevia stood up and smoothed the black bands along her skirt, wiping the tears from her face with the back of her hand.

"Mother must be beside herself," she whispered. I hadn't thought of Mother since I'd run from the house this morning.

"You're right," I said. "I just left her with Bessie and Tom. I didn't even think to tell her where I was going. All I could think about was John and . . . and Franklin and finding them."

"We need to go to your mother's house now," Henry said, turning to Mae. "We need to find your brother. Maybe John is there, too." He paused to glance at me. "And for the love of god lend your sister a proper dress."

Chapter Nineteen

The Loftin House
BRONX, NEW YORK

Franklin wasn't home and John wasn't there either. I knew that the moment I walked through the door. The house was startlingly silent save for sobs coming from the drawing room.

"Is that Mother?" Alevia whispered behind me. Mae nodded and trailed down the hallway on my heels. An ear-splitting shriek came from upstairs. Mae's eyes met mine and she sprinted up the stairs. Bessie. I started running down the hallway, wondering if something else had happened while I was gone. I stopped at the sight of my mother doubled over on the love seat in front of a dwindling fire. Her face was red from the strain of crying. She hadn't even heard us come in.

"Mother?" She stood slowly, crossed the room, and hugged me. She was still wearing her nightgown.

"Thank goodness," she whispered. "I was so worried about you, Virginia. Did you find Frank and John?" I tried to swallow the lump in my throat.

"No, but Alevia was at Mae's." I couldn't bear to tell her that the Hoppers' house had been ransacked, and that Lydia's body still lay on the floor of the drawing room.

"That poor girl." Mother started to cry again. "And my dear Franklin. He loved her so." Alevia walked into the room, placed a hand on Mother's back and they both sank onto the love seat.

"I can't imagine life without her," Alevia whispered. "At first I was frightened that she'd steal Franklin away from us, but she gave him . . . all of us . . . so much vitality."

I sat down in my father's leather chair, John's face in my mind. John loved me. Surely he wouldn't leave without sending word, without coming for me—unless he'd lied all along, unless he'd never loved me. The sinister thoughts came from nowhere and I pushed them away. They weren't true. He'd proposed twice; he wanted to spend the rest of his life with me. Then again, I thought I'd been sure of Charlie and he'd betrayed me. My thoughts flit to John's reputation, the blemish on his character I'd so readily believed untrue. Maybe he hadn't fled to escape Lydia's death at all. Maybe he'd only fled to escape the promises he'd proposed to me.

None of us said anything, choosing instead to stare at the fire, absorbed in our own minds. I could hear Mae trying to calm Bess, her voice lulling serenity to Bess's intermittent hysterics. Alevia began to hum the opening notes of Mozart's Piano Concerto No. 23. The tune was dreary and slow. Mother sniffed and wiped her eyes.

"There's a letter in the post for you today, Ginny." Mother straightened. She reached to the table in front of her, extracted a letter, and handed it to me, as though diverting the subject to something mundane had the ability to shift our minds from worry and grief. I stared at the choppy cursive handwriting on the envelope. I didn't recognize the hand and there was no return address.

Dear Miss Loftin,

Mr. Tom Blaine sought me out a few days back to inform me that the story we printed, attributed to him, was not, in fact, his work but yours. I certainly hope you will trust that myself, our staff, was entirely in the dark as to Mr. Blaine's plagiarism. The thought that we have printed your work as his absolutely horrifies and appalls me. Please accept my sincerest apology. A correction will appear in this month's issue.

In earnest regret,
Mr. Richard W. Gilder

I folded the letter and placed it back in the envelope. Yesterday, I would've rejoiced at the news. Today, amid all of the confusion and sadness, it meant nothing. Why had Tom decided to admit his wrong? It couldn't have been John's doing. He hadn't had the opportunity to speak with Tom prior to last night. A pang went through me at the thought of John.

"Mr. Gilder is going to print a retraction. Tom admitted that the story was mine." My voice came out in a sigh.

"What wonderful news," Mother said, as sincerely as she could. Alevia's eyes met mine.

"Oh," she said. "I'd almost forgotten."

"So had I," I said.

"No." Alevia shook her head. "Not about your story. I ran into Charlie a few weeks back. I was on my way to Symphony rehearsal when I saw him walking by Wanamaker's. He mentioned reading Tom's story in *The Century* and said he knew it was yours." She pulled her handkerchief from her pocket and blew her nose. "Apparently, he was on his way to depart on a holiday, but had decided to pay Tom a visit before he did. He said he told

Tom you'd shared an early draft of the story with him and that he still had it in his possession. Charlie threatened to show it to Mr. Gilder unless Tom confessed. The threat apparently worked." I stared at her, unable to fully register this piece of news. "Please don't be cross with me for hiding this from you. Charlie begged me to keep his actions in confidence in case Tom didn't comply. He was quite awkward about explaining why he was interfering. He kept saying that anyone would do the same for a friend, that it was the right thing to do."

"Of course," I said. "I'm not angry with you, Alevia." It had been kind of Charlie, but any thought of his gesture faded as Bessie's voice echoed through the quiet house.

"I love you!"

"Is Tom still here?" I asked, wondering if Bess's outcry meant he was with her.

"No," Mother whispered. "I'm afraid he's not." Tears threatened her eyes. "He's furious about something and hurting. He told Bessie he never wanted to see her again, that we'd all be ruined, and that he couldn't stand to spend another moment in Franklin's home staring at the sister of a . . . of a murderer." The words shocked me. Mother clearly hadn't mentioned them earlier because she hadn't wanted to tell us. Mother started crying again and I shook my head. It wasn't true. Tom was being irrational. He was mad with grief and looking for someone to blame. Whatever had happened to Lydia wasn't Frank's fault. He loved her, so did John, and the thought that they'd harm her was insane.

"It's not true, Mother," I tried to say softly, but could hear the defensive edge to my voice. "You know Frank. He'd never lay a hand on anyone, let alone the woman he loves." Mother sniffed.

"I know, Ginny. It's just that I don't know where he is and the longer it takes him to get home, the more I worry about him.

Where is he?" Her eyes searched mine as though I knew a secret she didn't.

"I don't know," I said. "But he can't be gone forever. He'll be home soon and John will be with him." My mind flashed to the destruction of the Hoppers' drawing room and I prayed that I was right. "Where are you?" I whispered, as though they could hear me.

*I*t had to be two or three in the morning, but I hadn't slept at all. I doubted anyone else was asleep either, but the house was silent. I stared at the curtains puffing and deflating with the fall wind seeping in from the crack in my windowsill. I'd been listening for the creak of the front door for the past eight hours, ever since I'd returned home, but no one had come in or out. Mae and Henry were in Mae's old room, too shaken with sorrow and perplexity to forge the journey back to Manhattan, and Alevia had insisted on sleeping with Bessie—a gesture Bessie had refused over and over until she'd simply run out of energy to argue. We'd all slept together as girls—Mae and I in one bed, with the occasional midnight addition of Frank, and Bess and Alevia in the other. As the oldest, Bess had been tasked with making sure our youngest sister didn't fall out of bed in the night. It was a comforting sort of thing, to know that your sister was beside you, that you weren't alone. If Mae hadn't had Henry I would have petitioned her to come to bed with me tonight.

I'd thought Frank would come home in time for dinner and that he would bring John. As crazy as the assumption seemed now, hours later, I kept thinking that perhaps he and John had been trying to find Tom or had gone to talk with the Blaines and that they'd make a point to be home by dinner. That way, they would know we'd all be here and could fill us in all at once. Instead, dinner, which had consisted of cold meat and bread, had been consumed in silence. The only conversation we'd made had been through glances from one miserable, swollen face to another, though during that time, I'd made up my mind: if they didn't show up by morning, I'd go looking for them again. This time I'd check all the places I could possibly think they'd be and I'd find them.

"How'd you ever get over it?" A soft voice came from the doorway and I jolted upright, finding Bessie's silhouette. She sat down on the foot of my bed. Her auburn hair hung down her back, tangled from tossing and turning. She opened her right hand and stared down at a burned cracked hazelnut shell in her palm. We'd played the game years ago as young women, writing the names of our favorites on the shells and tossing them into the fire to see if they'd crack or remain whole, to see if our supposed love would stand the test of time or end. Mother always reminded us that it was only a silly game. When we played, Charlie's name had always emerged from the flames burned but whole—proof that it was just a silly, childish amusement. The memory made me think of what he'd done for me. I didn't know why he'd felt the need to defend me after everything, but I was thankful that he had. I leaned forward to take the shell from Bess, but she pushed my wrist away, hand closing tightly around the hazelnut.

"I don't know," I said. "I suppose I had to." I recalled the sting of Charlie's proposal, the melancholy that gripped me at every suggestion of him for months afterward. I didn't know if I could endure that kind of misery again. "However, this time I don't know if I'll be able to if . . . if—" I couldn't finish the sentence. I'd spent all day trying to block the possibility that John could've left me, too, that in less than a day's time we'd gone from talking about marriage to silence. Bess was still staring at me, oblivious to my worry about John and Franklin, absorbed in her own. "You'll never forget him, but eventually, you'll learn to live with the heartache and you'll be able to move on."

"I'll never move on," Bessie said fiercely. "I'll never forgive Franklin. He's ruined my life."

"You don't know what you're talking about," I said. "Lydia died less than a day ago. Tom is hurt. You know Frank would never hurt Lydia. Tom was probably just reacting out of anger. He'll come around."

"No, he won't. I know him, Gin, better than anyone, and he won't. Whatever he believes, even if it isn't the truth, it's real to him, and he won't ever change his mind."

"What exactly is it that he believes? He's a liar through and through," I hissed and then closed my eyes to calm my anger. I couldn't believe that Tom thought my brother a murderer. "He didn't tell you anything at all about why he was mad at John and Franklin? He didn't mention anything about last night?" I asked gently. Bessie shook her head.

"I don't know. And I already told you he didn't tell me anything. He didn't even give me the chance to ask. As soon as you left, he said . . . he said he never wanted to see me again and stormed out," she said, her eyes pooling. "I swear I'm going to kill Frank when I see him," she said, fidgeting with my quilt.

"And if he never comes back?" The question was out of my mouth before I thought it through and Bess stared at me, lips pressed together in disdain.

"I hope he doesn't," she said evenly. "And I hope wherever he is, John is with him. They can rot in hell together." Her words knocked the breath from my lungs and I felt my hand lift from the blankets. One more word and I would slap her.

"I know you're upset, we all are, but you're being dreadfully heartless." She glanced at my hand hovering a few inches over the bed, and crossed to my doorway. I heard a sob echo in the hall as she shuffled back to her room and I collapsed against my pillows. I tried to focus on Franklin's warm smile and John's face pressed against mine, but couldn't. All I saw instead was a harrowing vision of both of them dead in an alleyway. "Please," I whispered to the darkness. "Let me be wrong."

Chapter Twenty

Central Park
NEW YORK, NEW YORK

*T*he day was uncharacteristically frigid for September. Suiting, I thought, as I huddled into my shawl. I'd been wandering the city all day, staking out any place that meant anything to John or to Franklin and so far had found nothing. Wind swept over me, lapping the water in Central Park Lake onto the shore. I looked out at the stone bridge. An old oak leaned over the water right before it, its leaves barely dappled with yellow almost masking an elderly woman in a gray wool cloak clutching the stone railing, watching a wooden sailboat glide under the bridge. A couple laughed at two little boys squealing in delight as water sprayed their faces and matching cape overcoats.

Reminded of John and Franklin, I turned and started up the hill toward Fifth Avenue, determined not to look back at the unoccupied white cast-iron bench under the cherry tree across the lake, but did anyway. John had told me that he came out to the lake when he needed to get away, when he couldn't think. I could picture him there—notebook in one hand, staring out at the water while park-goers promenaded and picnicked around him.

"I love you. I do," I said, stricken by the possibility that I might never see him again. I pushed the thought from my mind. It had only been a day and a half, I reminded myself. I closed my eyes, retracing the steps I'd already taken in case I'd overlooked something. I'd started at Randall's Island, at the rocky point where Frank always loved to picnic in the summertime. Finding a cluster of fishermen, but no sign of Franklin, I'd boarded the next boat and had practically sprinted to the park when I'd reached Manhattan. Whether it was desperation or my blatant refusal to believe they'd disappeared, something in my gut told me that I would find John here. But I was wrong again. Perhaps I was wrong to trust my intuition at all. It had only led me to false hope and heartache.

I reached the street in front of Ward McAllister's gargoyle-adorned mansion. A carriage stopped on the side of the home and a finely dressed gentleman got out, tipped his hat at me, and smiled. I stared at him, unable to move my lips to return the gesture. It was difficult to comprehend how my whole life could fall apart overnight while the rest of the world kept moving along undisturbed.

The Hoppers' home was just a block away to my left. I focused straight ahead as I neared the edge of the mansions that would shield me from the towering brick home, but at the last minute I couldn't take it. I gave in and looked. Gasping, I ran into the shadow of the house next to me as if the group of men dressed in black suits standing on the Hoppers' front stoop would somehow see me from a block away and know who I was. My heart continued to pound in my chest as I made my way toward the main office of J. L. Mott. It was Monday; perhaps Franklin had gone to work.

Past the lull of carriages along Fifth Avenue, the streets were bustling. Beggars were shouting, calling out for change or food, and businessmen whistled cheerily as they went about their days. My stomach growled as I inhaled the sugary scent of sweet bread.

I hadn't eaten all day, but didn't reach in my pocket for a nickel to buy one. I knew I couldn't eat if I tried. Even among the crowds of the city, I felt alone. I turned down an alleyway, wishing Mother or my sisters were with me. Bessie had gone to our neighbors' wedding anniversary tea—an engagement she typically would've thought below her—in an attempt to avoid her misery, while Alevia had refused to go anywhere, alternating between crying in her room and playing straight through her books of Mozart and Stephen Foster tunes. Mother had declined on the grounds that Frank might come home.

"Out of the way, miss!" A fat man lugging the wasted carcass of a gigantic catfish shooed me out of the way. The sulfuric scent of rancid fish flooded my nostrils, clinging to the inside of my nose. My eyes watered. The man flung the catfish and I ran to get out of the way.

I emerged from the alley right in front of J. L. Mott. The building was made of plain brick with tiny windows running along each story. Not nearly as fancy as the previous headquarters in Mott Haven, I had a feeling old Mr. Mott would have had J. L. fired for moving it. I grinned a little at the thought, but felt my palms tingle with nerves as I started toward the front doors. I adjusted my trilby hat over my hair and slicked the stray wisps behind my ear.

"Good afternoon." I tried to sound pleasant to the man sitting at the reception desk, but my voice shook anyway.

"How do you do, miss?" He tilted his head at me as I gaped at him. I'd lost the ability to speak. Vaguely aware of the suited men walking from the interior of the building past me toward the door, I blinked.

"I-I'm sorry. I'm here to see Franklin Loftin." The man snatched a huge stack of paper off the top of his desk and flipped to what I guessed was *L* in the directory.

"There's no one here by that name." he said, still scanning the page.

"I promise you, he works here," I said, exasperated.

"If he's not on here, he doesn't. I just received an updated list this morning. You must be mistaken." I felt my face drain. It had only been one day. He should still be on the list even if he hadn't shown up for work.

"He travels. He's a salesman. Does your list include them? He only works here when he's in town and—"

"Yes, it does," he said, cutting me off. I stared down at the directory, fingers gripped to the front of his desk, knowing that it was the only thing holding me up.

I turned, stumbling dizzily toward the door.

"Are you all right, ma'am?" the man called from the reception desk. I ignored him and stepped out of the quiet lobby onto the busy street. My mind whirled, bringing me back to my visit to Frank's office in Mott Haven. I'd been so angry, so confused, until he'd reassured me that my worries were in vain. I'd been wrong to believe him. Franklin had been lying to all of us.

BRONX, NEW YORK

A vagrant sitting against the side of a new brownstone looked up at the sight of me, and scooted back into the shadows. The night was completely black.

As I'd expected, Franklin hadn't been home when I'd returned from the city and no one had heard any updates. I'd spent the afternoon pacing around my room avoiding my family, alternating between fury at Frank's lying and panic that he'd never, return.

There was no reason to tell the others of Frank's deceit yet, of the job he'd lied about. It would only alarm them, so I'd kept the news to myself in hopes that he'd appear and tell us the truth.

I made a valiant effort to get some sleep, but darkness always tended to give reign to the devil, and the worst possible thoughts tormented me. The most horrible curse of all was that in the past hours I'd remembered what had been said the last time I saw John. *"God, Virginia, how you break my heart."* John's words rang once again in my head, watering my eyes. I'd told him I loved him. Why hadn't I said yes? I cursed myself for being so fickle. And then, I thought of my brother. He had come to my room to try to convince me to be happy, insisting that John and I were right for each other, and I'd yelled at him to get out. Regardless of my anger at his lies, I couldn't bear the thought of that being his last memory of me. I prayed he knew how much I loved him, that they both did, but I couldn't be sure.

So I left the house, deciding that rather than wait until tomorrow, I'd look around Mott Haven. In the haze of early morning, it had seemed like a promising option. If they'd fled Manhattan, they could easily be hiding out here, a reasonably far distance from Fifth Avenue and the Hoppers' mansion. So far, however, I'd seen barely anyone at all.

I cut down a side street, through a grove of oaks to the sprawling lawn of St. Anne's Church. We were Presbyterians and most of us had only been to St. Anne's a handful of times for the odd wedding or funeral, but Franklin had told me a while back that sometimes on his way home from work, he'd find himself walking toward the church. He said something drew him there. Without him saying what, I knew it was the history, the strange need to hear the whispers of Lewis Morris III in the graveyard rambling about the Declaration of Independence or the first Gouvernor Morris arguing about his edits of the Constitution. Franklin and I had always reveled in the past, fascinated by not only our family's history but also by the history of the people our family must have known.

The brown stone seemed to gleam against the darkness. I tugged at the iron door, but it didn't budge. The handle was freezing in my hand, but I gripped it hard and tried again. The door screeched open. I scanned the pews and my heart dropped to my stomach. Unless he was lying down, he wasn't here. I walked toward the front anyway, past the Gothic stained-glass windows to the flickering oil lamps illuminating the cross.

"Father, please," I whispered. "Help me find them. I can't do this on my own." I stood there for a moment listening to the wicks pop, and then turned up the aisle and stepped outside, letting the door slam behind me.

I walked back across the lawn and through a thin patch of trees to a side street that ran next to the river. I suddenly felt hopelessly alone. John and Frank had abandoned me. They'd left me to agonize over the possibility of where they'd gone and what they'd done. I thought of the rest of my family at home. They'd been able to settle their minds—at least enough to sleep. Perhaps that was my curse. Perhaps I loved too strongly, gave my heart away too readily to people who gave little consideration to mine.

I could see the row of piano factories in the distance. The white block lettering on the Estey building was so huge you could spot it from about any point in the Bronx. I wondered if Alevia had gone to play after her appointment at the Carnegies'. She hadn't been in several weeks. Symphony practices had taken up much more of her time than she'd planned—not that I thought she minded.

Realizing my hand had been balled in a nervous fist in my pocket since I'd left the church, I stretched my fingers out as

I turned up Third Avenue. I hadn't seen anyone for at least five blocks and doubted anyone would be headed out toward the last bit of forest left in the Bronx at three in the morning. The moon was still dim overhead, but hung at eye level now.

"Where are you?" I wondered aloud for the hundredth time. I stepped off the road and strode up the small hill. The early-morning dew soaked through the bottom of my skirt and stockings, freezing my ankles. I was breathing hard under the strain of the incline by the time I reached the entrance to the cemetery. I didn't visit my father's grave much, mostly because I knew his spirit wasn't there. In life he'd thought cemeteries sinister and tended to avoid them, so I doubted he would be hanging around one now. Even so, sometimes I just wanted to talk to him, and knowing that the shell of his body—the smile I'd loved, the arms that had held me—was still there comforted me.

I tapped my grandfather's headstone and then my great-uncle's as I walked under an ancient oak. All of my family members on my father's side were buried here, sprinkled randomly throughout the graveyard. My father was at the very back of the cleared land in a secluded spot at the start of the forest. He'd ended up there because they'd run out of room in the graveyard proper, but at his burial I remember thinking that he wouldn't have minded. He'd loved the wilderness like his father before him and had resented modern conveniences like the trolley line, commenting often that Grandfather would turn over in his grave if he knew that the whizzing noise was drowning out the call of hungry owls and the crickets' hum.

As I advanced toward the patch of forest, my heart stilled with worry. Lost in thought, I almost didn't register that Franklin was in front of me. Kneeling at our father's headstone, his back was to me, heavy black overcoat pulled around his neck. I nearly screamed. Instead, I stepped toward him cautiously, afraid that if I spoke his name, he'd run. Two feet away, I started to reach out and touch him, but thought better of it.

"Frank," I whispered loudly. He whirled on his haunches and backed away, stumbling over a headstone behind him.

"Virginia," he breathed, eyes wide with shock. "Get . . . get away from me. If they see you with me they'll . . ." He stopped midsentence and glanced around the cemetery. I kept walking toward him, but he held his hand out, keeping me back. Even in the dark, I could see that his face was haggard, stubble uneven and scraggly against his chin.

"What's happened to you? Where've you been?" Franklin backed into the woods and I followed. He remained half-crouched. "No one's here, Frank. I just walked through the whole cemetery." He straightened a little at my words, grabbed my wrist, and dragged me further into the woods. He smelled awful, like unwashed skin. Frank turned to look over his shoulder, jerked me behind a mossy boulder, and forced me down next to him.

"You can't be seen with me, do you understand?" he asked softly, though there was a sharp edge to his voice.

"No," I said simply. "I don't." A thousand questions flew into my mind.

"We're . . . I'm being hunted and if they see you with me, if they see me anywhere near the house, they'll come for you to get to me. After Lydia . . . Tom sent the authorities to find me, John, and Doctor Hopper. Someone shot at me today as I was getting on the train; the police know I'm here." Wind swept over us, unsettling the dry leaves on the ground, and Franklin's head twitched toward the noise.

"Why?" I asked. My hands began to shake in my lap and I gripped my fingers together to steady them. Frank leaned forward, dropping his head into the shadow of the stone. "Why are the police after you? Why have you been lying to us?" Anger swept through me, but I forced myself to calm, bracing myself for what he'd say.

"Lydia," he whispered. His voice cracked in the night, the high notes of despair echoing through the treetops. I started to look at him, but kept my eyes on the patchy grass instead. I'd asked him a question. He needed to answer me. "They're after us because of Tom. After she died, he threatened us. He said he'd have us killed. I didn't think he was serious, but John did. The minute Tom said it, John left the room and started packing his things. I thought he was being ridiculous and tried to reason with him, but he said that Tom had the money to hire a toxicologist and that we would be tried like that doctor William Palmer for murder." Franklin stumbled over the last word and my heart stopped in my chest. He turned Grandfather's gold band around his pinkie.

"That's impossible. Frank, you couldn't . . . you couldn't have had anything to do with her death. I know you. You would never hurt anyone. You don't have it in you. Neither does John." I noticed my voice was raised in a hysterical cry.

"Ginny, you know I did," he said bluntly. "You had to. Even if you didn't know how, you had to know that something wasn't right. It was the drugs, Ginny." Frank looked straight at me. My stomach lurched.

"What are you talking about?" At once, I felt Lydia's fingertips trembling against my arms, saw her eyes wide and staring, and didn't know if I could handle what he was about to say. I started to open my mouth to tell him, but closed it, forcing myself to hear the answer that would confirm a truth so harrowing I hadn't let myself imagine it.

"Doctor Hopper . . . that night at the opera he told you he was an innovator, an inventor, remember?" I nodded. Frank's hand pressed down on my sleeve to stop my shivering, but I jerked away from him. His eyes flashed with understanding. "About a year ago, Doctor Hopper invented a drug, a combination of drugs actually, to help cure John, Tom, Lydia, Marcus, and a few others after Will's death. They were going insane with depression and nothing was working." I stared at him, unable to say anything, but needing him to continue.

"John told me about the drug the day I met him on the train, after I mentioned that I was in sales. They were looking for someone to sell the concoction. He said that the going rate was ten dollars a bottle and that people were already begging for it. You know me, Gin. I'll hear anyone out about an opportunity." Frank's lips turned up slightly, though his eyes were dull with pain. John had lied to me. Fury washed over the pain of his absence. "John made me swear right there that I'd keep the solution a secret whether I took the job or not. He said that Doctor Hopper wouldn't allow advertising or the mention of it to anyone but the patient and that he'd only consider patients that he approved first. I remember thinking that system couldn't possibly be profitable and mentioned the same to John. He laughed and said that his father would approve about anyone. Doctor Hopper only had that policy because he didn't want to patent the medicine for fear the government would tax it." I wanted to scream, to beat my fists into his chest, but I couldn't move or speak. I could feel the fringes of my nerves fraying, threatening to snap. Selling drugs without a patent was illegal. Frank stared up at the treetops, pulling the lapels of his worn brown jacket around his neck.

"I talked to Doctor Hopper the next week and took the position on the same conditions that John had stated on the train. Hopper reminded me again that he didn't want me talking about the drug to anyone but the patient. And even when I discussed it with the customer, I wasn't supposed to mention the ingredients because he wanted to protect his recipe. It's not made of uncommon drugs. People could go down to the corner store and make their own if they knew." Franklin grabbed a handful of dew-soaked grass and yanked it from the ground with a tug. I tried to make sense of it all, but the only thing I understood was that my brother and John were swindlers. Everything I thought I'd known about either of them was just a façade. The charismatic, talented writer I loved seemed distant and foreign. The memory of his proposal, the careful, kind way that he loved me felt fictional, a character I'd dreamed up. My heart that had hours before been so full of affection for him shriveled in the grip of reality. He'd been wrong to say that he loved me, that we were equals, and I'd been wrong to believe it. Our souls were worlds apart. I felt the same about Franklin, the one person I'd been absolutely certain I knew inside and out. My head snapped toward him.

"You lied to me," I hissed. "I asked why you hadn't been at work and you lied to me. I've never deceived you. I never could. How dare you!" It was all coming together: The Benz, Lydia's extravagant necklace, Franklin's tailored suits. I'd caught him in a lie, but he'd talked me into accepting his explanation. I'd trusted him—just as I'd trusted John, as I'd trusted Charlie. I'd been a fool.

"I know," he said softly. My body finally caught up to my mind, and I swung my fist into his chest, knuckles striking the pewter buttons along his coat. "I'm sorry, Gin. I'm so, so sorry." Frank's hand grasped the back of mine, stopping the assault, and he started to cry. I wrenched my hand from his grip.

"Why would you?" My voice was icy, so quiet I doubted he heard me.

"It was good money," he said. "We needed it. And I thought the drug was helping people. I believed Hopper. I thought he was a good man. I still do." I suddenly remembered what Franklin had said when I'd first attended the Society, that I would never lose love again because of money.

"You didn't do it for me, did you?" As angry as I was at him, my heart ached with guilt. Frank shook his head.

"For all of us. We'd been living on the brink for so long. It was easier than selling iron and the money came fast. There are a lot of people on the verge of insanity. This drug made them happy. It stopped them from taking their lives or going through the pain of a lobotomy. Doctor Hopper called it Optimism Solution. At first, I only saw the good side effects. John, Tom, and Lydia were on it. They were normal."

"What was in it?" The traces of guilt disappeared and I could feel resentment taking hold.

"Cocaine and morphine. The cheapest drugs you can buy," he said. "Five hundred fifty milligrams of cocaine and forty-five milligrams of morphine. Patients inject it into their arms using a hypodermic needle once a day. It seems like a simple combination, but the cocaine relieves the depression and the morphine eases the anxiety."

"How could that combination possibly kill Lydia? We took those drugs as children, oftentimes together. Doctor Adelman used to give us cocaine for toothaches and morphine when we couldn't sleep." I was trying my hardest to hold to my belief that John and Franklin couldn't be at fault. I turned away from him, to the rows of crooked gray headstones.

"She'd had too much. Doctor Hopper emphasized that the mixture is only supposed to be administered once each day, but some didn't pay him—or me—any mind. The amount she injected was excessive." He slammed his hand on the ground.

"I saw her body," I said. Bile rose in my throat at the memory.

"When?" I could feel his eyes on my face, but I stared up at the last remaining leaves on the gnarled tree limbs above me.

"Tom came by the house the morning after. I was sleeping, but I heard Bessie scream. He told us about Lydia and then said something about you and John. I just knew the two of you were involved somehow, so I went straight to the Hoppers' to find you and she was right there on the floor."

"No one . . . no one covered her or called the coroner?" Even in the darkness I saw his face pale. His shoulders shook as he started to sob. "I can't stand it." His voice faltered. "I'm sorry, Gin. I'm so sorry I tangled you in this mess. I'm sorry I introduced you to John; I'm sorry I encouraged you to marry him. I didn't know it would turn out this way." I didn't acknowledge his apology. I couldn't believe him. Not anymore. "At the beginning, I only saw the good effects, but then I started noticing that people were going crazy without it, even worse than they were before. They'd be fine and happy while they were on it, but when it wore off they'd break down."

"Were you on the drug, too?" The question came out in a sharp snap and Frank's eyes narrowed at me, then relaxed.

"No. I tried a dose once to see what it was like, but it made me feel jittery. John told me from the beginning that I shouldn't take the drug since I didn't need it. He said it would make me sick and it did." Franklin let his head fall back against the rock. "That night, Lydia was coming down from the effects of it. She was crying hysterically and ripping out chunks of her hair and threatening to kill herself. After Marcus, I knew something was wrong. I knew that the solution had killed him. I just felt it. I asked Doctor Hopper about it, but he refused to engage. He insisted that Marcus's cause of death was the same as Will's—a hereditary heart condition—but there had been other deaths. I couldn't overlook them." I felt the echo of unease swirling in my gut, remembering the whispered speculation in the drawing room after Mr. Carter's funeral. Edith had been right. So had I.

"There were others?" Frank pinched the bridge of his nose.

"Four up north, in the country. I should've stopped after that, but I wanted the money. I wouldn't give it to Lydia, though, and I tried to keep it away from John, too, but I couldn't. I'd steal his bottles, but he'd just go to his father and get more." The vision of John's face that night in the study, his crumpled body, flashed in my mind. He'd needed more. That's why he'd been shuffling around in his cabinet. He'd needed to find the needle and bottles to calm himself.

"The other night at the meeting, Lydia needed the solution. She could feel the low coming on and begged me for it, but I refused. When she started screaming, John and I took her into the study. John gave her some, but it didn't work. She kept screaming and crying and scratching her arms until they bled. John was coming down himself and kept injecting her over and over thinking that if he gave her enough she'd come back to us. I got in his way a few times, but he turned on me and said that if I didn't let her have any, she'd kill herself and it would be my fault." He whispered the last words. "Eventually, she stopped struggling in the study and stumbled back out to the drawing room. One minute she was standing laughing and the next she was on the ground convulsing for breath, like she was having a seizure." Franklin held his head in his hands. I felt as if I were hovering somewhere outside my body. Who were these people? The pain of losing who I thought they were was killing me. Franklin stood and walked into the trees, a dark silhouette framed by the moon's white glow. After a while, he came back and sat down beside me.

"Was Tom with you in the study? I thought John was going to dismiss him from the Society." I couldn't bear to look at Franklin, so I looked at his boots. They still held polish, evidence of another life.

"At Alevia's first Society meeting, Tom had injected the solution twice, one more than normal, and fainted in the middle of writing." The vision of the small brown bottle emblazoned with a Celtic circle knot and the welt on his forearm the first time I met him flashed in my mind. "When he woke up, he knew the drug was dangerous. He mentioned it to me, but at the time I said I doubted anything was wrong with the formula and he kept taking it." Franklin pressed his lips together in regret. "He wasn't there when we took her out of the drawing room. He walked in at the end. He'd come back to fetch Lydia home, and saw John injecting her for what was probably the fourth time, but he didn't see me try to stop him. I don't blame Tom. I don't think I'd believe him if the same happened to you." I pulled my arms across my chest, suddenly wondering why Franklin was alone.

"Where is John?" I looked around, half-expecting him to materialize from the dense woods.

"I don't know," Franklin said and I heard a sound, deep and guttural come from his throat. I realized, as Franklin's face dropped to his hands, that John hadn't only been mine. He'd been Frank's, too, his best friend. "Wherever he is, he loves you, Gin," Frank said suddenly. "He was mixed up in his father's world, but if . . . when he comes back to you, you'll see. He's still the man you know."

Regardless of his deception and my anger, I knew that John had never intended to kill Lydia. He loved her. We all had. I had no doubt he thought he was saving her. I shut my eyes to stop the sting of heartache. In spite of everything, my soul longed for the John I'd known—for his strength, for his surety, for the stability I'd always felt in his presence. I knew he wasn't a bad man. All of this was Doctor Hopper's fault: Frank's ruin, John's destruction, my love for a man that I didn't know if I would ever see again.

"Damn you," I said under my breath.

"I lost John when I went after Tom," Frank said. "Tom ran out after Lydia collapsed and I followed him, but I lost him in midtown, so I turned back. By the time I got back to the Hoppers', they were gone. I have no idea where." I gripped Frank's arm. His muscles were tight. I was still angry, my heart shredded with anguish, but I wanted my brother back, to have the chance to know him again.

"Come home, Frank. We'll get this sorted out and—"

"No," he said. "The authorities will come for me and if they find me with you, they'll think you're involved, too. If they find me, I'm dead, Ginny."

"But you didn't do anything!" Regardless of the fact that he'd provided the drug, and as livid as his lying about his job made me, he hadn't killed anyone. If anything, he'd tried to save Lydia.

"Tom knows half of the families of the four others who have died. One was the daughter of his great-aunt up in Rhode Island; the second, a political supporter of his uncle's in Greenwich. If he realizes there's a connection . . ." he said slowly. He shoved his hands in his pockets. I had a sudden memory: Cherie's mention of her husband's friend who'd supposedly passed on of heartache. Franklin began to speak again. "When I sold to them, I made them sign a disclaimer that we weren't responsible for any injuries or deaths. It was something Hopper heard he should do to avoid being taken to court, just in case of any accidents." He rubbed his eyes. "Since Doctor Hopper never patented the solution, it'll seem like he knew the risk and poisoned them intentionally, that I was conspiring with him. Most of the deceased were family friends of the Hoppers. They trusted us. If Tom thinks of it, he'll make sure these families know how their children and brothers and sisters actually died. He'll turn them against us."

"What about John?" I asked. Emotion balled in my throat.

"Doctor Hopper's own son took it, too. It's not as though he'd try to kill John."

"They'll find a way to make it seem as if John took something different or took less. John can't prove otherwise. They'll say Doctor Hopper cautioned his son against taking too much, but didn't tell the others." Franklin pulled his hands from his pockets, extracting a few crumpled dollars and some change. "The autopsy will confirm that Lydia died of heart failure and the toxicology report will find massive amounts of morphine and cocaine. And the rest will all have copies of the disclaimer somewhere in their homes, proof that their loved ones took the drugs before they died." He stood suddenly. "I have to find John before it's too late."

"I'll come with you. I can help you find him. I don't know if I could ever trust him again, but I still love him." His eyes met mine.

"I know you love us and I know you're worried, but you have to go home. Don't tell Mother or the others that you've seen me or what I've done. It'll be best that way, in case the police come to question you all. I'm going to disappear for a while, Ginny, but I'll be all right."

"No." As much as I tried to hold on to the hope that I'd see John again, that life as I knew it would resume, I knew it wouldn't and I couldn't lose my brother, too. "You're coming home with me." I knew I wasn't being rational. He was right. If he and John—wherever he was—were being followed, our house would be an easy target for the authorities. But we were alone right now, no one was around, and there had to be a way.

"You really loved him, didn't you?" he whispered. I nodded, realizing I hadn't told Frank that I'd gone to see John.

"I saw him before the last meeting. I went to refuse him. But then, I changed my mind . . . it occurred to me that I might be able to have a happy marriage and a successful career after all." Our conversation felt distant and meaningless. "Now I've lost him. I can't lose you, Frank."

"You haven't lost anyone," he said, voice strong and rumbling in his throat. "I promised you that you wouldn't again and you won't. I'll find him. John's a tortured soul, Gin, but I know that he loves you." His arms squeezed tight around me. "And don't tell the others, but you know I love you best. You've always been my favorite."

"I'm glad," I said. "But I'm still not letting you go." I pulled his arm across my shoulders and reached for his hand, but something moved behind us. I heard the sound of leaves scattering and Franklin stepped away from me and ran. I raced after him, but he turned around and pushed me firmly to the ground.

"Stay. Here," he growled under his breath, eyes scanning the forest above my head.

"Where will you go?" I paused. "It isn't safe!"

"I'll get out of the city somehow. I don't know where. But I'll come back when I can . . . we both will. Don't worry." He forced a smile, turned around, and started to sprint. I ran after him, but lost him to the darkness. My brother, my best friend, was gone.

Chapter Twenty-one

The last place I wanted to be was here, sitting at a table by myself waiting for Fred Harvey who was fifteen minutes late and counting. I didn't have anything for him anyway. I'd barely touched *The Web* since we'd met last and certainly hadn't thought about writing since Lydia's death three weeks ago. I read the menu from the first entry—bisque of shrimp—to the last—brandy pears—for the eighth time and scanned the restaurant. It was crowded, but most of the guests would depart in an hour's time to see Frank Mayo's *Davy Crockett* at the Academy of Music. A group of people were laughing a table over.

"Are you sure I can't get you something while you wait, miss?" the waiter, an eager young man at least five years my junior, asked for the fourth time. I knew he was just doing his job, so I swallowed my annoyance and forced a grin.

"No. I'm fine, thank you." He tipped his head and left, zigzagging past guests and other waiters. I watched him as he passed table after table of black suits and elaborate hats. He disappeared into the bustling kitchen and my eyes landed on a man at a table next to the swinging doors. He was talking animatedly to two men with their backs to me. His eyes were bright with possibility and he stopped for a moment to take a sip from his water glass before talking again. I kept watching, very aware of the fact that I was staring, but unable to look away. Something in his manner reminded me of Frank. My eyes blurred and I turned toward the empty seat in front of me, blinking back tears.

I hadn't told anyone I'd seen him, even though it killed me to keep the secret. I'd panicked watching Bessie pay the month's charges. Although Frank's income had left us with a decent amount in our account at the bank, I doubted it would last us very long. And then what would we do? Bessie, Alevia, and I only earned enough to make up half of what we needed to sustain the household. Beneath her worry for Frank, Mother had to be wondering how we'd survive if Frank never returned. I'd noticed the way she kept glancing over Bessie's shoulders to look at the ledger. Mother had retired early that night, and the familiar and awful sound of her sobbing had echoed softly through my walls until well past midnight. In truth, the news of what Frank had done would destroy her, especially since he wasn't here to explain himself.

I'd heard nothing from him since that morning in the cemetery and still hadn't heard from John. I had no idea if they were alive or dead. It was strange; sometimes their memory and the thought that they may never come back knocked me down so hard I could barely pick myself up, but other times, when fury overtook my sadness, I was able to force all feeling away. I dabbed the corners of my eyes with my linen napkin. Anger flared up, sweeping from my stomach to my neck.

It was their fault as much as Doctor Hopper's. Frank and John had willingly participated in his ridiculous plan and sacrificed our happiness in the process. John was a liar. He'd convinced me that we were the same, encouraged my love for a man whose talent and kindness was a guise masking darkness and deceit. He was worse than Charlie. At least Charlie had had the decency to face me, to tell me why he'd decided to throw our love away. Meanwhile, Frank's absence was killing Mother, and his secret was killing me. It wasn't fair.

"Sorry I'm late, Miss Loftin." Harvey's deep voice startled me and I dropped the napkin to greet him, hoping I didn't look like I'd been crying. "Got caught up talking to Walter Damrosch on the way over. Said he's been practically living in the Hall practicing for the Messiah. Suppose your sister's been slaving away with him."

"Actually, she hasn't," I said, a little too curtly than I intended. "Damrosch dismissed her a few weeks ago." Harvey stared at me for a moment.

"Why ever on earth?"

I shrugged. "I suppose he changed his mind about allowing females in the Symphony." That was a blatant lie. The truth was that he'd cornered Alevia before rehearsal a week after Lydia's death and said he couldn't allow her to play. He'd spoken to Tom, and until Franklin was cleared—if he ever was—Damrosch couldn't permit Alevia's presence. Alevia had asked him outright what Tom had accused Franklin of, but Damrosch had shaken his head, saying he couldn't possibly tell her in the event she'd warn Franklin. She'd told Damrosch that she hadn't seen our brother since the night Lydia died, but it didn't matter. Damrosch had already turned his back and told her to leave. Alevia hadn't come out of her room for days after, and when she did, she swore that if Franklin ever turned up, she would never speak to him again, regardless of his explanation.

"That's complete nonsense," Harvey said, shaking his head. "I thought Damrosch was more progressive than that." His brows furrowed and he shook his napkin open. "And where in the hell is John? He was supposed to have a draft to me two weeks ago." I gaped at him. I wasn't expecting the question and had no idea what to say. "I heard some rumor that he and the doctor left town unexpectedly. Is that true?" He stared at me over his wire-framed glasses. My fingers curled into fists, gripping hard into my palms. I didn't want to answer the question, nor should I have to. John should be here to explain himself.

The Blaines had been strangely quiet after Lydia's death, but rumors swirled anyway. Thanks to Franklin, I knew why. They were waiting for the autopsy results. They'd already talked to the police, but they couldn't implicate John, his father, and Franklin until they knew for certain. Without the Hoppers' dramatic exit, I had a feeling no one would have had a clue as to what was brewing under the surface. The trouble was, of course, that the Hoppers lived on Fifth Avenue, and anyone could see they'd left their home in shambles without bothering to call the coroner before they went. Mr. Harvey reached across the table and shook me.

"Miss Loftin," he said softly. "Are you all right?" I could tell my face had drained, but I nodded.

"I'm sorry," I said. "I was thinking of something else."

"That's quite all right. I was just asking if you'd heard from John. It seems that he's avoiding me . . . and everyone else for that matter. He wasn't even at Lydia Blaine's funeral." Harvey shook his head. Lydia's funeral. The realization that she was dead still shook me. I'd never lost a friend. She'd wanted to be my sister; I would've readily accepted her.

"I haven't heard from him," I said softly. The last time Harvey had asked me about John, I didn't want to discuss him because I hadn't been sure I wanted to marry him. Now I wasn't sure I would ever see him again or sure that I wanted to. "I, um, I believe that he and Doctor Hopper may have gone out of town." Harvey placed his hand on top of mine.

"You seem as confused as I am, my dear. John has hurt you and I'm sorry for it." His eyes held mine.

"It's all right," I said. "It's not as though he's severed my writing hand." I held up my left hand, hoping to change the subject. The waiter bounded up to our table, notepad poised to finally take an order.

"Two glasses of scotch, straight up. Oldest and finest you have," Harvey barked, not waiting for the waiter to speak. I glanced at Harvey, half shocked that he'd openly ordered spirits for a woman. Alcohol would only chip away at my façade and I didn't want to burst into tears in front of my editor.

"Thank you. It's been a challenging few weeks," I said. He smiled at me.

"Were you friends with Miss Blaine, too?"

I nodded, unsure how much I should say, but decided there was no point in holding back. He'd likely know my family was involved eventually.

"Yes. We were very well acquainted." I remembered her smile the first time we met. "She . . . she was . . . involved with my brother." Harvey's eyes crinkled.

"Is that so? Did you know the funeral was a few weeks back?"

"Yes." I cleared my throat. "We had to miss it, unfortunately. We were all quite ill." With heartache, specifically. That, and we'd all been afraid to attend, knowing Tom thought Franklin at fault. Instead, we'd had our own sort of memorial for Lydia. Even Mae had come in from the city to have tea and reminisce.

The waiter materialized with our drinks and Harvey immediately raised his to his lips. I lifted my glass and took a sip. The memory of John's late-night kisses in the study tried to force their way into my mind, but I blocked it. The liquid burned down my throat and I took another long drink, treasuring the sensation.

"I hesitate to ask, but I must—how're the revisions coming?"

I set the glass down and looked at him. "They're not."

"Ah. I had a feeling. If I may?" His eyebrows rose in question and I nodded for him to continue. "Years back, I had the pleasure of meeting the esteemed Emily Dickinson." My mouth went dry at the mention of her, remembering Frank's words after Charlie had crushed me. *"I'll not allow you to wither away like that poor Dickinson woman."*

"She was the most miserable soul I've ever met. She was quiet and awkward, so paralyzed with grief that she couldn't stand to be around anyone. But she was an amazing writer." I thought of the weeks I'd spent writing after Charlie's betrayal. The days I'd poured myself onto the page without knowing what day it was or what time. Those words had been my best. "You won't be like her; you're too strong. But learn something from her. She channeled her grief into marvelous writing. Do that. It'll get you through."

"Thank you," I said, raising my glass. I drained the last of the scotch and Harvey squinted at me over his glasses, likely wondering if he'd inadvertently signed a drunkard. "Thank you for understanding."

"You're meant to do this, you know," he said. I stared at him blankly and he laughed. "To write." I grinned, genuinely this time. "You have a story to tell, one that people need to hear. Tell it."

*H*ours later, stomach still stuffed with filet of beef, preserved asparagus, and renaissance pudding, I clung to his words. It was only five in the evening, but the late October sky was already dark as midnight. The house was hauntingly silent. Alevia hadn't touched the piano since she'd been dismissed from the Symphony and Mother was out at a neighborhood women's sewing group— something I'd forced her to attend. She hadn't told anyone about Franklin's absence. I didn't blame her.

I braced my notebook on my knee, sinking back against the couch to look out the front window. It was time to begin again. I stared at the blank page, wishing inspiration would come. I couldn't let my dreams vanish along with Frank and John. The crowd of commuters from the city still trickled past, wandering down our street to their homes. They huddled in their coats carrying briefcases or lugging bags of tools or sweat-soaked clothes from working in the factories all day. A man turned around in front of our fence, waiting for someone I couldn't yet see.

I saw John's face and the memory of Frank propped in the corner of the Hoppers' drawing room. The strange burn of anger and pain drifted through me. Though it had been nearly a month, I still didn't know how to grieve for them if they never returned. I remembered the news of the Mud Run Disaster in Pennsylvania in '88. The pictures of the sixty-six people who'd died on that train had been in the paper the next day, taking up five full pages. Whole families had been killed, but the worst was the story of a young woman who'd lost four siblings as well as her parents. I hadn't understood, even then, how she could mourn all of them at once. At the time, I was heartbroken over losing my father. He was one person. Now, as angry as I was, I had no idea, if it came to it, how I would find a way to live with the fact that both my brother and my near fiancé were gone forever. I kept going to Franklin's room to sit among his things— the scattering of travel pamphlets on his dresser, the discarded half-finished paintings under his bed—and then something, a memory or the scrawled writing on a letter would remind me of John and my mind would switch to him, equally broken and confused.

"I'm going out. I'll be back on the last train." Bess materialized in the foyer balancing her supply trunk. Her bruised eyes were a startling contradiction to her cheery Christmas-red hat with pluming green feathers. "Here." She withdrew an envelope stuffed under her arm. "It's the new edition of *The Century*. Came in the post today and got jumbled with my things." I took it from her and set it down on the hard upholstery beside me.

"Where're you going?"

"The Carnegies'," she said blankly. "Louise has written me five times begging me to come over and fit her for a new hat for the holidays. I don't want to go, but . . ." Bessie pursed her lips and shrugged, not bothering to vocalize the obvious—that we needed the money. I'd found out gradually that Doctor Hopper was related to the Carnegies through Andrew's father, William Carnegie. Doctor Hopper's father, Thomas, was his cousin. Though I knew the Hoppers had never been close to their distant cousins, they were family nonetheless and I wondered . . .

"If they mention anything—" I started, but Bessie cut me off.

"If they so much as utter the name of . . . of those men or my brother, I'll leave, I swear it." As promised, ever since Tom had left, Bess hadn't spoken their names. I'd overheard her telling Alevia that she'd tried to call on Tom last week—likely because he hadn't responded to any of her letters—but had been quickly turned out of the Blaines' drawing room.

"I know you hate them," I said softly. "But you don't know what happened . . . none of us do," I amended, catching myself. "John and Frank's hearts aren't suited for murder. There has to be an explanation." I paused briefly, knowing even the clarification wouldn't change anything in her eyes. They were liars. Soon there would be newspaper articles slandering their names and calling them killers—unless someone knew where they'd gone and could go after them. They could come clean about the Optimism Solution. Even if Doctor Hopper hadn't patented it, the ingredients weren't illegal. It was the high dosage that had taken Lydia's life.

"I don't care," Bessie said, reaching for the doorknob.

"Please." I started to get up from the couch when Bessie turned to look at me one last time. Chilly air blew in from the open door. "Surely someone knows where they've gone. Please, Bessie. Pay close attention for me." She shook her head, but as she stared into my face, I knew she'd agreed. She was my sister and could tell I was miserable. She'd help me if she could.

The door slammed behind her and I watched her amble across the lawn, sling open the fence, and turn back to close it. Life confused me. The mix of pain and love and suffering and happiness didn't make sense. Neither did the timing of it all. I opened the envelope beside me and withdrew the magazine. I flipped past the index to find a short note from Mr. Gilder printed before the first story. I scanned it, found my name among the words, and closed the volume. A month ago, this page would have filled me with satisfaction and joy. Now, I felt nothing. Charlie's efforts on my behalf had been selfless and kind, but thinking of him at all only reminded me that I'd been deceived by every man I'd ever loved. I flung the magazine across the room, satisfied with the loud smack of the spine meeting the wall. I plucked my notebook from the arm of the couch and my pencil from the table beside me, thoroughly angry with everything and fully prepared to pour all my bitterness into my novel.

Chapter Twenty-two

DECEMBER 1892
The Loftin House
BRONX, NEW YORK

Alevia was sitting on the spoon-backed velvet armchair in the parlor staring out at the blue sky through the frosted window-panes. There had been clouds or rain for the past two weeks, ever since the first of December, and a bit of sun was welcome.

"Beautiful, isn't it?" I sat down on the tufted couch behind her and opened my notebook, relishing the warmth from the fire in the hearth. I'd poured myself into my novel over the past month and had finally worked out a daily routine, though I still had days where I did nothing but make myself sick thinking of John and Franklin.

Alevia's hair was down, black waves cascading down her back, and she nodded, without bothering to look at me. It was ten in the morning, but she hadn't dressed. She hadn't changed from her sleeping gown for days now.

"Are you all right?" I asked, fully knowing she wasn't. I wasn't either. Our bank account had dwindled to nearly nothing. Yesterday, while Mother, Bessie, and Alevia gathered around our ledger trying to figure how we could survive the next months, I'd retreated to Frank's room. With the sound of my family's muffled worries in my ears, I'd cursed him until my rage turned to despair and I'd crumpled on his bed weeping, guilt threatening to overtake me. Frank said he hadn't agreed to sell for Doctor Hopper on account of me, but he'd begun right after Charlie's proposal, right after Charlie had made it clear that he'd asked for Rachel's hand because she had money he needed.

Alevia sighed, eyes rolling toward the whitewashed ceiling before finally making their way to mine.

"Of course I'm all right. What do you think? I'm positively thrilled that I've been dismissed from the Symphony." Her sharp response startled me. I'd expected a muted "no." She kept her gaze fixed to mine and I noticed the swollen bags under her eyes. Her misery filled me with remorse. If I hadn't let Charlie's betrayal consume me so entirely, perhaps Frank would've remained at J. L. Mott, leaving us poor but safe from ruin. "I didn't mean that. I'm sorry, Gin," she said softly.

"You can't let Damrosch defeat you. He's only one conductor. There's still the Philharmonic and the Women's Symphony. You can't let him stop you from playing. You're too talented."

"You don't understand."

"Really?" I said angrily before I could stop myself. I was tired of Bessie and Alevia moping around as if they were the only ones who'd lost everything. "You of all people should know that I've stomached my fair share of disappointment. I was rejected from *The Century,* only to find out that a work Tom plagiarized was accepted. You were there when I lost Charlie and you've watched as I've suffered through the great possibility that I've lost John as well, not to mention our brother." Alevia looked down at her hands, long fingers drumming anxiously in the air.

"I know. But Harvey hasn't stopped believing in your work. You know I've never cared much about men or marriage. All I've ever wanted is to play the piano and Franklin has taken that from me."

"That's ridiculous. He has not. In fact, if it hadn't been for Franklin, you would've never met Lydia and Damrosch never would've accepted you." Alevia remained silent. "Futhermore, Franklin hasn't stolen your ability to play. You still have all ten fingers and I guarantee that if you sat down at the piano right now, you could play whatever piece you wanted." I pursed my lips at her, trying to channel Mae. I didn't have her gentle-mannered bluntness and wished she was here. She'd come to loan us some money yesterday with the promise that she'd return after school today. She and Henry had come to the house for dinner almost every day since Frank's disappearance. I was thankful for their company. Although I was certain her nerves were as frazzled as everyone else's, she was a calm presence.

"That's not what I meant, Virginia," Alevia whispered, though her words were edged with ice. "I could sit in the corner and play brunches and parties until I'm too old to see the notes, but I don't want to. That's not excellence, that's average. And I had finally made it. Now I'll never have another chance." I started to disagree, but Alevia kept talking. "I know what you're going to say. I love you for trying to cheer me, but Damrosch won't change his mind. Franklin isn't here for a reason. Whatever he's done, he knows he can't return and Damrosch won't consider me unless Franklin redeems himself, whatever that means. And I won't audition for the Philharmonic again. They won't hire a woman." Alevia took a deep breath and rubbed her eyes. I had never heard her speak this directly. Tragedy and worry had hardened her, as they had Bess. Anger had drawn them closer together. In contrast, I found myself rattled, vacillating between moments of calm and alternating fury or melancholy—though I never let my family see me break. I couldn't, lest they believe that I, too, had turned my back on my brother and John.

"I *am* right," Alevia said. As much as I wanted to argue with her, I couldn't. "You love Franklin and nothing he could ever do, even this, will make you stop loving him. You've always been his pet and him yours, but he's ruined us, all of us . . . our livelihood, our dreams. I've watched you try to write. It takes you hours to pick up the pencil. I know it's because you're worried. He's killed your creativity, your ability to breathe." She was wrong. True, I was worried, but over the past several weeks, I'd written better than I had in months, writing through my pain, using it for good.

"Don't act as though you don't love him, too. He's your *brother*, Alevia, and whatever he's done—" She cut me off, shaking her head.

"I hope that I'll be able to forgive him later, but right now, I am too angry. I hate him." She said it quietly, turning her gaze to the jumping fire. I remembered his face stretched with worry in the dark. He loved our family. Alevia's words would break him. I inhaled the yeasty scent of baking bread as the logs popped in the hearth. Mother had been making a loaf first thing in the morning for the last few days.

"Hate him if you want, but it won't change anything. It's Damrosch you should be angry with. He let his emotions get in the way of his work." I stood to leave before she could disagree with me. I started toward the front door. I needed to walk, even if it was just to the end of the street and back. The gloominess of the house was weighing on me.

The street was silent save the distant clanging from the iron factory. My breath hovered in front of me. Smoke trailed from the chimney of each house, puffing toward the blue sky like steam chugging from a train. A door echoed up ahead and two children sprinted down the front steps chasing each other and laughing. Obviously not siblings—the boy had a full head of bright red hair, while the girl's was raven black—they ran round and round the yard until the boy pulled up a handful of grass and threw it into the girl's face. Her smile drooped and she stopped running to wipe the blades from her eyes. The boy stopped then, too, and walked toward her.

"I'm sorry," I heard him say as I passed. He hugged her, little arms wrapping tightly around her back. She threw hers around him in turn and tossed him to the ground. She laughed at his surprised face, and at once I was reminded of Charlie. We'd only been children, maybe eleven or twelve, and we'd been playing cowboys and Indians in the snow during that lazy lull of a week between Christmas and New Year's. Santa Claus had given Charlie a bow and arrow and Frank a cap gun. Though I hadn't received anything remotely useful to bring to the game—my stocking had been filled with colored pencils and an orange—I'd insisted on playing, too, wielding a sling shot made from a leather strap cut from one of Father's old suitcases and whatever rocks I could find. Charlie and I had been chasing Frank, and after our third lap around the house, I'd decided to hide in one of the bushes and scare him. Hearing a running stride, I'd jumped from my hiding place at the wrong time, startling Charlie instead and causing him to scream at the top of his lungs like a little girl. Thinking it hilarious, Frank had doubled over laughing, but Charlie's face had burned red and he'd leveled his bow and arrow at my chest. The felt-tipped arrow hadn't hurt me, but his anger had, and before I could think twice I'd raised my slingshot and hit him in the forehead with a rock. I'd regretted it immediately, but he'd touched the red spot, raised his face, and laughed.

The familiar feeling of Charlie's friendship flowed through me and I urgently wished he were here. Even though I'd always been a believer in the idea that things happened the way they were supposed to, I couldn't help but wonder how differently things would have turned out if Charlie and I had married. I know I would have been happy because of my love for him, but also because I wouldn't have known anything else. I would have written exclusively for the *Bronx Review* until I felt like quitting. I never would have written my novel nor gone to the Society nor fallen in love with John nor met Frederick Harvey. The thought of John made my heart still. If I concentrated, I could feel the way his gaze set my stomach tumbling, longing for his touch, and the way his surety, the promise of his love, settled it. But his memory was so muddled now. I longed for the man I'd known, grieved for the torn part of him I hadn't, and despised the darkness he'd hidden from me. In spite of my confusion, the possibility of how different my life could have been without him was startling. Even given the hardship, I was glad for the opportunities I'd been given.

I started back home. After the rain, the sunshine made the paint slathered on each identical home look surprisingly fresh. I waved at Mrs. Jacobson who'd stepped onto her porch in her late husband's buffalo fur coat to collect her paper. Nearing eighty, she was the oldest and last original owner of the houses on our block.

"Do be careful out there, Miss Virginia. It's been raining for days and bound to be icy!" she called out. I nodded at her and kept on, refreshed and glad for the warmth when I finally made it inside. I unbuttoned my kid leather boots and left them on the front rug. As I'd come to expect, the house was quiet save the sharp dinging of the grandfather clock in the drawing room.

Hanging my mink coat on the rack next to the door, I started toward the stairs. I paused as I passed the dining room. Mother had just set out the plain white china bowls—we were having barley stew again for lunch—and was staring at the portrait of my father. Tears gathered in her eyes, but she didn't blink. A cup of coffee steamed next to the open newspaper in front of her and I walked into the room and sat down across from her.

"Mother," I whispered. She didn't acknowledge me at all, but kept staring over my head at Father, hand pressed to the lapel of her gray flannel walking suit. "Mother," I said again. This time her eyes landed on mine.

"Now I know why he hasn't come home. Your brother . . . he's ruined. He's ruined us." She said it evenly, but her words stung like a stitch threaded through an open wound.

"What do you mean?" I started to think she'd lost her mind before she lifted her hand from her lap and scooted the newspaper across the table. I didn't want to look, but forced my eyes to the page. The headline, *"Blaine Family Suspects Murder in the Death of Daughter"* was in bold on the right-hand side of the front page next to an article detailing Jack Astor's new home plans. Suspects, not confirms. I comforted myself before I started reading.

Authorities in Manhattan are searching for self-made physician to the elite, Doctor Jacob Hopper, his son, Mr. John Hopper, and business partner, Mr. Franklin Loftin. A source close to the Blaine family of Manhattan says that the three suspects have been prescribing and distributing an expensive unpatented drug called Optimism Solution, prescribed to patients for depression. After much digging, it appears that the drug, injected intravenously, was verbally said to be perfectly safe for use, but according to a waiver that many users were forced to sign ahead of time, Doctor Hopper, his son, and Mr. Loftin knew that there was a possibility that the drug could be lethal. Thus far, it has been determined that Miss Blaine's death was not the only casualty. Others, including the death of Mr. Marcus Carter, are thought to be a result of high dosages of this drug. Authorities fear that the Hoppers and Mr. Loftin fled the city after the death of Miss Blaine. The source has disclosed to us that a toxicology analysis found Miss Blaine's body to be flooded with lethal doses of both cocaine and morphine. An official warrant has been awarded authorities in order to bring these men to justice.

I dropped the paper and looked at Mother. Her face was pale, wrinkles etched deeply into skin taut with worry. I cursed under my breath. Damn them for doing this to us. Regardless of what I'd promised Franklin, I had no choice.

"I saw Franklin." Mother's eyes flashed at my words and I stood from my chair. "I'm going to get the others. It's time you knew."

*H*e's destroyed us."

That was the first thing Bess said after I'd gone on for nearly half an hour explaining how I'd come to see Franklin, what he'd said, and why I hadn't told them any of it. She glared at me, fluffing her enormous gigot sleeves. I slammed my hand on the oval walnut dining table and stood up. Mother's head jerked up from her lap.

"Don't you understand?" I said. "Frank and John didn't know—well, Frank suspected, but he didn't know for sure. Our brother is somewhere out there running for his life and all you worry about is our reputation?"

"Sit down," Mother said and I did, seething. None of them understood, not even Mother. As horrified and filled with rage as his actions made me, I'd seen his remorse. I knew his heart.

"Do you honestly believe he'd kill someone? Franklin, our brother, killing someone? He made a mistake . . . a bad mistake, one we'll all pay sorely for, but still." I looked from Bessie's stony glare to Alevia's eyes filled with tears to Mother's tapered lids fixed on my face. No one spoke.

"You've broken my trust," Mother said. "To keep this from me, Virginia, knowing all the time I've worried—"

"It would've made it worse, Mother. I didn't know how it was going to turn out, neither did Frank. He didn't want anyone to worry unnecessarily."

"So he hoped to get away with killing her? The woman he supposedly loved?" Bessie asked flatly. "I hope they hang him." I heard Alevia gasp as my hand met Bessie's face. My palm pulsed with the sting of the impact and Bessie clutched the red print on her cheek.

"You little twit," I said. "Didn't you hear what I said? John administered the drug but he didn't know either. He used it himself. He trusted his father and his father refused to see that people were misusing it, that it was dangerous." My head started to spin with anger at John for his deception, anger at my family, and I stumbled into my chair. I clutched the edge of the table, trying to steady. The edges of my vision were hazy and I knew that if I didn't sit down, I would faint.

"Where is he now?" Alevia's sweet voice drifted through my ears. Comforted, I looked up at her, thinking she'd finally come around, but her eyes, blurred with wasted dreams, said otherwise.

"I don't know," I breathed. "He said he was going to get out of the city for a while." Still light-headed, I turned my back on them, toward the portrait of my father leaning back in his leather chair. His stony glare hit me and I knew then what I had to say. I whirled back around and looked at my mother. "He's your son, your blood," I started. I plucked the newspaper from the table and held it in front of her face. "And you're going to take the word of a stranger over his?"

"I believe the only news I've heard. He didn't care to tell me," she said. I rolled my eyes.

"I found him. Otherwise, none of us would know." Mother was softening. I could see it in the slump of her shoulders. Bess and Alevia both stared at me, neither conceding, and I looked from one to the other, wishing I could shake them.

"The two of you can think what you want, but it's disgusting, really, how quickly you'll forfeit our brother to the wolves," I said. "If heaven forbid you should stumble off of your self-righteous paths someday, don't count on us loving you." I left the room. No one spoke as I slung on my cloak and buttoned my boots in the foyer. My one ally, the one person besides me that I knew would always love him wasn't here and I needed to go find her. Someone had to tell Mae. But as I reached for the handle, the door flung open. Mae's eyes were burned red, her cheeks chapped from the sting of the wind over her tears. She was clutching the newspaper in her fist.

"Mae, I—" Before I could begin to explain, she lunged at me, buried her face in my cloak and wept.

"Our brother. How could he?" She sobbed into my shoulder. "We'll never see him again. He's forfeited his life, he's given up everything to sell that drug. He'll never come home now, and I'm so angry and sad that I can hardly bear it."

Chapter Twenty-three

The Loftin House

BRONX, NEW YORK

Silent night, holy night. Son of God, love's pure light." I was dreaming the hymn. Yawning, I opened my eyes to the windows displaying a perfect Christmas Eve. The snow had started falling in the afternoon and was still pouring from the sky in fluffy flakes. We'd shuffled through the thick of it on our way to church tonight, letting our boots dry where we stood in the standing-room-only sanctuary. I closed my eyes to go back to the hushed silence of the packed room lit only by taper candles. I could see the light flickering off the limestone walls and onto the stained-glass image of the Good Friday Jesus at the front. I'd focused on his face the moment we'd stepped through the door tonight—at his mouth pinched in pain and his eyes turned up to the heavens. Christmas was supposed to be warm and soothing, a time to revel in joy and forget grief, but I'd needed the reminder that I wasn't alone, that an anguish much greater than mine had been endured by our Lord. I'd stared at the image throughout the entire service, barely aware of anything around me, until Pastor Worley called Alevia to the front to play "Silent Night." At the last verse, right before we sang "*with the dawn of redeeming grace,*" Mrs. Aldridge, who was for some reason alone on Christmas Eve, crossed all the way from the front of the church to the back to put her arms around Mother. The gesture had gripped me, bringing to mind the grace God continually poured out on even the most undeserving—even Franklin and John.

It wasn't that the backlash from the article had been particularly awful—at least in Mott Haven. If anything, our neighbors and friends had responded with pity, but across the river in Manhattan we'd been blacklisted. It hadn't been obvious at first, but when Alevia—who'd slowly started playing again— wasn't hired to play at the usual families' Christmas soirees, the message was clear. The only families brave enough to employ her were the Vanderbilts and the Astors and that was because they tended to disregard the social stigmas and rumors originating in any home but their own. Bessie's business had been slowing for the same reason. It seemed entirely unfair that they should pay for Franklin's transgressions, but that's how it worked. One misstep could devastate an entire family's reputation with the upper class—Mother was right about that—and our income had been ravaged to the point that we'd sold the Benz and had to put in an inquiry at the Building and Loan. I'd volunteered to go into town and request the loan, to face the penetrating eyes of the banker who'd either grant us a moment's peace or strangle us further. The whole way there, I'd blinked back tears. At one moment despair would hollow my soul, but then I'd recall the source of our agony, and my nerves would ache with fury until I wanted to scream.

I pulled the quilt up over my shoulders. The small fire I'd made from kindling had gone out hours ago and the cold whistled in through the cracks in the windowpanes. Huddling on my side, I tucked my arms under my pillow, praying the loan would be granted. The banker hadn't been sympathetic nor callous. I didn't know what his decision would be, but we'd find out next week, which seemed like aeons from now.

I must've drifted off for a moment before I was jarred awake by a sound downstairs. I stilled, listening, until I heard it again—the muted screech of wood sliding against wood and the soft rattling of a window. The sound was coming from right below me in the drawing room. Over the past weeks, a few neighbors had reported their windows knocked out and Christmas presents stolen. Robberies tended to happen more often this time of year, which is why we hadn't put our gifts out until tonight. Thinking of the packages beneath the small balsam fir in front of the window, I knew they were easy targets. A deep grunt and the thump of what sounded like boots kicking the side of the house came from the first floor and I jumped out of bed. Grabbing my cloak, I glanced around the room for something to use as a weapon, finding nothing save the decorative knob on the top of my dresser. I twisted it off. Only about a foot long, I doubted it would do much. My hands started to shake and I clutched the knob harder. Tiptoeing out of my door, I glanced down the hallway, thinking that I should go down to Mae's room and wake Henry, but a thud hit the floorboards below me and I sped down the stairs. By the time I woke Henry, the intruder would be gone.

My heart pounded in my ears as I crept toward the foyer, but the scrape of wood against wood again quickened my pace. I sprinted toward the drawing room. Even though our gifts to each other were nothing but small trinkets—eyeglasses for Mother, a scarf for Bess, a day planner for Mae, music to Alexander Scriabin's Piano Sonata No. 1 in F minor for Alevia—I wouldn't let the thief take them. Not this year. Entering the room, knob thrust out in front of me, I stopped dead.

"Frank?" I whispered. I didn't believe what I was seeing. I rubbed my eyes, but he was still there when I looked again. His hair had grown long, curling around his ears, and he hadn't shaved, a beard overtaking the bottom half of his face.

"Merry Christmas, Gin." He took two steps and gathered me in his arms. He smelled awful, but I didn't care.

"Thank god you're all right," I whispered into his shirt. "It's been months since I saw you and the news hit the paper a few weeks ago. I thought you were dead." I was babbling, but I didn't care. My brother was alive and safe and home. He laughed softly. I heard the echo of it in his chest and stepped away to look at him. "Why didn't you knock?" I asked, eyeing the cracked window.

"It's the middle of the night, Ginny," he said. "In any case, I tried to open the door, but it was locked?" His eyebrow quirked up in question. We never locked our doors.

"There've been robberies."

"Which is why you came down wielding the almighty dresser knob." He chuckled. "I was hoping to sneak in and leave without waking anyone. I'm not staying, Gin. I only needed Father's gold watch from my dresser. I haven't any money, but if I sell it I'm thinking I'd have enough to travel abroad—probably out of Canada so they won't recognize my name." He stared at me. "I'm sorry." His voice was soft, edged with strain. "I know I've left all of you in a terrible place." I nodded, unable to pretend that we were all right. "Sell everything I own, Gin . . . my suits, my cuff links, my shoes, all of it. I'll send money as soon as I can. I need to get out of here." He started to push past me, but I grabbed his filthy wool jacket, yanking him back.

"You can't leave again, Frank. Just go to the police and explain.

They'll see you're innocent." My throat strained with the thought that I would lose him again.

"No. They need a scapegoat." As much as I didn't want to admit it, I knew he was right. "And they won't find the Hoppers."

"What do you mean they won't find the Hoppers? Where are they?" I'd convinced myself John hadn't written for fear that a letter would be intercepted, but it had been months and I had yet to receive a token of love or apology. The thought of his reputation pushed its way into my mind. I envisioned him reveling in a new life somewhere else, wooing women who would fall into his arms. Perhaps he'd only craved the pursuit. Franklin shook his head.

"I haven't found them. I don't kn—"

"Franklin?" Mother stood in the doorway in her cotton night-gown, arms clasped to her sides. Even in the dark, I could tell her face had drained completely, as pale as the white ruffled collar below it. Frank lunged toward her, gathering her in a hug so tight she had no choice but to remain still, though she stared blankly over his shoulder, dumbfounded.

"I'm sorry. So sorry for what I've put you through." Mother started sobbing as she clung to his jacket. I heard the creak of floorboards above me and held my breath. The others were awake. "I promise I'll explain," he said, patting her back. "It's not what it seems."

"I told them," I said. Frank jerked away from Mother and turned to glare at me. "Please don't be angry. I had to. I stalled as long as I could, but when the article came out, I couldn't let them believe it." His face softened as an onslaught of footsteps rained down the stairs. "Come on." I pushed Mother and Frank toward the parlor. "We can't stand in here. I know it's late, but in case anyone passes by . . ."

We got to the parlor in record time, about three seconds before the rest of the family materialized in the doorway. They stared, hovered in a cluster of white cotton, bookended by Henry in a blue nightshirt. I stood between them and Franklin as if I could somehow save him from the anger radiating from Bessie and Alevia's faces. Mae moved first. Stepping away from Henry, her lips lifted into a smile as she passed me and hugged Frank.

"We've been worried sick," I heard her say behind me. "I'm so glad you're home." The rest of them—including Henry, who'd been only mildly suspicious of what Frank had told me—remained in the corner of the room.

"Do you know what you've done?" Bessie's snarl cut through the silence. Her hands were coiled in the tiered lace at her sides, teeth gripped. "You've ruined us. Tom won't answer my letters, he won't see me because . . . because of you." She stalked toward him, but I grabbed her arm.

"He's our brother and if you can't control yourself, get out." Bessie twitched away from me, stepped toward Franklin, and smacked him. He stared at his filthy leather boots, head hung in shame, as the red splotch from Bessie's hand burned his cheek. I heard Alevia's hushed voice start then, unfurling across the room like a toxic fog.

"Why did you do it? Please, Franklin. Tell me why. Damrosch let me go from the Symphony because he said he couldn't bear to see my . . . my face." She sank down and began to cry, rubbing her fists into her eyes as if it would somehow numb the pain. I turned toward my brother who had so far said nothing and saw my mother's face beginning to cloud.

"No," I whispered. The initial relief of seeing him was over. My sisters' words had made Mother remember what he'd put us through. "Mother," I started, but she stepped away from Franklin to stand next to Bess, who'd begun to weep.

"Explain yourself, son," she said bluntly. "We need to hear from you." Franklin lifted his face to the room, bloodshot eyes scanning the faces of the family he loved. At last, his eyes settled on mine. "I love you," I mouthed silently. His lips twitched to a grin and then dropped back down.

"I know I've put all of you through hell, but I've been through my own," he started. Unable to look at anyone but Mae and me, he alternated from our faces to his boots. He told the same story I'd told them, but when he got to the part about Lydia's death, he paused for a moment. "I didn't give her the solution that night. I wouldn't let her have it at all after Marcus's death. Something just told me that it had killed . . . Marcus and the others. I couldn't let her take it. Not that it mattered what I thought." His words were a lightning bolt striking through Mother, and she stepped toward him.

"If you knew there was a possibility of death, why did you keep selling it?" she asked. "You were playing God with people's lives. How dare you."

"I asked Doctor Hopper. He said I was being ridiculous, that it was safe." Frank's voice was strained, cracking over the words. I desperately wanted to rescue him, to wipe away what he'd done, but there was no way I could.

"And you believed him? Even knowing in your heart he was wrong?"

"I . . . John was on it, too, and assured me it was harmless. He said there was no way it had killed them and that his father was right, Marc had died of heart trouble like his brother," he protested, voice rising.

"But you didn't give it to Lydia, because you knew the truth," Bessie screamed as tears ran down her face. "You knew people were misusing it, that they were dying. Why? Why did you do it anyway?"

"How could you?" Alevia whispered from the corner and Mother's voice rang out, strong and demanding.

"Answer Bess's question. Either you've fooled all of us and are capable of murder like everyone says or there is a reason." Franklin stared wide-eyed over my head at the oak door.

"I made a mistake," he said.

"Yes, you did," Bessie said. Franklin's hands were shaking against his dirt-smudged gray pants and he threaded his fingers hard through his hair.

"Answer me!" Mother snatched his chin. Frank's eyes flashed and he jerked away.

"I already told you. They . . . they needed me. John asked me to keep selling it. He said it was helping people, that it was helping him."

"But you knew it wasn't. How could you let him convince you?" Mother was trembling as she screamed into his face, spittle gathering in the corners of her mouth. Franklin slammed his fist on the mantel beside him.

"Because I love him!" he shouted. I froze at his words. He hadn't meant to say it. The look on his face was pure horror. The room silenced. "Because I love all of you," he continued. "I . . . I knew we needed the money." He stumbled on the words and his face flushed. His eyes met mine and stayed. He was pleading with me to forgive him, to understand. He'd meant what he'd said. Franklin had been blinded. He'd wanted to believe John about the drug because he loved him. I covered my mouth to keep from crying out in pain for myself, for Frank. His wanting me to marry John, the amount of time he'd spent with him—my head spun and I closed my eyes to stop the dizziness. The image of John and Franklin side by side, both grinning at me from the other end of the drawing room popped into my mind. I couldn't blame myself for not seeing it before. I'd never suspected it, not with his involve-ment with Lydia. I opened my eyes to his and the question sprang into my mind: did John know?

"Get out. Get out and never come back." The sound of my mother's voice was gritty, like nails sliding down a sheet of iron. Franklin blinked dazedly at her and nodded. "You're a disgrace, a disgrace to our name and I never want to see you again."

"Mother, no!" It came out of my mouth before I realized I'd said it and she spun on me.

"You'll mind your place," she said, lips pinched in anger. Franklin began to cross the room. Everyone stood silently, watch-ing him go. I couldn't stand their passivity; my mother had dis-owned her son.

"Tell him. Tell him you don't mean it." I shouted at her. She glared at me as the sound of Franklin's footsteps disappeared into the hall. I turned and ran after him. I caught his sleeve and he stopped to face me.

"I won't blame you if you hate me for keeping this from you, Gin," he whispered. "I didn't mean to say it but . . . I can't help it. I don't want to love him." His eyes searched mine and his hand squeezed my fingers. I couldn't fully wrap my mind around it. Just last month he'd been in love with Lydia . . . or so I'd thought. I stared at him, unable to form words. "I need you to know that I've never said anything to John. He doesn't know and he's not like me. He wouldn't feel the same. Wherever he is, he loves you." My heart lifted with the thought that John loved me, but deadened with the loneliness of Frank's words—and the fact that despite loving me, John wasn't the man I'd known.

"I'm sorry." I didn't know what else to say. Nothing seemed adequate as I tried to make sense of what I was hearing.

"What could you possibly be sorry for?" He smiled at me,

though his eyes held misery. "I wanted him to love you and you to love him. You have no idea how badly I wanted the two people I love the most to marry each other. I thought you were perfect together, that you would be happy, and I would be forced to get over my feelings." Anger began to burn in my stomach. Frank had pushed me toward John for his own happiness, not for mine.

"I didn't want him, I didn't want any man after . . . after Charlie, but you kept on. I fell in love with him and now he's gone." I said it bluntly but softly, and Frank's eyes filled.

"I know. I'll never forgive myself as long as I live for what I've done to you. When I saw you in the cemetery that night, when I saw the way you loved him . . . I thought that everything with Lydia would be sorted by now. I thought he'd come back and the two of you would marry and it would be all right, but it's not . . . Ginny, please." He stared at me, begging for my forgiveness. I knew he was in earnest. I knew he hadn't done it to hurt me. "I prayed every day that I would wake up and stop loving him, but I didn't. I wish I were dead." His words knocked any arguments from my lungs. He turned to walk away, but I caught him, hugging him so hard he coughed.

"I love John, but you're my brother. I love you more." He sniffed and looked down at me. "Surely there will be someone else, someone who will love you back. You'll not lose the next one," I said, echoing the words he'd once said to me. "I can't bear the thought of you lonely."

"You're rare, Virginia," he whispered, and then his eyes drifted to the banister, toward his old room and around the foyer to the drawing room. "If I never see you again," he started and I shook my head.

"No. You can't go."

"If I never see you again," he repeated. He threaded his arm across my shoulders, drew me close and reached for my hand.

Chapter Twenty-four

JANUARY 1893
The Loftin House
BRONX, NEW YORK

Since Christmas, since Frank's appearance, time had seemed to stop, each day a depressing replica of the one before it. Weeks later, no one dared discuss what had occurred that night. I needed to talk about what Franklin said and how I'd find him this time, but I had no one to talk to. My mother and sisters were distressed and angry. Their fury blocked out everything else. They'd barely acknowledged the relief that came in the form of a loan from the bank. It hadn't been a large amount, but enough to make up our monthly expenses. I'd rejoiced when the letter came, but everyone had simply stared at the paper with a resolute, withered look on their faces. Since then, I hadn't bothered to initiate conversation with anyone, especially about Franklin. Mae, the only person I would think to confide in, was away in the country—a holiday Henry insisted she needed after her students' parents caught wind of her relation to the Blaine scandal.

I rubbed my eyes, exhausted by all of the unanswered questions. I'd woken up on Christmas morning truly thinking I'd dreamed the night before—until I spotted the post from my dresser lying unattached on my bedside table. Even now, I marveled at my behavior that night, at the way I'd instantly understood Franklin and jumped to defend him, though his confession had shocked me. I'd read articles on homosexuals before, on the treatments offered to cure them. Physicians said that it was a mental illness, but Franklin hadn't spoken as though it was something to be cured, only something to attempt to ignore. I thought back, trying to see his adoration for John, but the only thing I could remember were Frank's random glances across the drawing room during meetings. He'd said that John didn't know and I knew he was telling the truth. To everyone but Franklin, they'd simply been close friends.

Sitting at Frank's desk, I closed the novel I'd checked out from the library, *Born in Exile* by George Gissing, and plucked the first of eight travel brochures off the desktop in front of me, wondering if he'd planned to leave anyway, even before Lydia's death.

I opened the first brochure. *"New York to Paris. The finest staterooms in the world for the lowest fares."* Photographs lined the pages, featuring rooms with canopy beds draped in white linens and balconies stretching over the river. I set the brochure back on the desk, unable to look anymore. He'd never make it there. He couldn't do anything but run at this point. Father's watch, his last ticket out, was still here. I leaned against the wooden chair to stare at the sky through the window. I kept telling myself that Mother hadn't meant it, that she'd write to Franklin and set things straight, but no one knew where he was and her silence indicated that she wouldn't change her mind or discuss it again. He was no longer a part of this family.

I crossed to his armoire, and opened it. His fancy tailored suits still hung there, flanked by black bowler hats. I was supposed to be going through them, sorting what we could sell. I ran my hand down the wool coat hanging on the door and lifted the sleeve to look at the filigree cuff link. His clothes already seemed like mementos of another life. I felt hollow with sorrow. I glanced at Frank's tarnished pocket watch on top of his dresser. The chain was tangled, as if in a few hours he'd come home and shove into his pocket. The memory of John and Franklin, Lydia and Tom all laughing in the drawing room materialized in my mind. I could smell the thick smoke, feel the itch of it in my eyes, and see the vibrant jewel tones of the ladies' dresses through the haze. I felt the anticipation that came with knowing that in the course of a night, a conversation or introduction could forever change my writing. I would never go to the Society again. I sank to the floor and started to sob, but no sound came out, only quiet gasps. John and Franklin had left us all in shambles. Out of nowhere, I felt the solid grip of John's hand on my arm, but it was gone just as quickly and I cried harder, wondering if I'd ever stop grieving.

"There is a sacredness in tears. They are not a mark of weakness, but of power. They speak more eloquently than ten thousand tongues. They are the messengers of overwhelming grief, deep contrition, and of unspeakable love." The Washington Irving quote surfaced in my head in Charlie's deep whisper. Hours after my father's funeral, I'd been crying in my room and had apologized to Charlie for it. I could still remember the way he looked at me as he shook his head at my apology and whispered the quote in my ear. I'd agreed with Irving back then—back when I cried five, maybe six times per year—but now I wondered, if one cried daily, if the tears were still sacred. Surely, Irving would tell me that I'd exceeded my holy allotment by now.

Sniffling, I picked myself up off the floor and shuffled back to my room to dress. I glanced at the stack of paper on my bedside table. I had no idea how it had happened really, but through my pain I'd managed to finish revisions on *The Web*, typing it to perfection on the typewriter in the early mornings when my brain wouldn't shut off to sleep. I had to mail the manuscript to Frederick Harvey today. It was high time I escaped this house anyway.

I was halfway out the door when Mother stopped me. Thick bags lay at the base of her eyes and her black-silver hair hung limply against her pale skin. She looked like she'd aged ten years in a matter of a few weeks. Though it was cruel and wrong to think, I was glad for it. I wanted her to worry, to torture herself for what she'd done.

"Where are you going?" Her voice was breathy, but her blue eyes were sharp, eyeing me as though I were about to go rob the corner bank. I considered ignoring her, glancing over her shoulder at Bess making a hat for Caroline Astor despite our scandal, because Mrs. Astor found her new milliner unsatisfactory. I could feel Mother's eyes on my face. I didn't know what she was after and didn't feel like trying to figure it out.

"Post office." I lifted the bulky manuscript in front of my face. "I need to mail this to Mr. Harvey." I turned to go, but Mother grabbed my arm.

"You listen to me. You'll go to the post office and come right back. I'll not have you raking the city for . . . for him again."

I laughed, a short, huffing sound in the back of my throat.

"Him? Who's him, Mother?" I'd never seen this side of my mother. It was as if another soul had taken over her body. She stared at me silently, daring me to say another word, but I did anyway. "Franklin? Is that his name? The son you named yourself?"

"I don't know who that is," she said mechanically.

"You of all people," I whispered, unable to lift my voice higher. "You're supposed to love us no matter what. I've always wondered where Bess got her ability to be so cruel. Now I know." I stepped outside into the frigid winter wind, letting the screen door slam behind me.

"Love and acceptance are two different things!" she yelled. Her words shocked me, crawling along my brain like stinging ants, but I ignored her and started toward town, determined to forget them.

It was only ten in the morning by the time I arrived at the post office. Mr. Markos, the old Italian postman who'd been working there as long as I could remember, was alone at the counter. He smiled as I walked in and I winced in return, my mind still reeling from my conversation with Mother.

"How do you do, Miss Loftin?" His eyes crinkled as he said it, surveying my face. My nose was running from the cold and I sniffed.

"Fine, Mr. Markos. I hope you're the same."

"I've been on this earth for seventy-one years. You're not fooling me, dear." His dark eyes softened as he leaned across the counter. I rubbed my puffy lids and looked at him, unsure of what else to say. "It's everything going on with your brother, isn't it?" I opened my mouth to answer, but decided I couldn't speak without crying. "It'll be all right. I've seen Mr. Loftin walkin' 'round this town for years now. He didn't murder that girl. Young men are dimwitted. He's just gone off because he doesn't know what else to do. He'll be back, young lady. He'll be back." He patted my hand gripped to the width of my manuscript. If only that were the case, I thought. "I'm guessing you'd like to mail that," he said, and whirled around to find something large enough to fit it before I could answer.

"Thank you." I grinned as he forced the manuscript into the envelope, tugging at the rigid casing. He set the sealed package in front of me and handed me a pen.

"When will it be published?"

"There's no telling." I scribbled Harvey's name and address on the front. "It all depends on if my editor likes it."

"He'll love it," Mr. Markos said without hesitation. "It's a rule. Good news has to follow bad."

"Let's hope," I said on my way out the door, thinking that so far, bad had followed bad all year.

I trudged back toward Mott Haven, burying my neck and face in the collar of my grandmother's mink. Cold still seeped through, permeating my ruched gray organza bodice. I didn't want to go home. It had become as eerie as a funeral parlor and I got the feeling that it would remain like that for some time—cold and silent, my family too paralyzed to remember it hadn't always been that way. Just months ago, our home had radiated with happiness and warmth, with the sprightly arpeggios of Alevia playing the piano and Bessie's laughter.

Back then, it had seemed we were all on the cusp of something. Franklin had received a promotion at J. L. Mott and was in love, or so we'd thought; Mae had just been married and employed as a teacher; Bessie was finally going to marry the prominent man of her dreams; Alevia had been accepted into the Symphony, and I was on my way to publishing my book and a potential marriage myself. Now, all that remained was the possibility that *The Web* would be published. Everyone's lives and aspirations had been stalled with Lydia's last breath. Until the article, I knew that underneath their anger, Bess and Alevia had held a small flicker of hope that their dreams would all come back as swiftly as they'd gone.

My mother, however, was a different story. I wasn't certain what had caused her fierce anger at Frank. I didn't dare ask, though I figured it was a combination of seeing the treachery on Alevia and Bessie's faces as they sobbed on Christmas Eve and Frank's confession that he loved a man. I'd wondered at first if they'd even caught that part. For a moment, I'd thought that there was a chance that they'd missed it, that maybe they'd thought he'd meant that he simply loved him like a brother, but I'd known immediately in the wide-eyed panic on his face and figured everyone else knew it as well. My mother's words this morning were confirmation.

"How do you do, Virginia?" Absorbed in my thoughts, I jumped at the sound of my name. Cherie's mother waved at me from her front porch and started down the steps. I sighed and waved back. I knew why she wanted to talk, why everyone wanted to talk. It was the same reason *The Atlantic Monthly* had decided to print photographs of the dead during the Civil War. People were attracted to tragedy.

"I've been meaning to pay your dear mother a visit." Cherie's mother was a short, overweight woman with a beautiful cherubim-like face. She smiled up at me, small cap shading her eyes from the sun.

"I'm sure she'd like that," I said, waiting for her first mention of Franklin. My instinct over the past few weeks had been to pre-empt any conversation with, "Thank you for your concern. We're fine, and no I haven't heard from my brother." Even though my family currently hated Frank, they hadn't mentioned his random appearance to anyone. I assumed they didn't want to draw unnecessary attention to themselves.

"I've been so sad for all of you," she cooed. She quickly pulled me into a hug and I found myself standing awkwardly with my arms at my sides as she squeezed me.

"It's been hard, but we're coping with it." She clucked her tongue and pulled away.

"I'm sure you know, darling, but we've had a time with Cherie recently as well. I knew that she wasn't happy, but early this year William wrote to say that he feared she was going insane. The baby was only weeks old, but she didn't want anything to do with him." She shook her head. "I can't understand it. I went up to see her the moment I received the letter and she seemed completely fine, very happy in fact, but then I went up to visit at Christmastime and she was awful. She cried all day, would barely come out of her room, and kept saying she needed to see Franklin, and why hadn't he come." I heard the sharp intake of my breath as her words sank in. He'd been selling to Cherie and her mother knew it. Her eyes met mine and she gripped my hand tight. "It's all right. She is okay, Virginia," she whispered. I was amazed at her demeanor. She wasn't the least bit angry; in fact, she was wholly sympathetic. "At first, I thought she wanted to see Franklin because she'd loved him all along and couldn't stand being married to William. We all knew almost immediately after the wedding that theirs was a bad match." She rolled her eyes. "But when I saw the article about Franklin in the *Times,* it all made sense. She'd been on the formula, too." I blinked at her, speechless.

"I'm sorry," I said. "He loves Cherie. I know he'd never hurt her on purpose. I'm sure he thought he was—"

"You don't have to explain it to me, dear," she said softly, squeezing my hand again. "I've known your brother since before he could put two words together. He wouldn't knowingly do any-thing to hurt her, and if she was taking it when I went to see her in the fall, then it really was a miracle drug . . . with awful side effects."

"I'm glad she's all right," I said, horrified by the knowledge that Cherie could've been one of the casualties. "I don't know for sure, but I think Lydia and the others . . . I think they took too much."

"It's hard to tell," she said finally. "All I know is that when I asked Cherie about it after I read the article, she denied it. In any case, William seems to think Cherie has recovered from whatever insanity or depression spell she was under, but I know she's unhappy still and has been for some time. I wish I could say that William's growing love for her blinds him to her actual state, but the truth is that he's always been a stranger to her heart."

"I'll have to call on her soon," I said, leaning in to hug her. "Rest assured she'll not get more of the solution. I doubt Franklin or the Hoppers are anywhere near the state." I hoped I was right, that they were safe.

"I'm not worried." She patted my back. "Cherie will learn to live, if not in happiness, in contentedness. Eventually the baby will make her happy and she'll be fine. I'm more concerned with all of you. I heard about Alevia's dismissal and Bessie's failed relationship with that Blaine fellow." She pulled away and lifted her palm to my cheek. "You've always been the strong one. You and Mae. But you've lost so much, Virginia." I stared at her, expecting to feel the grief hit me, but when it didn't engulf me, I realized the shock of John's disappearance was dulling. Subconsciously I suppose I'd begun to accept the fact that I'd likely never see him again.

"I'm all right. I have my writing and they'll never fully disappear in my stories."

"Ah. I see," she said. And she did. Her daughter lived through her art like me.

"I better be going, but I do hope you'll call on us soon," I said.

"And I will," she said, squeezing my hand. "My thoughts are with you, dear Virginia." I tipped my head and walked away, fleetingly wishing that a little of her grace would rub off on Mother.

I clenched my fingers into my palm. Why had Franklin been dealt such a horrible fate? I bit the inside of my lip to keep from screaming in frustration.

"Ginny!" A deep familiar voice startled me, echoing between the rows of homes and over the whir of the trolley as it whizzed past. He was wearing a felt bowler over his curly brown hair, eyes piercing mine. I stopped in the middle of the road, heart pumping in my chest, and then he smiled. Without thinking, I ran to him, purple satin skirt whipping around my legs, lungs jabbing against my stays, and then I was in his arms.

"Charlie . . . I'm so glad you're here." Half-crying, I ducked my head to hide it, but he tilted my chin up.

"What did I tell you about tears?" He laughed under his breath and I grinned at him, comforted by his presence. Charlie was one of the few people, if a person was lucky enough to have one at all, that you may not see for months, even years, but the minute you saw them, it was as if nothing had changed.

"I'm sure even Irving would've grown irritated with my tears by now," I said. Charlie's arms clutched hard around my back, pulling me closer.

"I'm sorry I haven't been here, Gin. I came the moment I heard." I sighed. It had been a month since the *Times* article. I doubted he'd just heard.

"It's not your responsibility to comfort me," I said without thinking, not intending to sound so sharp. John had been my near fiancé; *he* was supposed to comfort me. But he hadn't even cared enough to write. Charlie's eyes flashed cold.

"Of course it is," he said. "I . . . I love you." The words shocked me. I hadn't heard them in so long that I didn't realize I was gaping at him until he laughed. "What? You thought I'd forgotten about you? I already told you that would be impossible." Leaning down, he hesitated, then kissed my forehead. His mustache tickled my skin and I closed my eyes, remembering the last time we'd been this close. "God, I've missed you," he whispered. "To think you've been by yourself all this time. I was away, in Europe. Rachel and I . . . we both needed a break. I went alone and just returned last week. I'm sorry I let you down."

"Charlie, it's all right," I said, trying to pull away. "And, you haven't let me down. You've done so much for me, with Tom and *The Century* . . . it was generous, what you did." I found it rather silly that he thought he had to be there for me. He shouldn't be holding me like this. He was married. He had his wife to look out for.

"Oh. So Alevia told you." A grin touched his lips. "I suppose I told her she could if my efforts were successful. I knew it was your work. I was on my way to the ship, but I couldn't bear to leave until I'd had a word with Mr. Blaine."

"Thank you," I said. I started to shift his arm from my waist, but he refused to let me go.

"Regardless, my absence is not all right." His palm flattened on my back. "We've always helped each other through, Gin. I'm never going to stop and I know you wouldn't if it were me." At once, our memories flipped through my mind—us as six-year-olds hiding in the cabinet in his library working on our project for the Centennial time capsule, the sweet fragrance of the lily of the valley he'd picked for me after the first time he held my hand—and I knew he was right. We'd always be linked by our history, like it or not. If the same had happened to him, I would be there.

"I know, but you have other—"

"No. Listen to me." He cut me off. "I told you before and I meant it. Marrying Rachel was the biggest mistake I could've ever made. It's my fault and I know that. But you and I need each other, Ginny, and as hard as I've tried, I still love you." His eyes searched mine, pleading. My stomach fluttered. As much as I'd tried to forget him, as much as I'd tried to convince myself that my love for him had deadened, I'd never truly stopped.

"I love you, too," I said softly, though I had to force the words. It wasn't only that I didn't want to tell him; I didn't want to love him. Even though he'd been mine long before he'd been Rachel's, he was still married to a woman who adored him, and if John hadn't disappeared, I would have been near married myself. Charlie exhaled in relief and hugged me close.

"I suppose Mother would have told me if you'd had, but have you heard from Frank at all?"

"No." I hated lying to him. A year ago I would've told him. But things had changed.

"I'm so sorry, Ginny. He couldn't have done it, at least not intentionally. I hope he's somewhere safe." His face was serious, forehead crinkled in worry. He'd grown up with Frank and loved him. He also knew how close we were. I stared at Charlie, waiting for him to ask after John, too, to ask how my heart was faring, but he didn't. Perhaps his distaste for John ran as deeply as John's for Charlie, or perhaps it was simply that he didn't want to hear my answer.

"Me too." I pulled away a little and Charlie let me, but kept his fingers gripped on my arms. I glanced at Charlie's house, eyes scanning across the porch to the library window. It seemed like decades ago that I'd stood looking out of it, thinking that he was about to propose to me. That was the first night my life had been rattled out of place and the last time anything had made sense. I looked away, but not before Charlie noticed and followed the path of my eyes.

"Ginny." He turned back to me, eyes dark with a heaviness I couldn't place. He lifted his hand, fingers trailing up my neck to rest against the side of my face. "Every time I think of that night, I hate myself." His voice was coarse with strain. I knew he was telling the truth. Even though I'd never forget it, the pain felt distant. "You have to know that when I . . . when I proposed that night, everything, all of the things I said about her, they were about you." Goose bumps rose along my arms and I looked at him, stunned. I could still remember every word and hear his voice shaking as he said them.

"Please say something," Charlie said. A cluster of children rode down the street on their wheels, one of them wobbling unsteadily behind the rest. He held me closer, smoothing the hair back from my face. I didn't know what to do. "I wanted so badly to disregard Mother. To just turn to you and take you in my arms and tell you that I wanted you so much that I'd die if you wouldn't have me. Well, I've died all right."

"Don't say that," I said. His words reminded me of Frank's and I couldn't bear the weight. "I've wanted to hear you say that for so long. Thank you. But it's too late for us." The last words came out in a whisper and he stared at me in disbelief.

"No, it's not," he said. "The whole time I was away, I thought about what I'd do when I returned. I want to divorce her. I don't care what people think. I just want you, Gin." Without warning, he kissed me. His lips were soft, opening my mouth slowly. He tasted like cinnamon, like the candy his mother kept in the drawing room, and I clutched the back of his head, unthinking, forcing his mouth into mine, and he groaned. The sound jarred me out of the moment and I stepped away. It wasn't right.

"I can't. You can't do this, Charlie. It's been too long. It's too late." His lips fell and he shook his head.

"You keep saying that, but I promise it's not. I'll have the papers drawn up tomorrow and filed by next week." He said the words so quickly, I stared at him for a moment trying to process them.

"I'll always love you," I said. "But I can't." Charlie pulled away from me. His hands fell to his sides, jaw working, as if he were either about to punch something or cry. A year ago, I would have accepted him without hesitation, but I'd changed. His words, his ardent promises reminded me of John's. At once John's face flashed in my mind—the last time I'd seen him, the last time I likely ever would—every line etched in desire and pain. My heart wrenched. He and Charlie had both said they loved me, but I could no longer stake my future on broken promises. As much as I wanted to trust Charlie, I couldn't. And over time, I'd learned that I didn't need to. I had my writing to fulfill me, to give me purpose.

"Why?" he barked, voice cracking. "For the love of god, Virginia. Am I to be punished for the rest of my life for the one mistake I've made?" He started to reach for me, but thought better of it, leaving his hand hovering in the air.

"No," I said, though I knew the real answer was probably yes. Unfortunately, I'd recently found that the decisions we made could either ruin or save us entirely. Franklin, wherever he was, understood that well.

"I swear I will go insane. You're mine, damn it. I'm yours. I always have been. Every time I see you it's the most euphoric, miserable torture. Please. I'm begging you." I wanted him. I always would, but I couldn't concede. I suddenly remembered my book, what I'd imagined would happen if he ever came back to me. Even if I said yes, it wouldn't be as simple as he was claiming it would be. He would go back and forth between Rachel and me, between his love for me and his responsibility to her. I was stronger than I'd been before. I couldn't say yes. I'd given both him and John my heart and they'd fractured it. It wasn't whole and I didn't know if I could bear to give it away again for fear it would shatter.

"I just can't, Charlie. Not right now. Maybe . . . maybe someday."

"Someday when we're old and sickly and gray?" He laughed once, though his eyes were heavy.

"Perhaps," I said. "Maybe then things won't be so complicated." I stood on my tiptoes and kissed his cheek. I stayed there for a moment, feeling the warmth of his skin against mine.

"I don't know how I'll live until then."

"We're strong, you and I," I said, remembering Franklin telling the story of my grandfather. "We'll be all right," I said. Charlie shook his head, his hands pressed to my back.

"Or you could marry me now," he said softly. "We wouldn't have to go through life alone."

"You know it's not going to be as easy as you think," I said honestly. He started to open his mouth to argue with me, but I clapped my hand over his lips. "I love you and know you'll always love me. That's enough for me right now. I wouldn't be able to take it if it didn't work out the way we planned. Regardless of what you say, it would be difficult, and Rachel . . . it wouldn't be right." I pulled his head down to mine, pecking his mouth once before taking his hand.

"Come with me," I said. "This house needs some cheering."

I turned to lead him up the rest of the walk and into the cold tomb that had become my home.

Chapter Twenty-five

Would you like us to walk you in?" Alevia held my arm lightly. I'd stopped on the side of the road to stare through the two-story arching windows, past the line of glittering gold chandeliers to the reception area of the Henry Holt Publishing Company.

"No, I'm fine," I said. I hadn't stopped because I was reluctant or nervous to go in alone, but because if I allowed myself to walk any further, the top of the publisher's building would give way to the white block letters of the J. L. Mott building behind it, and I couldn't bear to see it. Staring through the windows, I examined the marble floor as though it were the most interesting thing I'd ever seen. I needed a moment to collect myself before I went in to talk to Mr. Harvey.

"Go on, then," Bess said. I glanced at her and she shooed me forward, her breath disturbing the ridiculous black blusher hanging from the brim of her hat. She'd started wearing black when she found out about Franklin's involvement in Lydia's death and had continued to wear it in mourning for her relationship with Tom. Her daily letters to him had gone unanswered. She situated a crow's feather back into place at the top of her hat. The dark color made her pale skin look sickly against the gray sky.

"Yes, do. You'll be wonderful." Alevia smiled at Bessie and then her dark eyes flit to mine. As at odds as Bessie and Alevia were at times and as close as Alevia and I were, Frank's disappearance had driven a wedge between us, shoving her closer to Bessie.

"I certainly hope he's planning to pay you today. God knows we need it," Bess said to me. She pinched her faded black muslin skirt, nose crinkling. "Great-aunt Rose would turn over in her grave if she saw me right now." My eyes started to roll, but I stopped them, deciding to ignore her instead. Mother had sold all of Franklin's belongings for two hundred dollars only weeks ago, buying us a little more time until we spent through the last of the money from the Building and Loan. We had just enough this month, but I worried that any purchases beyond groceries and paying our household fees would sink us further into debt.

"I suppose we should be getting on to the Vanderbilts'," Alevia said, letting go of my arm and looping hers through Bessie's. The gold filigree design along her sleeves seemed to glow against Bess's demure black. *Thank goodness for the Vanderbilts.* In spite of Mrs. Astor ordering a hat from Bessie last month—an olive branch that should have rippled throughout the upper class, but hadn't yet—Bess and Alevia had still been employed regularly by the Carnegies and Vanderbilts, the only households that had continued to hire them directly after the scandal. "Alice will be unhappy if we're not there in time to fit her for a hat before the luncheon. Your meeting will go wonderfully, Gin. I just know it." Alevia's nose was pink in the early February cold. I nodded once and walked toward the doors. The street was vacant for a

Tuesday morning. Those who had decided to brave the weather were snuggled down in heavy coats, eyes barely peeping over their collars. I opened the door to the lobby. Condensation gathered on the steam radiators along the front wall and I stood there for a moment, warming myself.

"Can I help you, miss?" A young man's voice came bellowing down the long entry from the reception desk.

"Yes. Thank you," I called out, starting toward him. Mr. Harvey had asked that I meet him at Delmonico's again, but I'd replied to his letter declining and asking that we meet at his office instead. Both times I'd gone to meet him at the restaurant I'd been at the crux of a major decision or crisis. Though I wasn't superstitious in the least, I couldn't stand to sit there continually being reminded of John, wondering if something else would come crashing down around me.

"I'm Virginia Loftin, here to see Frederick Harvey," I said when I finally reached the desk. The man stared at me over the rim of his steel-framed glasses. I could tell he recognized my last name and wanted to say something, but didn't quite know how. Glancing down the asymmetrical white silk and lace insert below my high maroon collar, I avoided his eyes, praying he wouldn't ask.

"If you wouldn't mind me asking . . . I've heard about your brother and Mr. Hopper. Have they been found?"

"No," I said quickly and swallowed hard. I wondered at what point, if ever, people would forget and stop asking me about it. For the most part, we'd all begun to go about our normal lives. I was writing; Bessie was immersing herself into the little amount of work she had, Alevia was playing again, and Mother had begun talking to us. They had yet to say Franklin's name, however.

"That's too bad," the young man said, shaking his head. "I'll call for Mr. Harvey. Have a seat over there if you wish." He gestured toward a circle of leather chairs situated on a red oriental rug and I took a seat with my back to the desk.

I ran my hand along the smooth leather. Had John sat here before me? The hollow feeling of betrayal and abandonment started to rise, but I refused to let it overtake me. *"You'll never be alone, Gin. I'll be here. I promise."* Charlie's voice. He'd stayed in Mott Haven for a week, spending every waking moment in our company. On the last day, I'd been unable to let him go. I could still feel the grip of my fingers holding on to him next to the front door. His presence had done what I'd hoped. For a while, it had prompted my family to talk again—old friends tended to know just the thing to do to block out misery—and for a moment, while we'd all sat laughing around the fireplace, I'd tricked myself into believing the peace was permanent. As he'd gone to leave, though, I could feel sorrow seeping back in and worried the moment he left we'd go back to our own rooms, to silence. "Write. Art has always healed our wounds," he'd said, touching my face. "But there's no escaping the scars and I hate that I've contributed to them. Please know that I have one, too." He'd traced his index finger across my chest as he said it and then across his own. "But mine will never close up. Even if you'll not allow me to be with you, I can't stay away. I need you."

"Miss Loftin." Fred Harvey's deep voiced boomed from behind me, disturbing the memories. I smiled as he walked toward me, realizing I hadn't had to fake it. The void in my chest was gone.

"Good to see you," I said. His lips turned up and I noticed that his mustache, usually trimmed to immaculate precision, hung long across his top lip. "Are you all right?" He looked around and nodded.

"We'll discuss in my office," he whispered. "Can I have any refreshment brought up, Miss Loftin? Coffee, tea, water?" he asked, much more loudly. "Scotch?" he asked softly, eyebrows quirking up. I laughed and then cleared my throat.

"No. I'm fine, thank you," I said. "Actually, scotch sounds wonderful," I whispered, even though it was still morning.

"Thank goodness. I need it today." We didn't speak as the elevator launched upward and stopped at the fourth floor.

"Here we are." He led me into a sizable office lined with inset bookshelves on three of the four walls. A picture window overlooked the city . . . and the side of the J. L. Mott building. My breath hitched in my throat when I saw it, and I looked away. Harvey circled his desk and gestured at the chairs in front of it. I took the seat with its back to the windows. Reaching into his desk, Harvey pulled out a crystal decanter and poured us two large glasses of scotch. "Here," he said, setting it in front of me. "I know it's not yet noon, but it's been a difficult day already. The law paid me a visit first thing this morning asking me yet again if I'd heard from John. They've come every week since the first of January— the three-month anniversary of the filing, I suppose. I figured I might be called if it went to trial, but didn't think they would bother potential witnesses beforehand. They're probably just getting desperate thinking they'll never find them." Harvey took a long sip of scotch. "I certainly hope they've had the decency to leave your family alone."

"They haven't. They don't come every week, though. If we were in Manhattan, I'm certain they'd come more often. It's a haul out to the Bronx to hear the same response each time." They'd come for the third time two weeks ago while Charlie was in town. It had been Detective Barfield again, a short waif of a man who—you could tell from his tone of voice—hadn't wanted to ask us again. Unfortunately for the detective, Charlie had reached the door before any of us had had a chance and told him in a cacophony of curses and shouts that no we hadn't heard from Franklin and that he couldn't believe he was bothering us during this difficult time.

"I'm just tired of it all. And worried for John, too, I suppose. He was . . . is a good young man. I'm sure your brother's the same. I can't imagine they'd hurt Miss Blaine." Harvey sighed and lifted the glass to his lips. He gulped the scotch as if it were water and leaned back in his chair. "But that's not why I asked to meet you, Miss Loftin." He swirled the liquid around and set the glass down on the desk with a clink. I lifted mine, took a small sip to steady my nerves, and nearly gagged. It was scotch all right, but very low quality. It smelled like rubbing alcohol and tasted the same. "Suppose I should've warned you." Harvey laughed. "It's a friend's homemade formula. A little stronger than the bottled variety."

"I'd say," I said and waited. Harvey stared at me as though he'd asked me a question. "You were going to tell me why you wanted to meet?"

"Ah, yes." He took another swig from his glass and stood up, pacing behind his desk chair. "You took my advice. You channeled your heartache into something truly remarkable. I thought that you nailed the revision." His tone was flat and emotionless. "The trouble is . . . Mr. Holt did not. I'm sorry, Miss Loftin, but I have to release you from our contract." I stared at him, feeling the breath flee from my chest. "I'm so sorry. Please know it wasn't my decision—"

"Just like that?" Surprised I could find my voice at all, it came out in a screech.

"Excuse me?"

"You're saying that Mr. Holt found my book so awful that he forced you to fire me without a chance at revision? What was wrong with it? Did he hate the characters? The plot? Is it because I'm a woman?" Words were flying from my mouth as quickly as

I thought them. I tried to calm down, but couldn't, and started to stand. I had to get out of there.

"Of course not. Please, Miss Loftin. Let me explain."

"There's apparently nothing to discuss." I opened the door, but Harvey edged in front of me and slammed it shut.

"You deserve the truth," he said. His eyes were watery, and I noticed on second glance that veins had started to snake across them as if he'd been up for days. "Please sit." He whispered the words and when I complied, he exhaled loudly and ran a hand across his face. Practically falling into his desk chair, he yanked the wire-framed glasses from his eyes and pinched the bridge of his nose. I waited, counting the muted ticks coming from the cuckoo clock on the wall so as to keep my composure. In truth, I wanted to throw something. I wanted to go to John and let him tell me how unfair it was, to hear that he'd endured similar hardships, but he was gone and the Society that had inspired me gone with him.

"This is hard for me to discuss, Virginia, as I don't agree with any of it," Harvey started. Reaching into his drawer, he pulled out the decanter and poured himself another glass. He took a gulp and cleared his throat. "It comes down to this: the association with . . . with your last name. Mr. Holt feels that we can't afford an additional connection to this scandal without compromising the firm's reputation and—"

"That is absurd!" I was out of my chair before I could stop myself. I slammed my hand on his desk, rattling the pens in his holder and sloshing the liquor in his glass. "I don't even know where my brother is! Why should I have to pay for what he's done?" Harvey pressed his lips together. He wasn't going to say anything because he didn't have the answers. I whirled away from him and glared out of the windows at the J. L. Mott building that I'd worked so hard to avoid minutes earlier. "I hate you, Frank."

The words came out so softly that I barely heard them myself. I knew Mr. Harvey hadn't heard me, but I clapped my hand over my mouth, shocked by the words I loathed hearing Alevia and Bessie say, words that I'd said countless times in my head but never permitted myself to say aloud. I swallowed hard, hoping to dissolve the lump in my throat, but it didn't budge. "I didn't mean that," I whispered again, as if he could actually hear me. "Please. Just come back."

"You shouldn't." Harvey's voice came from behind me. I faced him, not entirely sure what he meant. "You shouldn't have to pay for what he's done," he clarified. Running his finger around the rim of his glass, he shifted in his chair and the old wood screeched. "It's not fair and I told Holt the same, but he won't listen. For what it's worth, Holt has asked me to revoke John's contract, too . . . if he's ever found." He flipped his hand at the desk, but his breath hitched on the last syllable. He clenched his jaw to stop the emotion.

"I know they couldn't have done it on purpose if they did it at all," I said softly, looking down at my hands. I heard Harvey sniff once and glanced up at him to find his eyes dry. I wasn't quite sure why John's disappearance was affecting him so deeply—other than the nuisance of having officers barging into your workplace once a week. He didn't say anything, but plucked the glass from his desk, stood, and swirled the scotch once more. Staring out of the window at the street below, he shook his head. Unable to bear the silence, I tapped my fingers on the arm of my chair. "A while ago you told me to turn my sadness into something good. I think it helped," I said. "Perhaps you should try it."

"I know," he said, gripping the top of his chair. "You're probably wondering why I care so much—or maybe you're not." I shrugged, figuring he had his reasons. "It's hard to explain, really, and you may not understand, but I chose not to have a family. As a young man, I wasn't interested. I was too involved in my work. When I met John, I knew I'd met the man my son would have been if I'd had one." Harvey's words didn't surprise me. John's kindness and wit had affected so many people. "I know it's silly, but with him gone, it's like I've lost a son, and a writer, and I worry for him."

Harvey took a deep breath and sat back down in his chair. He yanked at a drawer, withdrew a checkbook, scribbled on it, and handed it to me. "It's only for half of what I promised you, but it's all I can personally afford."

"I can't take this." I pushed the check back on his desk. As much as we needed the money, I couldn't.

"You'll take it. I promised publication and failed you."

"You didn't fail me. It's not your fault." I fiddled with the ivory ribbon at my waist and concentrated on keeping my breath steady. Even though my greatest dream had been dangled in front of me and taken away, I couldn't blame Mr. Harvey. It was done—at least for now—another casualty of Franklin's misstep, and neither of us could do anything to change it.

"Look at me," he said. I met his eyes and he smiled. "I know this is a defeat, but this is not the last the world will see of *The Web*. Someone will take the chance on it. I promise you. Just give it time. The world will know your writing, Miss Loftin." I nodded, appreciative of the words, even if I didn't believe them. So far, he'd been the only one to take an interest in my novel. In three months I had yet to hear anything from G. P. Putnam's Sons or Charles Scribner's Sons.

"Thank you for believing in me."

"I don't say it to humor you either. It's the truth." He grunted as he leaned across the desk, snatched the check, and forced it firmly into my hands. "And you *will* take this," he insisted and then leaned back in his chair and laughed. I looked at him as if he'd gone mad. "I'm sorry. But it just dawned on me. The saying is right. You know the one—money can't buy happiness. In this case, it can't. Not even close. If it could, I'd clean out my checkbook." He reached once again into his drawer, and lit a cigar. The sweet smell of charring tobacco drifted through my nostrils.

"If only it could." I flattened the check onto Mr. Harvey's desk. "It would have been a pleasure to work with you." Mr. Harvey started to insist that I accept the payment, but I shook my head and left his office.

*P*lease don't tell me any of you have forgotten Father at Great-uncle Edmund's funeral." Mae started laughing and I coughed, choking on the sourdough bread I'd just shoved in my mouth. Even though I'd tried to forget Mr. Holt's rejection and move on—I couldn't do anything about it, after all—I hadn't laughed in weeks, and it felt good. Mother started giggling at the head of the table.

"I don't think there's any way we could," Alevia said. "We were all shoved into Edmund's little general store on the corner sitting two to a chair around his open casket. The priest—"

"Who just happened to be wearing some unofficial yellow robe on account of the fact that he'd been defrocked," I interrupted.

"Kept droning on and on about what a good man he was," Mae continued. "It was so hot in there and suddenly a loud snore rose up next to Mother."

"He never was one to fake interest in something," Mother said. She glanced at the portrait of Father over my head.

"I don't think it was a matter of interest. The man couldn't sit down without falling asleep. Mr. Mott always said he'd fall asleep on a break in the middle of the iron plant during peak hours,"

Bessie said. Her lips turned up slightly and she tucked a loose auburn tendril back into the black paste jeweled pin at the side of her head.

"I did try nudging him during the funeral. It *was* rude." Mother swirled her fork in her mashed potatoes and Alevia giggled.

"But he didn't wake up. He snored through the entire thing and everyone else just pretended they didn't notice," I said, remembering my father's head tilted back against the chair, mouth gaping open.

"Until the end when—" Bessie stopped abruptly, momentarily forgetting that Franklin was no longer a part of the family. Only six years old at the time, he'd pinched Father after an especially loud snore. Father had jumped in his chair and bellowed "damn it" at the top of his lungs, right into the face of the priest.

I laughed to myself, but the rest of the table sat in silence. I looked around at my family. Merry just moments earlier, their faces had suddenly turned to stone as they stared at their plates. I recalled Mr. Harvey's words dismissing me and clutched my fingers into my palm, willing the fire away. I was tired of it—tired of our anger. I'd lost my brother, a love, the Society, my chance at publication, and still, despite my fury at Franklin, I missed him.

I glanced down at my half-eaten rosemary chicken breast and set my fork down. In the few years since we'd lost Father, we always had a family dinner on his birthday. We laughed about our memories, what he would say about the mischief we'd gotten into over the past year. Franklin had been here last year, sitting at the head of the table across from Mother. I could still see the way Mother had looked at him as he'd told a story, the way her eyes had gleamed with simultaneous hilarity and grief. Franklin had always reminded her of Father. He had his sense of humor, but more than that, he had his heart.

"Ginny?" Mae nudged me, forcing me back to the silence of the dining room. Silverware scraped across china and I had an urge to yank the tablecloth with all of its contents off the table. "I thought you'd fallen asleep like Father."

"If you'll excuse me." I stood from the table. I could feel everyone's eyes on me, so I turned at the doorway. "I'm not feeling well," I said, knowing the tone of my voice had given me away.

"Don't do this, Virginia. Not now. We've been having such a pleasant evening. I've made Father's favorite, Grandmother Loftin's coconut pound cake. Have a seat and celebrate with the rest of us." Mother's blue eyes were soft with fatigue. For a moment I felt sorry for her—sorry that my father was gone, sorry that she couldn't reconcile the faults of her son—and then the pity flung away as quickly as the drawing of curtains at a play. Did anyone else miss Frank? My hands clutched my silk skirt and I scanned each of their faces, at Bessie then Alevia, who was wiping a drop of mashed potatoes off her brocaded bodice, and finally at Mother. None of them seemed to mind that he'd been removed from our family, that he was gone forever. The front door flew open down the hall and I jumped.

"Hello, Gin." Charlie smiled at me. His cheeks were rosy with cold and he was covered head to boots in snow. He held a box and turned for a moment to brush the top of it before stepping inside. At once, my fury settled.

"Charlie? Is that you?" Mother called from the table.

"Yes, ma'am," he said. "Give me a moment to dry off and I'll be right in. I'm sorry to interrupt your dinner. I know it's a special day." Charlie glanced at me, eyes flickering in the candlelight. He set the box down next to him and hooked his black bowler hat on the coatrack. I left the dining room and started down the hall toward him. He stared at me, gray wool coat dripping on the rug. "Wait a moment, I'm soaked," he said, but I didn't listen. Relieved at the sight of my oldest friend, I wrapped my arms around him, fully aware of the snow melting down the front of my dress.

"Recently, you seem to appear the moment I need you most," I whispered into his ear. He leaned back, and planted a kiss on my forehead.

"I'm glad for it," Charlie said. His eyes dropped to the ground in front of him, but I could see his telltale dimple emerging. "But if you're not going to agree to be my wife, you can't keep doing that to me."

"What do you mean?" His eyes met mine and his head cocked to the side.

"As if you don't know," he whispered, glancing down my neck to the saturated pink silk now clinging to my body. "The moment I walk through the door you throw yourself into my arms and press against me. It takes all of my willpower to avoid pulling you down on that couch right there." His words conjured John, the way he'd pulled me onto his couch the last time, the way he'd kissed me. In spite of the melancholy that seeped in at the memory, my stomach fluttered with desire for Charlie. As much as my heart longed for me to accept him, my mind refused. I didn't know if I could trust him, and until I could be sure, I couldn't consider his offer. I grabbed his hand.

"I'm sorry."

"No, you're not." He laughed hoarsely and reached down for the box.

"Did you bring Father a gift?" I asked, and Charlie glanced down at the sagging cardboard under his arm.

"I don't think he needs any gifts where he is. This was on your front porch." We walked into the dining room and everyone looked up from their plates to smile at Charlie. Mae's eyes met mine, widening as they traveled down my dress.

She started to mouth at me, hand drifting down the front of her white shirtwaist in illustration. I crossed my arms over my soaked bodice, hoping to block the manner in which it clung to my every curve.

"Did you bring a gift, Charlie? How kind," Mother said, standing up from her seat to hug him. Charlie set the box down on the buffet.

"That's what Ginny just asked. No, it was on the front porch. I thought I would bring it in."

"Oh, I'd forgotten. Cassie said she was going to send a few ribbons over to the girls. She bought more than she needed in France." My aunt Cassie had never married, lived with her older sister and her sister's husband in Newport, and pretty much went about her life as she wished, beholden to no one.

"Perfect. Then I won't have to buy more next week for Catherine Vander—I mean LaFitte's hat." Bessie started to move toward the box, no doubt more thrilled than ever about the possibility of what she could make for Cornelius's newlywed daughter.

"After cake," Mother said, motioning for her to sit down.

"It seems that I've arrived just in time," Charlie said, taking a seat between Bessie and Henry. Alevia leaned across Bess to squeeze Charlie's hand.

"I'm glad you're back," she said.

"What is it that you tell your wife when you come here?" Bessie asked, refusing to look at him. She glanced at me instead, eyebrows rising at my indecent appearance.

"That I'm going to visit my dearest friends and my mother," Charlie said calmly. He plucked Henry's fork from his plate, swiveled to his other side, and shoveled a sizable amount of Bessie's mashed potatoes into his mouth. "Those are delicious, Mrs. Loftin," Charlie said through a full mouth. He set the fork down and grinned at Mae beside me who was laughing under her breath at his complete disregard for Bessie's question.

"And she believes you?" Bessie persisted. Her neck began to flame in blotches from the black lace neckline of her dress. In her eyes, the love of my life had come back to me—even though that wasn't the case—but Tom hadn't even allowed her the kindness of a word. In spite of the way she was questioning Charlie, I felt for her. She'd gone down to the Blaines after her appointment at the Vanderbilts this afternoon, only to be turned away again. "She doesn't mind that you're . . . that you're embarrassingly in love with my sister?"

"That's enough," Mother snapped from the doorway. She'd gone to get the cake and stopped to narrow her eyes at Bessie, cake tray balanced in her hands.

"It's all right," Charlie said. His face paled for a moment, but then he lifted his eyes to me and shrugged. "They're fair questions considering I *am* married." My heart began to pound. "She knows about all of you. She knows what you're going through and she knows how much I care for this family, so yes, she believes me." He kept his eyes on me as he spoke.

"We know, Charlie. You're like a b-brother to us." Alevia stumbled on the word, no doubt finding it difficult given the fact that she'd disowned the one given to her by blood. "We're glad you're here. You don't have to answer Bessie."

"And as for understanding how deeply I love Ginny, she couldn't possibly. No one can," he said, disregarding Alevia. My face burned, but as uncomfortable as I was, I understood why he hadn't ignored Bess's question. My family was as close as his. When he'd hurt me, he'd hurt them, and he was trying to make things right. Charlie cleared his throat. "I'm sure Rachel minds, but I've never been dishonest with her about it. She asked me once, right after we were married, if I'd ever loved anyone else, particularly Ginny. I told her that I had and always would." Mae gripped my leg under the table. I hadn't known he'd ever spoken of me to her. The weight of the shame I'd felt for loving him suddenly lightened.

"I went to find Gin at the Society that night. I was feeling tremendously guilty that I didn't love my wife and prayed that when I saw Ginny, I'd feel either homesick for Rachel or nothing at all. Instead, I burned for her more intensely than I ever had. I was disgusted with myself." I blinked at him, instantly recalling the way he'd avoided my eyes that night, leaving me standing alone on Fifth Avenue. "All of you know that I've loved her since I was a boy. My marrying someone else was a tragic mistake . . . one for which I'll have to pay for the rest of my life. But, embarrassing or not, Bessie, I can't stop loving your sister. As wrong as it is, I can't." Bess's eyes blurred with tears and she stood from the table with a clatter.

"Then he never loved me," she said. "He wouldn't have been able to let me go." She started to walk out of the room, but Mother grabbed her wrist.

"Sit," she hissed. "Tom is still in crisis. He can't think of anything but the death of his sister."

"Shall I play while you cut the cake?" Alevia asked. She started through the pocket doors toward the piano before she got a reply and I was glad for it. We all needed a distraction. Mae squeezed my leg under the table again and tipped her head toward Charlie. His face was cast into his lap likely in an attempt to avoid my family's reaction to his confession.

"It's too bad things didn't turn out differently," she whispered, so low I could barely hear her. "Good lord, you have him under a spell."

"I wish I didn't," I whispered back. "Too much has changed.

Even if . . . even if he divorced her, I don't think I could marry him. Not now . . . not after everything."

"But you love him."

"I do," I said. "But I can't be his wife." The largest piece of coconut pound cake I'd ever seen landed in front of me. Flakes drifted off the top to the floor of the plate, mimicking the snow pouring down outside. Alevia was playing an upbeat tune I recognized. At once, I was back in the Hoppers' drawing room coughing through the smoke. I could see Lydia's blue eyes focused intently on the music in front of her, arm barely moving on the strings, and Franklin watching behind her.

"If you're not going to eat your cake, I will." Henry's voice woke me from the memory.

"I'm sure Mother will be happy to give you another slice," I said, still reeling from the notion that half of the people I'd cared for that night were gone or dead. I took a bite, though the spongy cake and toasted coconut turned to mortar in my mouth. Mae patted me on the back as I coughed and I could feel Charlie's eyes on my face. He didn't say anything, but I knew he was wondering if I was all right. I shook my head just enough for him to see.

"I think it's high time we found out what was in that box," Charlie said cheerily, still staring at me. Bessie jumped up from her chair.

"It's only fair that I open it," she said, crossing to the buffet. She looked from Mae to me and back again. I shrugged. I didn't care if she took all of the ribbon. Alevia's hands lifted from the piano and she materialized in the doorway.

"At least save me a few, Bess. I haven't had new trimmings in months." She pulled the tattered end of her navy blue ribbon toward her face in illustration.

"Very well," Bessie said, though as she turned away she rolled her eyes. Mother handed Bess a small knife from the buffet drawer.

Suddenly Bessie screamed beside me and then I heard my mother sob, a deep, gutting hiccup in her throat. Whirling around, I saw a bit of white drop back into the box. Bessie backed away, mouth hanging open.

"What?" I asked alarmed. Alevia and Mother were staring at the box as though whatever had come out of it had turned them to stone. No one would answer me, but I noticed that Mae had begun shaking. My eyes locked on Charlie's across the table and I watched as he craned his neck forward and swallowed hard.

"Ginny," he said hoarsely. "It's . . . it's . . ." Mother was bawling. I could feel tension starting to constrict my neck, blocking my breath. Bessie was on the ground now, face between her knees, but Alevia still stood staring at the box, tears pouring from the corners of her eyes. No one could talk. I paced toward the box and threw the edges open. The crisp white sleeves of a gentleman's shirt were balled on top and the tightness in my chest gave a little as I clutched the fabric and pulled it out. I couldn't breathe, but I could feel my body trying to, lungs begging me to inhale. An enormous brown-red ring stretched from the collarbone to the waistline, dried and crusty along a torn gap in the middle. Snow had leaked through the box, wetting the dry material, and the metallic stench of spilled blood filtered through my nostrils. Alevia was whimpering behind me and I was barely aware of my mother and my sisters sobbing as I fell to the floor. The room was spinning and the sides of my vision seemed to close in. I forced my arm toward one of the table legs to steady myself.

"Gin, you're all right. It's all right." Charlie's fingers locked around my arms as a water glass was pressed to my lips. My dizziness slowed as the water trickled down my throat and down my neck, mixing with tears.

"My brother," I whispered. I pitched forward. Charlie's finger-tips were rough across my chest as he forced me back up. My heart had torn in two.

"I don't think this is Franklin's." Charlie's voice sounded like he was speaking through a funnel, but I lifted my head. He was holding the edge of the shirt. "It's a seventeen and a half by thirty-five. Franklin is a sixteen by thirty-five. I know. We used to get fitted together when the tailor came to the neighborhood."

"His size could've changed." Mae's high voice came from above me. "Or maybe he was wearing another man's shirt." *John*. Charlie had said it was a 17.5 x 35. That shirt would have been small on John. The only option was my brother.

"It has to be his. Why else would someone send it here?" Henry's voice was calm amid the hiccups and sobs echoing through the room. Bess, Alevia, and Mother had yet to speak. Franklin's grinning face jumped into my mind and something sparked in my chest. Maybe Charlie was right. Maybe Franklin was still alive.

"I don't know. To make everyone think he's dead? To scare your family? I'm telling you, I don't think it's his shirt. It's not right." Charlie was looking at me. I could feel his eyes on the top of my head and then his arms wrapped around me and he pulled me into my chair. "You've got to have faith, Gin. I don't believe it," he whispered.

"I'll not have this in my house." Mother's voice trembled with hysteria and I looked over Charlie's shoulder in time to see her clutch the box and walk out of the door. I jumped to my feet to go after her. I didn't know what she planned to do, but she couldn't get rid of the only thing I had left of my brother.

"Let her go." Charlie grabbed my arm, but I glared at him and pulled loose, running down the hallway. I could see Mother's slight frame pacing toward the back door and the white shirt gripped in her hand.

"Mother! Mother, stop!" I yelled, but she didn't listen to me. She opened the door and flung the shirt into the snow. She exhaled loudly into the silent night and then the door shut. She turned and her icy blue eyes prodded into mine. Her body was trembling with what I guessed was fury and I pushed past her toward the door. She caught my arm. "Leave it. He's gone."

"He was your son. You're supposed to forgive him. Father would have." Before I could duck, she lifted her hand and slapped me.

"I love all of you," she growled. "But he ruined us, all of us. Even you."

"Franklin," I said out loud as she went back toward the dining room, wishing more than anything she could find it within herself to say his name. I stared through the window at the brown-red blotch on pure snow. The wind was blowing hard now, scattering flakes over the ground. I couldn't move from the window. The snow was covering the shirt. I closed my eyes, praying that wherever he was—dead or alive—he could be freed of the guilt, of his part in Lydia's death, of his knowledge that what he'd done had stolen all of his sisters' dreams. A strange sense of calm drifted through me and I opened my eyes to the yard, once again covered in white. The red was gone.

I continued to stare out the window, at the old oak tree with its gnarled branches, remembering the ribbon Franklin had hung from it to make a May pole for Mother's birthday two years back—something she hadn't had for her birthday since she was a girl. I remembered how touched she'd been and the tears in her eyes as she'd hugged him. Somewhere inside, I knew she still held him in her heart. I'd give my life to hear his voice one more time. The pain hit me. The past—good and bad—would never go away.

I could feel Charlie standing behind me. I hadn't even heard his footsteps, but knew he was there.

"I knew she was angry with Frank, but I didn't expect this." He said it gently so that he wouldn't upset me further. Charlie's arms came warm and solid around my waist. I leaned against him. His untrimmed chin tickled the top of my forehead.

"Mother disowned him," I said. "She couldn't accept the drugs and Lydia and the fact that he . . . he loved John." Saying the last bit made it sound so inconsequential, and as far as I was concerned it was—even given the fact that John had nearly been my fiancé. My fiancé. I couldn't help but wonder when we would have married. I pushed the thought from my mind. It was pointless. Charlie was silent and I started to pull away from him, sure he'd react to Frank's love for John like most of my family had—revulsion on top of their hatred and disappointment—but his arms tightened around me, refusing to let me go.

"Oh," he said finally. "John, eh?" Charlie smiled. "I didn't think he'd prefer a man like John." I stared at him.

"John didn't . . . doesn't know," I said. "How did you know about Frank?" His confession had taken me completely by surprise. As far as I knew he'd been in love with Lydia. Charlie reached for my hands and I let him. I searched his eyes needing to know what he knew.

"Well, I suppose I didn't know for sure, but I wasn't feeling so well after Mrs. Windemere's fiftieth-birthday luncheon, remember?" I nodded, recalling Charlie's clammy skin and pale face. "I excused myself to the library thinking I'd lie down and when I opened the door I saw your brother and a dark-haired fellow I'd never seen before standing a little too close to each other. Frank was leaning on his chest when I walked in. He babbled something about catching up with an old friend and then they both left immediately. I never mentioned it to him, of course, but thought it was a bit odd." The thought that my brother had been interested in multiple men made his memory feel foreign. I blinked, holding back tears. He'd lived his entire life feeling he had to lie about who he was, who he loved.

"And it didn't make you angry?" I asked.

"I don't think I'll ever understand it, Gin, because I don't feel that way," he said. "But no, it doesn't. Then again, it could be because Frank's not the first man I've known with that, uh, preference. My uncle James. Not that he or anyone else would have ever admitted it, of course, but he never married and from time to time one of us would find him in a compromising position with his butler." I smiled at that, wishing more than anything that I could kiss him.

"Ginny, you've got to believe me. It's not his shirt. I feel it. He's not dead," he said.

"And if you're wrong? We may never know. Even if he isn't, I don't think he'll ever come back." Charlie wiped the tears falling now from my cheeks.

"If you never see him again, dead or not, at least he knew you loved him with your whole heart." I looked down. "What is it?" Charlie kissed my mouth, a soft, closemouthed peck that made my heart skip in spite of my grief.

"He'd be alive if it wasn't for me," I whispered. "At Christmas, he snuck in to get Father's gold watch to sell for ship fare. I was so relieved to see him that I woke the others. That's the night Mother disowned him. He left without the watch." Charlie pressed the side of his face to mine and I felt his chest lift with a deep breath.

"Frank's fate—whatever it was or will be—wasn't dealt by your hand. He's one of the cleverest men I've ever known. If he wanted to find a way out of the country, rest assured he did, even without the watch." Pulling back, I looked at him, doubtful. "Guilt and I have become well acquainted over the past years, but most of my regret is earned. Yours isn't. He loved you, Gin. He wouldn't want you to blame yourself." I thought of Frank's hug in the grave-yard and his words as he left, *"Don't tell the others, but you know I love you more than the rest."*

"I miss him."

"You always will," Charlie said. In all of the chaos, I'd forgot-ten that Charlie had lost a brother, too. "Not a day goes by that I don't think of George. At the beginning—well, you know how I was—the thought that he was dead had the power to knock me down with guilt for letting him get hit by that sleigh. In those days, I wondered if the pain would ever stop. Now I know it does, but you'll never stop thinking of him." Charlie hugged me tightly and then let me go.

"I'll be in Frank's room if you need me," he said. I watched him walk down the hallway and up the stairs, thankful that he'd decided to stay. I needed him here.

I turned back toward the window and looked out at the lawn where the bloodied shirt lay inches under the snow. The house was completely quiet, save the familiar striking of the grandfather clock in the parlor. I shivered at the draft seeping in from the crack in the back door. *"Remember."* That was the last thing Franklin said to me before he'd disappeared into the Christmas Eve night.

"How could I ever forget you?" I whispered to the silent house. I thought about Father, about the way we continued to celebrate him and the stories we told about Grandfather. Even though there was no way I'd ever forget Franklin, he'd thought it important to remind me anyway. By that point he knew the rest of our family would do their best to forget him. I looked away from the window and started down the hallway.

There was a puddle in the foyer. Moonlight gleamed off the moisture where the snow had melted and dripped from Charlie's jacket. I grabbed a rag from the linen closet. My body felt heavy as I leaned over to soak it up. Patting the spot, I moved one of Charlie's boots and an envelope fell from the space between them. The paper was wet, ink bleeding down the paper, but I could still make out my name scrawled in an unfamiliar hand. I sank to the floor, my finger hesitating on the seam, chest gripped with dread.

> *Dear Miss Loftin,*
> *I so appreciated the opportunity to read your book,*
> The Web.

I paused at the first line, never so relieved by another rejection. Turning my eyes back to the page, I figured I would go ahead and read it. Right now none of it mattered.

> *I know that it has taken me quite a long while to get*
> *to your book—it is embarrassing to think that I have had*
> *it since August—but I would like to arrange a meeting at*
> *your convenience to discuss a possible partnership.*

I blinked at the words and read it again.

> *Your storytelling is remarkable both in your novel*
> *and in your work on Mrs. Emilie Helm in* The Century.
> *I began reading* The Web *last week and was immersed*
> *in the characters from the first sentence—in their deep,*
> *unrealized desires—but was most impressed by the theme.*
> *You see, I find it speaks to a rare but beautiful truth:*
> *that how, out of incomparable loss, some of the most*

brilliant art emerges. As I know you are aware from your
mention of it in your cover letter, my father was quite
intimately acquainted with Washington Irving. He was
an interesting sort of man who once told my father that
the ills he had undergone in this life had been dealt to him
drop by drop and he had tasted all of their bitterness. He
lost the love of his life, his fiancée, Matilda Hoffmann,
at the young age of seventeen to consumption. It was
always my father's belief that it was his grief that drove
his determination to prevail. Though he never married
or got over losing Matilda, he poured his undying love
and loyalty to her into his writing. I am telling you all of
this because—and I hope you won't find it too forward
of me to say—I believe you have done the same. This
story is too honest to suggest that it was created from pure
imagination. I also hesitate to mention, for fear that I will
grieve you by doing so, that I have heard of your brother's
disappearance and alleged involvement in the death of
Miss Blaine. Please know, Miss Loftin, that though we
have never met, I have kept your family in my prayers.
My hope is that through all of this you have been able to
canvas your pain in the solace of your words as I often do,
as Mr. Washington Irving often did, while facing adversity
beyond our control. I look forward to receiving your reply.

> *Most Sincerely,*
> *George H. Putnam, President*
> *G. P. Putnam's Sons*

My hands shook as I finished the letter and ran my fingers
over the writing. *George Putnam* wanted my book. My greatest
dream had just been realized and yet all I could think about were

Putnam's last words—his encouragement to canvas my pain by writing. It reminded me of Franklin, of his smile as he'd lugged the easel into the study encouraging me to paint, to write. I closed my eyes, hearing the creaks and groans of the winter wind shaking our quiet house. Franklin had known how desperately I'd wanted this moment. So had John. They'd been my greatest supporters. Even though I had the support of one of the most respected publishers in the world, I still couldn't believe how much I'd lost.

Picking myself up from the floor, I stumbled up the stairs, barely able to hold myself up. I ran my hand along the wall, turned into my room, and collapsed on the bed. Staring into the dark, my eyes caught the spine of the thin notebook on my dresser. A few months ago, it had held the first chapter of a manuscript about the Society, but after Lydia's death, I'd torn every page out save the first. I smiled remembering the one scrawled sentence I'd kept: *"My brother was notoriously attracted to adventure, which is why, as I stood at the edge of the grand drawing room filled to the brim with eccentric artist-types and smoke as thick as the clouds, I was nervous."* I reached for my pencil on the side table and stood to grab the notebook. I'd do what Putnam said. I'd channel Irving and write through the pain. I'd done it before and knew Frank would want me to do it again—and so would John and Frederick Harvey— because they knew it would save me. Once again, Franklin's last whispered word rang in my head and I lit a new taper candle and flipped to a clean page. In the pages of a book, a person could become immortal.

Epilogue

Franklin's disappearance no longer startled me, but remembering that he was gone—that he'd been gone for so many years—still made me ache. I looked down at my notebook, at the aging hand holding it, and then out at the vacant field across the street. Instead of the green, sprawling expanse, I saw his face—smiling as he glanced at my window and ran up the porch, street dust clouding round his boots. Alevia had been playing in the drawing room. I could still hear the effortless sound of her fingers on the piano and smell the sharp piney scent of turpentine radiating from the oil paints. His name echoed in my mind though I hadn't spoken it in forty-one years. None of us had. I'd forfeited my desire to talk about him in order to salvage my relationships with the family I had left, the family that refused to acknowledge that he'd ever existed. Eventually, even Mae had asked that I stop mentioning Frank. She'd said that it wasn't because she didn't think of him or love him, but she thought his memory was best left in the past so that all of us could heal.

"Hello, Gin." My eyes lifted from the notebook to Charlie who'd materialized from the French doors behind me. He pushed his cropped gray hair from his face and sat down in the wicker chair next to me. "Nice day for an art show," he said, looking out at the field. I nodded and waved at the gardener starting to mow the far end of it, reveling in the earthy summer smell of cut grass.

"Is everything set downtown?" I asked.

"As set as it can be. You know artists, they'll be tweaking their work till the last minute. Speaking of," he said. Stepping inside, he returned momentarily clutching a small canvas. "Do you know whose this is? It was in the stack with the others, but no one's iden- tified it." He turned it around and I gasped.

"Mine," I said, feeling my hand turn to stone around the pencil. I stared at my painting of the Hoppers' drawing room, the evidence of the one and only time I'd taken Frank's advice to paint the image I was trying to write. I could taste the cigar smoke on my tongue and hear the orchestra playing Tchaikovsky's *1812* in the corner over the chatter and laughter. I hadn't seen it in over forty years and had no idea how it had ended up here, one hundred miles from our home in the Bronx.

"Really? It's yours?" Charlie asked. The crinkled skin around his green eyes deepened as his eyebrows rose. "It's not half bad."

"Where'd you find it?" I swallowed hard. It was June 17, Franklin's birthday, and it was rather coincidental that it had turned up today of all days. Doubting my random premonition had any- thing to do with why it'd suddenly materialized, I looked around the porch and down the hill to the field anyway, as though the brother I hadn't seen in four decades would miraculously appear.

"I suppose it was in the cedar chest you gave me years back. It must have been in the bottom. Some people dropped their paint- ings off early and I stored them in there for safe keeping." He shrugged. "I don't know why I hadn't noticed it before, but then again, I don't think I've opened the chest since it ended up in my house. What's it of?"

"The Hoppers' drawing room, of course." I narrowed my eyes at him as though he'd lost his mind, before realizing he'd only seen it once. "I'm sorry. I forgot you weren't really there."

"You've never really forgiven me for those years, have you?" Charlie asked. He sat next to me, looped his arm across my shoulders, and reached for my hand. Goose bumps prickled my skin. Charlie had never embraced me like this—the way Frank and I had embraced since birth. I glanced down the hill at the field again, sure I'd felt Frank strongly enough that he was near, but he wasn't.

"Of course I have," I said, pushing Frank from my mind. "You've been the most important person in my life for sixty-three of my sixty-six years. Sometimes I forget that you weren't there for a time." Rachel had died of pneumonia in December of 1893, a tragedy that had left Charlie with an immense sense of guilt and heartache.

"I would say it's more like sixty-five of sixty-six. I was only really gone for a year, you know. Even if it wasn't right, I couldn't stay away after . . ." He let the final words of the sentence drift away in the summer breeze. He was right. He'd frequented Mott Haven much more often than he had his own house in the year between Frank's disappearance and Rachel's death. In those days, he'd always made the excuse that he kept calling on account of his art, that he created his best work in my presence, in his mother's library, though every few months he'd plead for my hand. As difficult as it had been at times, I'd remained true to my word, refusing to allow our relationship to progress further than friendship. Instead, I'd poured all of myself into my writing. I pulled Charlie down beside me and leaned into his chest, lacing my fingers around the back of his neck.

"I know," I said. "And you'll never understand how much that meant to me." He grinned and leaned away to snatch my lemonade glass from the table beside us. He took a long drink of Mother's famous recipe, reducing it to two small ice cubes. I sighed, suddenly thirsty, and he looked at me and laughed.

"Don't worry. I'll get you more." He stood to do so, but paused in the doorway, staring at the painting propped against it. "Now that I know it's yours, it's obvious that it is the Hoppers' drawing room," he said. "I vaguely remember it, but the colors and the feeling are just the way you described it in the book." He disappeared into the house and I stared at my painting, unable to tear my eyes from it.

I hadn't seen or heard from John since the night of Lydia's death, though from time to time his final words to me still rang in my head. *"God, Virginia, how you break my heart."* I closed my eyes and saw him standing in front of me, eyes full of want, and prayed, as I had every time I'd thought of him since, that wherever he was, his heart was finally full. I'd never stopped looking for him and Frank and never would. Over the years, I'd come to believe, as Charlie had from the beginning, that they were both out there somewhere, even though the rest of my family preferred to assume they were dead. Even now, the thought of my family's bitterness, their hatred, upset me. If they ever regretted their treatment of Franklin or of his memory, they'd never let on, but their reactions changed the way I saw them. As much as I tried to convince myself to love my sisters and Mother the way I had before, in my heart, I didn't. I would never understand how they'd so easily forgotten Frank.

After *The Web*'s marginal sales and dismal reviews that spring, I knew I needed to get out of the city. One night, I'd woken in my room sweating. I'd dreamed about John and Franklin and felt as though I'd die if I spent one more night in the old Bronx home. The next morning, I wrote a resignation to the *Bronx Review* and booked travel to all the places Frank's brochures had described. I'd been saving as much as I could and had just enough to buy a third-class ticket to France. Everywhere I went, I looked for Frank. I went from there to Scotland, where in a small inn outside Edinburgh, Charlie found me. After Rachel's death, he'd come to Mott Haven, intercepted my latest letter, and boarded a ship. I remember asking him months later, as we fished in the archipelago in Karlstad, if he thought wherever Franklin was—if he was still alive—if he'd been able to forget about the horror of what had happened. Charlie had looked at me, eyes meeting mine straight on. "No," he'd said. "Have you?" I knew then, two years later, more clearly than ever before, that I couldn't escape my memories. They'd always be a part of me, no matter where I was.

We'd returned to the Bronx a few months later and I started writing seriously again, much to the relief of George Putnam, who'd immediately published in *The Century* three short stories on my travels, illustrated by Charlie. Over the years, we'd found a home for our work in the magazine, publishing several pieces per year until its last print run in 1930. Tom, however, had never had anything published again—in *The Century* or otherwise—and seemed to give up writing after Lydia's death. I'd also finished what I'd started of *The Society* a year after my return to the Bronx and realized, as I wrote the last chapters, how much it had meant to me and how much I missed it. Charlie had begun drawing again, illustrating and etching for books and magazines, and one night, as we sat working in his mother's library, I proposed the idea of creating an artists' colony. We'd heard of many during our travels in Europe, towns full of small vacation cottages where writers, artists, and musicians came together to live and create. As strongly as Charlie and I supported each other's art, he knew he needed the company of other illustrators for his art to keep progressing, just as I needed other writers.

"Here you go." Charlie's voice startled me from my memories. He set the glass of lemonade on the table next to me and sat down, eyeing the painting. "I think there are about three hundred pieces in the show tonight," he said. "Three hundred," he reiterated. "Sometimes I'm still stunned that you and I have created something this large. When we bought the land what did we think? Ten houses tops?" I took a sip and nodded. A friend of Charlie's had shown us a ninety-acre plot on the outskirts of sleepy Lime Rock, Connecticut, fifteen years back. At the time, it was all we could afford, but it was also our dream, a place to share the art we knew we'd never stop creating. It was close enough to Manhattan, we thought, to attract some of the artists there, but over the years our small colony had grown to a small town.

"It shows how crowded the city's becoming. It seems like everyone is dying to get out . . . at least in the summertime," I said.

"Everyone but our families." Charlie rolled his eyes. Alevia and Bessie still lived in the Bronx house with Mother, who was as spry as ever at the very old age of eighty-nine. Mrs. Aldridge, who had been battling some chronic illness for the last decade, lived next door and refused to move in with my family even though she and Mother had reconciled years before. Alevia was still playing for society events and had just retired from the Philharmonic, which had finally accepted her in 1902, and Bessie was making hats and vying for eligible widowers. Neither of them had married, though it wasn't for lack of offers. Alevia never took male attention seriously. Bessie had caught the eye of a handsome neighbor, Mr. Calvert, a few years after Tom had stopped speaking to her, three months after her final attempt to call on him at the Blaines'. Mr. Calvert was a supply manager at Estey Pianos who lived a block over in Mott Haven. Although it had been clear that she was mad for him from the start, Bess thought his post well below her and rejected his proposal, only to carry on what she thought was a secret affair with him for the next thirteen years, an affair we all knew about after Alevia followed her back and forth to his house a few days in a row. Their relationship ended when he moved back home to New Jersey to care for his aging mother and Bess had absorbed herself into her work, insisting that his absence didn't bother her in the slightest.

"Mae and Henry got out, though," I said. They'd finally moved to the country permanently—to Greenwich, Connecticut—with their two girls and two boys around the turn of the century. "The others are just content there, I suppose."

"We were happy there, too, for a while," Charlie said. His eyes drifted out over the field, occupied from time to time by people crossing back and forth from the colony to the village. "I remember that there was a span of a year—I was about twenty, I think—when I couldn't wait to come home from work because I knew you'd be in my library reading *A History of New York*." I leaned back to glance through the window at the tattered spine of Irving's book on my shelf.

"I still have it memorized." I cleared my throat ceremoniously and conjured up my favorite part. "'*Upon this, my wife ventured to ask him, what he did with so many books and papers? He told her that he was seeking for immortality; which made her think, more than ever, that the poor old gentleman's head was a little cracked.*'" That quote always made me think of Franklin. Eventually, he had been immortalized in the pages of my book. As much as George Putnam had pushed me to do so at the time of its completion, I hadn't let him publish *The Society*. It was finished too soon after the Blaines finally realized they would never find Frank or the Hoppers and dropped the charges—four years after Lydia's death. Even though I'd changed some things, I knew that Tom and the others would recognize it, and at the time, I hadn't wanted to risk the backlash. As years passed, I started to think that I would never want to publish it, but after I heard of Tom's passing three years ago, I thought it was time. George Putnam was in his final years, retired, and in poor health, so I approached Frederick Harvey. Nearly eighty-seven, he'd refused to retire, and jumped at the chance to publish it as one of the last books of his career. To my surprise, *The Society* came out to sensational reviews and excellent sales last November, placing it at the top of the second *New York Times* bestseller list. I published it under a pen name, James Laughlin, and one of my greatest joys had been hearing whispers in the bookstores where I browsed, speculating that the book wasn't entirely fiction, and wondering who the author actually was.

"I'm glad to know that you haven't lost your memory yet," Charlie said.

"You know I could quote the entire book if I wanted to." I slung my arm to swat him, but he caught it, fingers circling around my wrist.

"Come here," he said, under his breath. "I need to ask you something."

"What?" I smiled as he pulled me onto his lap. His fingers drifted over my cheeks, down my face to my lips. I closed my eyes, feeling the rough calluses he'd earned from years of gripping charcoal pencils float off my face and settle at the back of my neck. I felt his lips on my mouth. He tasted sweet from the lemonade. I could feel his heart pounding against my chest. The way he loved me, the way I loved him, still took me by surprise. Through all the years, it hadn't ever faded. Charlie pulled away.

"I know that you asked me not to read *The Web*," he said softly. I froze. I'd asked him—begged him, actually, since the day it came out not to read it because I knew he'd recognize us. All this time, I thought he'd listened to me.

"If you—" I leaned away from him, voice rising as irritation and nerves balled in my stomach. He clapped a hand over my mouth to silence me and forced me back to him with the other.

"I have, but only the other day. A copy was lying on your table and the temptation was too great," he said. "I read it in a night. It's a triumphant book, Gin. It tore me up." His eyes met mine, a spark of fire in them, and a smile touched his lips. I knew that look well. I'd seen it countless times over the years. It meant he was proud of my work. At once, my mind flitted to Mr. Smith's face. Although Cherie had eventually taken to painting again in spite of his blatant disapproval, I'd never been able to forget the insensitive blankness in his eyes as he'd appraised Cherie's misery in her painting. Charlie cleared his throat. "I presume I'm Carlisle?" I started to shake my head to lie to him, but couldn't.

"It was a long time ago, Charlie."

"I know. But, at the end," he said. His voice sounded strange. "Ginny, you know I love you. I tell you that all the time." He looked away from me, dug in his pocket, and withdrew a piece of paper— the permit for our show this evening. He flattened the folded document on the table in front of me and withdrew a ballpoint pen from the drawer below it. *Charlie and Virginia*, he signed at the signature line. His hand shook.

"And I love you," I said back, hoping to settle whatever anxiety had overcome him. *Aldridge*, Charlie signed after my name, and set the pen down. I stared at his fingers, waiting for him to correct his mistake, to add Loftin as he hadn't all those years ago on our Centennial Time Capsule project. I felt his eyes and lifted my gaze to his.

"Years ago, I begged you to marry me. It wasn't the right time. I was married, you were heartbroken and then after . . . after Rachel's death, I wanted to ask you again and should have. But we were young and scared. We'd watched promises shatter love too many times." He stopped and swallowed hard. I wondered, fleetingly, if my heart was still beating. I hadn't expected this. "At the end of your book, Carlisle . . . he's old, but he asks her to marry him and she finally . . . finally agrees." Charlie lifted his hand to my cheek. "I told you I'd always love you and I always have. Now please, will you be my wife?" I nodded and at once, the green field and the open doors of my cottage faded and I found myself standing in the Aldridges' packed drawing room, hands balled in my skirt, heart pounding, as Charlie turned away from Rachel Kent and knelt in front of me.

The End

Author's Note

Dig around in your family's history long enough and you'll start to find stories behind the names and dates on your pedigree chart. Every family has them—tales of triumph and victory, love and tragedy, of tumultuous lives and simple days well lived.

For as long as I can recall, my family has made a habit of telling our ancestors' stories—a way to keep them alive in a world that has long since forgotten them. Because of this, I can't remember when I first heard of the real Loftins—Alevia VanPelt and William Lynch and their children, Annie (Bess), Virginia, Alice (Mae), Franklin, and Alevia—but I've always been entranced by this family of extraordinary artists.

My great-great-grandmother was Alice—Hunter College graduate, educator, and the only one to marry and have children. My grandmother, Alevia VanPelt Jenkins Ballard, often told me how lovely and kind and smart she was, but she also told me of the others—of Annie the milliner, Virginia the writer, Franklin the salesman, and Alevia the concert pianist. They have each captured hours upon hours of my thoughts, but when I sat down to write a story based on this family, it was Virginia's voice I heard, a voice I found rather fitting considering her profession.

Not only was Virginia an artist but also in her soul she was an adventurer. She traveled the world, seemingly unperturbed by the difficulty in doing so at the turn of the twentieth century, wrote several books—mostly nonfiction—and articles for the *Bronx Review*, painted, taught, organized a women's suffrage group, and helped establish an artists' colony in Lime Rock, Connecticut. Though she never married, I'd like to imagine that she'd had the option. Her diaries suggest her interest in a man who proposed to another woman quite without warning. The character of Charlie is fictional, but his profession is roughly based on lithographic illustrator Berhardt Wall. Wall illustrated Virginia's book *Washington Irving's Footprints*, but their relationship was likely much closer, as evident by his inscriptions in several of his own books to various members of the family. In later years, they both lived in the artists' colony in Lime Rock.

To this day, no one knows what became of Franklin. The prevailing rumor is that he was disowned for disappointing his parents, possibly for doing something corrupt, possibly for being gay. In my narrative, the latter option was so difficult to reconcile on its own, that I decided to create a fictional plot using the murky twentieth-century drug industry. After the blood-soaked clothes were delivered to their home, it was said that Virginia went searching for him, but he was never found.

Though only imagined, the Hoppers, Lydia and Tom, and the Society are a conglomeration of the colorful friends, artists, and groups mentioned in Virginia's diaries and Virginia and Alevia's letters to Alice. Alevia never sought acceptance into the Symphony or Philharmonic, though she did make her living both playing for hire and testing pianos at several of the local factories.

The place where the old Mott Haven home once stood on the corner of Morris Avenue and 142nd Street is now a parking lot, but the story of this remarkable family lives on each time it is told, made immortal by our remembrance.

Acknowledgments

Writing this book was a true gift to myself, a time I spent thinking of ancestors I'd never met but had often dreamed of meeting. It is a captivation like no other—to hear about the adventures of those that have come before, those whose legacies are entwined with ours. For the gift of the Lynch family story, I will thank Gran, Alevia, first and foremost. My love of family history was ignited by your influence.

I want to thank God for the miraculous blessing of perfect timing and the gift of imagination.

To my family—to my mom, Lynn, who has read and deemed genius every word I have ever penned, even the countless horse stories I wrote as a child, and who fostered my love of books. To my dad, Fred, who has always believed in my dreams and stressed the importance of chasing them. To my brother, Jed, one of my very best friends, whose relationship served as the basis for Ginny and Frank's close bond. To Gramps, Ed, a man whose surety in my success propelled me forward. To Momma Sandra and Daddy Tom, for their influential love of reading and unwavering support. I love you all so much.

To the best friend that ever lived, Maggie Tardy, who has read all of my work, even the embarrassing early attempts at novels.

Thank you for the lifelong friendship, the laughter, the definition of sisterhood.

To the early readers of this book, thank you for your comments and encouragement.

To my Lynch cousin, Dana, thank you for sharing not only our family's mementos, but your passion for our ancestry.

To my writing buddies—Sarah Henning, Renee Ahdieh, Cheyenne Campbell, Liz Penney, Alison Bliss, Sam Bohrman—thank you for the time, the sharpening, the friendship. I love and appreciate you more than you know.

To my dream team—to my savvy, whip-smart agent, Meredith Kaffel Simonoff, thank you for your ceaseless support and belief in both myself and this book. And to my editor, the brilliant Maya Ziv, whose keen eye and love for this story has molded this novel into something I am truly proud to share.

To the exceptional minds at Harper—Amy Baker, Dori Carlson, Jane Herman, Jamie Kerner, Joanne O'Neill, Kathryn Ratcliffe-Lee, Mary Sasso, Oriana Siska, Audrey Sussman, Jillian Verillo, and Sherry Wasserman—thank you for all of your hard work and time.

Lastly, to my little family—to my children, Alevia and John, you are my happiness and my heart. And to my husband, John, for your enthusiasm for my work and steadfast belief in me. Thank you for being a true partner in all things. I can't imagine going through life without you. I love you.

P.S.

Insights,
Interviews
& More . . .

✱

Meet Joy Callaway

Laura J. Meier

Joy Callaway's love of storytelling is a direct result of her parents' insistence that she read books or write stories instead of watching TV. Her interest in family history was fostered by her relatives' habit of recounting tales of ancestors' lives. Joy is a full-time mom and writer. She formerly served as a marketing director for a wealth-management company. She holds a BA in journalism and public relations from Marshall University and an MMC in mass communication from the University of South Carolina. She resides in Charlotte, North Carolina, with her husband, John, and her children, Alevia and John. ∾

The True History of the Loftins

DIG AROUND in your family's history long enough and you'll start to find stories behind the names and dates on your pedigree chart. Every family has them—tales of triumph and victory, love and tragedy, tumultuous lives and simple days well lived.

For as long as I can recall, my family has made a habit of telling stories about our ancestors—a way to keep them alive in a world that has long since forgotten them. Because of this, I can't remember when I first heard of the real Loftins— Alevia VanPelt and William Lynch and their children, Annie (Bess), Virginia, Alice (Mae), Franklin, and Alevia—but *I've* always been entranced by this family of extraordinary artists.

My great-great-grandmother was Alice—Hunter College graduate, educator, and the only one to marry and have children. My grandmother Alevia VanPelt Jenkins Ballard often told me how lovely and kind and smart she was, but she also told me of the others—of Annie the milliner, Virginia the writer, Franklin the salesman, and Alevia the concert pianist. They have each captured hours upon hours of my thoughts, but when I sat down to write a story based on this family, it was Virginia's voice I heard, a voice I found rather fitting considering her profession.

Not only was Virginia an artist, but in her soul she was also an adventurer. She traveled the world, seemingly ▶

The True History of the Loftins *(continued)*

unperturbed by the difficulty in doing so at the turn of the twentieth century, wrote several books—mostly nonfiction—and articles for *The Bronx Review*, painted, taught, organized a women's suffrage group, and helped establish an artists' colony in Lime Rock, Connecticut. Though she never married, I'd like to imagine that she would have. Her diaries suggest her interest in a man who proposed to another woman quite without warning. The character of Charlie is fictional, but his profession is roughly based on lithographic illustrator Berhardt Wall. Wall illustrated Virginia's book *Washington Irving Footprints*, but their relationship was likely much closer, as evident by his inscriptions in several of his own books to various members of the family. In later years, they both lived in the artists' colony in Lime Rock.

To this day, no one knows what became of Franklin. The prevailing rumor is that he was disowned for disappointing his parents, possibly for doing something corrupt, possibly for being gay. In my narrative, the latter option was so difficult to reconcile on its own that I decided to create a fictional plot using the murky twentieth-century drug industry. After the blood-soaked clothes were delivered to their home, it was said that Virginia went searching for him, but he was never found.

Though only imagined, the Hoppers, Lydia and Tom, and the society are a conglomeration of the colorful friends, artists, and groups mentioned in

Virginia's diaries and Virginia and Alevia's letters to Alice. Alevia never sought acceptance in to the Symphony or Philharmonic, though she did make her living both playing for hire and testing pianos at several of the local factories.

The place where the old Mott Haven home once stood on the corner of Morris Avenue and 142nd Street is now a parking lot, but the story of this remarkable family lives on each time it is told, made immortal by our remembrance. ∾

Family Relics
Found Material That Contributed to *The Fifth Avenue Artists Society*

THESE ARE SOME of my most treasured Lynch family mementos—relics that gave life to stories that at times seemed too romantic to be real. When I look at this collection, only fragments of full lives, it is as if they are reaching through time to remind me—*We promise. We were here.*

Virginia's passport applications

Family Relics *(continued)*

Several photos of Virginia, Alevia, Alice, and Anne

Virginia Lynch

Alevia VanPelt Gorton (mother)

Alice Lynch Gorton (Mae)

Anne Broome Lynch (Bess) ▶

Family Relics *(continued)*

Portrait of Alevia VanPelt Gorton

Alevia, the pianist

Bernhardt Wall's sketch of the Lynch home

Family Relics *(continued)*

Photo of the Lynch home

Alevia (mother) and William in front of their home, 1895

Written by Virginia Lynch; etched by Bernhardt Wall

Family Relics *(continued)*

Other material that contributed to *The Fifth Avenue Artists Society*

- Virginia's diaries—three years
- Virginia's obituary
- Virginia's article in *The Bronx Review* titled "An Old Bronx Home"
- Virginia's handkerchiefs
- Several mentions of Alevia playing at parties in the *New York Times*
- Three of Virginia's paintings
- Old maps of Mott Haven